The Days Fly

C.L.Quinn

Blak Kat Publishing
June 2015

One

It had been nearly a week now. Sarah stood in front of the fogged mirror in her small apartment and looked over her body. *Yes, it had changed.*

Without clothes, so that she could see her body fully, she noticed that her muscles weren't as hard or defined as they had been, and she looked slightly smaller than she had a week ago. The differences showed most in her face, which was narrower, almost emaciated, the cheekbones too defined, her large eyes seemed bigger yet. Even though she had always known that when she stopped her daily dose, her body would convert quickly back to human, it was still startling. So, six days after taking the last sip of Xavier's vampire blood, it appeared that she was fully human again. Each day, she'd felt the changes as her body reverted to what she was born to be.

"I think I need to eat," she told the overly slender woman in the mirror.

It felt odd, like she'd lost something important.

As soon as she thought that, she smiled. Of course she had. For ninety two years she had been blood-bonded to one of the most powerful vampires on this earth. Her body had been protected from illness and aging by the tiny amount of his blood that she had ingested each day. The gift of health and longevity, the connection to power and legend, every element of her human life, had been enhanced by Xavier's blood for nearly a century. So the loss was real, and now, nearly a week after ending her blood-bonded life, her body had purged the last of the effects from Xavier, and she could begin again.

Human. Just like everyone else walking around in this lovely city by the sea. Boston, her parent's hometown, was now home for Sarah as she worked to accept her human body, the life she'd chosen, and all that it meant to be fully human again.

TWO MONTHS LATER

Spring. Sweet air, softly scented from fresh rain and new flowers. Blue skies were dappled with cotton-ball clouds that gently floated by above newborn grass and baby leaves. Birds fledging, insects sliding out to test the damp ground and moist foliage, people emerging from behind closed doors. Winter was over and life returned in abundance to fair days ahead.

Sarah hadn't enjoyed springtime in decades. She sat on the ground, uncaring that her jeans were wet from the grass and watched people passing by quickly on their way to their jobs or home to family. People living their lives. Human, like Sarah. Like she was *again.*

"Are you kidding me? This is how you want to eat lunch? On the ground like a kid? Girl, I have got to retrain you!" Naji barked as she arrived.

Amused, Sarah stood and tried to tamp down her damp and wrinkled pants, but it was impossible.

"I had to feel that grass. Naji, it's springtime in Boston! And after the winter you've had, this has to be the most beautiful day."

Naji shook her head. "I don't care *how* beautiful it is, my three hundred dollar skirt isn't sitting on it!"

Fair enough. Sarah watched her lovely new friend take a seat on a bench after carefully inspecting it.

Elegant and graceful, Naji sat, her legs crossed immediately, because, she'd once told Sarah, this particular position highlighted her sleek, gorgeous legs and her designer stiletto heels.

"Presentation, presentation, presentation," Naji had tried to pound into Sarah since they'd met.

Naji was right, Sarah had seen it work over and over for the striking woman with skin the color of coffee with a touch of cream.

Pulling Sarah down beside where she was strategically displayed, Naji clicked her tongue.

"Love, you are not rocking that awesome body of yours!"

"Awesome? Average, at best. And tending towards sickly, I think."

"No, now, your body is nice, we just gotta fill you out a little more, and *that*, I can do. *Micelli's*, tonight, and wear something sexy."

Sarah let her eyes roam over the park, past it to the pier, and back to this vivacious woman, the first friend she'd made when she came to Boston a few months ago. They'd bonded instantly when both reached for the same cupcake with sky-high frosting at a bakery downtown. It had been the only one left, and when neither wanted to give it up, they finally ended up splitting it, laughing over their shared sweet-tooth. At one of the bakery's outdoor café tables, the two women from different parts of the world, with radically diverse backgrounds, found something in each other, a connection neither had felt before. Since that day, the bond had only strengthened.

Sighing, she realized that sitting here on this bench, her first spring fully human again, talking about getting dinner, was the first time she'd really felt that she was living the life she was supposed to live.

Dinner in a popular restaurant with Naji, who would keep the conversation amusing and boisterous, who wouldn't let her shy away from meeting new people, was exactly what she wanted to do. Without knowing it, Naji was teaching her to live like a human being again. Naji had no clue at all that the vampire world Sarah had lived in all of her life even existed. Luckily, she was going to stay that way.

Sarah had been blood-bonded to a vampire, not just any vampire, either, but an ancient, enormous, incredibly

4

powerful vampire that had been on the earth for the better part of a thousand years. Xavier was first blood, a rare race of vampires *born* vampire, not *made* from vampire blood. He was handsome, perhaps the sexiest man she'd ever seen, and a womanizer, drunkard, arrogant…and kind.

But she'd been ready to step out of the endless life she'd lived for too long in the vampire world. She'd prepared and was now ready to live as humans were meant to do, day by day.

And that included aging. She hadn't done so since she was twenty-nine years old and bonded by blood to Xavier so that she could remain twenty-nine forever.

Eight years ago, when she first considered leaving the blood-bond, she had been standing before the old mirror in her bedroom. Her fingers had moved across her cheeks as she scanned her face…such smooth skin and rich brown hair. That would change if she decided to do this. She would age and eventually die.

Life, with an expiration date, as it was meant to be.

Until recently, her days had been unchanging, day to day life in service to a first blood vampire was all she had ever known. Sarah was a sixth generation blood-bond behind her mother and father, who had been with Xavier for the previous century. They were both gone now, left the vampire world the way that most blood-bonded humans eventually did.

Released from service at their own request, they'd moved out into the world to finish their lives, grow old, and die. It was the way most blood-bonds chose at some point. Living forever, endlessly youthful, it turns out, isn't as great a gift as people would imagine. At some point, there needed to be purpose, accomplishment, and change.

"What is going on in that pretty little head of yours?"

Naji's voice broke into Sarah's reverie. Smiling, she placed a hand on Naji's knee.

"Nothing that a good meal and night out with my girlfriend can't fix. You're on. But Naji, you know I don't do sexy."

"Let me change that. I'll come by with a few things and we'll have you va-va-va-vooming all *over* that joint. I'll bring out the wildcat in you."

Now Sarah laughed. "Me? A wildcat? You've been smoking something again!"

Naji grinned, her perfect teeth artificially whitened to beyond anything natural. "You haven't seen my work. I'll pick you up."

"Okay. I just have a few more errands to run and I'll be home in time to stand listlessly in front of my closet and wonder what the hell I've gotten myself into."

"Sarah, you hardly went out last month. It's past time, and you know I can hook you up."

"I'm not looking for a hook-up, Naj. You know that."

"No, you *tell* me that, but I'd be doin' you and a lot of hot men in Boston a disfavor by letting you spend your weekend nights alone in that shoebox you call an apartment."

"I'll trade up, when the time comes."

"Yeah, well, for now, you need to redecorate."

"Redecorate?"

"Um, hmm. With a six-pack and a long hard one."

Sarah pushed off the bench. "You are incorrigible!"

"I am. Now come with me and I'll get you a hoagie and some fries. You *do* have a hot little body, but you need a little more meat. I mean the kind that comes when you zip a man's pants down, but for now, we'll settle for the hoagie."

Coming from the world of vampires, a very erotic community, frank talk about sex never bothered Sarah.

What *did* bother her was that Naji was right. Sarah's sexual experience was probably on the same level as a girl in high school. She'd been in an oversized protective mansion for her entire life, so her romantic relationships numbered exactly zero. And sex for her? Well, four times, and all singular events. Naji was right, she needed to explore her own human sexuality, but not tonight. It was only the second month of her new life, she just wasn't ready for *that* intensity of new experience.

Naji stood and stretched out her long legs, glancing at a group of three men just passing on the sidewalk. She let her dark eyes, ringed with bright eye-liner, the kind men called *bedroom eyes*, move slowly over each man, top to bottom, and lingered on the area just below their belts. Then she slipped her fingers through the long dark ringlets that surrounded her face, fluffing the curls to draw their attention.

Sarah felt the air around all of them rise several degrees when Naji turned, her lips in a sensual smile as she took Sarah's arm and walked away from the three men. They hadn't moved.

"And *that's* how you do it, my dear friend."

Shaking her head, Sarah had to work to keep up with Naji, who was taller by several inches and moved like she was late for a date with God.

"I don't have that. But I truly enjoy watching you work it."

"We'll get you there. The raw material is all here, we just have to bring it out." Naji stopped and sifted several strands of Sarah's dark hair though her fingers. "This is lovely, but we need to bring out your eyes. You need some highlights. Come with me."

"I can't, I have to…"

"Uh, uh, *uh!* You *have* to come with me!"

Sarah mentally accessed her list of tasks, decided she could do them before work tomorrow, and shrugged. "I am yours to mold. Consider me a big lump of clay."

"Well that's elegant! Get in the car."

Later…

Sarah shook her hair and scanned her image. *She was blonde!*

"Perfect. You are now officially a fucking goddess!"

Naji looked extremely pleased. "I'm *so* good at what I do. Now, where do I start next?"

Pushing her hands out in a defensive gesture, Sarah stood. "Naj, I don't think I can take anything else right now.

I need to recover from this makeover. I mean, it's amazing, but really a *big* change."

"You bet it is, love." Naji had a habit of randomly adopting a British accent. She was a self-professed anglophile, which made Sarah laugh.

"Have you been to England?" she'd asked Naji after they first met.

"Nope. It's on my bucket list, though."

"Bucket list? You can't have a bucket list at thirty, surely."

"Baby, you don't know how long you'll get in this old world, things change on a dime. Here today, a memory tomorrow. So, yeah, I got a long bucket list, and nearly half already marked off. Guess what item number one was?"

Sarah had only known Naji for about a week at that time and was afraid to say. "I really couldn't."

Naji had sidled in close to her and raised her eyebrows several times quickly, a sparkle in her eye.

"Sex with three men at once."

"Really? And you've done it?"

"Uh, huh. And guess what is at the bottom of the list?"

"Sex with three men at once again?"

"You got it. Only I might change it out. I'm straight as a pole, but I've always wondered how it might be different with a woman. We'll see. Like I said, things change on a dime."

After a few more outrageous conversations like that, Naji's indomitable personality and spirit won Sarah's heart, and she knew that they would be good friends. From that moment forward, they were.

Naji interrupted Sarah's memories. "All right, Sarah. I'll drop you off and pick you up tonight at seven. Don't do *anything* to that blow out. It's sexy and tousled, so don't you make it flat and managed, okay? Tonight is my treat."

"No, you've done me the favor, I'll get dinner."

"Don't counter me, love. I've got this. Besides, it's all on my expense account anyway."

"You are *loving* this promotion."

With a wide smile, Naji nodded. "Absolutely. I run that entire gallery now, and it's finally just as it should be. The new car and expense account are nice, but being able to make that place the way it should have been all along is my real joy. And not answering to anyone. Like Cleopatra, I was always meant to rule."

Laughing again, Sarah glanced out the window of Naji's prized corvette. The city was coming alive after one of its toughest winters, and watching people return to the outdoors, their effervescent joy at the end of snow and cold days, filled her with such a sense of well-being. She was here, finally, living as part of her own race. Leaning out, she breathed deeply of the fresh air and closed her eyes to just immerse herself in this moment.

Too soon, the car came to a smooth stop.

"Here you are," Naji announced. "I'll be here at seven sharp."

Sliding out and closing the door, Sarah fished her keys from her bag. "I will be ready. Thank you for the re-do. I needed it, but I wouldn't have had the flair or the courage to do this myself."

"It was my pleasure. Tonight." Naji revved the engine to a soft growl as she pulled away from the curb too quickly and moved into traffic, gone in seconds.

Sarah loved her tiny one-room apartment, which was three floors up with no elevator, but she enjoyed the climb to reach it. Every time she entered her apartment, she always felt a little tingle in her belly that this was all hers and that she was home.

Scanning the room brought satisfaction as she looked at the pale, flowered sofa, multiple layers of off-white tulle over the windows, and above the bed. The place looked like a fairy's bedroom, which suited her newly developing sense of style. She had Jacob to thank for the wonderful furniture.

Her old friend had come from Africa to help her settle in to her new life. He'd used compulsion to get her an entry level position as an ER doctor at Massachusetts General Hospital. Her credentials alone might not have done it, since she'd never practiced in a hospital setting before, so she'd needed a vampire's help to begin. From here on out, her true job history would serve for a reference, but

Jacob's skill gave her the opportunity to work as a doctor, earn a living now that she was responsible for her expenses, and take care of people who were injured or ill and needed her.

After helping her settle into her new life, he'd headed back to Zambia to his village near the Victoria Falls, to a lovely blended family, first blood children, and the love of his life waiting for him. If she needed any more help, he'd told her to just call, but she didn't plan to. She would manage her life just like everyone else in Boston did.

After pouring a glass of red wine, and dropping onto her softly patterned sofa, Sarah let herself relax completely for a few minutes before she had to go search for appropriate clothing for her night out with the queen of sexy.

Naji lit up any room when she walked into it. Sarah had spent her life in a quiet mansion in Paris, taking care of business for an extraordinary man. She was accustomed to blending *into* any room, and she was okay with that. It wasn't her personality to seek notice. Tonight would be fun only because she really enjoyed watching her new friend get her *groove* on.

Shaking her head, Sarah finished off the wine and stood. She wondered if she herself *had* any *groove*. Time to dress.

The next morning

Sarah's head was still pounding, even after four hours sleep. Naji had kept her out far too late, and while they'd had a wonderful time, Sarah had the early shift today and the precious sleep she needed had been torn in half.

As she hurried through the wide double doors, she nursed a huge, hot cup of coffee. In France, she'd barely indulged in beverages other than water and wine, but since working long hours in the emergency room here in Boston, she'd adopted the habit, and pleasure, of highly caffeinated coffee to help her cope with long hours, late nights, and often high stress shifts.

But she loved it. This was the life she'd wanted when she left Paris. It was hard work, but so much more satisfying than she'd ever imagined. Challenging and raw, the busy moments intertwined with quiet ones, intense drama followed by appreciated dull downtimes.

Last night had gone exactly as she expected. Blonde hair hadn't changed who Sarah was inside; she was still the quiet, introspective observer she'd always been. Watching Naji work the room, and the two men that she really *had* invited to meet Sarah, had been a blast, but it was Naji who took a tall, caramel-skinned man home for some after-hours R and R.

Slipping off her jacket, she slid on the white coat that she would wear for the next twelve hours or more. Her mind went to the handsome man Naji had kissed and made promises to before she drove Sarah home last night.

Sex, she thought. She hadn't had *any* in over six years. As a blood-bond, it was not easy to meet men. With her responsibilities to Xavier and his household, and her studies over the past seven years, there hadn't been much time anyway. Most of the time, sex was tucked into a corner of her mind as something that, eventually, she would like to explore. Never at that time, and it was never imperative. Now, though, with life so real and so limited, it had been on her mind again. And this time, with some sense of urgency.

Not this morning, though, with her shift beginning and an ambulance just arrived. Leaving her personal belongings in her locker, she swung her stethoscope around her neck, pulled back her newly brightened hair, and headed toward the examination bays.

"Sarah," a voice travelled to her from behind.

Turning, she nearly crashed into an intern she'd been working with off and on from her first night here at Mass Gen.

"Trixie, just coming on?"

"No, just going off. Beat to shit! Dr.P is on tonight."

"Oh, that's nice. You get some sleep, then, Trix."

Trixie brushed a hand against Sarah's sleeve.

"Yes, I will. And *you* enjoy Dr. P's company," she said with a sly smile as she hurried toward the locker room to gather her things and get out of the hospital before someone asked her to stay.

Embarrassed, Sarah knew what Trixie meant by that comment. As much as she tried to squash her attraction to the gorgeous, aggressive, but ridiculously charming doctor that ran the pediatric center in trauma care, it hadn't worked. *He* was the major reason that her mind was on sex too much this past month. Working with him, remaining professionally detached, was her toughest challenge since she'd arrived in Boston. Since Sarah worked side by side with Trixie many nights, the astute young doctor had long ago seen Sarah's flushes and quickened breath when Leo Peretti walked into a room.

A call from the nurse's station let her know that she was needed in exam room 6 for the patient the ambulance team was bringing in.

As she arrived, the quickly moving EMT gave her his report on the victim. A 69 year-old woman, normal vitals, but every sign of a stroke.

Sarah's mind closed off everything else and went to work.

Exhausted, Sarah dropped into her bed after a quick shower, still damp, and pulled up a sheet. Although she closed her eyes, it took several long minutes to shut off the events of the day. It was after midnight and she'd been on duty nearly every minute of the past sixteen hours.

After two months, she was still adapting to the brutal requirements of an emergency room doctor. While it was gratifying to help people in desperate need, it took its toll on the medical staff that worked with dedication to save lives.

Eyes closed, she rolled over and sighed. There had been no time to speak with Leo about anything other than their patients tonight. It was frustrating because she'd decided to let him know, subtly, that she was interested in him as more than an admired associate. While there would be plenty of other opportunities, that didn't exactly help the twitching between her legs tonight.

Eventually, the sandman brought sweet oblivion.

A raucous disco-era song woke Sarah abruptly, shooting her from her sleep, upright, confused, her eyes reluctant to open. Seconds later, wakefulness let her recognize Naji's self-installed ringtone, *Funkytown.*

Fumbling for her cell phone, Sarah finally stopped the annoying tinny music and answered while she pressed a hand into her eye. "Naj, I was asleep."

"I'm sorry, kitten. It's nearly five. You missed our yoga class this afternoon."

"Ah, I'm sorry. We had a long shift yesterday and I'm on again tonight. I went out right away when I got home and I must have slept through the alarm."

"I forgive you. Make it up to me and join me this weekend for a trip to the country with my new boy and his roommate. Separate rooms, if you want."

"I have to work the entire weekend."

"I thought you were off this one."

"Originally, yes. But one of the other doctors traded this weekend for next. She has a graduation to go to."

"Well, hell. Doubles are always more fun, and especially with *you*. Okay, you're out of it, but you need to promise me that next week, we'll get a nice dinner and talk about my birthday party."

Birthday party? "I didn't know that. Of course we'll celebrate."

"You bet your pretty little ass we will. Everything is ready, but I want you to know that I intend that you have a plus one."

"The party's already set?"

"Oh, girl, I don't leave important details to other people. Of course my party is set. Invites were sent out three weeks ago and my guest list is long. This might be Boston's party of the season."

No surprise that Naji would throw her own birthday celebration. She wasn't kidding when she said that she wouldn't leave her own birthday soiree to just anyone.

"I didn't get mine."

"You get a personal invitation. You're my soul sister, love."

Sliding from her bed, the floor too cool on her bare feet, Sarah hurried over to a rug in front of her sofa. "I am honored. If you need any help with the party, you must let me know. And speaking of that, I understand that gifts are customary for birthday parties."

"Customary? Mandatory, love. I'll get the list to you."

Sarah laughed as she pulled a robe around her shivering body and made it into the kitchen to put on a kettle to heat water for coffee. She'd be back on duty before she knew it, so it wasn't too early to begin preparation for her next shift.

"Okay. Sorry again for missing our date."

"Nah, no worries. I'll see you next week."

"Enjoy the weekend trip."

Naji purred. "You *know* I *will.*"

Ringing off, Sarah set a cup on the counter and filled it with coffee grounds and a generous amount of sugar.

A weekend trip to the country. Sex with a stranger.

Grinning, she spoke out loud. "It's just not me."

Turning, she went to her small closet to pull out a lightweight sweater and dark blue slacks. The pale amber sweater would bring out her eye color, which Naji said was *astounding,* just in case she and Leo might have a chance to speak tonight. Maybe that weekend trip could happen for Sarah sometime in the near future. The twitch between her legs returned.

Two

THREE MONTHS EARLIER IN SIBERIA
BENEATH LAKE BAIKAL

Nikolai came awake, confused, freezing. After a few seconds, he tried to sit up, but he knew by how he felt, by the extreme cold, that his body was near hypothermia. He couldn't feel his extremities at all, and each breath hurt. When he was able to open his eyes, they met pitch darkness except for a weird hard column of light near his feet that shot straight up until it disappeared into darkness again.

Trying to scan his surroundings, he considered what he knew, where he could be, how he came to be here. Like something hit him in the temple, the memory crashed back to him. *He'd fallen through the ice!*

Several attempts to push upright failed, so he rolled to his side and shakily got up on all fours. His eyes landed on the light source, grateful to realize that it was his flashlight lying on its end and that it still worked. Other than that one device, whatever cave he'd landed in was very deep and would be the definition of absolute darkness.

A slow crawl brought him to the light and he curled stiff fingers around the handle to lift the flashlight and begin to assess his surroundings. The light was bright for the moment, but he knew that when it began to die, it would do so quickly. Nikolai had no idea how long he'd been out and how long it had been burning.

The flashlight revealed that he was in exactly the situation that he was afraid of. He was in a dark cavern well below the one that had held the vampire graves. It was devoid of ice, of which he was grateful, but still dangerously cold. When he shined the light on the ground around him, the broken corpses he'd so carefully worked around lie shattered along with the ice that had encased them.

His situation was dire indeed. No one would check on him, so no one would know that he was missing and arrange for a rescue. His only chance was that many of these subterranean chambers could be traveled to possible openings somewhere on the surface.

"If only I survive long enough to do so," he said out loud in his native Russian.

Taking a deep breath, painful though it was, he made a strong push to stand up, and achieved it, but his right knee would not support him and he crashed back to solid rock. Pain shot through him that was so intense, he sucked in air and couldn't release it. Seconds later, it expelled violently as he fell back onto the ground.

Assessment, then. He was injured, badly, probably couldn't *walk* out of here. It was Friday night, and someone would come to the cave above this one after the weekend, but by then, he'd either have found a way out of here or he would be dead. His cell phone didn't work this deep in the ground.

"You are not so good, my buddy," he said, again out loud, the slight echo somewhat comforting. "You are screwed." He thought of this discovery, the find of any archeologist's career, and that it would also be the end of him. Was there some twisted cosmic justice here? Or did it mean that the universe had a sense of humor? It didn't matter, he wasn't ready to die *yet*.

Once he gathered his strength, Nikolai rolled onto his side and pushed against the hard ground that seemed to push back. Eventually, he regained his footing, the pain in

16

his knee nearly driving him back down, but he surged to the left to where he'd noticed a wall and pressed himself into it for support. Relieving all weight from his right leg, he rested. Several long moments later, he carefully tried to step forward on the damaged leg to see if there was any way he could tolerate the pain enough to walk. Sharp stabs ripped through him, but he knew that he was strong enough to deal with it.

Unfortunately, the injury was so egregious, he fell again, forward onto the damaged leg, catching himself before he hit the ground once more. He could have tolerated the pain in an attempt to hike out of this underground grave, but the damage to his leg was too severe; it would not hold his weight.

"Fuck me," he whispered, no longer comforted by the sound of his voice as it echoed off the high walls of stone.

Looking around, he wondered if he might be able to cobble together a brace and realized immediately that the most likely possibility down here would be the bones of the long-deceased vampires. What sacrilege, that he must consider such an act, but this was all about his survival now.

Nikolai reached for the flashlight, and as his fingers curled around the handle, the brightness dimmed.

God, it was failing! In moments, he would be trapped beneath the earth in total darkness. Rapidly swinging the flashlight around the cave, he scanned the area and tried to memorize the objects and their positions, and the chambers as they led off in four different directions. Within seconds, the light dimmed again, so much so that it barely illuminated his hand. Then, it was gone.

He didn't move. First, because the pain was so awful, he dreaded the moment when he would have to crawl across the ragged rock to the nearest skeletal remains only a few yards away. And mostly, because everything about this seemed wrong, like karma would smite him just for his arrogance. But it had to be done. To survive, to try to find a way to brace the damaged knee, he would have no choice but to break apart the precious remains of the most ancient first blood vampires ever known.

"Forgive me," he said, his head tilted up, because it seemed appropriate to look towards heaven when asking God to grant him permission for this horrible act of desecration. "I do this only because I must."

Scooting the flashlight out of his way, Nikolai advanced in the direction he was sure to find the skeleton that he'd been looking at when the floor gave way, the one whose spirit amulet had begun to glow, the one that attracted him back into the cave and put him in exactly the right place to get trapped. A niggling feeling in his stomach tried to convince Nikolai that the dead man deserved this for not dying properly and *staying* dead.

Pitch darkness, it turns out, can totally fuck any sense of direction. He wasn't sure if he would be able to find the skeleton after all, but, crawling on two hands and one knee while dragging the damaged leg, his fingers struck a hard bone.

Between the cold, the pain, and the exertion, Nikolai collapsed onto his back as he wrapped his hand around what felt like a femur. Closing his eyes was automatic, but there wasn't any reason to, he could see exactly the same black nothingness. As he lay still to allow his body a chance to recover enough to begin to construct a brace for his leg, his mind wandered over this vampire gravesite.

He'd been dumbfounded when his team uncovered the ice-encased remains in the subterranean cave here in Siberia. Shocked further when it became apparent to him that these were no ordinary remains, he'd contacted his dear friend Olivia, who had been vampire for centuries, and asked her to come verify that these really were vampire remains. They had indeed been exactly that.

She'd come, as he expected her to, but along with another vampire, and ultimately, a vampire that blew his mind. This vampire was not *made* like he thought they were by changing a human with blood. He was *born* as a vampire. And so, too, it turned out, were the bodies of those he'd uncovered under Lake Baikal. Here he was, unremarkable Nikolai Zalesky, conservation biologist and archeologist, among supernatural beings that nearly no one else on this world even knew existed. He'd been overwhelmed and humbled.

He still was. It's just that now, all of his fine plans and ideas would dissipate like smoke across water because his life would end the same way as those vampires of centuries ago…white bones locked in blocks of ice in a place no one would ever find him. It was sad to think that he would end so unceremoniously.

Olivia would grieve, she really cared for him, but she was hundreds of years old, she knew how to move on after loss. He would be soon forgotten, not even a memory on this earth.

"You've had your cry, now get that brace made and get out of this hole." His skin was so cold now, he tried to smile at his *better self* telling the *complainer* to fix this and get the job done. The smile didn't come. Hypothermia was setting in. Trying to push back up, lethargy worked against him and he dropped back down.

What had he been doing? Hmmm…there was something…

Nikolai knew that he was losing focus, another symptom of the extreme cold. His body was trying to shut down. *He couldn't let it!*

In desperation, and with the greatest effort of his life, he grasped the bone and held on tight, as if it could imbue him with the strength to accomplish his task of walking out of here. Somehow, it seemed to, for he rolled over again, pushed up, breathing hard, and pulled himself closer to the vampire's fragmented parts.

But with the absence of light, the devastating cold, and aware now that he'd been losing blood all of this time, as well as the ability to think clearly, Nikolai knew that his chances were sliding away by the second. He would die here, this night, the struggle of life over, and, hopefully, go on to a cosmic reward for a life well-lived with kindness and gratitude.

Heat surged in the back of his head, and he thought it was the fight or flight trigger. Emotionally, intellectually, he wanted to fight for life, but his body was succumbing to factors beyond his control. He was just too injured and in a

19

deeply inhospitable place to survive, but the heat burned on, and sparks of light twinkled in his sight behind closed eyelids. He wished for the peace of heaven or at least a place in the stars from which he could watch eternity as it unfolded on earth.

Brightness interfered suddenly and blinded him. His eyes were still closed, so he knew it wasn't real, but the light persisted and he opened his eyes, expecting to see the unkind blackness that surrounded him. The light still invaded the space, a glow, golden with warm edges, filled the area just above his head.

What the hell? Was someone here? Would he be rescued after all?

He had enough strength to turn his head and tilt it up.

There, just out of reach, the glow, the light…

What was it?

It hit him suddenly. There was only one thing that it could be…the spirit amulet that had started this whole nasty event. What should have been dormant, *dead* in fact, according to the first blood, Xavier, had begun to glow above, and now, at the moment when Nikolai had accepted his fate, it was doing so again.

While he didn't know what it meant, he did know one thing. He *had* to get the thing. For some reason, he knew that he had to get to it. One thing that Olivia had taught him over the years was that, while life followed its own haphazard path for many people, sometimes, often, a path is drawn, guided, by destiny's hand. All that person has to do is to make the right choice.

What made him think that this might be true for him?

Because it had to be. In the back of his mind, in his heart, in his soul, and even in this broken body, Nikolai knew that it was never his destiny to die alone in an ice-cave before he ever had a chance to leave his mark upon this world. The heat in the back of his head pushed him to get up, and he knew it now for what it was. It was something from beyond him, from beneath this earth, from above the sky, it was hope and purpose, a future that he still had to make.

"I'm not finished," Nikolai said, out loud, but so softly that even in the deathly still cavern, he couldn't hear his own voice. But he believed every word.

Now, ready, and knowing that the strength would be there when he needed it to be, Nikolai shoved himself across the jagged rock. Even though it tore at his skin, he pushed and pulled, and crawled, until the fingertips of his right hand touched the central stone of the glowing amulet.

Warmth surged into his fingers, through his hand, up his arm, and into his body. The heat felt like hot water, coursing through him in a furious flood, and, *oh, God, it was good!*

A second push against the ground pulled him close enough to lift the amulet off the rock and hold it to his chest. He could feel moisture on his face. Tears, that there was hope. Grateful for the warmth, the light, and the chance, Nikolai pulled the amulet around his neck. It took what seemed like an eternity to slip the simple hook over the small circle to latch the amulet, but once he had, he collapsed again.

It was done, what he'd been urged to do, the amulet rode against his body. It had been very warm, and now, lying still, his attention only on the brilliant stone in the center of the amulet, he knew that, for first blood vampires, this thing held unimaginable power. What it would do for him, only human, he did not know.

Even if he was mistaken, even if it didn't save his life, even if it didn't mean that he had a special destiny, the warmth was life-saving. It meant that he still may have a chance to get out of here alive.

Lying still, his eyes closed again, Nikolai allowed himself to *feel* the amulet, and what it was doing to him. The pain was gone, the cold too. He felt as if he floated on a cloud, high above the world. If this was death, he embraced it. His mind floated and he lost consciousness again.

Nikolai opened his eyes to darkness, only this wasn't total pitch black absence of light. He sat up, easily, no pain, no discomfort at all, and scanned his surroundings. He sat high on a cliff with a vertical drop just below him, a deep valley beneath with distant villages lit for the night. A sea lay beyond, illuminated by an overly bright full moon that seemed so close he could touch it. As bright as the moon was, stars competed for their place in the sky that, too, seemed too intense to be real. A soft breeze lifted his long hair and moved the grass back and forth in a slow dance.

Where the hell was he? He stood with no resistance, no pain, and moved his arms and legs to check out his body. It was perfect, better than ever. Even the persistent ache he'd had in his neck for years from arthritis was gone.

Don't be ungrateful, he thought. "Is this heaven?" he asked out loud.

"No, but as close to it as you can get," a deep voice behind him answered. Nikolai slowly turned to see who did so.

He was tall, built like what Nikolai envisioned a god would be, his eyes black in the night, but sparkling with silver lights. He wore his dark hair like Nikolai did, long and pushed back over his shoulders.

"Where am I?" Nikolai asked. "And who are *you*?"

"Good questions, both. Sit, we will discuss this. I am only now learning about this new journey we travel."

"Journey? *We?*"

The huge man sat on the edge of the precipice with no concern for safety. Automatically, Nikolai scanned him, his graceful movements, quiet, calm demeanor, plain clothes, though archaic. He was shoeless.

"Sit beside me, please. You have a lot to learn before the change begins."

"Change?"

Nikolai did as requested and dropped down beside the stranger. "Change? What change?"

"We will come to that. The first answer of who I am to you is a simple one. You and I are one. My spirit rides within the amulet that you wear."

His hand moving to his chest, Nikolai felt bare skin beneath a dark tee shirt he wore in this strange dream. The amulet he remembered putting on in reality was not there in this dream.

Nikolai's eyes crinkled as he grinned.

"Funny. Dreams can get so bizarre," he said to the man beside him, who, for some reason he couldn't figure out, he could not take his eyes off.

"Yes, they can. But…" The big man looked out at the sea breaking against the shoreline far below. "This is not a dream."

His odd eyes went back to Nikolai. "I am Mies. Or I was. Many, *many* years past. I was one of the first of my kind to settle on this special world, but those days came to an end and I was able to rest at last. I was done with life and I was okay with it. After a thousand years of living, I *desired* the eternal rest." He paused again.

Nikolai didn't speak because he sensed that, whatever this man had to tell him, even if it was in a dream, as he believed it to be, was grave and monumental.

Mies continued.

"It appears that the ancient powers that command the universe have decided that I am not finished after all. I am already exhausted at the idea of returning to a corporeal body."

"Can't you tell them no?"

"I cannot command the sun or the moon, or the stars that wander through eternity. Like all living things that are, that once was, that are yet to be, I must bow to the justice of the universe. I sense some capriciousness, I believe the fates may have a wicked sense of humor, but I still have no power to change this decision."

"Huh." Nikolai didn't know what else to say. He felt as if he was the most inconsequential being ever. That led him to the question he needed to ask.

"Why am *I* here?"

Mies turned and faced Nikolai.

"You are dying. There, on the globe, the planet beneath your damaged body, you are leaving your life. Nikolai Zalesky, this is not my choice. I need to tell you that I am being sent to earth again, to live again, in your body that is, even now, being changed by the spirit amulet that holds all that I am, all that I ever was, and all that I will be again. I am, too, now merging with you, physically, and spiritually, soul to soul, lifeforce to lifeforce."

None of this made sense. It was as crazy of an idea as Nikolai could have ever dreamed up.

He laughed. "I never realized I had such a good imagination. I've spent too much time among the vampires recently, I must think that I can become one of them. It is all too hilarious."

He watched Mies smile and lower his head. "It *does* seem unreal. You are not even vampire, so you are coming from a place where you can't conceive of the power of destiny's hand. Reality will convince you quickly, unfortunately, as soon as your spirit is returned to your body."

"Sure, yeah, okay," Nikolai responded with a laugh.

"This has never been done before, my friend. I have no idea how it will work. They did not want to sacrifice you, the powers-that-be say that it is our combined lifeforce that will lead us to where we must be. I am glad that you have a sense of humor, Nikolai. We will both need it in the days to come."

"I'm going to play along with this weird-ass conversation since obviously I am the one who dreamed it up. What the fuck are you talking about?"

"It is nothing normal, I must agree. Nikolai, your body is damaged beyond the ability for you to survive. Right now, your body is dying in that cave deep beneath the land of the mother. I am a first blood, one of the first vampires to ever exist in this world. My people died thousands of years ago. It is my own spirit amulet, dead for all of those years as I was, that you touched in that cave. You brought it alive, and me with it, and now, having donned the amulet, your body is changing to become vampire, to become a vessel, to become first blood. You will inhabit that body again." After a brief pause, he lifted his eyes to command Nikolai's. "But not alone."

Quiet for a few moments, Nikolai's smile waned. "I don't know what you would mean by that kind of comment. If this were real, I'd be concerned."

24

"You would have to be. And you *should* be concerned, it *is* real. You will understand that soon. I have no more idea than you how this will work. It must be possible, though, or they would never have put us where we are. We are here at this moment for me to let you know what to expect when you are returned to your body and find me there. Can we agree that neither of us want this and that we must attempt to make the best of this for *both* of us?"

Nodding, Nikolai continued smiling complacently to the dream.

"Sure, sure. Don't worry, my friend, we will be like peas in a pod." Then, laughing, he slapped Mies on the back. "My, but you are big. You will be disappointed to be plopped inside of my puny body."

"Do you remember me commenting about the *change* and that you would be first blood?"

"You mean I am going to get bigger?"

Mies smiled too. "Yes, Nikolai, you are going to get bigger."

Suddenly, he looked up into the canopy of stars.

"It is time. I will see you on the surface. Good luck, my companion."

Before he could respond to Mies, Nikolai watched him fade into nothing.

He shot up and scanned the landscape but he was alone.

"Alone," he whispered. What a ridiculous idea, that he would be put back into his body, and that he would not be alone there.

Sighing, he looked up at the super-sized moon.

"I'm going to be really disappointed if I survive this and don't get my huge vampire body."

Dizziness struck fast and Nikolai pushed himself away from the fatal drop off the cliff before he lost consciousness.

Three

PRESENT DAY ... BOSTON

Sarah had never seen anything like Naji's birthday party.

The determined woman had the entire thing catered by the top catering company in the city, *Bebe's Best*.

"Naj, everyone in the city must be here tonight!"

Dressed head to toe in sparkling crystals, Naji nodded.

"Nearly. My guest list topped three hundred. Don't look at me like that, I know a *lot* of people. Besides, a girl only turns thirty-one once, am I right?"

Only once? How would Naji like being thirty-one forever? Sarah knew without question; Naji would love being vampire. If anyone deserved it, this vibrant woman did, and she would make an exceptional one.

"Love, I know it's *my* birthday, but I have two gifts for you." Naji's purloined British accent was really getting a workout tonight.

"What?" Sarah said, surprised. "I don't need anything. Really, you don't have to give me anything."

"Yes, I do. Look over by that ice sculpture of the tigress. See that man that looks like he needs to be licked from head to foot?"

A big man with a spray-on tan and bleached blonde hair cut very short posed near a buffet table grazing on shrimp hors d'ourves, his nice body well showcased in overtight pants and a jacket that barely buttoned.

"Yes?"

"He's yours," Naji whispered.

"No, he's not."

"Yeah, I bought him for you. You told me at dinner that you were horny."

"I didn't use that word. I said that I needed some localized stimulation in the nether regions."

"Yeah, *horny!*"

"Well I didn't mean for you to *buy* someone for me!"

"Oh, it was a bargain. I got a *buy one, get one free* deal. The other one is gift-wrapped on my bed right now."

"You're crazy!" Sarah laughed. "I appreciate the sentiment, but I'm not taking that man home!"

"I figured. A girl's gotta try. Okay, then, here's the other gift. Put that in your bag, it's non-negotiable." Naji handed her a shiny black rectangular box. "And at least go get another drink and hit that dance floor. This band cost me a *fortune!*"

"You make me laugh, Naj! That's just one of the many reasons I've fallen in love with you."

"Me too, doll. Well, I need to get back in there."

"I'll have to head out shortly, they have me on early tomorrow."

"Ooh, I hate your hours!"

"Sometimes I do too. Happy Birthday, my sweet friend."

"Thank you, Sarah. Make sure you have some cake. It really *is* to *die* for!"

Naji danced away, her body and feet glittering in the lights created by stringing white LED bulbs all over the ceiling to cascade down the walls, all behind pale blue tulle. Whoever designed this was very good at their job.

Sarah did as requested. After snagging a red wine and a large piece of vanilla cake with raspberry icing covered with chocolate shavings, she slipped out the door and grabbed one of the hired cars that the hotel had provided for Naji's guests.

27

Once home in her small space, dressed in a low-necked plain white tee shirt and thick socks, Sarah fished the box out of her bag.

"What the hell, Naj? It isn't *my* birthday!"

When she lifted the lid, she grinned.

"Oh, my God," she whispered.

It was silver, and an odd shape, with some weird protrusions at one end, and a battery compartment at the other. She read the card attached to it.

I knew you wouldn't take the guy, so this will have to do. And it does do the job very well! It's called the King Kong, so take it to bed and climb that Empire State Building!

Sarah squealed and grinned. After pouring a glass of wine, she killed the lights and stopped to look out at the city through her small window. Naji's party would go on until daylight, but by then, Sarah would be back at MGH.

With the glass of wine in her hand, she wandered over to her bed, but before she did, she picked up the box.

Early shifts were still tough for Sarah. After over a hundred years with vampires, she was so accustomed to nighttime hours that the brightness of early morning still felt punishing at times.

As she finished tonight, she headed to the doctor's lounge and the locker room beyond. Off early at only seven, her mind was on returning to bed as soon as she got home, even though it wasn't that late. She'd found that she tired much easier than she had when she was blood-bonded. Worse, her back ached after long shifts, and that was completely new.

Even when she'd decided to discontinue the vampire blood, she hadn't expected that her body, which had arrested at age twenty-nine, would have any medical problems. It appeared that working twelve and fourteen hour shifts, on her feet most of the time, bent or lifting much of it, took its toll on even *young* human bodies. Now that she was off Xavier's blood, her aging had resumed at a normal rate. By this time next year, she would celebrate her *own* birthday.

For now, though, an NSAID and some rest was what she needed as she found the sore spot on her back. Slipping off her lab coat, she looked up as the door to the doctor's lounge swung open.

"Finished for the night?" Leo Peretti said as he opened the door to his locker, his smile charming as usual.

Sarah felt her cheeks heat. "Yes, thankfully. Too many guests today." Without realizing it, she continued to massage just above her tailbone with her fingers.

Seconds later, she felt another set of fingers, bigger, stronger, replace hers.

"Sore? See if this helps." Leo kneaded along her backbone, sliding dangerously low as he leaned closer.

Damn, he smelled good! There had been some erotic moments recently when Sarah had daydreamed about his hands on her, and while they weren't exactly on her *back* in the dreams, this was close. Leo's fingers felt amazing as they worked the tired muscles. *And turned her on.* Without realizing it, a moan escaped.

She felt his breath on the back of her neck and dropped her head forward. When she felt his lips there, she bucked back away from him.

Leo held his hands up as if in surrender. "I'm sorry, that was probably too forward. I just...well, that just happened, it wasn't planned. Somehow, it felt right, like it was something that we both needed."

He paused as he slowly lowered his arms. "Am I right? Surely you've noticed that I've been attracted to you from that first day we met a few months ago."

Trapped against her locker, Leo's broad chest well revealed now that he'd removed the white coat, Sarah looked up at him. This near, she admitted that he was probably the handsomest human male she'd ever seen.

Clearing her throat awkwardly, speaking with men didn't come easily for her, Sarah placed a hand on his chest as a way to let him know that she'd reacted badly. And that he was right.

"I'm sorry, that was a strange reaction. Especially since…" She trailed off, her eyes shooting up to his. Pale blue, long blonde eyelashes, the prettiest touches of yellow in the iris…she was distracted. "Um, what I mean to say is that yes, you're right. I do find you fascinating…attractive, I mean. *Um*, I mean, I *am* interested. Shit, I suck at this."

"I get what you're saying, and no, you don't." Leo moved closer again, placed one hand on the locker on each side of her head, effectively pinning her between his body and the thin metal.

"I've wanted to do that for such a long time."

One hand slid down the locker to land on her waist, curling around her as it slid lower and lower, curving to move sensuously against her buttocks. The thin skirt she wore didn't block him much.

Sarah didn't answer, her attention fully on where his fingers were and what they were doing. Her eyes lifted to his, locked for several seconds while his fingers continued their exploration unstopped.

"So many things I've wanted to do," he whispered, just before he leaned down to kiss her, a gentle tease at first. As their kiss deepened, the door opened and an intern entered, whistling, stopped in his tracks as he noticed Leo and Sarah's passionate kiss.

"Sorry," the young doctor said quickly and backed out, the door closing with a gentle *whisp*.

Sarah pressed against her locker, then slipped from under Leo's arm to step aside.

Leo smiled. "So, now that we've settled that we are both interested, how about a proper date?"

"I…yes, I would like that."

"Why don't I pick you up next Saturday evening at seven? I checked the schedule and we're both off. Do you like Italian?"

"I do."

"It's a date then." He paused, then his voice lowered slightly. "Sarah, I'm really looking forward to this."

"I am too, Leo. It will be interesting."

"I guarantee it."

Leo hesitated long enough to finger a loose strand of hair before he walked out of the room. Sarah fell back against the locker once more.

"Holy shit," she whispered. She had a date with Leo, her first since she'd returned to her human world.

"Holy shit," she repeated, as she hung her lab coat in the locker and walked out of the lounge.

Shaking her head, she wondered how well this would go since she was so damned ignorant of human relationships.

"Holy shit…"

Exhaustion was setting in, maybe a little shock. It was time for sweet unconsciousness.

IN SIBERIA

Nikolai dropped his gear on the table top and lowered himself into a chair that probably would no longer support him. He'd already damaged the other three in his cabin. This new body brought by his merge with the ancient first blood vampire had taken a long time to get accustomed to.

Who was he kidding? He hadn't adjusted at all and didn't think that he ever would.

These past few months had been impossible. Not only did he share this huge new body with the vampire, but his mind as well. For a man who had spent most of his life alone, and had been happy with that, now, to never be alone, *ever*, even inside his own head, was tortuous. There were moments when he wanted to take a bullet to his temple just to find that precious privacy.

He never would, he was a survivor. Even if he really wanted to end this miserable existence, he wouldn't have been able to. It had become very apparent that he did not have control over his own body unless the vampire gave it to him. There was no doubt…*Mies was dominant.*

Mies. His new best friend. Forcibly, of course, because they shared everything now. It was creepy in ways Nikolai could never have imagined. His sense of self remained, but even now, he could feel it waning. Mies was getting stronger, and Nikolai knew that he, only human, was fading away. Mies assured him that was not the intention, but Nikolai believed differently. Mies may not even know it, but Nikolai did.

The small lifeforce that was Nikolai Zalesky would be buried beneath the superior lifeforce of a being so ancient, with such magics, it would smash his tiny life. He would soon be gone, he was certain of that.

Even now, he wished that he could be unconscious to his own existence. *This*, this *half life*, this strange merge where he could *feel* Mies's thoughts and emotions as if they were his own, he did not want to go on like this.

For now, he tried to manage the remnants of his life and go about it as normally as he could. For now, much of the time, Mies was the one who sat on the inside of consciousness silently.

Nikolai knew that Mies did not want to be like this either. Both were trapped, victims of some cruel, as yet not understood idea of fate's game. Even Mies had no idea of their future or what was expected from them. So they had spent these past few months trying to discover how to live like this. Neither of them had been able to.

They had, however, finally forced themselves to co-exist.

Conversations between them, in his head were, oddly, both disquieting and comforting. While both men hated this circumstance, each admitted that their existence was dependent on the other.

Nikolai had been dying, he knew that with absolute certainty now that he had access to the spirit world and had felt his lifeforce ready to go.

Mies had been gone for many centuries, and while he had no interest in living again, he had to admit that being resurrected thousands of years beyond his own lifetime fascinated him.

So Nikolai would have passed out of this world, and Mies would never have had the chance to see the far future that this world had built, and he really wanted to do so now.

Bound together as they were, they had a lot of mental dialogues.

We need to break this bond, find a way to separate our lifeforces into two bodies. Is that even possible?

Mies had taken a few moments to answer.

This I do not know, my friend. One of us would have to find a second body to move into. That would repeat what has been done to you and it would not solve this problem for me. If it can be done, the method would likely be available on the spiritual plane. And I do not believe it is something they would reveal to us.

I know several first bloods; they are brilliant, part of a community of vampires in France. I want to contact them.

They have connections to the spirit realm too. I do not believe that is a safe inquiry unless you want to warn the universe of our intention.

Then what? What can we do?

We live, as we have been made to do. I am sorry, but we must learn what we are meant to accomplish, Niko. After, then we will pursue it.

No. NO!

Your choice is made. My choice is set. This is who and what we are, my brother. When you are ready, I would like to go out and travel the different lands to see this world and to meet the people of this millennium.

I'm not ready.

You won't be, not until you do what you must do. Niko, I wish to do this as a cooperative unit. Please do not make me force this upon you. Whatever we must do, whatever mission we have, whatever we must learn, it cannot be here in this small cabin in Siberia. We must go.

Yes, I see that will suit you. I know that you can force me to do anything you want. I am aware that you are

33

sensitive to my needs, but you'll do what you want anyway. Why bother to pretend to ask.

No pretense, you can feel that. Do not be petulant, you are not a child. This we will do.

I realize that. Then could you grant me one request? I know of a human who is not only incredibly bright and intuitive, but she is also very familiar with the first blood race and even with your ancient people. In addition, she is a physician, trained to know the physical body very well. Will you let her be our first stop out into the world? She may be the one person who can help us. We will need someone out there on our side who is aware of what we are.

Mies was quiet. This was one of the moments when he did not share his thoughts or feelings with Nikolai. He was considering the repercussions of revealing their nature to someone who was not even vampire.

You indicated that it was not wise to involve first bloods because of their connection to the spiritual world. She is an excellent choice.

Still, Mies did not answer.

Mies?

Finally, he responded. **I agree, Niko. We will seek your friend. Where is she located?**

France.

Then we will travel to her. Tomorrow, we will begin the next part of this journey. We will rest well this day.

Spasibo.

Removing his clothes carelessly, Nikolai ran a hand over his body, sliding down to palm the oversized cock he'd received with his *first blood* conversion. As much as the invading Mies wanted to take it out into the village and play, Nikolai had deliberately refused to let him, and yes, he knew that it deprived himself as well, but he couldn't help it. The thing was half-erect most of the time, and if he even got *near* an attractive woman, it hardened further. Nikolai was horny as hell all the time, too, but for now, since Mies was trying not to force this without Nikolai's

34

agreement, it gave him too much satisfaction to blue-ball both of them.

Dropping onto his bed, he stretched his width over the entire mattress, a new one that allowed for his extra bulk and weight. Now, he had the daunting task of trying to sleep. Shutting off his own mind and any thoughts that penetrated it from his companion was immensely more difficult than his ability to do it well. It had been over two months since they had been merged, and he didn't think he was any better at coping with the day to day, or in this case, night to night, moments of trying to live a life. All of the components that came along with it were exponentially harder now.

Even trying to select food was a challenge…Mies didn't recognize anything that Nikolai liked and wanted things that Nikolai wouldn't touch. Sleep gave him his best rest once Mies fell deep into his slumber. It was the only time that Nikolai felt alone in his own head and body. He cherished those moments, which is why he was highly sleep deprived.

While Mies rested, he tried to stay awake…and enjoy the moments when he could just *be Nikolai*.

I cannot reach her. Sarah must have changed her cell number. I will try her master's home in Paris.

You say that she's a blood-bond to a first blood vampire? Why would she have her own access? Would you not just call her master's fortress?

The world doesn't work like that anymore. For the most part, everyone is equal and free. Blood-bonds have their own lives, their own phones, sometimes their own residences. Sarah is an amazing woman in her own right.

I see. You can understand my desire to get away from this small village and see how the world has changed. Niko, this is the most interesting thing to me now, after centuries on the spiritual plane, to see what people have done with this world.

I do understand. You are right, it is past time. I apologize for being difficult. I have taken my anger out on you and I know that you are just as much a victim as I. But I am human and this part of your world is so alien to me.

Yes, it must be. I have never experienced anything like this before either. Truly, I don't think that anyone ever has. I think that we are unique in history.

I can't imagine we are anything else. Okay, I'm going to call Xavier's household.

Once his call connected, Nikolai greeted a pleasant female voice who answered in French.

"*Parlez-vous anglais*?" he said with a bad accent.

"*Oui.* It is the language of the household. May I help you sir?"

"I hope so. My name is Nikolai and I am a good friend of Sarah's. I need to speak with her."

"I am sorry, sir, but Sarah has left her service with us here. She is no longer in the country."

"I don't understand. Isn't she blood-bonded to Xavier?"

The woman hesitated. "I cannot confirm anything, you are unknown to me. If you would leave a number that I can reach you by, then perhaps I can assist you further. The household is at rest."

"Of course, it is much earlier in Paris than it is here in Siberia. Yes, please, if you could let me know where I can reach Sarah, let her know that it is urgent."

He left his name and cell phone number with the young woman, who was cautious, and rightfully so since the vampires were private about their natures, and sighed. He went into his mind to discuss the discovery with Mies.

Later, then, when she reaches Sarah, we will find out how we can connect with her.

I look forward to seeing this city of lights you speak of.

It's lovely. Mies, this world will astound you, excite you, and overwhelm you. I will try to shelter you from it somewhat, but it is bright, loud, and busy. It bears no resemblance to the world you would have known over six thousand years ago.

I am ready, my friend. Your guidance is welcome, because I know, even as first blood, even as a magical being, I have no idea what to expect or how I will react or adapt. Never has a man been more out of his element. Do not let me fail.

Nikolai laughed and reached for a bottle of Vodka.

Let you fail. You mean let us fail as a pair.

I trust you, you know. We need to work in tandem to make sure that whatever is required of us, whatever the universe needs, we will succeed. You will get your body back, as a singular man, human again, if you desire, if I can possibly ensure it. I promise that I will seek your freedom from me.

But what would become of you?

It is irrelevant. You host me, and you should not have to do so. This body, this world, this time...it isn't mine, it is yours, Nikolai Zalesky. Once we achieve our mission, I will give it all back to you if they allow me to do so.

That is the first good bit of news I've had since I fell through that hole in the earth.

Let us hope that we find nothing but good news from this day forward. Toast?

Da. Toast. To our success, brother.

Da. Now, with an understanding and a truce in place, can we seek a blood meal? I am starving.

I hate this part most, you know.

Sorry, but it is essential. For you, too, since your body is vampire. And Niko. Please, could we find a woman?

Vampire, the idea of having sex, like this, like we are, a trio, for all purposes, I don't know if I can do that.

You are as in need as I am. It will be all right. I believe we can both find pleasure without feeling compromised by the other. And Niko, sex as vampire is much more satisfactory.

Really?

Really.

The conversation stopped. Mies could feel Nikolai's hesitance. He could feel his confusion. And he could feel that Nikolai was as frustrated as he was.

Da, okay. When we get to France.

Mies sighed. *Thank the Gods! Soon then.* He could block Nikolai from observing if he was more comfortable with that. He thought he might like to feel how it would be to have sex as vampire.

But Mies would be driving the act. He was hard as stone in this body and in his mind.

Hours later both men occupied Nikolai's body, sprawled drunk on the bed from copious amounts of vodka. They were filled with food and resting in the underground chamber where his friend Olivia had stayed this past winter. Now that his body was vampire, Nikolai no longer slept in his room in the cabin above this dugout basement.

When his cell phone began to ring, he rolled upright and looked around the room.

"Ah, there," he said, out loud, obnoxiously so, and grabbed the phone.

"Yah?" he barked.

"Mr. Zalesky?"

Her voice brought him to the edge of the bed, his hand massaging his soft cock, happy now that it had gotten what it needed.

"I spoke with Mr. Xavier and he verified you. Miss Sarah does not have a telephone that we can reach her by right now. For the time being, she's left the vampire community. She is living in Boston, in the U.S. She is fully human again and working there as a doctor. We are very proud of her."

Nikolai thanked her and pitched his phone onto a table nearby. Boston.

Okay, then. "Boston, it is."

Four

IN BOSTON

"Excellent," Naji agreed. "Sexy without being slutty, but definitely a *come hither and bite my ass* kind of look."

Sarah smiled into the mirror. "Just the look I was going for. No, Naji, it's perfect. Elegant, classy, and, yeah, you're right, sexy."

"Girl's gotta look a-ma-z*ing* the first time she goes out with the man of her dreams."

"I don't know if *that's* the case, but I am really attracted to Leo, and, yeah, I'm looking forward to finding out if we might have something. And, yes, Naji, I mean hot sex."

"You got your juices flowing now girl, and only *one* thing will *tap* that flow. A downright *great* fuck."

It might not have been the word that Sarah would have used, but she had to agree, that really was exactly what she needed…*a really great fuck*. While it was a coarse term, she had visualized Leo naked, crawling on top of her, and plunging into her. Shit, even now, with Naji grinning at her, she felt a pulse between her legs.

"Um, hum. I recognize the look. Saturday can't come quickly enough for you two."

"Why am I so obsessed with sex right now? Good heavens, this really isn't me. I haven't had sex in what seems like a century."

Laughing, Naji watched Sarah spin in the black halter-top dress she'd bought from a couture studio next to hers. The dress cost over eight thousand dollars retail, but she'd never tell Sarah. She knew her dear little friend would never accept such an elaborate gift, and nothing was going to stop Sarah from blowing that man's mind, and perhaps other things, when they had their first date this weekend.

Her dark eyes moved over Sarah's body. Grateful that her friend had filled out some over the past few weeks, Naji tilted her head. She hadn't known what it was, but the moment she'd met the pale girl who'd just arrived in Boston a few months ago, she'd felt a kinship, a sisterhood, with her. After all her years working to get to the top of her field at the gallery, after all the bad years before that, it felt right to be with someone she could trust so completely.

Sarah carried a joy of life that she'd never seen in anyone, a faith that all was as it should be and that it was not only okay, it was going to *be* okay. That life was for the living and that time here was tragically limited, so you must love every second.

Over her entire life, Naji had never really connected to anyone on a deep level. Empathy was the last thing anyone would ever have accused her of, and Naji would agree with them. Her childhood had taught her distrust and to defend her emotions at all costs. Because of how she'd been raised, she'd had numerous friends and nearly as many lovers over these past years, but had always kept them at arm's length. With Sarah, though, without realizing it, she'd let her in…into her mind, into her heart, into her life. For Naji, Sarah had become family.

She leaned in and answered Sarah's question.

"Sex, love, is pure pleasure. It doesn't need anything else, nothing but the feeling of hands on skin, or mouth on skin, and especially, skin on skin, that leaves you lying in a pool of orgasmic perfection that you can't get anywhere else or any other way. It doesn't matter how you get it, girl

40

on girl, girl on guy, or even that pretty silver tube I gave you in the box last week. It just matters that you do it."

"I know that sex is your go-to for just about everything. I bet you could teach me things that I really need to know, but I want you to understand that it isn't anything I've ever done casually. I think I need a real connection to someone to be that close. Is that weird?"

"No. Just puritanical, ancient, and kind of dull."

"God, I think you just described my life in three words."

"Not quite. Beautiful, brilliant, soulful. There you go."

Moving close, Sarah hugged Naji. "I love you, my dear sister-friend. Thank you for welcoming me to your world."

"Thank you for transforming mine. Now don't go around telling people I said that, I'll have to deny it. I got my rep to protect."

"I have your back, Naj, you know that."

"I do. Now, get this dress off, I'll get it back into the bag, and then you'll destroy that man when he sees you in it."

"I hope. For now, I'm on for a full shift tonight so I guess I'd better get some sleep."

"And I have a handsome new artist waiting for me. I'm going ahead with my idea to do a summer exhibit showcasing local talent. It's been done before, but not like this. And you know me, I may have to sleep with every one of them to get a good *read* on their talent. Now you know I don't ordinarily go for girls, but there's this new sculptor with a body like men only dream about and purple curls down to her ass. I may just have to make an exception."

"You love your shock value, and you're good at it, I'll give you that, but I know your sexual tastes by now, and they tend to run to hard pecs and cocks."

"Ooh, girl, look at you pulling out that word."

"I'm no prude, really, but I told you, I'm still kind of a sexual newbie. You'll get me to speed, I know."

"Love, that hot doctor's going to do my work for me."

"At the risk of repeating myself, boy, do I hope so. Have a good day, Naj. Thanks for the dress. Are you sure I can't pay you for it?"

41

"No, darling, it's a sample. No charge. Too small for me, of course. Sleep well."

After a needed restful day of sleep, Sarah arrived at the hospital to begin a long overnight shift. It was quiet when she walked out of the lounge, her lab coat in place, ready for whatever trauma walked or rolled through the door. The diversity of people and their situations made the job fascinating. This was precisely what she'd been looking for when she changed her life so dramatically. While her choices weren't irreversible, Xavier would welcome her back with open arms, she hoped that this life would bring what she sought; meaning and purpose.

"Hey, you too, eh?"

A sweet, almost childlike voice came from her left and Sarah turned with a welcoming smile. Dr. Tracy, young and driven, a full attending at only twenty nine. While many of the departments wanted her, she loved the ER for the same reasons that Sarah did.

"Hot chocolate or coffee?" Sarah asked. Both Tracy and Sarah needed a lot of caffeine on these overnights.

Tracy tilted her head as if considering the difficult decision.

Walking away, Sarah laughed back at her. "As if you would choose anything other than hot chocolate with those strange marshmallows pellets."

"I can see that I'm too predictable. Bring me a V-8."

"Okay," Sarah called back as she went through the swinging doors to where the vending machines waited at the end of a long hallway. Seconds later, a voice carried down the hallway.

"Don't you dare get me anything but chocolate!"

Never, thought Sarah. It would be a long night, but Tracy's ebullient personality made the hours fly by. Tracy was slightly shy but she had a sneaky sense of humor that surged at the most unlikely times. Emergency rooms and some of the bizarre complaints offered endless opportunities for harmless observations by the staff about specific events and life in general. And a lot of smiles.

Well aware that Tracy knew it would be the chocolate, Sarah safely delivered the paper cup into Tracy's eager hands.

"Sarah, I wanted to ask if you would be able to cover for me Saturday afternoon?"

"I'm sorry, normally I would, but…" Sarah couldn't help herself, she was grinning ear to ear. "…I have a date."

Tracy's eyes widened. "Really? You gotta tell me who…shit, is it Doctor P?"

Now Sarah's eyes widened and her jaw dropped. "How did you know that?"

Shaking her head, Tracy sipped her beverage carefully. She loved her hot chocolate, but she'd burned her lips before and she'd determined to never experience *that* again. Lowering the cup, her eyes sparkling, she answered Sarah. "Please. Everyone around here can feel the heat when you two are near each other. Hell, if you'd been here this past winter, you guys would have reduced the snowfall here in Boston."

Really? Her cheeks flamed. "Surely we are not *that* obvious."

Tracy, diving into the hot chocolate, nodded vigorously between sips. "Oh, yes, you are," she explained, a little sing-songy to make her point.

"Ugh!"

Sarah pushed her way past Tracy and two nurses who leaned against the desk, smiling.

Shortly after that, their night became busy. Mostly simple things, no traumas, just the usual steady issues, easily cared for, the patients through and on their way home quicker than was often the case in emergency rooms.

Around midnight, Sarah walked into exam room 4 to deal with a repeat customer. Sally was in her mid-thirties and an internet hypochondriac. Whatever was trending, whatever latest ailment she'd found by searching through medical sites on the internet, she often presented at the

ER with symptoms of the issue or rare disease that she was certain she had.

Sarah didn't mind, but try as she might, she'd never been able to get Sally to stop searching for her next self-diagnosed illness. Truly, the girl was very healthy, according to all standard medical tests, which had been performed on her no less than twelve times since Sarah had been there.

She pulled back the curtain. Sally smiled up at her.

"Hi, Sally. So what's going on tonight?" Sarah asked patiently with the same warm smile.

Outside on the streets of Boston

I can't believe all of this.

Mies watched the masses of people moving around on concrete with shiny steel and glass rising everywhere up into the sky above Boston, the city lit by millions of lights now that the sun had long dropped. He'd been shocked by the plane ride, and had given Nikolai some alarming moments, too, when Mies's terror nearly overcame him on lift-off and while landing.

This is what the world is like now. I told you before we left that it would be crowded, noisy, and filled with things you wouldn't recognize or could understand. It's going to take some time for you to adjust. I can't even imagine how I would feel in the same situation. I understand, Mies, but you must be careful and let me guide us through.

Indeed you did warn me, but you are right, this is so much beyond my experience. I didn't think that even the world now could overwhelm me, but I see that I was wrong. Yes, my friend, this is all yours. I will stay in the background and just observe.

Good choice. Just enjoy, old vampire. You were right when you told me that the idea of getting a chance to see the future like this is such a gift. Mies, it will be years before you stop being amazed.

Years, Nikolai thought. God help them both if they were still trapped with each other years from now. Would either of them ever adjust? Would this shitstorm of a situation ever seem normal? He couldn't imagine. And for his own sanity, he couldn't allow himself to think about it another moment. For now, they just needed to find Sarah, to see if there was any chance at all that she could help them, or would know someone who could.

He remembered her sharp eyes and quick smile, and the softest manner. Everything about the slight woman spoke of intelligence and elegance. He remembered, too, that while she seemed delicate, she could command the world in a few words. He needed her help, yes, but he found that he was also very much looking forward to seeing her again.

When I searched online yesterday, I hoped to find a safe hotel, I'm sorry it isn't luxurious, but it'll do. Since we've dropped our luggage now, we can begin our search.

My gratitude. I feel lost and useless, I am sorry, my companion. Please know that I will get up to task soon and then I can help with our mission.

No concerns. Just relax and let me drive this body.

Mies was fine with that. Just the noise alone here in this bright and frightening city was enough to disorient him. How could he ever get accustomed to this madness?

He watched as Nikolai stepped from the curb at an intersection where four roads met beneath strange red and green lights. Several people stepped into the road and began to cross to the other side.

His attention was drawn to a group of teenagers pushing each other and laughing raucously. It was late and he wondered where they were bound unsupervised.

One of the boys shoved a blonde-haired girl with a ring through her nose. She shoved him back. Then he shoved her so hard that she lost her footing and flew backward.

What happened next happened so quickly, no one saw exactly how it went down.

Mies scanned the scene and saw a large vehicle, Nikolai had told him that they were the major conveyance now, an automobile, traveling at a high rate of speed

45

toward the spot where the girl landed. He knew that the massive thing would hit her within seconds. Using his first blood abilities, he took control of the body from Nikolai and surged forward to push the girl out of the path of the vehicle. Even his quick vampire speed only had time to assess the situation, command control, and get the girl to safety. He knew within a split second after he moved her out of its path that he and Nikolai would be hit. He wasn't worried, they were vampire and they would survive this assault.

It still hurt like hell when the speeding mass of metal slammed into them. Mies could feel Nikolai's intense fear as their body was struck.

I'm sorry Nikolai. We'll be all right. Have faith.

Pain ripped into them and welcome unconsciousness came.

At Mass-Gen

"Sally, how are you tonight?"

"I'm so sick. Doctor Sarah, it's just awful. All these months, all this time, and I finally know what's wrong with me."

"What are your symptoms?"

"Rashes, all along my arms and legs. And headaches. And look!" Sally lowered her head, her fingers moved through her hair, lifting strand after strand. "I'm losing my hair!"

"That doesn't sound right, does it? We'll begin with…"

"But I already know what's wrong with me. It's plain once you see my symptoms and realize what's going on."

"And what do you think is wrong?"

"I think that I'm an EHS."

"EHS? Sally, you've never had any problems before and there isn't much evidence to support that type of diagnosis. It's a set of symptoms that have no verifiable physiological basis. I'm not saying that it can't occur, but…"

"I'm sure of it, Doctor. I have every symptom."

"Okay. Okay, well, let's just get your basic vitals, make sure that there's nothing that I need to treat tonight. If everything looks okay, you know the only way to truly tell if you are electro-hypersensitive is to go somewhere technology-free with no electromagnetic waves or wireless signals. That's going to be tough, EMR is all around us, but it *is* your best bet."

"But I work here in Boston."

"See, that's going to be hard. Everyone here is bombarded by cellphone, television, and radio transmissions. Don't worry, we'll figure this out."

For the past few moments, Sarah had noticed activity outside of the examination room.

"Sally, I'll be right back."

When she reached the corridor, she saw one of the nurses hurry by.

"What's going on?" Sarah asked.

"Level one trauma. A hero hit by a speeding cab. Dr. Tracy's started trauma protocol."

Sarah followed her to trauma bay one where a large man lay on a gurney with his shirt ripped open, the usual IV's begun, a nurse checking for BP pulse, Tracy leaning over him.

"Sharlene, call up to prepare surgery, and get me an epi. Sarah, hi. This one's bad. EMT said the accident scene is horrible. The car hit him head on doing about fifty. On a city street! I could use a second set of hands."

"You've got them." She turned to the nurse. "Can you have someone finish with Sally?"

Sarah went to the man's left and began an exploration for injury to his neck and head when she stopped, her hands frozen above him.

"Oh, my God…" she whispered. *The man looked like Nikolai from Siberia*. Her eyes moved over his body.

No, it couldn't be. This man was huge, heavily muscled, taller than Nikolai, his frame much bigger than the slight sweet scientist she'd met in Siberia, but he looked so much like him. Shaking her head, she went back to work. Both legs had fractures, and deep lacerations scored his left leg and arm. Save him first, *then* figure out who he was.

"Do we have any ID?"

"Yeah, they've already been through his wallet. His name is Nikolai Zalesky and he has a Russian passport. He's about thirty five years old and no sign of any prior health issues. He has an airline ticket in his pocket. Sarah, the poor guy just got here tonight. What a welcome, eh? How cruel."

How could this be Nikolai? Sarah lifted his left eyelid to check his pupils. Nik had pretty pale blue eyes but this man did not. Dark iris's met hers as she felt his body suddenly jerk and his head turn to her, all doubt removed when he spoke before he lost consciousness again.

"Sarah?" he said.

Tracy looked up. "You know him?"

While she worked, Sarah answered. "I guess I do. He's, um, changed."

"Let's save his life, and you'll have to tell me all about him later."

After assessing the extent of the damage, Sarah and Tracy's eyes met.

"He has internal bleeding, but I can't find the site."

Sarah nodded. "I know, Tracy."

"Surgery is ready. Let's get him stabilized and get him up there."

Once they'd done all that they could do to prep him for exploratory surgery, Sarah cleared her throat.

"Tracy, would you let me attend? He's an old friend."

"Sure you want to? He may not make it, Sarah."

"I'm sure."

"Okay. Well, I wish him luck. He's going to need it."

"Thanks."

Tracy left the bay as Sarah waited for transport to wheel Nikolai to surgery.

She felt fingers close around her wrist and looked back down. He was awake again.

"Nikolai, we're getting you to surgery. You're going to be all right."

"No," he said, weak, almost too quiet to hear. Then, louder, his voice deeper, his eyes more intense, his fingers tightened on her arm, he managed to say, "Sarah, no surgery. I will be...okay."

"Nik, you're seriously injured. We have to..."

"No! Sarah, listen." Nikolai closed his eyes. When he opened them again, Sarah thought how unsettling it was to see the dark instead of the ice-water blue. This time he spoke clearly.

"Sarah, I'm first blood. I'm vampire, don't let them cut into me. You must gather the blood samples."

Oh, the poor guy, he was hallucinating, Sarah thought.

"Nikolai, you've had a bad accident. You're confused. You are *not* vampire."

And yet, as soon as she said that to him, her eyes moved over the massive, redesigned body, the jawline that was definitely more defined than she remembered, the eye color change, the fact that, as badly injured as he was, he seemed to be getting stronger by the minute. His body was reacting very like that of a first blood vampire. But that wasn't possible. *Was it?*

I will compel the woman to do what we need her to do.

No, Mies. She is a friend and well acquainted with your race. She is a trusted ally and you will not fuck with her. Let me handle this!

We cannot let the human surgeons cut into us.

They won't. Let me speak with her. Trust me!

After several moments of hesitation, Mies relented.

As you wish. You are trusted too.

"Sarah," Nikolai said, as his hand slipped around hers.

"You must trust me. I am just as amazed as you are at the idea, but I am first blood, perhaps the first one in history that was not *born* first blood. But I house the spirit,

49

the lifeforce, the soul, of an ancient first blood. Sarah, you can see that I continue to improve when it is medically impossible."

Everything he said seemed true except for the claim that he had become first blood. And what the hell did he mean that he *housed* a first blood spirit? That was the part of his claim that seemed the production of a confused man.

"Let us take you to surgery and see what we need..."

The hand around her wrist tightened. Sarah tried to pull free, but it was impossible. "Nikolai, you're hurting me."

"I am not Nikolai. And you will do as I command."

From force of habit, she dropped her eyes.

What was she doing, Nikolai couldn't compel her!

Lifting her gaze back to his newly darkened eyes, Sarah confronted him. "Stop this. Let me help you."

"You will do as we ask. I will not circumvent your will, I have promised Niko, but you cannot allow humans to operate on this body. I understand you are a bright woman. Think about what you have seen. Allow that the impossible might just be possible. I am not well enough to get up from here, yet, but I will be within this hour. Protect us, Sarah the doctor. Get us out of here."

Sarah couldn't move. Even though the sound of the voice was the same, she knew, instinctively, that the man who spoke to her now was not her friend, Nikolai.

"You are cutting off the blood to my hand. Let go of it and tell me who you are."

Eyes that were *not* Nikolai's stared into hers. The man held on a few moments longer before he slowly unwrapped his grip and let her hand fall free.

While she shook out her numb fingers, Sarah kept her eyes on Nikolai's body, moving carefully from the torso, which was definitely huge enough and ripped enough to be a first blood, to his legs, clad in scraped and torn jeans, up past the obvious bulge between them, to stop on his face. Pulling loose a bandage near the knee on his left leg, she nodded to herself. It was true, the deep lacerations were already healing.

Without realizing she was doing it, she moved the fingers of her sore hand up and slid them along the heavy jawline. As she perused every detail, she brought her eyes back to his.

"This *is* Nikolai's body, but it has been transformed. So I can only think that he's been converted. I can't explain *you*, though."

The lips moved into a smile. "No one can. It appears that I am something that has never been before. You believe me then."

Mies watched the lovely woman while she considered him. He could see everything that Nikolai had told him about her in her eyes. She *was* brilliant and she very well might be exactly what they needed.

"I believe that you are not my friend Nikolai. Once I get you out of here, two things are going to happen. You will explain to me, in detail, exactly what is going on with you two. And you will let me speak with Nikolai again. You understand?"

"I will comply, my lady."

"All right." She paused, her arms folded, as she walked towards the door.

Sighing, she turned to face the man lying on the gurney watching her every move. "This will take some doing."

Five

"God, I'm going to be fired."

Rolling the gurney out of the elevator, she pushed it into a maintenance room that was never used at night.

"I'm going to try to track down your blood samples, but for the love of the world, stay here."

Nikolai's body sat up and swung around so that his long legs touched the floor.

"I am healing enough to help you."

Sarah rolled her eyes. "Yes, because no one will notice that the critically injured patient we just received half an hour ago in trauma care looks remarkably fine all of the sudden. No. Stay here."

Mies watched the door as she closed it behind him.

I don't believe I've ever had anyone, let alone a human female, speak to me so forcefully.

Get used to it. Women are a formidable lot now. They are beautiful, smart, and capable, now that the cultural bonds that people used to place on them are gone. You will like them, I promise.

Mies didn't want to tell him that he already did. Sarah intrigued him. In his eight-hundred years on earth, he'd never found his mate. While he had always been highly sexually active, and always satisfied, that hole in his life had been deeply noticed. Would it be possible that he might find a mate, here, in this time, in whatever semblance of a life he might be able to carve out given the unusual nature of his return? Whatever his future held, he reminded himself of the grave circumstances they faced. This was not the time.

Twenty minutes later Sarah came back through the door quickly, closing it as if she was afraid someone else would follow her through it.

"Success?" Mies asked.

"Shit. No. I couldn't get around the techs in the lab without being suspicious. They haven't fully processed them yet. They've tried to type one sample, though, and they can't. You're going to have to use compulsion after all. I hate to do it, but there's no other way."

Mies nodded. "I will go. Please show me the way."

"Not like that. Here. I got the largest I could find."

Sarah threw a set of scrubs and a lab coat to him.

"Hurry. The longer we wait, the greater the chance something will get out of our hands."

Immediately, Mies dropped his pants. Sarah shot her eyes to the floor, but not before they lingered on him. He'd been commando, and his huge organ just poked out after he removed the ruined jeans he'd been wearing.

Oh, I didn't need to see that, she thought. She'd been so sexually charged these last few weeks and now all she could think of was the size of that beautiful cock. *Not the time, not the time*, she repeated to herself as she counted the tiles on the stained floor.

"Are you ready?" she asked without looking up.

"I am. Do I look like one of you?"

Her eyes moving over the huge man in front of her, dressed in too-tight blue scrubs, Sarah held her breath for a few moments. She didn't see her friend Nikolai in him, she saw instead the stranger who wore his body. His heavily muscled arms flexed as he tried to put the surgical cap over long dark hair to further hide his identity.

"No, but it will have to do. Come with me and let me do the talking."

"Little doctor, there will be no need."

Nodding, Sarah led him from the small room. He was right, from here on, his vampire skill of controlled compulsion would be their best recourse.

So much for a vampire-free life, she thought.

53

Even though he followed beside her, she watched him stride confidently, his eyes missing nothing, as they headed toward the lab. He moved like he owned the world, and if he truly was a resurrected first blood, he probably thought that he did.

"Here. Just do this quickly and efficiently. We need to get out of here as soon as we can."

The vampire stared at Sarah. "Madame, I do everything quickly and efficiently."

She stared back, rudely she thought, but she was already impatient with his self-imposed superiority.

"Just…get this done."

As they entered the room, Tio, the man who handled labs almost every night, looked up and grinned. Always the first to smile, Tio was one of the most pleasant people in the hospital.

"Ms. Doctor S, you still need something?"

Before she could speak, the vampire moved in and captured Tio's gaze.

"Show me all blood taken from the man who was hit by the taxicab."

"All blood tests for Nikolai Zalesky, Tio," Sarah explained.

Wordlessly, he complied.

"Tio, are there any reports prepared yet on the results from this patient's blood tests?"

"Here, on my clipboard," he said.

Sarah gently removed the folder.

"Clear him," she said to the vampire and walked to the door.

"You will not remember either of us coming here, or anything at all about the blood or tests for Nikolai Zalesky. If anyone asks, you know nothing."

Tio nodded.

Silently, but with a sigh of relief, Sarah led Nikolai's body from the room. She needed to go back to the ER and redirect everyone, make them think that someone else had the emergency patient tonight so no one would question his disappearance.

Traveling back to the ground floor, she steered the vampire to a set of sliding double doors.

"Go outside and stand in the shadows so that no one sees you. I'll be there in a few moments."

His eyes landed on hers, and a split-moment of wills ensued. He didn't like to be told what to do, even if he knew that he needed her help.

"Go outside and do as I asked you to do," Sarah repeated, knowing it would piss him off, and smiled because of that, then she went back to explain to Tracy that she had to leave.

Mies watched her go, dumbfounded.

Get used to it. Women in this time do not defer to men and even if they knew that you were some kind of powerful supernatural creature, they wouldn't defer to you either.

She's magnificent.

Da, she is. Mies, she is not for you. She's left the vampire community that she lived in for over a hundred years. She's done with your kind.

We shall see, my friend.

Pushing open the door to her apartment, Sarah motioned to her unexpected guest.

"Go in. It's small, but it's where I live."

"We've engaged a room in this city," Mies informed her as he wandered through the door. It took a mere moment to scan the space from one side to the other. "This will not do."

Stepping in, Sarah closed the door. "It will have to. Daylight is around the corner, and you are still badly injured. I should keep an eye on you the rest of the night and tomorrow. Then, I want to know what the hell has happened to my friend. After you reveal that extraordinary event, we'll find out what you want from me, see what I can do for you, and get you back to your hotel. Okay?"

"I do not think so. This room has an opening to daylight."

"It does. See that door there? That will be your room."

Slowly, Mies walked over and opened the door to the bathroom. He flipped on the light switch, and looked back at Sarah with a grimace. "Hardly. That room is inadequate in ways I cannot possibly list."

Amused, Sarah dropped her bag onto a side table near her kitchenette. "It will do. All you need is a place to rest."

Mies stood completely still for several seconds before he walked over to Sarah, his size normally intimidating, but not with *this* woman.

"You show no fear or respect for this first blood vampire. I do not understand why."

Sighing deeply, Sarah walked around the counter and started a kettle to heat water. "I do not disrespect your race. I do not disrespect you, either, but your sudden shocking appearance somehow merged or conjoined or, I can't even imagine, with an old friend has thrown me from my game. Not to mention, I respond to how I'm treated, and you, sir, have a lot to catch up on when it comes to contemporary human relationships."

"I am sorry that you do not like how I've treated you. I will endeavor to improve."

With a long release of breath, Sarah nodded. "I'm sorry, too. I can't even imagine how this feels for either of you. So let me get us some coffee, and we'll sit down and find out what the hell is happening. You're here with me for a reason, *that* I've surmised. You wouldn't be in Boston otherwise."

Mies didn't respond at first.

Don't be a shit, vampire. Sit down and let this woman in. I've already told you, she's brilliant. We need her.

This is not easy for me.

None of this is, but it is time to let someone else help us. That's why I brought you half way around the world. Neither of us can keep doing this, agreed?

"Agreed," Mies said out loud, and he meant it to both voices in his head. He watched Sarah's movements as she prepared the hot beverage that Nikolai often made for them at Lake Baikal. He'd grown fond of it. Her movements were efficient and moments later she handed him a mug with steam rising from its rim.

"Then we're on the same page. Come with me to the sofa, you don't look well."

"Then I look like how I *feel*. That vehicle that struck us was traveling so quickly, I didn't have the time to even use air displacement to be somewhere else when it reached where we stood. I believe there is considerable internal damage to this body."

"I *know* there is. You were on your way to surgery to find the bleed. Although you'll heal on your own, I have some narcotic pain relievers that may help temporarily, even with a vampire's fast metabolism."

"It would be appreciated."

"Certainly."

Mies dropped onto the soft surface beside Sarah, who'd taken a seat on the left end and placed her coffee on her knee that she'd drawn up onto a cushion.

"Will you let me know how this happened? Or, forgive me if I'm blindsided, let me know *what* happened? I have never encountered anything like this, I doubt *anyone* has."

"It is necessary. I should allow your friend to tell the story, but I think you'll be better served to hear what happened from *each* of us in our *own* voice. That will give you an impartial and better rounded view of what we are experiencing."

"Rashomon, yes. Alternate versions of events as seen by differing points of view. I agree about that. I also agree that you are the best place to begin."

"Yes."

Sarah watched as he sipped the coffee, stopped, raised his eyes to hers, then sipped again. "This is sweeter than the coffee Niko gives me. It suits me."

"Sugar, the drug of the people."

"I am first blood vampire, you are now aware of that, yes?"

"Quite."

"Nikolai has told me about your history with my people, that you were blood-bonded to one of my kin. But you do not know the clan that I rose from. We were alive on this world six thousand years ago."

Startled, Sarah said nothing, but kept her eyes on his. Six thousand years ago? That meant he was with that *first* group of vampires *born* of the race and buried beneath ice caves in Siberia. All of those people had died centuries ago.

"I see you realize the significance. Here is what I know. I was in my final resting place, bound to the spiritual plane for the rest of eternity. It was a place of ultimate serenity. I was done with life and grateful for it. Immortality isn't as perfect as you imagine it is."

"You'd be surprised. Let's just say I concur. You have my attention, vampire. May I ask your name?"

The big man who dwarfed her sofa tried to bow slightly, but he set off a sharp pain that stole his breath.

"Shit. I'm sorry. Here." Sarah fished a bottle from her bag. "These should help with the pain, at least some, anyway."

Nodding his thanks, Mies slid four of the white tablets down his throat. "I am Mies, and I was leader of my clan. It was a peaceful time in my people's history. When the sickness came that should not have been a sickness for us, it devastated my people."

"We know of it. When your graves were uncovered, the strain of that virus was released in Switzerland and tried to spread. We realized quickly that it had the makings of a global event, so we stopped it. In fact, we used a scroll from your people to defeat it, so I need to say *thank you* for the cure."

"It killed all of us in time, there were so few left when it was over. I was one of the last to go, but there was nothing that I could do at that point to save my race. It is my greatest sorrow."

"Something like that is out of the hands of any one man, vampire."

"Perhaps. Yet many thousands of years later, I still feel responsible. That is my background. What happened three months ago changed the end of that tale, when it comes to me. Nikolai fell through the ice-supported floor of the cave where he found my people's remains."

She watched the hard jaw flex.

Mies continued. *"My* remains. He was badly injured and dying. He reached out and touched my spirit amulet, dead too all of these centuries, as I was. His touch reached from his dying body to my first blood spirit, my soul, that had gone to its reward beyond the stars. All I know is that the powers that exist to guide this universe released me to live again, corporeal, on this world. They sent me with the message that I had a mission, and that I would not be alone. I could never have dreamed what they had in mind. In my spirit realm, this man appeared and I knew, somehow, I just knew what the future held for us."

"I get some of it, but it can't be right. You are both, both men, both souls, in Nikolai's body? Together?"

Mies nodded. "Imagine *our* surprise."

Sarah shook her head in disbelief. "Oh, God. How in the justice of the cosmos can they expect you to live like this?"

"We've tried for about three months now. We can't. That's why we've come to you. Nikolai believes that you can help us."

"Me? What can *I* do?"

"He has faith in you. In your excellent mind and instincts. Having met you, I think I see why."

"I don't understand why you haven't sought help from the other first bloods. We have three communities of strong, talented, spectacular first bloods vampires who can help."

He leaned closer, and Sarah felt light-headed. *Was that his scent assaulting her?* It was primal, pure masculine pheromones. This couldn't be good in the tight quarters of her apartment with her own sexual appetite so fired up. She scooted deeper into the corner of the sofa.

"It is the spiritual realm, the order of the universe, that has designed this path for Nikolai and myself. I am certain that it is unwise to involve my race. Their tether to that realm is close and it may compromise our attempt to separate our lifeforces. Sarah, I honor the choices of the powers that rule events in this world, but we cannot live this way. If I am here for some noble reason, some critically vital mission, I will do everything within my power to achieve it. But not like this. Nikolai is a good man, with a heart of gold. He doesn't deserve this."

Holy hell. Within inches of this big man, his pain palpable, his heart open, his body singeing hers, she wondered how in the world someone as small as she became part of something so huge. This was the work of the universe, of forces beyond any measure of power, beings that guided the future. This man had been here at the dawn of humankind, and had been drawn from death to live again to perhaps affect the course of human events.

Only one thought kept repeating in her mind.

"I'm not worthy," she whispered.

Without warning, Mies was beside her, her hands in his, his knee touching hers, his forehead against her palms. "We need you, Sarah of Boston. I believe you are more than worthy. I now believe you were always meant to be part of this journey. You have a place in this story, my beautiful lady."

His voice lowered to just above a whisper. "Please, two strong men need you and beg you to rescue them."

He looked up at her then, dark eyes weaving into her soul. She really liked Nikolai and seemed to be bonding against her will with this man who should not exist. More than the fact that she couldn't say no to them, she *wanted* to help them, *needed* to give them everything she could, even though she knew, it might be more than she had.

"I will do all I can, whatever that is, but I can't make any promises. I am no more than a universally powerless human woman."

"I have faith. Thank you, little doctor."

Suddenly, his touch threatened to overwhelm her, so Sarah pulled her hands from his.

"Um, all right, Mies. Please let me speak with Nikolai."

He no sooner nodded than his intense demeanor changed. The body relaxed and a charming humorous smile spread across his face.

"Nikolai," Sarah said in welcome.

"Damn, we found you." He scooted closer and gave her a warm hug.

As she held him, she realized that the strong attraction that she'd felt to this man's physical presence had subsided. The huge vampire was still here, now in her arms, but that overt sexuality that compelled her had gone.

"Oh, this is *so* bizarre," she said out loud.

Nikolai scooted back. "You don't say, my friend. I have been living this way for months. I have had very little contact with anyone else because I've lost my sense of self and that vampire has control over this body whenever he chooses. So we've done nothing but fight and eat this whole time, with weekly visits to get blood meals, which...yuck!"

"Poor Nikolai! I assume that each of you knows anything the other knows, right?"

"It's unavoidable."

"Then, his version of what happened, it's how you see it too?"

"Pretty much. My team and I had finished for the day, I stopped to make sure the site was secure before I left when I saw a glow near the back of the cave. One of the spirit amulets had come alive. Naturally, I was curious, I tried to free it from the ice when the ground gave way. I would have died, I know that, but suddenly, there I was, in the spirit realm, with this guy. It's as he told you, we've apparently been recruited for something. Neither of us have any idea what."

"All right. When tomorrow night comes, after you two have gone down for healing rest today, we'll begin. Would you like another coffee?"

"*Da*. When he is in charge of the body, I cannot fully experience what he does. Somewhat, but it is not the same thing."

"Okay," Sarah responded, picking up the empty mug. "I'm sure you're hungry too. I don't have enough food to satisfy a vampire's needs but I'll order some delivery."

As she poured hot water into the mug, she glanced towards Nikolai and her eyes went past him to something hanging on a hook behind the couch."

"Oh, shit."

Nikolai looked up at her. "What?"

"Tomorrow is Saturday."

"Yes? You have to work?"

"Actually, it's my first weekend off in six weeks."

"That is good, yes?"

"It was."

"Ah. You have plans."

"Had. I'll change them."

"You sound regretful."

"No. Well, yes. It was my first date here in Boston. I was kind of looking forward to it."

"Sarah, you must go."

"No, this takes precedence. Leo will understand."

"I think that Mies will agree with me that we don't want to interfere with your life."

Sarah laughed. "You're kidding, right? I've already risked my job. I think you are aware that I left Paris to live a normal human life. *This*, whatever this *is*, is beyond any human experience. So, my life is well and truly already completely interfered with, but that's all right. Nik, you are a good man and you have a great need. It's true that I am probably your best bet. If I can't help you, then the only choice would be to go to the first bloods. Until I've done all that I can, this human life I'm trying to build is on hold."

"I guess. There aren't words strong enough to convey our thanks for your help."

"You know that I am happy to do so. Today, though, you'll get some rest and heal." She stood and set her coffee mug on the table beside her. "Before you do, though, let me look at the worst of the wounds."

Nikolai slid off the scrubs, lay down on the sofa, and pulled the shirt over his privates so not to embarrass her as Sarah did a quick check over his entire body.

"This is certainly first blood healing, even the deep lacerations are over half closed already. By tonight, you'll be almost back to normal. Why don't you go get a shower and I'll get you some bedding for the bathroom floor. It'll be a little cramped, but safe."

"It will be fine, Sarah."

"Your company bitched about it."

"Water off a dog's back. It won't hurt him to get a glimpse how we *normals* live."

"I was thinking the same thing. Nik, I've missed you. And it's *duck's*."

"Duck's?"

"Off a *duck's* back."

"Oh, I've always wondered about that."

Nikolai went into the bathroom and reached for the shower nozzle.

Closing the door, Sarah pulled a couple of thick blankets from a closet to make a pallet. She assumed that he wouldn't need much in the way of covers since she kept the apartment pretty warm. The outside temperature had been steadily rising over the past few weeks anyway. She smiled when she heard Nikolai groan dramatically once the generous jets of water reached him from the pulsating shower head that Naji had suggested she install. It *did* have a strong pulse of hot water that did wonders for sore muscles.

Several long minutes later, seated on her sofa again, her mind moved back over the wild events of the past few hours. When the door to the bathroom opened, a column of steam surged from the opening. Through the mist, Nikolai walked out, a towel low on his hips, barefoot, his hair wet and wild where it touched just below his shoulders now that it was released from its band.

Only, it wasn't Nikolai. She could tell by his demeanor, and that erotic scent again, that Mies was in command now.

"Refreshing," he said, as he walked towards her.

There was no other way to describe him…he was breathtaking. He walked with the confidence of a god, and for all purposes, on this earth, he was pretty near to one.

The attempt to take her eyes from him was a total failure, so she just watched him moving smoothly across her small space. She wished that he was wearing a lot more than the towel that barely covered his genitals…and wished that he was wearing a lot *less*.

"May I have another cup of that sweet coffee? I find it comforting. Also, I hate to impose, but I need a blood-meal to continue healing. I assume that you are accustomed to feeding a vampire. Would you do so before I go to rest?"

No. Oh God, no! How could she tell him that it would be a bad idea, a very, very, bad idea right now? That she thought that she would jump his ass if they did.

Just exactly like that, she thought, *just a firm no.*

"Could you make it until tonight?" she countered.

Inches from her now, Mies squatted in front of her and she raised her eyes forcibly, afraid that the towel would part and reveal what she knew was an enormous cock.

"Please, doctor. You must know that it will aid my healing exponentially."

As compelling as his unclad body was, it was when she looked into warm, dark eyes that she was lost.

"I…" Was there any safe way to do this? "Mies, I have to tell you…" Sarah didn't know how to tell him that if they entered the intimacy of a vampire feeding, she would want to have sex with him, but she didn't *want* to want it.

His huge eyes stayed on hers. "What? What are you not telling me?"

"Just that it wouldn't be wise for me to feed you right now."

"Why?"

Shit, how was he not aware of her ragged breath, her increased heartbeats, her sexual stimulation?

"It's just that, um, with the sexual nature of a blood meal…it isn't a good idea right now."

"I would service you when we are finished."

"Perhaps I don't *want* you to service me."

"I don't understand why. I am highly desirable."

"Pretty cocky, aren't you?"

He stood and dropped the towel. "I am well endowed, so yes, I would say so."

As the towel dropped, she glimpsed his partially erect penis when her eyes lifted for a split second and dropped again. Yes, it was gorgeous.

Don't look, don't look…! Sarah repeated in her mind. *And for heaven's sake keep your tongue and hands where they are!*

Her best choice was to keep her eyes on the torn threads of the rug he stood on. Damn, even the big feet that led up to hairy calves were sexy.

"I didn't mean…oh, hell. Please put that back around you. In fact, could you put some clothes on?"

"But this body is very pleasing."

"Look, just do what I ask."

"You are a confusing, argumentative woman."

"I am. You asked me to help you. Be courteous enough to follow my requests."

As Mies wrapped the towel back around his waist, he bowed. "As you wish."

He disappeared back into the bathroom, and as the door closed, Sarah collapsed against the back of the sofa.

"I can't do this," she whispered out loud to the empty room.

Sex had never been a priority for her, and while the few times she'd had it, it had been pleasant, she'd never been horny or desperate for it. With this vampire in her tiny apartment, though, she felt like a cat in heat.

"I don't know what to do with these feelings," she whispered out loud once again, as if someone would answer her. Naji's voice came to her immediately afterward.

Yes, you do. You ride that magnificent beast!

No. She'd never been with a vampire, and she knew she never could be. They were sexual creatures, and if she did so, the comparison might make sex with a human male unsatisfying and that would wreck this normal life she was trying to build. So, no, that would definitely never happen.

"I have to be strong. I can resist those freaking pheromones."

No, you can't. Your libido is on fire right now, and he's like gasoline. Even the fumes will get you.

The door to the bathroom opened and Mies stood there, his eyes on hers again.

Why did even his *gaze* affect her so?

He bowed his head. "I will wait until tonight and get a blood meal from someone else. Niko tells me I am greedy to require it from you since you are doing so much for us. I

65

apologize." His eyes moved to the back of the sofa. "Is that bedding for me?"

Sarah had to pull her concentration from his body.

"Um, yeah."

"Then I will retrieve them and be out of your sight for the rest of the day. Thank you, doctor, for helping us to get out of the hospital and eliminate any threat of exposure."

"You are welcome, Mies, Nik. Um, I put two extra towels in there, just shove them under the door. Sleep well. If you need something, I will be right here."

After a brief smile and curt nod, Mies closed the door for the last time.

Sarah downed her cold coffee and went to her bed. Without undressing, she dropped onto the mattress and rolled to face the wall. No vampires, no. *No, no, no.*

She fell asleep with those words repeating in her mind.

Even with the drapes drawn and the plastic blinds pulled, weak sunlight still leaked in.

Exhausted from long shifts, and now the concern and worry with this situation, Sarah startled when a voice invaded her sleep and she floated into awareness. Was someone speaking to her? They couldn't be, she was alone in the apartment. *Wasn't she?* Moments passed before she became fully alert and memory returned…no, she wasn't alone, not even close. Two men whose fates were intertwined slept just a few feet away.

Was someone calling her?

Pushing out of the bed, she went to just outside the bathroom door, put her ear close to the panel and listened.

The silence within convinced her that she'd just imagined a voice, so she went back to her bed, but removed her clothes to slide into her satin nightgown and crawled back into the bed, this time under her covers.

Minutes later, in that twilight zone between wakefulness and sleep, she heard the voice again, quiet, but insistent.

Flipping the blanket back, she went to the bathroom, hesitated only a moment, then opened the door carefully.

"Nik? Mies?" she asked beneath her breath.

No one in the darkened room answered, so she entered.

"Are you all right?" While she wanted to let him know that she was there if he needed her, she didn't want to wake him either if he really hadn't called out.

He was breathing deeply, and a little uneven. She could see him in the filtered light that slipped through the narrow opening, lying on top of the blankets.

Of course, he was naked and uncovered again. Now, she couldn't stop herself, she looked. Hard lines, sharp definition, and smooth skin covered the body that was much larger than Nikolai had been. His big arms looked like they could cradle the world, and she couldn't help but think that that might be one of the reasons Mies had been sent back.

But the sleeping man was silent now, so she started back out of the room when a low voice said, "Sarah, stay with me."

It was Nikolai. When he spoke, much about the voice was different. Mies's presence brought a deeper timbered tone than Nikolai's sweet gentle one.

"Are you all right?"

"I haven't been all right for months. Sarah, I'm terrified that I'll never be myself again. More than that, I'm pretty sure that when all of this is sorted, I'll fade away and all that will be left is my vampire invader. It isn't his fault, I know that, and he doesn't intend that it will go like that, but I know. I know that I will just fade into nothingness and just be gone as if I never existed. I'm scared, Sarah."

"Oh, Nik." Sarah felt his pain, her empathic ability weak since she no longer had a connection to Xavier, but remnants remained, and her heart ached for him.

Stepping cautiously over the pallet, she slid down and put her arms around Nikolai's big body. He pulled her close and buried his face into her hair.

"This is the first human contact I've had since I nearly died," he whispered. "You feel so good. So human."

"I will keep you safe, my friend, if there is any way on this earth or through the universe, I will take care of you. Sleep, Nikolai, this body is still very damaged and the rest will heal you."

"Stay, please, just until I fall asleep again without the dreams."

"I will. Dream good dreams, *da? Sladikh snov.*"

After a sigh, his breathing slowed and she could feel his muscles relax. His hair was still damp and smelled sweet from her scented body wash. She held him close and kissed his forehead.

Sighing, she looked up into the darkness, worried. Sarah had always known she was bright, and tenacious, but this was such an enormous thing. Did she have the knowledge to help fix something so huge? Something that the universe had put into place, could a single human woman affect that event at all?

She would have to. There was no doubt at all, she must help Nikolai get his life back. The big vampire who wore his skin would have to seek different dwellings.

"I won't let you take him," she whispered into Nikolai's ear. Relaxing against him, she, too, fell back asleep.

Sarah moaned. *Ahhh*, that felt incredible. She was dreaming that Mies's fingers were moving across her belly, the place between her legs pulsing as it begged for the same attention. When she felt lips and teeth replace the fingers to travel from her navel and lower, she began to wake, and groaned the word *no* because she didn't want to. Dreams were safe, she could explore this unwanted sexual desire with him in that shadowy place in her mind because it wasn't real. *But not if she woke too soon.*

Sliding her hands down to bury her fingers in his long hair, she held him close to her skin and heard him chuckle.

"This will be perfect," his deep voice said on a growl.

"I can't believe I'm dreaming of you," she mused out loud.

"It's all a dream," he answered, as his tongue moved up her body and curled around a nipple.

When a piercing whine interrupted the erotic moment, Sarah wondered what the hell it was. Her head felt leaden as realization struck. It was her alarm clock, but why was it ringing in this dream?

She woke completely seconds later and knew. *This wasn't a dream.*

With force, she shoved Mies away from her.

"Get off me," she hissed.

The room was too dark to see him clearly, but she knew that if her alarm had gone off, it was night and safe to open the door, so she surged up, pulled the bathroom door open and raced into her living room.

Her nightgown fell back into place, but everywhere he'd touched her still tingled. She raised her eyes to look at him as he walked from the bathroom, his cock fully erect, his stride easy. Standing before her, naked, ready to take her, the most glorious man she'd ever seen, she couldn't take her eyes off him as much as she begged herself to look away. The offensive orbs kept straying to the hard organ between his legs. She suddenly realized he'd been speaking to her and raised her gaze back to his.

"I don't understand. You enjoyed my attentions. I want you, can you not see that? It may have been a long time since I was with a woman, but I can promise you an orgasm like none you have ever experienced. And you came to me, I did not come to you."

"Yes, I was with you, but...I mean, I was there for Nikolai. I'm sorry if you misunderstood. This isn't your fault, but I don't want to have sex with you. You need to believe that."

He smiled and pushed the thick hair back from where it had fallen over his forehead. "I would believe that more if you had not responded so deliciously. Why do you deny this attraction?"

"Because..." She didn't know how to explain it without implicating herself. It was time to just tell the truth.

"Mies, you are first blood and one of the sexiest creatures I've ever seen. But I've lived with vampires my entire life. When I decided to move to Boston recently, it was difficult to make the commitment to living my life as a

69

normal human. I don't want to be involved with you on a sexual level because you're right. I know that once I have sex with you, no one else will be enough for me. And I need to be able to bond with a fully human male if I plan to live a normal human life. You understand?"

"I understand that you are attracted to me, that you want me, but that you don't want to *lie* with me."

"I was blood-bonded for most of my life to a first blood, you already know that. He was extremely masculine, extraordinarily sexy, but I was never attracted to him in that way. I never wanted to be."

Mies seemed to take offense. "Sexier than this body that I inhabit? You know that when my lifeforce takes control, it changes, don't you? This body is not the same when I imbue it as when Nikolai does. Have you not seen a difference when I walk in this body than when your friend does?"

"I have." Sarah expelled a long breath and looked up at the ceiling briefly. "Oh, yeah*, have I.* This is what I'm telling you. I want to help you, both of you, but I don't want to make love with you. It's just that straightforward. That's the deal, Mies. You either accept it or find another way."

It must have been her overactive imagination that made her think that he looked hurt by her curt demand. Even so, he nodded, and walked back into the bathroom.

Good God, what a fine ass! He had the perfect buttocks, and she knew that because, once again, her eyes betrayed her and watched him every step of the way.

"Coffee," she groaned, and hurried to the kitchenette to start the kettle. They both needed the beverage as a distraction when he came back out.

Moments later, he walked out carrying the blankets. She knew right away that it was Nikolai who laid them on the back of the sofa and joined her in the kitchenette.

He offered a tight smile. "Good evening, Sarah."

"Evening, Nik." Her eyes moved over his attire, which was the set of scrubs from last night.

"You need to get to your hotel room."

He glanced down. "True. Or get a job in the hospital."

Sarah offered a slight smile. "Coffee?"

"Please. What a night. Dreams, wild ones that carried both Mies and myself into weird landscapes that left us wondering what the hell they meant."

As she prepared his mug, Sarah nodded. "It makes sense, I think. Neither of you know what you're here for or what is expected of you. No one has any idea how this will turn out in the end."

She hesitated as she slid the mug to him and watched him take a sip, then leaned closer, her eyes frozen on Nikolai's. "And you don't believe you'll survive this."

Nikolai took long sips, then set the cup down.

"No, I don't."

"I won't let that happen. I'm going to fix this, Nikolai. You know I rarely fail when I start something. I'm like that assassin in those Terminator movies, I keep going until I get what I want."

She made him smile, thank God.

Then Nikolai's smile faded. "But this is cosmically sanctioned."

"Bah. I have a few cosmic connections of my own. No less than 10 first blood vampires who have spiritual ties well beyond this plane. Make no mistake, Nikolai, I will use every tool I can to make sure that you are still standing when the smoke clears on this."

"My little tiger."

"I like that. A glorious animal with sharp claws and teeth. Very few things on this earth will mess with it."

"I would never bet against *you*."

"Wise man. Let's get to your hotel, get you some clothes, get some food in you, and, God help me, let Mies find an appropriate blood meal."

Nikolai rolled his eyes. "It's been difficult. I'm aware, of course, that he needs to feed, but I find the process quite distasteful."

"It's necessary, though, for vampire health. He really does need the blood."

"I know, I've felt the effects when we have gone too long between feedings. He's wanted sex, too, but I've asked him not to, and he's been kind enough to comply. But he's not happy about it."

"I wouldn't imagine he would be." Sarah thought about that engorged penis, and now that she knew he had been celibate, she felt even guiltier for turning him on and then turning him away.

But she had no choice. She would not lie with a vampire and upset her entire plan.

Hopping up, she snagged Nikolai's sleeve.

"Let's get moving."

The hotel room was kind of dismal, but it provided exactly the type of protection a vampire needed from daylight. After putting on clothes still too small for his current size, Nikolai followed Sarah back out of the building.

"We're starving," he commented, as they slid into a waiting taxicab.

"I'm taking you to *Transparency*, a restaurant with delightful food. I figure that you two have been through so much, I would treat you to the best. My girlfriend takes me there once in a while, and it has become a favorite. Not only mine, but this entire city."

Minutes later, they pulled up in front of a building on a busy street. The entire front was a series of windows with elaborate etchings, the glow from the interior threw soft amber light into the darkened street. Several groups of people waited outside.

"There are a lot of people here tonight. I'll see how long it's going to be, but we may have to seek another restaurant."

"That is okay, Sarah, whatever you can do." He followed her into the busy space, and although a lot of people wandered around the lobby, and voices could be heard, it was pretty quiet. The acoustics were designed to soften sound within the room.

Nikolai leaned against a glass wall as Sarah waited to speak with a tall red-headed hostess behind a frosted glass pedestal. Several women passing him stared or did double-takes. He smiled back at them, aware that his body was now what women called a stud. Two stopped and

72

actually ran their fingers along his arms, the heavy muscle apparent in the strained shirt.

Sarah watched from where she waited, a smile on her lips. That *was* a spectacular body, naturally he would be noticed. The blatant touches surprised her, but she noticed that he didn't seem to mind. She remembered that he hadn't allowed Mies to have sex the past few months, and of course neither had he, so the attention was probably welcome.

Two more women stopped dead in front of him and one actually leaned close and put her lips to his collarbone.

Why did that bother her? It wasn't *her* business. Perhaps it was just that she thought that the woman's behavior was too brash.

Sarah sighed. *No, it wasn't.* She knew that some part of her was jealous that this man she was unexpectedly attracted to would have sex with a woman very soon, and in spite of her determination not to be with a vampire, she wanted it to be *her.*

"Unreasonable bitch," she said out loud.

"I'm sorry, ma'am, what did you say?"

Crap, the hostess had finished with the previous guest and was talking to her.

Sarah winced. "Sorry, not you. Just…" It was obvious that the woman didn't care.

"How long before you can seat a party of two?" Sarah asked.

"At least an hour and a half, if not two," the hostess said, a cold smile plastered on her lips.

"I thought so. Thanks, anyway," Sarah answered and made her way back to Nikolai, whose left arm was entangled by a woman with long hot-pink nails and a whole lot of exposed cleavage.

Sarah knew that when she smiled at the woman holding onto Nikolai, it had to be as cold as the hostess's insincere smile.

"Nik, it's going to be too long, so we'll just find somewhere else."

"Oh, you must stay!" Hot-pink nails proclaimed loudly.

Sarah shook her head. "Not happening."

73

"Sarah!"

Turning to the loud voice, Sarah saw Naji making her way through the waiting diners.

"Sarah, join us!"

Ah, this she didn't need, not tonight.

"Hi, no, I'm here with a friend and…"

"Friend? Ooh, who is it?"

Naji's eyes scanned the crowd waiting for tables and when they landed on the huge man behind her, they widened. "Don't tell me this piece of prime beef is your date?"

Sarah jumped in. "No, no, he's just a friend."

"Um, huh, I wish all of my *friends* came with that equipment." She surged forward, a smoldering look focused on Nikolai.

Was he blushing, Sarah wondered.

"Hi, I am Nikolai," he said, his Russian accent more pronounced than usual.

With her inimitable style, Naji wrapped a hand around Nikolai, the other around Sarah, and led them through the standing people.

"This is going to be an interesting night," she announced. She captured Sarah's gaze. "Sweetheart, you have been holding out on me."

"No, he just got into town last night. He's come a long way, so I wasn't planning on keeping him out all night."

Naji's electric personality was on overload. Sarah knew that it was because she sensed the strong pheromones Nikolai's body emitted. And she knew that Mies would show up at some point, because Naji was gorgeous, sexy, fascinating, and the perfect blood-meal and bed partner.

She wasn't sure that she could let that happen. Naji would have an experience like no other, and in that, it would be spectacular. Mies would use compulsion to make sure that she had nothing but great memories. But it breached the trust she had built with Naji. Secrets were dangerous and she'd vowed to keep them at a minimum. Then, there was the nasty jealousy that insisted on raising its ugly head. Being a pragmatic woman, Sarah knew it was unreasonable and silly. If she didn't want to have sex

74

with Mies, there was absolutely no reason to deny it to someone else. He needed the blood meal, and the sex would significantly improve both Nikolai and Mies's mood.

Still…

As the evening progressed, Sarah sat amazed. Mies did not show, but Naji and Nikolai were so mesmerized by each other, they barely noticed that Sarah was present. Through three courses of food, their heads bowed towards each other, forks in each other's plates, and several sensuous *feedings*, Sarah saw Naji glow like she'd never seen her. Three times Naji glanced over to Sarah, and her eyes sparkled with pure joy. Was she watching the awareness of love in Naji's eyes?

Naji had told her that she'd never been in love and couldn't imagine being so. "Too many creative partners out there to *ever* settle on just one," Naji had explained.

Tonight, though, there was a distinct difference in how she behaved with Nikolai. Sarah couldn't imagine why Mies hadn't pushed forward to make his mark with the lovely woman. She would certainly ask him later why he stayed under to let Nikolai enjoy the evening with her.

It was actually charming. Naji was usually the aggressor in her romantic pursuits, but with Nikolai, she was almost shy. While she ate her dinner, Sarah couldn't take her eyes off the sweet display. Nikolai kept brushing his fingers along Naji's arm, frequent shoulder bumps followed big smiles which led Sarah to think that something else might be bumping underneath the table. Maybe she was going to have to let Naji be with Nikolai after all, since Mies was so absent.

Naji's other dinner companions, an elderly man and his young companion, kept Sarah amused throughout the meal until Naji suddenly looked up at her guests.

"Dinner was wonderful tonight, everyone, thank you for joining us. I'll get the tab, so if you would like to go on with your night, I'll stay and take care of everything else."

She leaned across the table and offered her hand to the older gentleman. "Demeter, thank you for bringing Sofora to meet me. Sofora, I can't wait to see your work. I'll meet you at the studio tomorrow evening, all right?"

Demeter pushed back his chair, helped Sofora to her feet, took Sarah's hand and kissed it, then bowed.

"Such lovely company tonight, we are lucky men, eh?" he said to Nikolai. Nikolai, now standing as well, nodded.

"Da, no luckier in this city," he answered, but his gaze slid back to Naji.

Sarah tilted her head. Was *Naji* blushing now? *Into the rabbit hole*, she thought.

After Demeter and his lady had gone, Naji looked at Sarah. "My darling, would you mind terribly if I steal your man? I would like to *welcome* him to Boston, Naji-style."

Sarah was prepared to say yes, and leave them to it, when Nikolai turned Naji toward him, his fingers gently guiding her chin.

Sarah watched Naji nearly melt as he kissed her gently on the lips. Only it wasn't Nikolai that kissed her.

Mies lifted up from the soft kiss and caught Naji's eyes.

"We had a nice dinner and connected on a strongly sensual level, but you will go home now and think of the kind man you dined with. Your dreams of him will be erotic and satisfying."

Naji sighed with a smile, picked up her bag, and walked out of the restaurant without saying a word to Sarah.

Sarah looked up into Mies's eyes.

"Good evening," she said. "And welcome back."

He nodded, walked over to the waiter, used compulsion to take care of the check, and came back to the table where Sarah waited.

"The meal was pleasant and hit the spot. Now, I must look for a quick blood-meal. Do you wish to accompany me or do you prefer to go home?"

He'd get in trouble, in Boston, alone, with no real idea how busy modern cities worked. Nikolai was buried now, and she knew that Mies would not let him out too soon.

"No. This needs to be efficient and safe."

"It will be. Compulsion takes care of all risks."

"Like the accident you had when the taxi hit you? It isn't a good idea since you are so new to this world."

Hesitating before she said anything else, she almost bit her tongue. But she said it anyway.

"I'll do it. I'll feed you. This once."

Their eyes locked and he watched her pupils dilate while she held her breath. He didn't say anything, but nodded again, and led her out.

A waiting taxi took them back to his hotel room and once the door closed, Sarah walked to the window to look out at the city lights. It was on the fifth floor and the view was uninspiring.

His voice came from behind her. "Are you ready?" he asked.

For seconds longer, Sarah kept her attention on the cityscape below the window. When she turned, her breath hitched because he'd taken off his shirt and wore only a black sleeveless tee shirt. He stood ten feet from her, his arms at his side, the big well-defined muscles flexing as he flexed his fingers.

"Are you nervous?" she asked suddenly, surprised at the restless motion of his hands.

"No. Anxious. Excited."

"Excited? I'm just offering the blood-meal, buddy. If you wanted the sex, you should have let Nikolai take Naji home. I guarantee you two would have the best ride."

"No. I'm just hungry for blood. And I would have receded to allow them privacy, so it would only have been Niko and the lovely Nubian."

"You mean you wouldn't have to be present if they were together?"

"I can go into the spirit realm to let Nikolai have the body completely to himself, yes. I can send him there, too, if I need to do that. He prefers that when I take a blood-meal. He has never acquired the taste."

"I can imagine. So, yes to the blood, as I said. No to sex, sorry."

"I understand."

"Where do you want me?"

"Everywhere, but that is off the table."

"Funny. How about the sofa?"

"It will do."

Sarah walked around Mies as she took a seat in the center of the sofa to allow him access on either side of her neck.

He approached her slowly. When he dropped beside her, his weight shifted hers and she pitched into him.

"Ummm," he moaned as he slid his arms around her and gently laid her head back against the sofa.

"You know it will sting for but a second."

Sarah couldn't make the words come, but she nodded, her eyes closed, because this was already too sensual and she was aching like crazy between her legs. *Oh, this was every bit as bad of an idea as she thought it would be!*

His teeth grazed the skin beneath her left ear and she steeled herself for the punctures, but they did not come. Instead, she felt his tongue, hot and aggressive, travel from her neck to her collarbone, then back to her neck. His fingers moved against her belly and she put her own hands on top of his to stop them, but without conscious decision, she curled her fingers around the back of his hand and let them ride along with his as he slipped under her shirt and caressed just underneath her bra, then slid down to unsnap her pants.

The dual assault of his tongue on her neck and his fingers on her belly created a languorous feeling and Sarah found herself sliding down on the sofa as he pressed gently, his weight pushing her down.

"Just the blood," Sarah whispered.

"Just the blood," he agreed. Then his tongue slid deeper until it met the top of her bra, and he pushed beneath her shirt to nip a very erect nipple through the satin. "Unless you ask for more."

"No, I won't..." Sarah hoped that sounded more decisive than she thought it might. "Blood-meal only, Mies."

"Okay, but you know vampires need to play with their food."

He struck then, lightning fast, and she thought that the puncture might sting, might hurt, for a second, but the only thing that she felt was moisture surge between her legs. She wanted to feed her hand down there and press it against the wet opening to remind herself that she wasn't going to have sex, it might as well stop tweaking. It didn't listen, though. All she wanted now was to feel Mies there, any way she could get him, but mostly, she wanted to feel the big organ that was pushing against her leg right now.

Mies's tongue moved over the punctures, his teeth buried, as he drew blood into his body through a generous artery, and the feeling…*oh, fuck, was new.* It had to be the abstinence, but he thought he might ascend back to the spirit realm and never come back if he couldn't get inside of this infuriating woman right now. He'd promised both her and himself that he wouldn't touch her like that unless she asked. *Gods, she had to ask!*

Nikolai was blocked away from this body, sitting on a beach right now, and thankfully, unaware of the intensity of Mies's emotions.

Mies wasn't even sure he liked the sharp-tongued wench. There was no doubt that she was intelligent, stunning, and the sexiest thing he had seen since he came to this world. No…before that too. *He'd never been this enamored…it pissed him off!* And he still wanted inside of her worse than anything he could remember in this life or the last. As smart as she was, and as turned on, she was stubborn, so he knew that there was a great chance that he'd be in that shower and taking care of his own needs shortly.

No, no, no! Good God, how could he feel this sensuous?

"Uh…" That utterance was all Sarah got out before his tongue went flat against her neck and licked a wide path towards her breasts as it had earlier, along with searing heat and moisture.

She tried again. "When, uh, will you be finished?"

Mies lifted his head and Sarah noticed how dilated his eyes were, the lids heavy. He was dangerously close to a sexual thrall. "Mies, you need to get control."

"I have control. You need to let me use it. Your body is begging me…I can feel you…your stimulation, you want me. Little doctor, why can we not find pleasure in each other?"

His fingers had stilled, but were moving again, and this time, he held hers and led her own fingers below her waistband to slide under her panties and between her legs, which she widened to allow better touch. He pushed her fingers lower until she followed the line of the slick channel. When he pushed her fingers in, deep into the slit, his own piggy-backed with hers, she felt herself close around the thickness they made.

The groan motivated Mies and he moved his lips to her ear. "You must say the word."

Sarah heard him. *Say the word.* He was asking for permission to give her the orgasm of her life. She couldn't refuse now, her body wouldn't let her. But her mind took charge and *it* wouldn't let her accept him. There would be a price to pay for the perfection of sex with this vampire. Maybe someday she would be willing to pay, but she wouldn't make that decision just because she wanted to feel him, once, inside her. How would it feel to have him buried deep in her womanhood, moving, touching, feeling, exciting… *Stop!*

"Are you finished with your blood-meal?" she asked with a calmness that belied her real emotions.

Mies pulled back after sealing the wounds and got off the sofa.

"I guess that's the word. And yes, I am finished."

Sitting up and pulling her clothes back together, Sarah lifted off the sofa and walked to the window again. The brisk night air wasn't up to the task of cooling her down.

"Thank you," Mies said from the other side of the room as he poured a glass of Scotch. "Would you like something to drink before you go?"

"No, I'm fine. And I guess I should. Go, I mean."

"You may wish to know that your blood is potent. More so than an ordinary human's blood."

"Oh. I suppose it is because I was a blood-bond for many decades. Although it seemed that all of the effects of it had worn off since I have not had any vampire blood in three months."

Killing the entire glass of Scotch, Mies turned to Sarah, who still lingered by the window. He thought she looked extraordinary, standing there with the wind blowing her hair back, her clothes fluttering, her blouse gaping as the air raced down the neckline.

"It should have. I think that you have something beyond human in you. There may be elements of magic in you."

Sarah shook her head. "I don't think so. I'm smart, driven, thorough, mostly a scientist at heart, but I don't think I'm anything special beyond that."

"The blood says different."

She was uncomfortable with this conversation.

"Be that as it may, I think I'll head home."

As she reached the door, she turned suddenly.

"Mies, something's been nagging at me all night. Once my girlfriend snagged us and drew us into the restaurant, I expected that you would take over. She's hot, smart, and sexy. You were looking for blood and sex tonight. Why did you let Nikolai stay in charge?"

Without answering, Mies started to pour a second glass of the fine Scotch, but then set the glass back on the counter and lifted the bottle to drink directly from the lip.

"Nikolai connected with her right away. I had no right to interfere with a relationship that he was interested in building. So I enjoyed the company and the meal, and let him woo your vibrant friend. If one of us sleeps with her, it will be Nikolai. He deserves the feelings they developed almost from the moment they met. I could feel him, doctor." Mies smiled as he took another swig. "He's deeply smitten."

"All right. That was very generous and thoughtful of you."

Mies's eyes shot to Sarah's. "I am not a monster."

Sighing, Sarah walked to him, took one of his hands and pressed it to her chest. "I know that. This thing between us is complicated. We'll work it out eventually. Until then, get some rest. You still have some healing to do, and that blood meal will help. Do you have a cell phone?"

"The communication device that you can hold in your hand? Yes, we do. It's a piece of human magic."

Sarah laughed. "Yeah, it is. Let me have the number, and I'll give you mine. We must stay in touch as we begin this mission."

His eyes burned into hers. "I *want* to stay in touch."

"That isn't how I mean."

After entering her own number in Nikolai and Mies's cell phone and taking theirs, she left before she let herself change her mind.

Six

Please, call me. I know we missed our date, but we have to reschedule. You don't know how much I've been looking forward to this.

The voice mail from Leo should have made Sarah happy. Wrapped in a satin robe that Naji had given her, a sexy one of course, she perched on the edge of a chair while she nursed a hot milk chocolate with whipped cream three inches high. She smiled as she thought about how much Mies liked the sweetened coffee.

"You'd love this," she said out loud.

And that was the problem. A terrific message from Leo that he couldn't wait to be with her, and she sat here musing about how pleased that vampire would be with hot chocolate.

"Aargghh!"

Placing the mug carefully on the counter, she wandered over and pulled the curtain back to look at the soft light as night faded into a golden morning. God, she loved her mornings now. In Xavier's household, she usually got up in time to see sunsets, but rarely sunrises.

"I've missed the sunrises," she whispered.

Turning, she headed to the bathroom to take her shower.

"Today, I'm going to go and watch the Atlantic and just be out there with other people going through their *day.*"

Was talking to yourself an indication that you're going a little stir crazy? Probably. More than anything right now, Sarah needed to distance herself from that world that encroached again into the life she sought here in the U.S.

Dialing her phone, she waited.

"Who the hell?" a sharp voice whispered through the speaker.

"Naj? I woke you, didn't I?"

"I can't even see the sun, of course you did!"

"It's just rising."

"Just rising? Ugh! What time is it?" A loud groan cut off Sarah's reply. "Don't answer. All I need to know is that it is *too-early* o'clock. Love, this better be an emergency."

"It is. Life's short, it is a gorgeous spring day, and I need you to go boating with me this morning on sparkling waters with sparkling wine. Please tell me you are up to it."

After several moments of silence, Naji answered.

"Maybe. Will you bring that delicious Russian pastry with you that I had dinner with last night?"

"Ah. That's, uh, not possible."

"Why not? If I have to get rudely awakened by the sun, what puts him out of the realm of possibility?"

Because he's a vampire and the sun will burn him alive almost instantly.

"He has other plans. Unbreakable plans."

"Give me two hours. It will take me that long to wake up enough, get some coffee, forgive you for waking me so *early*, and get this mass of hair tamed."

"Thank you! I'll supply lunch."

"You know what I like. All right, let me go do this."

Good. A nice, normal day in full sunlight with ordinary-sized portions of food, and her favorite human companion who always made her laugh. Today would be a wonderful respite.

Two hours later, exactly on time, Sarah, waited on the stairwell outside her apartment building for Naji's little red corvette. As she searched her big beach bag for her sunglasses, she glanced up when a sleek silver Mercedes convertible slid to a stop in front of the steps. Dropping her eyes to continue her search, she looked back up when she heard someone clear their voice. Naji got out of the Mercedes and leaned against the hood.

"Coming?" Naji inquired casually.

Sarah stood. "That isn't your car," she commented, a little confused.

"It is now. My new buddy Demeter gave it to me."

"I'm definitely in the wrong line of work," Sarah said as she grabbed her wide-brimmed hat, and walked down the steps to slide into a luxurious cream-colored leather seat.

"Why did he give this to you?"

Naji tore away from the curb far too quickly, but Sarah was accustomed to her fast starts and faster stops.

"He told me that a beautiful woman should be in a beautiful car, and handed me the keys. My new job comes with some awesome perks!"

"I'll say."

"Plus, we're set up at his yacht club for a cruise on his yacht today."

"No!"

"Yes! Don't worry about lunch, he's catering."

"Naji, you are the most amazing person."

Naji's joyful laugh filled the air around them. "I know. I honestly think that I could fall into a pile of shit and crawl out with a handful of diamonds."

"I believe it."

Three hours later, sitting on the deck of a luxury yacht, sipping a smooth Mai tai, Sarah laid her head back against an exceptionally comfortable lounge chair next to Naji. Her eyes closed, Naji nursed a similar drink from a bright green straw.

"This is the life," Naji sighed, eyes still closed.

"Ummm, I agree," Sarah purred. "Someday, maybe, for me, if I can get my practice established."

"Soon, for me, because I'm going to marry that billionaire. I just have to figure out how to get rid of that bitch that has her hooks in him now."

"Bitch? I thought Sofora seemed sweet."

"Oh, she is. But she's between me and that gorgeous money bags, so I have to demonize her to justify getting rid of her hot Latina ass."

"You're too kind for that."

"Maybe. Speaking of hot. Where's your friend today?"

"Friend?"

"Oh, Sarah, you don't play stupid too well. You know precisely who I mean."

"I thought you had your sights set on money bags."

"I'd change them in a New York minute if I could snag that man, rich or poor." Naji opened her eyes, which were softer than Sarah had ever seen. "We really connected, love."

"Nikolai is a wonderful man. You two would be great together. But Naj, it's complicated and I don't know if that will ever be possible."

"He's married?"

"No, but he's…" There really was no way to let Naji know that Nikolai was in real trouble. "He's just unavailable, let's leave it there. I wish I could tell you, but it's kind of family secrets."

"Come on, love, spill."

"I would, but just trust me, I really can't."

"Too bad." Naji closed her eyes again and laid her head back on the lounge. "I felt something. Like maybe I could have finally found the one man that I would keep."

"Naj…"

"Forget it. Lots of hot men out there waiting for me, so he isn't *that* big a loss."

Sarah could see that wasn't true. Naji truly wanted a chance to see where a relationship with Nikolai could have gone. "I'm sorry, my friend."

Naji surged from the seat and poured a glass of wine to overflowing, capturing the spilling wine as quickly as possible with her tongue. "Don't be daft, there's nothing to apologize for," She said with a full-on British accent.

After a few moments, Sarah decided to let the subject die. "I'm going to take you to London someday soon."

"And I'm going to keep you to that promise."

The rest of the afternoon went exactly as Sarah had hoped; long leisurely swims in warm waters, plenty of wine and poo-poo platters, and several impromptu disco dance sessions. By the time the sun lowered to just above the skyline, Sarah and Naji were buzzed and grinning off the edge of the yacht as it headed back to its berth. Both were entranced as they watched long rays of light bounce off the water like giant pieces of scattered glitter.

"Sarah, let's never *not* be friends, okay? Where I come from, people lose each other. All the time, right? And I hate that. You and I are meant to be friends *forever*, I felt that from the first day. Yeah?"

"Yeah," Sarah said softly, leaning into Naji's taller form.

"Hey, let's do a blood bond? Like blood sisters, okay?"

Blood bond. The term that defined who Sarah had been all of her life. The bond meant nothing if she did it with a human, not really, but she understood Naji's need to make the metaphoric connection. It wasn't as if she was unaccustomed to blood.

Walking over to the poo-poo platters, she set her wine glass down and picked up a sharp knife meant to cut thin slices of cheese. She walked back to the railing where Naji lingered, tipped a little too far out over the water, stopped beside her, held up the knife and punctured her own index fingertip.

Naji smiled and held out *her* fingertip to Sarah.

"Do the honors," she said, and winced as Sarah did so without delay.

Holding the seeping fingertips to each other, Naji leaned down and placed her forehead against Sarah's.

"Thank you for arriving in my life when you did. My mother, God rest her bitchy soul, had only one good piece of advice for me. 'There's good folk and bad folk, child, learn to know the difference, and it will serve you well all your life.' She was right. You are good folk, Sarah."

"You've helped me, too, in ways I could never convey, so I think that your mother was right, and that we found each other because there is order to the universe, and sometimes, it gets it right."

They stayed there, finger to finger, forehead to forehead, for several more minutes, a merge of hearts, aware that their journeys through this life were merged now, too.

It felt good to have a companion on this journey. Sarah knew now, as much as at any other time, that she'd made the right choice by leaving Xavier and finding her own place in this world. She was human, and yes, it was exactly where she belonged. Exactly where she wanted to be.

As they moved apart, Naji drained her glass of wine. "Do you work tonight?"

"I guess. I'm scheduled and I haven't called in."

"Worried about your guest?"

"I am. I have to be. He's, um, unfamiliar with this city and how things work here. Effectively, he's kind of too innocent to leave alone too long. He'll get into trouble."

Naji's eyes twinkled.

"I know where he can go to wait for you where he won't get into *any kind of trouble at all.*"

"Ha, you wish."

"What, are you afraid I'll break him?"

"You actually might."

Placing a hand on Sarah's shoulder, Naji turned to face her. "Are you interested in Nikolai? Because if you are, of course, hands off, I promise. Hos before bros."

"No, no, Naj, not at all. I can honestly say that I have no romantic interest in Nikolai at all."

Although the hot vampire trapped inside of him was an entirely different thing that Naji couldn't begin to understand.

"Then why don't you want me around him?"

"He's just." Sarah really didn't have a good reason unless she told her the truth. And she was certainly *not* going to do that. Knowledge of the vampire world complicated human lives and she didn't want to do that to Naji.

"He's just not the right man for you. You have to trust me on this, okay?"

Several silent moments later, Naji nodded.

"I trust you. If you say he isn't, then you have a very good reason to do so. Too bad, though, I know we would have had the best sex ever."

"I have no doubt. Perhaps things will change. Until then, my dear friend, this has been the perfect day. Great warm spring weather, wine I could never afford, a luxury yacht, and *your* company. You'll never know how much I needed this very normal human day."

"Human?" Naji said with a smile. "I guess I do that pretty well."

The drive back to Sarah's apartment was quiet, both women relaxed and satisfied with everything in their lives at that very moment in time.

As the new car pulled up and stopped at Sarah's building, Sarah got out but leaned back against the doorframe.

"I'll see you soon. Goodnight, love," she said.

"Goodnight, love," Naji repeated, then pulled away once she saw the security door to Sarah's building close.

"Oh, I can't *believe* that you cancelled that date!"

Tracy finished off her precious hot chocolate.

Sarah finished putting away a box of bandages. It was a slow night in Mass Gen's ER.

"Family emergency, it couldn't be helped."

"Hah. I heard that you had a sexy visitor from your past show up suddenly."

Stunned, Sarah stared at Tracy. "Where would you have heard something like that?"

"From me."

Leo walked from the long hallway that led to the doctor's lounge.

As he approached, Sarah looked up at him. "Leo..."

He smiled casually, his hands in his pockets. "It's okay, Sarah. I saw you out to dinner with him. I ended up at *Transparency* with a colleague after you called to tell me about your *emergency*."

"Leo, I'm sorry." She started to explain when she noticed that Tracy hadn't moved, her eyes wide and both hands still wrapped around the now empty paper cup. Her eyes moved to Sarah when she stopped speaking.

"Oh, I guess I could find somewhere else to be."

"I appreciate that," Sarah told her with a nod.

Tracy hurried out to the nurse's desk as Sarah turned back to Leo.

"It's okay, Sarah. I get it. Someone from your past shows up and things change."

"No. Nothing's changed. Nikolai is an old friend and he'd arrived unexpectedly from Russia. He couldn't have managed here without my help. I'm so sorry, Leo, but he needed my guidance. I was going to give you more details when I saw you next. Which is now."

"Fine. I understand. So...you haven't changed your mind about dating me?"

"No! No, Leo, not at all. I meant it when I told you that I was disappointed that we couldn't get together Saturday."

"I was too. Very. So, can we reschedule? Soon?"

Her hesitation made him flinch. She definitely wanted to reschedule, but it wasn't a good idea until this situation with Nikolai and Mies was sorted out.

To make sure that he understood her, Sarah stepped close, glanced around the room to make sure they were still alone, took a firm hold of his tie and yanked him to her.

All of her sexual frustration poured into the kiss. After the shock passed, Leo pulled her against him and she could feel his body's reaction, the movement in his pants, his thighs pressed against her abdomen as if he wanted to wrap around her.

Once she moved back, Sarah looked into his eyes.

"I really do want to reschedule, but I can't make any plans yet. Will you still accept the date if I have to defer it for a little while?"

Leo was still tamping down the results of the kiss, a hand moving nervously through his hair. "Yeah, um, yeah."

"That was a reminder that I mean that, when we finally get to it, the wait will be worth it."

Blowing out a long breath, he turned from her, still feeding restless fingers through his loose hair. "I knew that all along, and now, whew, the wait, however long or short it will be, is already too long. See you, Doctor S."

Leo disappeared down the corridor and didn't see Sarah drop back against the wall, a smile on her lips, a gleam in her eyes.

"God, that was hot," she said out loud, but when she closed her eyes for a moment, it wasn't Leo's face that filled the darkness. Unwelcome though he was inside her thoughts, it was Mies.

She blew out a long breath like Leo had done moments earlier, but hers was from frustration. What was she going to do about him? She could not want him, she refused to. Still he stayed in her mind, and the mere thought of him made her horny.

"Am I going to have to fuck that vampire to get him out of my mind?" she whispered to what she thought was an empty room.

"What vampire are you going to fuck?"

Tracy stood behind her and when Sarah turned to her big grin, she rolled her eyes and followed Leo's egress down the corridor.

It was going to be a long night.

Three hours into the shift, the hour approaching one a.m., Sarah finished bandaging a deep gash on a ten-year old boy's leg. He'd fallen off the concrete steps in front of their apartment building and into a pile of construction debris.

"You're good to go, Paulie. I'll tell your mother she can come back in."

"Hey, mom!" he yelled loudly through the closed curtain.

"Really?" Sarah inquired. "I meant I would go *get* her."

"Sorry. We're all yellers in my family."

"I get that."

Shirley Malone came back through the curtain. "He's done? Oh, thank God! I can't stand the sight of blood. Just driving him here, I had to keep him in the back seat."

"Well, he's all covered now, and he's fine. It's a deep gash, but a few stitches and a clean bandage does wonders."

"Thanks, Doc."

After finishing up, Sarah left the nurse to do all relevant paperwork to get Paulie and his mom on their way back home.

Tracy joined her a few moments later as she leaned against the nurse's station. The two nurses who manned the desk had taken a quick break, and since the ER was unusually quiet right now, she'd offered to spell them for a few minutes.

"You get the kid with the leg injury?" Tracy asked.

Sarah nodded. "He was easy. How is Mr. Brooks?"

"The usual. He's having a tough go with the chemo. Too sick to keep anything down right now."

Each day here reminded Sarah of the fragility of human life, the extraordinary limitations of a mortal body that could be injured or die so easily. There had been a few mind-blowing moments where her heart raced at the idea that she'd given up immortality for this brief life, however beautiful and satisfying it had been. Would she be satisfied at the end of the few decades she had left? Would all that she'd won by returning to her nature be worth it as she lay ill, aged, and dying in what was certainly, by vampire standards, a very short time?

No. No, she would not allow her mind to wander back into that dangerous zone. Her choice had been made and she expected that it would, absolutely, be the life she wanted and needed. That someday, at the moment the time arrived, she would accept, gracefully, that her days were well-lived and move beyond this realm. She didn't know if humans found a place in the spirit world that seemed to be the final resting place for the first bloods, but she hoped that there really was a place beyond all of this, a *heaven*, for humans, too.

"Sarah?"

Tracy pulled Sarah from deep thoughts that had no place in the ER.

"I'm sorry, Tracy, what were you saying?"

She leaned heavily on the counter, facing her colleague. Tracy faced the front of the admissions area with an expression of surprise.

Confused, Sarah wondered what she'd missed while she had been spaced out checking her emotional baggage.

"Trace, what is it?"

"Um, you have a visitor," Tracy finally replied and pointed behind Sarah.

Before she even turned around, Sarah knew who it had to be. There was only one person, or persons, as it were, who would have caused that look of shocked surprise. As she lifted away from the counter and turned, Sarah prepared herself. Would it be Nikolai, welcoming, with a smile? Or the brooding Mies, who sent Sarah's libido into hyper-drive? By Tracy's continued state of awe, she knew that it had to be Mies.

Slowly turning, she confirmed that suspicion. No smile, but heat searing off him like compressed steam.

God, it should be illegal for anyone to be that sexually explicit just standing there.

"Doctor Sarah," he said quietly with supreme confidence.

I could throw him down right here and...

Stop! Sarah told herself. *Enough with the ridiculous mental images!*

"Mies," she acknowledged. "Didn't you get my text?"

"The message on the little box? Nikolai did. I didn't. We need to speak. Now."

Tracy touched Sarah on her arm, drawing her attention away from the huge man who stood in front of them, his dark eyes moving between the two women.

"Sarah, who is this man?"

"He's, uh, an old friend from out of the country."

Tracy's eyes moved over Mies's body, dressed again in tight jeans and the black tee shirt that showed every bulge.

She tilted her head. "Don't I know you?"

Sarah shook her head. "No, Trace. He just got into town, didn't you, Mies?"

Completely emotionless, Mies looked from Sarah to Tracy. He knew the young doctor was one of the people present the night he arrived in town and was hit by the speeding car.

Suddenly, he smiled. Sarah knew that she wasn't the only one who felt the full force of his sex appeal.

"Look into my eyes, little doctor," Mies said, only this time he was talking to Tracy.

She did not hesitate.

Sarah watched the silver lights begin to swirl again as he touched her on the wrist, his fingers wrapping around it seconds later.

"You do not know me, you've never seen me before and you will not ask anyone who I am if you see me again. Please leave us."

A quick nod answered his command and Tracy walked away. She passed the two nurses who manned the desk, returning from their breaks, surprised as Tracy walked by without looking at either of them when they said hi to her.

"Hey," Sheila said to Sarah. "What's wrong with Doctor Harrison?"

Beginning to respond, Sarah moved back, startled, as Mies jumped over the receiving desk and landed next to her. Both nurses moved back as well.

He grabbed Sarah's arms. "Don't make me use compulsion."

Snapping her arms free, Sarah pushed him using all of her strength, not surprised when she barely moved him at all. "You try that, and you're on your own. Ask Nikolai if I'll submit to that kind of treatment and betrayal."

"I'm sorry, but you waste time here on this irrelevant job. You need to devote all of your time to our problem. Do not forget that I can *make* you do what I want."

"What did I tell you about making demands? And threats? Mies, you need to get the hell out of here before I set your ass on fire."

Carelessly, using air displacement, he moved her from behind the desk to an alcove in the patient waiting area faster than humanly possible.

His fingers wrapped around her upper arms too tight, he suddenly lightened his hold, now massaging the bruised flesh. As he leaned down, his hair brushed her shoulders, and she thought that he was too close, and yet wanted to pull him closer. Because he was in a heightened emotional state, his overt sexual pheromones were on overdrive and assaulted her. In spite of her anger, Sarah could hardly think straight and she made the one critical error when confronted by a vampire; she looked up into his smoldering eyes.

He didn't steal the opportunity to use compulsion, though. His voice raw, his lips too near to hers, he drew a deep breath. "Sarah, we woke tonight drenched in sweat. We couldn't catch our breath, we couldn't move. Tears came, and that is rare for a vampire."

The silver swirls in his eyes were spinning. His voice dropped. "For me."

His fingers slid to her waist and pulled her into him. Without realizing she was doing it, her arms went around him as he leaned into her, her own fingers finding the hard muscles of his waist.

Mies whispered into her ear. "Help us."

The kiss began slowly, amber eyes sought dark ones, then they moved closer. Once his lips touched Sarah's, Mies slipped his tongue out to taste them. He ran his tongue around the top lip, then the bottom, and drew back to look into her eyes and seek acceptance. What he saw kicked him in the groin and he pulled her body to his, fitted her shape against him, and plunged his tongue into her mouth.

Sarah leaped into the kiss, urgency not urgent enough, body against body not close enough, his hot tongue inside her incredible…and not enough either. Somewhere in the back of her mind, she was aware they were in a place that, while in a corner, was still public. They would need to go somewhere else if she wanted him inside her, as she really did.

But as the kiss grew more intense, she felt Mies lift her and begin to carry her deeper into the alcove.

"Mies, no."

"Doctor, it is clear that you want me, and I need you, with a desperation that I am not certain I could refuse even if I wanted to. And I don't."

"Not now. Not here. Stop, please."

He *did* stop then, unmoving, silent, only his ragged breath in her ear. Seconds later, he lowered her.

"You're refusing me again?"

Sarah had no answer. She wasn't sure if she was, wasn't sure if she wasn't, but she knew that they couldn't do anything here in the hospital.

"Can you wait for me? I need to speak with Dr. Harrison."

"What would be the point? You refuse me, on every matter. I assume that I am unwelcome in your life, so I will go."

No sooner had he announced the intention, he disappeared.

Exhausted, shocked, Sarah dropped into a chair.

What the hell was she going to do?

He was right. She needed to attend to the situation with Nikolai and his unexpected passenger. It was apparent that she would have to take a leave of absence from her job and do exactly that. They deserved nothing less from her. After letting herself have a few more moments to adjust to the truth, she walked back out into the receiving room.

Tracy had returned to the nurse's station, her fogged reaction to Mies's compulsion gone.

"Hey, Sarah."

"Hey," Sarah parroted.

Tomorrow morning, she would let the hospital know that she had to be away for an undetermined amount of time.

Seven

Mies wandered for hours through the glittering city where everything fascinated him. Nikolai had tried to push forward to help him navigate, but he was tired of having others guide him and tell him what he needed to know about this enormous modern world. He was a first blood vampire...powerful, smart, capable. He'd figure it out.

You were hit by a taxicab the first night you arrived.

I've learned much since then. I'm tired of feeling helpless. Tired of trying to figure out what we're supposed to do and how we're supposed to manage this fucking mess.

You are certainly learning. Look at you with the modern curse word.

It fits. This entire life we're forcibly living is impossible. We both want different women and can't be with either of them. We need different things. What the fuck was the universe thinking to do this to us?

"What the fuck do you want?" he yelled explosively, out loud, startling other people passing on the sidewalk near him.

Get it under control, vampire. We don't want to draw attention to ourselves, and we certainly don't want to end up with a confrontation with the local law.

I can manage anything, certainly human constables.

Yes, I know that, but how about we pretend we aren't children and don't make the wrong choices to start with?

97

You make sense. I find that I am too hot headed and you are likely the smart one. Perhaps you have more magic than I have in this world.

Hardly. But I am your voice of reason. Your calm side, if you'll listen. Sarah will help us.

No. I have told her that we don't need her.

And you're wrong. Even now, I know that she is making a decision to dedicate herself to our needs. She is a good woman.

Mies thought about Sarah, just a few hours earlier, hot in his arms, her tongue matching his every movement as they tried to get as close to each other as possible when they kissed.

Yes, she is a good woman, but she has other concerns. She's human, Niko, and has a human life. She doesn't belong to us.

She is our best choice. Don't count her out. We need to head back to her apartment.

Why? She'll only refuse me again.

You really are a child when it comes to women, aren't you? Whether she sleeps with you or not, she will give everything she is to help us. You have never met a more amazing, determined woman, Mies. Turn around.

No.

Mies smiled suddenly. Yeah, he really was acting like child. Nikolai was right. It was time to go to the beautiful human doctor, his cock tucked back, his libido in check, and apologize. He had no right to make demands as he had done. However awful this life he and poor Nikolai had been forced into, Sarah was innocent and only attempting to help.

I've been an animal. All right, we'll go to her and I will throw myself on her mercy. Assuming she still has any when it comes to me. You, my friend, she loves.

I am not absent when I speak with her about you or when you control this body. I see and feel what you do, Mies, and it is obvious that she would like to show more than mercy to you. You understand her reasons, da?

Da. It doesn't make my friend go away, though. She sets me on fire, Niko.

That, I feel. Much as her friend did for me. We are a sad pair, vampire.

Da.

Mies gave control of the body back to Nikolai so that he could enjoy the walk back to Sarah's apartment, and so that *he* would be the one to apologize on behalf of *both* of them. It seemed the reasonable thing to do.

Nikolai sucked in the air and delicious smells as they walked past a neighborhood bakery. Sunrise would be in about two hours and someone was already inside preparing the baked goods for morning sales. He was of a mind to have Mies use compulsion to get them some hot pastries, but he didn't want to trade places with him right now. He just wanted to enjoy this American city. Neither he nor Mies had any idea how long either of them might have…either in this odd merged existence, or as the one surviving lifeforce in this body. Not a moment was to be squandered.

Warmth had finally hit Boston and seemed inclined to stay. As a man who lived in one of the coldest climates on earth, Nikolai lingered on the walk back to Sarah's place. Even this early in the morning, it had to be a good seventy-five degrees and on skin that was used to layers of fabric to protect it from frostbite, a warm breeze on bare skin was exquisite.

"Almost as good as sex," he said out loud, and could hear Mies laughing in his mind.

"Okay, not so much, but it is the best thing I have felt in a long time."

His face to the breeze, he closed his eyes for a moment and just stood there, the intersection he needed to cross still waiting for his footfall. His mind was calm but the thought intervened anyway.

"I'm not ready to leave," he told the universe when he opened his eyes, squinting to see if any stars were visible above the lights surrounding him. One was, and he wondered if it were a planet.

Jupiter.

"Jupiter," Nikolai repeated. "It's stunning. Everything is so vividly bright in Siberia. So few lights to compete with the canopy of stars and other celestial bodies."

A young woman leaning against a post smoking a cigarette looked at him abruptly. "You talkin' to me, mister?"

"No, ma'am, I was just remarking about the beauty of the night sky."

Jerking her head up, she stared into the charcoal darkness above the city for several moments. When she dropped her head back to look into Nikolai's eyes, she rolled hers. "Whatever."

Once again, Nikolai could feel Mies's amusement.

Youth hasn't changed in six thousand years, I see.

Shaking his head, Nikolai continued on his trek. "Da, some things never will."

Instantly, both men's minds shifted to one thing, to something else that never changed in the entire history of mankind. The need for connection, for love...*for sex*.

"Stop it, Mies. We are neither getting what we want. Not for this night, anyway."

The voice in his head was silent, and for the rest of the walk, so was Nikolai.

Several blocks away

Sarah had texted and called Nikolai's phone four times tonight with no response.

"Fine, you big, overblown, obnoxious...sexy asshole."

Pitching her phone onto the chair on the other side of the couch, she headed into the kitchenette.

"Late for dinner, early for breakfast. What shall I eat? Damn, this situation. If things had gone according to plan, I would be having a fancy breakfast with Leo in his high-dollar all-glass apartment downtown. But no, I haven't even had my date with him yet."

After setting the kettle on, she glanced up when a gentle knock on her door interrupted as she reached for a canister of cocoa.

Her eyes went to the clock. "Three am?" She placed the canister on the counter and started toward the door.

"Only one person this would be at this time of day."

She paused just before she flipped the catch to let him in and looked up. "Destiny, you're one vicious bitch," she said softly, and pulled the door wide.

Nikolai tilted his head and smiled. "Hi, lovely lady. We are here to apologize."

"I know. Come on in."

Once again, Nikolai's giant vampire body filled her apartment. She realized that she had watched his every movement as she closed the door.

"I was just going to make some sweet cocoa with a mountain of whipped cream. I don't even have to ask if you're interested."

"Never. Make mine as large as you can. Vampire appetite, you know."

"Boy, do I."

"We agree, by the way."

Pulling down a second much larger mug, Sarah looked up. "You agree?"

"Destiny. She's a nasty and creative bitch at times."

Nikolai grinned as he lowered himself onto her sofa.

"Vampire hearing, too."

"Yeah. I could never sneak up on Xavier. Even as a child, I'd try, and back then I was as light and quick as a fairy, but still I couldn't pull it off. Once, he tried to pretend like he was surprised, but I caught him at it, and I remember telling him that I would never want to win that way. If it wasn't a real accomplishment, it was useless."

"You've been good at everything you've ever done, haven't you?"

"No, but I've been pretty great at anything I really wanted because I knew that if you work hard enough, you can usually achieve anything you want."

"Mies, you hear that? We're in the right place with the right warrior."

Silence followed as Sarah watched to see if Mies emerged. She was thankful that he didn't. That kiss in the hospital still burned in her mind and she didn't trust herself with him right now.

"Here, Nik, let me get that cocoa to you. Are you heading back to your hotel tonight?"

"I think so. Your bathroom floor is, ah, a bit small for this body."

Those eyes that kept betraying her did so again as they went immediately to his chest and below, lingered where they shouldn't.

Nikolai stood suddenly. "Sarah, if you keep looking at me like that, Mies will come out."

"Shit! I know. I'm sorry. Sit back down, enjoy your cocoa. I have something I want to go over with you." She rolled her eyes. "With *both* of you."

Cautious, Nikolai took his seat again as Sarah scooted the large mug she'd placed on the table beside the sofa closer to him. A tower of curling white foam caught his eye immediately.

"I'm sorry, but I just needed to cool the two of you off a little." After taking a sip, a white mustache on his upper lip, which Nikolai licked off, he finished his statement. "You both run really hot."

"We aren't going to act on it, though. Look, I've done some research while I've been waiting. I had Tamesine send me the entire written history that we extricated from that magical tube that was buried with Mies's people at the gravesite. Luckily, she'd already made translated copies. So I'm familiar with basic elements of the lifestyles of the period, and the disease that ultimately sickened and killed them."

Sarah leaned over to reach a tablet computer lying on the table where she and Nikolai's drinks were.

Lifting back, she looked into his eyes, only it was no longer Nikolai.

"Tell me what you've discovered," Mies asked politely.

After a curt nod, Sarah handed him the top page.

"Your people had everything covered up until the contagion. Good lives that you shared with everyone. You

102

were fair and kind with other supernaturals as well as humans. I'm impressed with how lovely you all were. It appeared that the universe gave with both hands when it came to your race."

"We were very happy. When we began to die, and realized that we could not stop it, the tragedy was so deep, hearts so broken, that even if we had survived, I'm not sure we would ever have recovered."

"I understand, Mies. I got a great sense of your community as I read the pages your people left behind. You had beautiful lives and the loss was unmeasurable."

As she paused, her eyes lingered on his. What was it about this man that touched her so deeply? She had known numerous first blood men and none of them had ever had this intense effect on her.

In spite of her determination not to engage in a personal relationship with this ancient vampire, she still reached to him, her fingers finding his, a thrill hitting her belly when he curled them around hers without hesitation.

"We'll fix this, my friends."

Suddenly aware how easily that simple touch could evolve into more touching, she slipped her fingers from his quickly. *Back to business*, she reminded herself.

"So, here's what I think we may be looking for in these pages as they pertain to what we need to do. There is a section where the author of the pages…"

"Brio," Mies said suddenly.

"I'm sorry, what?"

"Brio. He was our scribe. *He* wrote the pages. The magic he bore was a connection to the universe beyond any of the other vampires."

"Okay. Well, Brio tells of the gifts and magic that the universe gave to your people. He said that you were all born of blood of the earth and the sky. It got me thinking that if you were *born* of the blood of the earth and sky, why couldn't you tap into the *magic* of the earth and sky? Think about it. If what is stated in those pages is true, you may already have the power that you need to fix this. You just have to know how to wield it and make it do what you need it to do."

"It's been centuries since I have used my gifts. When I was here before, they did not include a direct connection to the mother planet or the sky above her. Honestly, I'm not even sure *what* my talent may be now. Or if I even have one."

"It will take a special talent to do this. Mies, we need to contact the first bloods who live in *this* time. They are really good people who are not only talented, but kind and empathic. I know of two who have direct links to both the spiritual realm and the power of the earth. They will help."

"There is a danger in that, Sarah. I explained to Nikolai that if those who put us here, who have a mission for us in this body as we are right now, discover we seek to destroy the merge, they might stop us. Finding aid in those who receive their power from the universe may be an irreversible mistake."

"I don't think so. Mies, trust me, these people have accomplished remarkable things and they would not turn you in. In fact, I can guarantee they will be just as horrified as you are that the universe has done this to you and Nikolai. It's your choice, of course. I won't presume to make this decision without your consent. You would have to be compliant anyway for this to work. Why don't you and Nikolai think about it and let me know?"

"You do not believe that there are any other options?"

Lost in the depth of his eyes, Sarah forced herself to pay attention.

"I don't think so. This merge is sanctioned, designed, by powers that rule the way the planets move, tell the stars when to shine and when to die. You need magic, real universally-charged magic, to undo this deed. Too bad you don't have your spirit amulet."

"I have my spirit amulet."

"What? You do? How?"

"Before we left the caverns, Nikolai placed it around his neck. It is what alerted me that something had happened. It is what brought him to me on the spirit plane."

"Wow. Okay, then, in that case, perhaps I *do* have another idea." Sarah's mind raced now, aware that the spirit amulet that rode with any first blood through their life, and now apparently *beyond*, could tap into the primal powers of the universe. It may be all that they would need to find a way to reverse this odd and cruel fate.

"We can try using the amulet, and your power as it is enhanced by it, to change this event. But Mies, there is much to discuss before we seriously consider proceeding. Between me and you, between Nikolai and myself, and between *Nikolai and you*. We have to think about the consequences of this action. Even if it works, how might this end? What I mean is, what will happen to you two? Will *you* still exist on this plane if we succeed? On *any* plane? Will *Nikolai*? And if we can reverse this, if you both remain present, how can that work? Where would you go if Nik gets his body back? Once Nikolai has his body back, what will become of *you*, Mies? I don't have any answers to those questions. It's a lot to consider if we pursue this."

"Little doctor, we have already run the scenarios. Nikolai and I have long come to terms with how this might be once we unravel our merged lives. What we *know* is that we cannot live this way, neither of us. So, the results? Yes, we have no idea who may live or die, or if there is a way for both to survive. All we know with any surety is that we must try."

She couldn't move. All Sarah wanted at that moment was to memorize Mies's face, his eyes, those lips she'd experience only once, his expression of calm acceptance. He and Nikolai were both remarkable men and she couldn't imagine losing either one of them.

"I'll do all that I can to keep either of you from being swallowed by this cursed universal mistake."

The eyes that mesmerized her softened. With no warning, he surged forward and slid his hands up her arms.

"It is a cursed event, but I wouldn't call it a mistake."

One hand moved to her cheek, the fingers sliding across her skin to caress her jawline. "I wouldn't have met you if they hadn't sent me back. And I wouldn't have wanted to miss you."

He undid her. Sarah had never felt this kind of attachment to anyone.

"Mies, I will save you. And I'll save Nikolai."

He stood and walked to the door.

"Our heroine and warrior. I believe that you will. I must go now. If I stay another minute, I'll have you underneath me in seconds. Once I do, I'll ask permission, and you won't say no. So to honor your wish to avoid that, I'll leave. This is the most difficult part of our journey together, that I want you so badly and I cannot have you."

Sarah's mouth dropped. When she spoke a second later, she stuttered at first. "Mies. Uh, I...I don't know how to respond to that."

"I know. And I also know that you feel the same way. You want me, and you are miserable because you feel that you cannot have me."

He was right. No matter how badly she wanted to be able to refute it, he was right.

The silver swirls in Mie's smoky eyes had increased, more mesmerizing than usual. "It's all right, little doctor. I understand your reasoning because you are not mistaken. Once we make love, you will never want another man. I warn you, though. I plan to be utterly charming and ridiculously sexy, so guard yourself well."

As he was speaking, he slowly pulled the tee shirt over his head. "This is yours, Sarah. I will sleep with no other until it is you." His right hand curled against his swollen crotch.

She shot off the sofa. "No, Mies! Don't do that, don't wait for me. I can't, I mean it." After a pause, she sighed, a decision made. "Sleep with someone tonight. Pick a fascinating woman and fuck her until you both are satisfied. Or I'll give Naji a call and you can send Nikolai over to her."

Funny how the idea of Nikolai with Naji didn't bother her, but the idea of Mies finding a gorgeous woman and giving her the orgasm of her life...hurt.

"No. Only you. Good night, doctor."

Mies used air displacement to disappear and Sarah knew he was likely already on the next street and close to his hotel room. She fell back onto the sofa.

Oh, God, what had she gotten herself into? The vampire had challenged her and she knew that if he pushed it, even a small amount, he *would* be inside of her in seconds.

"And I want him to be," she whispered to the still air in the apartment as she sat alone. After another several minutes, she pushed up from the cushion.

"Hot chocolate. Now. Later, I'll deal with the hot vampire and my own crazy sex drive."

A chime interrupted, and as she pulled a clean mug from the cabinet, she glanced at the face of her cell phone.

"Leo," she said. "Sorry, buddy, I can only deal with one lothario at a time."

She let it go to voicemail.

Mies kept control of the body as they slowed from the inhuman pace to normal speed. He was still smiling.

I can't believe you said that to her. You told her that you wouldn't honor her wishes.

I told her that she would ask me to make love to her when the time came. And she will.

The woman has a sharp mind and a will of iron. She will not do anything she doesn't want to do.

Mies lifted his eyes to the stars that he could not see, the smile deeper.

That won't be a problem.

Eight

"Tamesine, hi, it's Sarah. I got the transcripts, thanks."

Sarah sat on the arm of her sofa, nervous, although she didn't know why. Tamesine was considered one of the most powerful of first bloods, but she was also one of the gentlest women she'd ever met. Still, she had to ask questions that might cause Tamesine to respond with her own questions.

"Good. I assume you're doing some further research? You saved my daughter, my race, and perhaps the world, so I hope you find what you're looking for. Will you let me know if you do? How are you? How's Xavier?"

Tamesine's beautifully-cadenced voice travelled well through the phone lines. Sarah remembered being a little smitten with her when she was in France with Tamesine and the other first bloods who lived on a high cliff overlooking the Mediterranean.

"I'm sure that he is well. I'm not in Paris, Tamesine, I'm in Boston. In the U.S. I live here now."

"How can that…oh. You aren't blood-bonded anymore."

"No, I'm not. Xavier was kind enough to release me from my responsibility to his stronghold. I'm human now. Completely."

"Ah. I hope that you are happy."

"I am. But I've a complication and it involves your world. May I ask some questions?"

"Sarah, of *course* you may. Any question at any time. You saved Dez, I would give you the world."

"How about the universe?"

"That's an intriguing request. Please continue."

Hesitating, Sarah cleared her throat. "Tam, you will understand if I tell you that, at this time, I can't divulge any details, right?"

"My past is perfect proof that there are times when you must have faith in someone. I trust you, Sarah. What do you need to know?"

"Your amulets. How do they work, exactly? Is there a way to access them? To, uh, use the power for a specific purpose. Believe me when I say that the thing which I inquire about will require a great deal of power."

"You do not disappoint."

For several moments, Tamesine was quiet. Sarah could almost hear her thinking about how much she should divulge to Sarah, who, technically, had no link to the vampire world anymore. Finally she spoke again.

"Sarah, the amulets are direct links between the first blood and the universe. It draws its power from all life, from the earth and sky, and ultimately, from that which is beyond heaven. That power is channeled to the first blood to which the amulet is bonded. This bond is lifelong, and will never die, even when the vampire does."

"I know." Distracted, as soon as Sarah made the comment, she realized that it was a mistake.

"You *know*," Tamesine repeated quietly. After another pause, her voice was calmer yet. "*How* would you know? Sarah, you need to tell me what you are playing with. The amulets are way beyond anything that you can imagine. They can change the course of a life, of many lives, of the future. You cannot mess with something of such great power unless you understand the consequences of your actions."

Another pause was interrupted by a quickly drawn breath before she began again. "Sarah, I *do* trust you, but I know that you have an overly sharp mind, that it is inconceivable to you that you can't achieve something if you put your mind to it. I'm suggesting that whatever you are involved with, whatever you might need this information for, you would be wise to let our community help you."

"I would love to do so. I suggested it to, well, the person who I am trying to help. He believes it would be *more* dangerous to involve your race because of your connection to the spiritual plane."

"Oh, Sarah, you need to tell me what you are doing. Whoever this is, whatever he is asking of you, you must not do it unless we can be there to guide you. This is out of your league, dear. No offense, but humans should never be messing with first blood magics."

"I couldn't agree more. All I ask is that you trust me enough to know that when I need to call you and the others in, I will. I've promised these…this person that I'll try first to deal with the situation. If I fail, if we get into trouble, I'll call you immediately. But I need to try. Tam, this is a one-shot deal once I call you in, so please, can you accept that I *do* know what I am doing and that I know when to call you?"

Dead silence met Sarah as she held her breath, her cell phone so tight against her ear, her fingers ached.

Please, Tamesine, please, she prayed silently just as Tamesine answered her question.

"I really don't know how to respond, so I'll give in to my baser instincts and trust that you will do exactly as you have said. Whatever it is that you need to do that involves accessing the power of a first blood amulet, it is dangerous."

"I understand and I accept the repercussions. So, accessing the amulet, how do I do it?"

"The amulet is still servicing its vampire, correct?"

"Yes. Yes, it is."

"Okay. This is so difficult, without knowing what it is you need to do, what you need from the amulet, how much power you need, and what the final outcome must be. But I will do what I can."

"You don't know how much this means to me and the person that I need to help."

"I hope I won't regret it. Okay. The connection to its source is the key. If you can tap into the power of the earth, of the sky, and move that power into the vampire, he will be able to accomplish a great many things. It isn't easy, but all first bloods have the potential to access this power and wield it, temporarily, to do feats well beyond anything any one of us has ever been able to do on our own. As you know, we recently discovered that combining our talents on the spiritual plane reaches levels that might rival that of a god."

"I'm so grateful that we were able to find enough information in time to save Dez and Park. That is the highlight of my life."

"It should be. Those are spectacular women and you are personally responsible for bringing events together that led to the cure we needed. That's why I wish you would let me help you now."

"I wish I could."

"All right, then. To do this, to touch the powers of the amulet, you would need a place with a deep connection to the earth. Somewhere close to her heart where the magic can stretch into the sky and down into the core. You need to be far from all of man's machinations. Somewhere that also carries magic. You don't want any interference."

"It makes sense. Any other advice?"

"At that point, you and the first blood must give in to instinct and just listen. I wish you luck, Sarah."

"Thank you. I'll let you know the result."

"Oh, you'd better. I will be waiting here immensely worried and curious."

"You and me both." Sarah's mind was spinning. She was half ready to go ahead and tell Tamesine everything and ask her to bring Koen, Park, and Eillia to help.

"Tamesine, what would happen if someone were to try to reverse a universally designed event? To stop a destiny made on the spiritual plane?"

Dead silence again. This time the pause lasted longer before Tamesine's sigh preceded her next words.

"Sarah, you need to tell me what you are doing."

"I will…"

"Now, Sarah. This sounds like it may have consequences beyond you and this unidentified vampire. I can't let you do this without guidance from our oldest first bloods."

Sarah's harsh laugh was abrupt. "You'd be surprised then that *that* isn't a problem. Tamesine, I'm going to let you go now. Thank you for your help."

IN SOUTHERN FRANCE

The phone call went dead. Tamesine just stared at the home screen of her cell phone for several long minutes.

"Oh, shit," she whispered and headed downstairs to find Koen and Eillia.

Something bad was happening, she just felt it. Sarah was one of the brightest people she'd ever met, human or vampire, and if *she* was nervous, this was serious. While Tamesine had no idea what this was, she knew that someone from her race needed to be there to control or at least monitor whatever the hell Sarah was involved in.

Reaching the main floor, she entered the dining room. Everyone had risen for first meal about an hour ago, and most of the members of the household were finished and gone, but Eillia remained, a spoon held out to her son. She looked up with a sweet smile as Tamesine entered.

"Hey. I'm heading into Paris shortly. Would you like to come?"

"Paris sounds lovely, but I was thinking that a little trip to the U.S. sounds better. Boston, in fact."

Eillia laid the spoon in a bowl still half-filled with ice cream. Her eyes closed briefly, the smile gone, and when she opened them, she sighed.

"What now?" Eillia asked.

"Trouble."

"It must be Tuesday."

"My favorite phrase. Yes, it's Tuesday."

"All right." Eillia stood and placed Caedmon on the floor. "Go find Daddy. He's in the living room."

The toddler raced from the room on plump legs, but he was now very steady, even at that quick pace.

"Give me the details."

"I don't have any. But wait until I tell you what I *do* know."

Ten minutes later, Eillia polished off the melting ice cream while Tamesine picked at a slice of chocolate cake with buttercream icing.

"Okay. I agree. This isn't something we can ignore. Sarah's too smart to discount your assessment. Trouble."

Tamesine nodded and scored all of the thick icing off the side of the cake. "Yep, trouble."

IN BOSTON

Sarah had spent all night online and made her choice.

"Close to the earth and near to the sky. Somewhere sacred and magical," she whispered.

She had to find a place to take Mies and Nikolai where they could try this. They needed to access the spiritual plane.

On her mind the entire time was the reality, the inevitability that if they did this…if they succeeded…one of the two men that she had come to care about would not be here afterward. Pressure persisted in her chest and the pit of her stomach. Several times, she thought that she might throw up.

The only thing that kept her moving toward this horrible task was what Mies had said to her. *"What we know is that we cannot live this way, either of us."*

"How can I do this? How can I let one of you die?"

The impossible question hung in the air and suffocated Sarah. Closing her laptop, she walked to the window to look out at the sunrise painting a new day in soft blue and rose watercolors. But she didn't want a new day, because when it ended, as it inevitably must, she would have to go to Mies and Nikolai and tell them to pack for a journey to the Appalachian Mountains.

When she turned a few minutes later, she slipped off her dress and just dropped onto her bed. Rolling over, tears threatened.

"Please let this go well, and let *both* men stay on this earth," she prayed.

And that was new for her, too. She fell asleep, aware that her cheeks were wet.

What the hell was that sound? Seconds later, blinking, Sarah realized it was her cell phone, disco music blaring into her sleep. She was so exhausted by the past 24 hours, her mind wasn't functioning at full capacity.

Normally, she would shoot out of bed and grab the offending phone, but her legs were stiff from a long shift and didn't want to mind the order to stand and move.

"God, I'm not sure this was such a good choice after all," she whispered to herself as she contemplated the effects of aging.

"Yes?" she called into the phone when she finally unlocked it and answered the call. For a full ten seconds, no one responded. She thought that she knew why.

"Mies?" she asked.

"Yes," his deep voice responded.

Why did her body respond immediately, just at the sound of his voice? A flush moved from her head down and centered at her core.

"Sarah," he continued. "We've risen and Nikolai wanted to know if you found anything. And he wanted to know something else, too."

Curious, Sarah dropped into the chair near her window. She needed to meet with them and talk to them about her conversation with Tamesine, but she found that she was more interested in what Mies said about Nikolai.

"What else does he want to know?"

"He would like you to let him spend a night with your friend. You know that he would treat her well, Sarah. He has had his life hijacked by this merge, the man deserves some pleasure. Won't you allow him to have it with the luscious beauty? He thinks of her nonstop."

The request stunned her. Mies wanted Naji to have sex with the body he now inhabited. Jealousy struck deep in her belly before she could tamp it down, even though she knew it was unfounded. Nikolai and Mies were *not* the same person. Not where it counted.

"Little doctor, I know what you are thinking, and it is not true. The chocolate-skinned woman is lovely, and I would be thrilled to have a night with her...were it not for *you*. Also, Nikolai has strong leanings toward her and I would not betray him. I told you once before that I would not be present if he were to be with her, and I will not. So please do not think that it is *I* who ask."

She didn't know what to say. "I'm not sure that letting them have a date is wise."

"It may not be, but it is important. Sarah, we do not know how this is going to turn out. Nikolai deserves a last evening if it doesn't go right."

A last good day. What terminal patients called the day before the disease claims dominance. There was a similarity. She could grant him something he wanted deeply. Was there any reason to deny him? No.

"All right. Yes, I will make the arrangement."

"Thank you." He was silent for a few moments. "I will not be there. It will just be Nikolai and Naji."

"Okay." What else was there to say? She wouldn't tell him that she was jealous and that she couldn't think about Naji lying naked with him, making love with him, touching him like she so desperately wanted to. That she wanted that same *last day* with Mies.

"I know. I know it won't be you. Just, make sure that she's okay before you leave. Be sure that she has memories that won't hurt if she never sees him again."

"You have my word on it."

"I'll call you when the date is set."

"Sarah..."

"Mies, I have to go."

Sarah felt guilty hanging up on him, but her emotions suddenly went wild as she considered how dangerous what they were planning to do really was. One or both of these men that she cared for might die. How could she live with herself if that happened? If *either* of them died? In spite of her assurances that she would try to save them both, there was little doubt it would turn out that way.

She should bring the other first bloods into this before it went wrong. Making the decision suddenly, she dialed the phone again.

Mies answered immediately.

"Mies, I know that you didn't want the first bloods involved, but this is too important and too dangerous. I'm going to call them."

There was no response.

"Mies?"

The line was still open, she could hear strange sounds, but he didn't respond.

"Mies? Answer me."

"No, you won't."

His voice was deeper than she'd ever heard it, filled with emotion, and it didn't come through the phone.

As she turned, Mies's big body filled her view. He'd moved using hyper-speed from his hotel room to her apartment and through the locked door.

Laying her phone on the back of the sofa, Sarah looked at him, breathing hard, but not from the exertion, his eyes searching hers. She was speechless. He wasn't.

"You can't, I forbid it. You must understand what forces we are playing with here. This must go well and it must go only one way."

Sarah's breath coming quickly now too, she returned his intense gaze.

"What do you mean?"

"There is one body, Sarah. One body, two men. You understand what that means."

Moisture surged unbidden, the amber iris's shining through tears. "Of course I understand. That's why I want to call in my friends. They may have a way."

"How? How can anyone fix this?"

Moving closer, his scent overwhelmed Sarah. His hands went to her forearms, warm fingers wrapped around them, and he spoke so quietly, she had to lean in to hear him.

"This body, the life in this body, belongs to Nikolai. I have been dead for several millennia. I do not deserve this life."

"But you're here, you have a reason, you believe it's destiny. You must stay."

Mies shook his head. "I cannot stay without replacing Nikolai. *That...*I will not do."

When tears filled Mies's eyes, Sarah was lost.

At the same moment, they moved in and held each other, so close, she felt every contour of him. She couldn't even imagine letting him go from here, return to his state on the celestial plane, and never have a chance to be with him, to touch, to kiss, to feel him on her, inside of her, part of her.

She pulled away from him just enough to speak, her lips so near his, they breathed the same air.

"Is Nikolai...someplace else?"

"He's on a beach in the spiritual plane. I did not want him to know that I plan to release his body to him and fade back to eternity."

On tiptoe, Sarah pulled Mies down and kissed him, lightly at first, then deeply, with everything she was. He responded desperately because she made it clear that she wanted him, and that the answer was yes.

Keeping the kiss going, he lifted Sarah into his arms and carried her to the bed, then followed her down to the firm mattress and lay on top of her.

Gods in all the heavens, she felt like she belonged there. He knew that she did. In all of his years those long centuries ago, he'd never found his mate, and the one thing he knew now, without question, was that destiny had brought him here for *her*. Sarah was the woman always meant for him.

Destiny, you heartless crone, he thought. *You give her to me knowing that I cannot stay. You've destroyed me and this perfect woman, too. You unkind soul, to do this, when she has served you so well.*

His lips against her throat, Mies whispered. "We will make love?"

Her fingers twisted in his hair, her body pressed against him, Sarah smiled. "We will make love. If you must go away, I need to be with you first, every way possible." She closed her eyes. "I give up my desire to remain connected fully to the human world. I want you, I admit it, damn it, with every drop of blood that pumps through me, I want you. *Why* I do, well, that remains a mystery."

"I'm irresistible," Mies smiled back to her. Then the smile dropped as he caressed her face, her eyes opened again and focused on his. "It's because we are meant to be, Sarah the doctor. I was yours the moment I looked up into those soulful eyes at the hospital. No, I was yours before they even sent me here. Destiny spoke."

"I don't believe in destiny."

"Yes, you do. You've seen its hand in the vampire world. Your human side is trying to subvert your own experience. Now, let me show you that destiny knows what she is doing."

Mies slid down her body, slowly pulling her slacks off as he went. He nipped her inner thigh, then licked the tender spot while his fingers caressed the skin along her side. She could feel his breath on the slit just above that place and couldn't stop herself from moaning.

Sarah reached up to the metal headboard to hold on for the ride of her life. She'd never had sex with someone she was falling for. Her experiences had been pleasant, the men had been attractive, but she hadn't really had any feelings for them. Mies...oh, hell, Mies was different.

Was this love? She didn't know. All she knew was that when she was with him, she wanted to crawl inside him...*every time*. When he wasn't there, she was thinking of him. *And the thought of him being gone forever...it tore her heart to pieces!*

Finishing his journey from her belly to her knees, little bites followed by long licks, Mies moved back up as he parted Sarah's legs and slid between them. Always aware that vampires could move hyper-fast, Sarah had never thought of the sexual implication of that vampire ability.

When Mies's tongue slid along the side of the sensitive slit between, he ramped up the speed and Sarah nearly exploded off the bed.

She could hear him laugh just before the tongue buried into her, fast and furious, skilled like she'd never known, pulling and twisting the clitoris and deep beneath. Her fingers tightened on the slim metal stiles of the headboard as she held on through a sensual assault she could never have imagined. *God, she'd been right! How could a human man compare to him?* Although she knew, she admitted it, he was more than just a practiced vampire sexual partner to her. He was in her heart.

It was going to hurt so much when he left...

But now, this second, he was making love to her in the most deeply sensual way possible. His tongue made its way all around the center of her sex, plunging over and over to suck and pull at the opening, to bring her to an orgasm so intense, she felt him pull her into his arms as he steadied her while her body bucked in ecstasy.

Mies wanted to feel her as she orgasmed, the most personal, erotic thing he could imagine in this world. He felt her body shudder and finally come back down from the electric orgasm that he knew was the best she'd ever had. Not because he was that much better than anyone else she might have been with, although he knew that he was, but because they were connected to each other.

Lifting away, Mies looked into her eyes. No words were needed, they both knew that the only thing that would satisfy either of them was for him to slide into her, and seconds later, all of their clothes abandoned on the cool floor, he plunged into Sarah and just let himself feel her. Buried deep, his skin against hers, he was still, satisfied, and when he looked into her eyes, they shined with unreleased tears. His own misty vision told him that his were, too.

When he began to move, he wrapped himself even tighter around her and let their bodies do what they wanted to do, in and out, over and over, friction burning them both with a fire they'd never felt with any other. He felt Sarah give in to him completely, her heart and spirit lost to him now. He felt sorrow that she would always want him and he wouldn't be there, and at the same time, an unbounded joy that she now knew that they were always meant to be together, like this, whether many times over many years, or just this once.

No matter the outcome of their intervention, he was grateful that the universe had sent him here, to her, so that even this one act was worth the interruption to his eternal rest. Later, when he was back on the spiritual plane, he would let them know that the chance to touch the woman who would have been his mate was worth any price.

Something inside of Sarah broke, a wall she'd always kept up, a barrier around her heart, protection from any pain that true love might cause, but it was blown apart by this connection that let her know it was well beyond just physical. Unbidden, *unwanted*, her attachment to this man, this supernatural being who likely would not be able to stay here with her, was deep and true and binding. She would miss him forever, an eternal need that would always be unmet. Until the day she left this life, she couldn't regret a moment.

This, this…merge, for that was what it was, would not be broken by Mies's return to the spirit realm or by her own death. All she hoped was that, as merely human, she would be allowed someday, to join him there, to have an eternal life with the one person she now realized she was meant to be with.

The best laid plans of mice and men…so much for being fully human again with a normal human life.

When their orgasms hit, blood magics flew, lights split the air, rainbow hues shattered around them, their bodies twisted together, hands to hands, heart to heart, their groans loud and erotic. As they dropped back onto the now-damp sheets, Mies lifted up on his elbows, his hands curved against Sarah's cheeks. Her eyes were still wet and searching his.

"You're glowing," she whispered. Silver swirls in his eyes, illuminated now, intense, bright, in the near-darkness of the room.

"First blood response to spectacular sex with an even more spectacular woman," he explained. "Are you all right?"

Sarah nodded, her head restrained by his hands, but she loved the touch and wished he would never stop.

"No regrets, Mies. I know we belong together. I felt it in you and inside of me."

"Never regret destiny or perfection."

"If this is destiny, then I have to thank it for bringing you to me and curse it for how it did so. If you have to go…"

Her voice cracked and she couldn't continue.

Mies knew of nothing that would console her, so he gathered her to him and held her. Sarah's arms went around his belly and they lay still, unable to untangle from their physical link, until the sun threatened the horizon.

"I must go," he whispered.

"I know."

Sarah slowly pushed off the bed and wrapped her satin robe around her body, the coolness too frigid without his warmth. She pulled it close, her arms tight against her chest as she thought that once he left, she might never be warm again.

Dressed in seconds, Mies came to her and kissed her on the forehead, the cheeks, and finally, a long lingering kiss on her lips.

"You are the greatest pleasure of my life."

Turning her head toward the window, Sarah cursed the coming daylight. Facing him again, she looked into his eyes, now calm.

"You already know how I feel."

"I do. And thank you for letting us be together. I am sorry if it ruins your plans."

"Plans, *ha*. Humans make plans and mostly watch them fall apart. Proves how very human I am now." She was quiet for a moment, then continued. "But I wouldn't want to have missed a moment with you."

"It would have been the greatest tragedy of the world."

"It might have been. Um. I'll still set things up for Nikolai and Naji. It's only fair."

"They will never know what we have known together, but I believe that they are also meant to be. The spirit realm has a lot to answer for with this decision."

"I'll say."

"I must go."

"Hurry."

He lingered a second longer, a hand curling into hers, his fingers touching each of hers in order, then he was gone.

After watching the misty light fill the morning sky, Sarah pulled the blinds and dropped onto her sofa. She had a mid-day shift, but she knew she wouldn't make it. In fact, she would phone the hospital and call off the rest of the week.

She would be traveling to the Appalachian Mountains by the weekend.

Moments later, in the hotel room

Mies threw his exhausted body onto the bed.

Where have you been, friend?

After a brief hesitation, Mies spoke. Nikolai noticed the sadness in Mies's tone.

I have come from Sarah's.

Nikolai paused before he spoke again.

You were with her all night?

We were together, yes.

I'm not going to ask what you did.

You needn't. You can feel this body. You can feel what I have felt, can you not? I will let you into my mind.

Emotions poured into Nikolai's mind and overwhelmed him. The love, the sorrow, the loss…

God, my friend, I am sorry for your pain. For Sarah's. You believe she is your destined mate?

122

I know that she is. My body recognized her almost from the first moment. Once we touched, it was clear. After last night, the inextricable bond forged. She is mine and I am hers. Forever parted, yet forever linked.

I cannot even imagine, but you do not know that, Mies. I expect that you will be victorious should this intervention work.

Nikolai waited for a response, and when there wasn't one, he became suspicious.

What do you know that I do not? What are you not telling me? Do not leave me out of the loop, brother, this is too important.

You will prevail. My intention is to leave this body as soon as the connection to the powers is made. I will not take what is yours. This I know, Niko. By the time this is all finished, you will be alone in this body, and I will be back where I should always have been.

You don't want to keep this body and stay with Sarah?

More than anything on this world and beyond. Other than taking this body that belongs to you, I would gratefully stay and live my life out with my mate at my side. But I will not live so that you must die.

Very noble of you. You would do that for me?

I would do that for anyone who was in this situation. This body is not mine. And I have become very fond of you. We call each other brother because of how close we are forced to be, but I feel that kinship with you, Nikolai. I will not live if you cannot. It is that simple.

I keep thinking that there must be a way.

One body, brother. One body. There is no way.

I believe in Sarah. She may be able to figure it out.

I believe in her, too, but even her extraordinary mind can't change what can't be fixed.

I won't accept that you cannot be saved.

Accept it, Niko. This is what must be. I am okay with it. To have had tonight with the love of a lifetime, it was worth all that I have endured. I just hope that it hasn't hurt Sarah too much to live out the rest of her life in joy.

She's resilient.

She'll need to be.

I guess, what will be, will be.

You guess correctly.

Strangely, if it happens as you expect it to, I will miss you, brother. I somehow realize that it will be very lonely when you are gone.

I bet you say that to all the parasitic ancient vampires who inhabit your body.

Yeah, well, you're my favorite.

It will all be okay, brother, I promise. Everything under the sun has its moment, its season, and moves on. Even immortal beings don't truly last forever.

I hear you. Too bad, though, that I don't get a moment with the woman who might have been right for me.

Sarah's sexy friend?

Da. I think we might have been just as good together as you and Sarah were.

Perhaps you will still have a chance to find out.

Doubtful. Sarah has already told her that I am not a good fit for her. She was protecting her, I understand that. Naji has no idea that supernatural beings exist and I have come to know that, for peace of mind, it is better that way.

Perhaps.

Perhaps? What do you know? Tell me.

Sarah is even now arranging for your date.

No.

Da. Niko, I intend to be the one to go when we do what we must do. But there are no promises that I have the power to protect you. There is a chance that you may be the one ejected, you understand that?

I have always thought that when the smoke cleared, you would be here and I would be gone. I still know that is very possible, in spite of your intention otherwise. Mies, I am grateful for the gesture, even if it turns out that I cannot remain.

I am sorry if that is so. I promise, I will do all I can to control this.

In either circumstance, I want that night with Naji. Thank you for that, at least.

It is my pleasure.
It is my pleasure I seek. And hers. I hope that I may use some of your skills.
I will make certain you can.
What a spectacular way to go!

And the next morning…

"Seriously? What changed your mind?"

Naji sipped her hot tea, her eyes sparkling.

"I *didn't* change my mind, Naj. I always thought that you two would be good together. It was obvious that night, but I told you, it's complicated. Now, though, I think that you two deserve a chance to find out if you might have something."

"Oh, we *have* something, all right. Sarah, love, thank you. I haven't been able to get that muscled god off my mind. I mean, he's hot, no doubt, but there was something *else* about him. I don't know what." She was quiet for a few moments while she took several lingering sips of sweetened tea that was mostly sugar. Setting the cup back on the table, her eyes went back up to meet Sarah's.

"You know a little bit about my history. I'm aggressive because I've learned that if I ever wanted anything in my life, I had to be. No one else was gonna get it for me. My mother did what she could, but I think that no one ever really loved her when she was growing up, so she didn't know how to love me or my little brother. I learned to take care of myself after he died in a car accident. My mother took up with some unsavory men, spent all of her time with a straw in one hand and a bottle in the other. So, learning to trust people, to feel anything for them, it's the hardest thing I'll ever do. You are the first one I've ever really let in. I mean, let close enough to really get to know me."

"I'm honored, Naji. No one would ever guess, though. You bring such brightness everywhere you go. Your interminable joy of life infuses everyone who meets you."

Taking Sarah's hands, Naji caressed her wrists with restless fingers. "Thank you. I told you that I figured out that if I wanted to be happy, it was up to me. Once I left Missouri, I never looked back."

She pulled Sarah into a hug. "Um, this feels right. Thank you, love."

Naji held Sarah close for several more minutes, Sarah holding on, too, then she walked away, wiping her eyes with shaky fingers.

"Well, I need a new dress. Something devastating."

"What you need is your awesome self. You blew him away the night you met."

"I wanted my hands on that man from the first moment I saw him."

"That was obvious. So, tonight?"

"Tonight. The sooner the better. Sarah, I don't know if I've ever been this excited."

"That's good, yeah?"

"It's a little frightening. Honestly, I have such high expectation for this…what if it isn't right? I think I'll be inconsolable."

"I've got your back, Naj, no matter what. But I know you won't need me. I saw you two at dinner, and you created some serious heat. You and Nikolai are destined."

"Destined? I thought you didn't believe in destiny."

"Maybe something's changed my view of the world."

"Maybe things are going to go right for both of us now."

"I hope so." Sarah knew better. Tonight, Naji and Nikolai would have their dream date. Tomorrow night, he might be gone forever. If Destiny really did guide things, it was a monster.

Nine

Nikolai dressed, his mind on the night ahead. His clothing choice was limited, so little fit the body created by his vampire house guest. He admitted, though, that nothing showed off the ripped and sexy body better than the tight jeans and tighter tee shirt. As he slid the shirt over his head, all he could think about was taking it off again, Naji's body against his, all of their clothing gone.

The sun had set, and Mies was in that heavenly landscape where he sent *him* when he needed to be alone.

Using normal human speed, he headed to Sarah's apartment, and, arriving early, knocked on her door.

Sarah opened it, her smile welcoming, her hand out to pull him in. He scanned the small room immediately and saw Naji standing near the window. She looked delicious and he felt his cock twitch.

"Hello, gorgeous," she said as she walked towards him.

"You stole my line," he responded.

"Aren't we a pair."

Sarah, waiting by the door, could feel that same heat coming off them again as it had at the restaurant. She opened the door wider. "You guys are raising the temperature. Get out of here and have a good time."

Nikolai held his arm out to Naji.

She slipped her fingers through it, caressing his forearm. "I concur. Ready to ride, handsome?"

At his wordless nod, Naji led him through the opening and they were gone. Neither noticed as Sarah closed the door.

Leaning against it, her arms folded, Sarah shook her head. They were already half in love, she could see it. Was it weird that, technically, sort of, Naji would make love with the same body that she herself had been with the night before?

Pushing away, she grinned.

"Weird is my new normal. I think this calls for pizza and a huge chocolate milk shake."

A moment of melancholy struck her as she dialed the pizza café just around the corner. She had a strong desire to call Mies to join her. How impossible was this situation?

The call connected and a young man asked what she would like.

"Hi, yes, I'd like to order a pizza for pick-up."

Naji watched Nikolai with frequent sideways glances. The enormous man filled her small sports car, his head so high, it would have touched the top if she hadn't lowered it.

The wind blew his hair around, he squirmed some in the small seat that wasn't designed for such a large body, and also kept glancing at her.

"We don't know each other," she finally commented, breaking the uncomfortable silence.

"We don't."

"But we're going to. And soon. I haven't stopped thinking about you since that night we met."

Nikolai's heart raced. "Pull the car over," he demanded. They had been passing a park and when she did as he asked, he rose from his seat and had her door open in seconds, pulled her out of the car and into his arms. With the old-fashioned street lamps that had been placed for aesthetic effect along the sidewalk illuminating Naji's face, he slid his fingers around her head and held her still so that he could just take her in.

"I don't want dinner. Are you hungry?"

Naji shook her head. "Yes, but not for food."

"Good. You have a place we can go?"

"I have an outstanding place on the water."

"Would you wish to go there and make love with me?"

His accent had deepened, and so had her desire.

"I cannot think of anything else on this earth that I would rather do right now than to make love with you."

"The sooner we get started, the longer we can do it."

"Love a man with a plan. Get back in my car."

After Nikolai had taken the passenger seat again, she watched his face for a few moments. Licking her lips, she spoke. "You've bewitched me," she whispered.

"There you go, stealing my line again. How long will this journey take?"

"Three minutes in this car with the way *I* drive. Hold on."

Nikolai did, onto the hand grip, but all that he really wanted to do was hold on to her. *Soon*, he kept whispering, *soon*. Thank the heavens that Mies was absent. He needed to be completely alone with Naji. If he had to die soon, he couldn't imagine a better last memory.

IN SOUTHERN FRANCE

"Xavier? Where in Boston?"

"I don't know. I didn't go with her."

"You feel no blood connection to her?"

"Not when I'm this lubricated."

"God, Xavier, you're such a..." Tamesine sighed. As if she could judge someone else's past or choices. But this phone call wasn't getting her any closer to finding Sarah in Boston.

"Okay, when you're tuned in, you'll see if you can find her?"

"Aye. What do ya want with her?"

"It's important, Xavier. *Very* important. It has to do with first blood magics and the fact that she may be playing with them."

Tamesine heard him snort a laugh.

"Nay, that's not so, for two unsurmountable reasons. My brilliant little blood-bond left me to return to the dull vicissitudes of ordinariness…she wanted to be fully human again. So, she's done with our kind and all of our drama, *and* she's way too smart to mess around with first blood magics."

"Well, she is, so you need to help me find her. Now. Is there someone there who can sober you up? I'll come right away if not."

"I think I can handle me own self, lassie!"

The drunk womanizer, Tamesine sighed to herself. He doesn't even know how much time he spent in his cups and up a woman's… "Don't go there," she whispered out loud.

"All right, but Sarah's life might be in danger," she said, instead of what she wanted to.

That was what it took. Call Xavier what you will, he took care of the people he loved.

"I'll call ya back in due time," he said abruptly, and Tamesine thought he already sounded more sober. The line went dead, and she rang off the call.

"Let's hope it's soon," she said, before she turned to her children who called from the main floor of the villa. Sarah needed help, but for now, so did two rambunctious and creative children with ravenous tummies.

As she wandered down the stairs, Tamesine yawned. It was nearly morning and time to finish the final meal, get the kids to bed and crawl next to her mate. She tired too easily lately, and she knew why. A troubled mind didn't rest well.

There were so many things to resolve right now, between forging a strong bond between her newfound daughter and great-granddaughter, finding her son, finding a vampire who should never have been one, and making sure that the family was safe. Now, Sarah's odd request that couldn't be ignored.

"All in good time," she said to the wall as she stepped off the final stair and got hit by two charging bullets followed close behind by three golden retrievers. Bed time could get chaotic around here, but it was one of her favorite parts of the day.

OUTSIDE PARIS

Groaning, Xavier pushed the two women still lying on top of him aside. His bed was enormous, so there was plenty of room to safely dislodge them. Swatting the buttocks of one of the women, he gave them a smile.

"Lasses, ye must go. It appears that I have to go to America."

One of the women pulled him back to her and gave him a hearty kiss. Struggling, Xavier slipped away from her. "Lass, I mean it. Ye both need to skedaddle. I've a woman to save. I think."

Striding naked across the soft carpet, he didn't notice the two women watch him until he disappeared into the obscenely large bathroom adjacent to the room.

One looked at the other, rolled her eyes, then commented to her companion in their native French.

"God, I can't decide if he looks better from the front or back. That yummy ass!"

"True enough, Josie. Well, it appears he's finished with us for now. Let's get out of here."

As they dressed, Josephine sighed. "I hope he is not gone too long."

"I will starve for him if he is."

"Of course you won't. Still, he makes my week when he calls us in. I wish he called more often."

"He used to. I think something is on his mind. He seems…different…lately."

Now clothed, the women left arm in arm. There were tasks waiting in the household other than this most favored one.

Scrubbed, Xavier walked back into his bedroom, aggressively towel-drying his hair. The length bothered him, it was too long, mostly because he just hadn't cared enough to have someone cut it. He hated that, recently, things were constantly changing and shifting and generally being a pain in his arse. What was wrong with the way things *were*?

He'd supported Sarah leaving, but it was just one more thing that made his life less enjoyable. God knows he didn't understand why she wanted to go back to the miserable state of being only *human*, but he'd supported her choice to do so.

Unexpectedly, he'd found that he missed her. She'd been with him for about a hundred years, and never, in all that time, had he needed to ask her for anything. Intuitively, and perhaps not, she always anticipated his needs and had him taken care of immediately. He liked that. Fuck, he *depended* on it!

Yes, he'd admit that he missed her gentle smile and those satiny amber eyes that had looked at him in disapproval almost as often as they hadn't. He would admit only to himself that he missed her like he might a daughter. *A hundred years! You miss someone that's been there for such a long time.*

"Sarah, what have ya gotten yerself into?" he said out loud as he reached for some jeans. "Whatever it is, ya know that I've got ya."

After shaking his head vigorously, the combination of the cold shower and the physical activity had cleared his head, which is precisely what he'd needed to do.

He smiled. The sex helped too. Josephine and Natalia were young, healthy blood-bonds who had sought him out twelve years ago and asked to be considered for blood meals and sex. Both women were gorgeous, motivated sexual partners, and remained his favorites when he was

132

at home. The trio of lovers had become comfortable and casual with each other over the years, the sex inventive and fulfilling.

Forcing his mind off the women, he reached into the world for Sarah. The blood tie was weaker now that she'd ceased taking his blood, so he had trouble making the link. While human blood was too weak to find through a blood draw, Sarah had taken *his* blood for decades, so there should still be a trace amount in her body.

Damn't, it wasn't working! He thought that maybe a good Scotch...*no!* No, even he knew that the alcohol dulled his senses and that wasn't what he needed right now.

He needed to burn off the rest of the fogginess, so he zipped down the stairs to the well supplied fitness room that he kept for his blood-bonds. Forty minutes later, sweating, tired, he raced back up the stairs and into the shower for another cold dousing.

This time, hair dried and yanked back with a tie, loose fitting sweat pants over legs that never needed a gym, he sat on his bed, pushing aside the messed up sheets.

"All right, little Sarah, let's find out where ya are." He spoke out loud as if she could hear him. Closing off all outside stimulus, including his eyes, he sent the search out into the cosmos, across the planet, to find his own blood somewhere in America. The search proceeded perfectly, and ten minutes later, he landed on her exact location.

Finally, Xavier opened his eyes. "Gotcha, lass," he said, and called Tamesine.

After a brief delay, she answered expectantly.

"Did you find her?"

"Aye. Ya need to have more faith. I know precisely where she is. When do we leave?"

"You needn't go. I'll have Park and Eillia with me, and you know what we can do together."

"I do at that. And I'm still goin'. She's family, and I'll see to it that she's safe. Ya can fill me in on the plane. I expect ye'll be pickin' me up in Koen's jet?"

He could hear Tamesine sigh through the phone and smiled.

"Aye," she said.

IN BOSTON NEAR THE WATERFRONT

Nikolai pushed up onto his elbows. Naji lay on her side while his fingers slipped up and down soft curves, her skin incredibly smooth and sensuous against his fingertips. Their lovemaking had been epic.

God, the woman was skilled! The past hour had been a long session of sex so creative, so nearly acrobatic, even this vampire body was exhausted. Now, all he wanted to do was touch her and watch her.

Nothing in his life had ever felt better than being with this woman who had a gentle soul, but didn't know it. She came on strong, but while he was inside her, while he was connected to her, he'd felt the fragile heart buried within.

As he caressed her taut, perfectly curved buttocks, he bent over and whispered, "I could have fallen in love with you if we had the time."

Naji's eyes opened suddenly. "What did you say?" she asked sleepily.

"I'm sorry, I thought you were asleep."

She rolled over and smiled. "I should be. We *both* should be. That was insane." Lifting a hand, she touched Nikolai's cheek. "And wonderful. I knew we would be good together, but...wow."

"I should be satiated, but I do not think that is so."

"No, you are not. We are *so* not finished tonight."

Lowering to her, Nikolai touched her lips with his tongue. He scored the edges, then slipped it inside to kiss her thoroughly.

"Boy, are you a good kisser. If that were an Olympic sport, you would take home the gold for the Russians."

134

"Only if they would let me use you for the performance."

Still smiling in the low light provided by a string of multi-colored lights strung along the top of a wall, Naji paused. "Nikolai, I heard what you said as I woke. What did you mean by *if we had the time*?"

His hand had been moving down her body, heading back to give her another orgasm when she asked that question. He didn't have an answer for her. This was likely a one-time moment and he didn't want to leave her with a disappearing lover and wonder for the rest of her life where he was or what she had done wrong. After tonight...no, before, he knew how precious she was, he would never leave her with that kind of memory chained to her.

"I simply meant that there wasn't enough time in the world to make love to you." He hoped that she would believe him, although it didn't matter. Mies would use his skills to compel memories that would leave her happy before this night ended. He didn't know what Mies had planned for her, but Mies assured him that they would be memories that would make her smile every time she thought of him.

"If you feel that way, why are we wasting time?"

Nikolai was shocked when Naji jumped from the bed, ending up spread across the bottom. She burrowed between his legs and looked up into his startled eyes. He didn't think he'd ever seen anyone other than a vampire move that fast.

"Hold on," she said, reminding him of her order earlier in her car. Only this was...

Nikolai groaned loudly. "Where did you learn to do that?"

Naji tilted her head. "Are you really asking me that now?"

"God, no. I really don't want you to stop."

"Right answer," she said as she wrapped her tongue around him again. Nikolai kept his mouth shut and just let himself experience her. He didn't think that he could speak anyway.

Two hours later, Nikolai stood above a sleeping Naji. This time she was truly out. He glanced up at a strange contemporary clock on the wall. It was time to go.

Was it everything you expected it to be?

And more. I am, at once, grateful that I was able to be with her, and furious that I may never be with her again.

You will be, if I have any say in the choice.

You know I appreciate it, but I really doubt that you do. The universe wanted you here and I was just the unfortunate vessel that was available to them. If one of us will go, it will be me. It's okay, Mies, I know that you are as innocent as I am.

We must go. You've said goodbye?

As close as I could. You'll make sure that she'll be okay?

I promise. Wake her.

Nodding, Nikolai sat on the bed and pulled Naji into his arms. She moaned, roused, then opened her eyes. A smile lit her face as soon as she saw him.

"Hey, handsome. You're still here. I usually send my lovers away as soon as I'm finished with them." She yawned. "I don't see that I'll be finished with you for a long, *long* time. I'm glad you stayed."

"Being with you is the highlight of my life. Thank you, beautiful lady, for every moment. I really could fall in love with you."

"Give me a few minutes."

"I wish we had them."

She pushed up and pulled away from him, lifting a hand to gently push back the stubborn locks of hair that fell over his brow and nearly covered an eye.

"That sounds like goodbye."

"It sounds like the beginning of love."

"So why do I feel like you won't be around for the end of it?"

Nikolai lowered his head and closed his eyes.

Mies, take over. I can't do this.

I've got her. You'll see how we leave her. You won't be disappointed.

I already am. But that's not something we can fix.

Naji's face registered deep concern.

"Nikolai?" she questioned, when he didn't answer her.

"Look into my eyes, Naji," he said suddenly.

Naji did, searching to understand what was going on. Something was, he didn't look right. His face was hard-set, his eyes...what was it that she saw in his eyes? Not the loving, kind man she'd been inside.

"Nikolai, what's going on? You seem...I don't know...different. Almost like you aren't...that doesn't make sense."

"It will," he said. "Naji, you had a marathon night making love with Nikolai. You will always have spectacular, erotic memories of tonight. You will feel love and acceptance whenever you remember it. You will not expect to see Nikolai again, but it will be all right. From now until you do see him again, you'll feel loved and loving. You will be able to move forward and love again even if you never see him again. Sleep now and wake with a warm feeling of sensuality and passion."

Mies lowered her gently back to her pillow and kissed her on the forehead. "*Solzinan*, little Nubian. I will do all that I can to make sure he comes back to you."

The young man had just left his apartment, climbed into the classic Porsche his father had purchased for him for his birthday, and prepared to head out. His mind was on the job his father insisted he take in the family business...and how to get out of it. He didn't quite know how to avoid it yet, but he figured if he got the fuck out of the apartment, and claimed that he'd forgotten his cell phone, at least today his father wouldn't be able to pressure him into it.

Just pulling out of his parking space, a huge man came out of nowhere and stepped in front of the car. Damn't, what was wrong with people?

He surged from the car, ready to confront the idiot when it struck him how unwise that might be. The guy was

137

heavily muscled and dwarfed him at an easy 8 inches taller and half again wider.

As soon as he got close to the big guy, he hesitated and plastered on a smile, deciding to just wave his hand, inquire as to if the guy was okay, and get back into his car. Trouble, he did not need.

"Hey, fellow, you okay?" he said, surprised when the guy was in front of him without seeing him move.

"Look at me," the guy demanded.

Once he did, he felt dizzy. The last thing he remembered was the guy telling him to take him to his hotel.

Mies glanced over the bright red Porsche in front of him.

Nice!

You like? Were you happy with Naji's compulsion?

I was. Thank you. Mies, if this goes my way, I want you to know that I'm going to miss you.

Mies didn't speak for several moments.

It will be too quiet on the spiritual plane too. Perhaps someday, we may meet again.

Da.

"Take me to my hotel," Mies told his compelled driver.

A slender young man dressed in a polo shirt and knee length shorts nodded and stepped back into the driver's side seat of the sports car. Mies dropped into the passenger side.

They would return to the hotel room before sunrise, and then go back to Sarah to see what she had found out after sunset. He felt…sad.

Another sunrise pushed Sarah from her bed. A deep melancholy wouldn't let up. Tonight, when Mies and Nikolai rose, she would talk with them about their journey to the Appalachians to perform the ritual she had designed using a combination of information from Tamesine, her long experience with first blood vampires, and a fair amount of exposure to their lore and magics.

Sorrow infused her morning routine as she tried to accept the fact that if she was successful in helping the two men who now shared one body, the world would be less one vampire or one kind human being far too soon.

Sipping on hot chocolate, since coffee wasn't enough of a mood enhancer, she perched on the arm of the sofa again, her feet buried in a cushion, her eyes on the rosy sky, and thought about the situation. So, last night, Nikolai and Naji should have been together. They would have made love, bonded, and said goodbye, all in that one night.

This emotional roller-coaster was playing havoc with her health. She hadn't eaten much since Nikolai-Mies came into her life. All her life she'd prided herself on her reliability and resourcefulness, but now, when it really counted, she wasn't sure that she could help anyone at all.

Curling her toes against the soft fabric, she admitted freely…she was afraid.

Afraid that Naji would be heartbroken, afraid that she wouldn't be able to help *either* of these men, afraid that she was making the wrong decision not to call the vampires in on this, afraid that after all was said and done, she herself would be lost and alone in this foreign city.

Her eyes moved to her cell phone, lying abandoned on the counter, turned off so that Tamesine couldn't have it traced. Although she'd told Mies that she was going to contact his people and bring them in, it had just been her fear and desperation speaking.

No, she would perform the ritual just as she had designed it. And may the gods in all the heavens have mercy on them. *Hell, if they were vengeful, they might even take her too!*

After another long sip of the chocolate goodness, she wondered, if the powers-that-be took her too, would there be chocolate on the spiritual plane? Would she even be sent there with Mies? Was a human allowed to go there after death?

"Oh, this is all so crazy," she moaned out loud.

"Oh, you bet it is."

Startled, Sarah looked up. Naji stood behind her, twirling her keys on her finger.

"I knocked, but you didn't hear me. Then I heard you speak, so I used my key. Hey, love."

"Hi. Um, how did the night go?"

"De-lish-us! If I didn't know better, I'd think that he was cut out of heavenly cloth and made just for me. It was a dream, Sarah. I think I could fall in love with him."

Sarah's heart skipped beats. This couldn't have been worse. She stepped off of her sofa.

"Naj, you know that he might not be able to stay here? In the U.S., I mean."

"Oh, I know that I might never see him again. It's okay, though. We had a wonderful night and that is enough for me. I mean, I'd love to be with him again, I understand that he might not be able to come back, but I'll always have these amazing memories."

Moving close, Sarah studied Naji's face and her eyes. *Did she mean it?*

She meant it, she really *was* all right with this man that she thought she could love disappearing forever. Sighing, Sarah walked over to the counter to fix Naji a cup of hot chocolate. So Mies had successfully compelled her memories to make the possible loss of Nikolai acceptable to Naji without destroying her.

"Thank you, Mies," she whispered as she built a tower of whipped cream exactly the way that Naji liked it.

"What was that, hon?" Naji asked as she slid onto one of Sarah's tall counter chairs.

"Nothing, nothing at all. Here."

"Ummm. Devastating sex and a mountain of whipped cream. *This* is a happy girl."

Picking her mug back up, Sarah smiled. "It's your morning. What shall we do today?"

"You don't have to work?"

Sarah hated lying. "No, I called off until next week. I have…um, something that I have to take care of tomorrow. I will actually be gone for a few days."

Naji's eyes lit up. "Oh, tell me! Can I come too?"

"You wouldn't want to. It's dull old family stuff."

"I would love to meet your family. What, are you afraid to introduce me? Too sexy for them?"

"Yes, you are far too sexy for my relatives. They're from the bible belt and you would scare the living shit out of them."

"All the more reason to go. Come on, I'll behave."

"Naj, it's dealing with some boring private family stuff. You really *would* hate it. Why don't I introduce you at some better time?"

After an intense stare, Naji shrugged and returned her attention to the chocolate. "Okay. So, today, then, why don't we have lunch at *Pier 41*, then go shopping. I need some new shoes."

"Don't you already have every shoe ever made?"

"Ha, ha. And yes, but that still doesn't stop me. I'll pick you up later. I have somewhere to go."

"Where, at this time of morning?"

"I have secrets, too. I'll see you in one hour."

"Okay."

Naji left quickly, taking her mug with her.

Sarah watched the door after she left, frozen in place. Just one thing left to do before she tried to enjoy the day with her best friend. She turned on her cell phone and texted Nikolai's:

Meet me at my place tonight after sunset. We will travel to a place in the Appalachian Mountains. I've devised a ceremony. If all goes well, this will be settled by tomorrow.

Sarah turned her cell phone back off and left it on the counter again as she went to change. Her footsteps felt as heavy as her heart.

"I don't want to do this," she said, as she stepped into the shower and just stood still to let hot water pulsate over her head, and hoped that it could wash away the pain.

Hours later, a long shopping trip behind them, Sarah stopped in front of her apartment door.

"Thanks, Naji. I had no idea that many types of shoes existed."

"Oh, you poor thing, such a terrible education. It seems that I have my work cut out for me. When you get back from your family trip, we'll begin."

"Okay, but I really don't think I need any more shoes than I have right now."

Naji's expression became serious and she took Sarah's shoulders in her hands. "Oh, love, I had no idea that you were this ill. *Nobody* can have too many pairs of shoes!"

Laughing, Sarah opened the door. "You'll have some trouble convincing me of that, but you can try. I'll see you sometime next week."

"Fine. Hope your weekend goes all right."

"Thank you. I just want to get it over with. Good evening, Naj."

After she closed her door, she fell against it.

She just wanted to get it over with? More like, she wished she never had to. But the men were right, this was no life for either one of them. Something had to happen, and for the moment, *she* was the one charged with the task.

She walked over to close up the blinds. Night was nearly upon them, and so was the coming journey. A small overnight bag sat inside her closet, ready whenever her vampire arrived. They would leave right away to make sure that they arrived before daylight. Tomorrow night, it would be over, one way or another.

It was safe to turn her phone back on, Tamesine couldn't possibly reach her now. Within the next half hour, Mies would arrive and they would go to the airport for a private flight to Mount Mitchell, the highest mountain in the Appalachians. She'd found a man who had a private runway, so they could fly very near to the spot she'd chosen for the ritual.

A text came up as soon as the phone finished booting, and she looked at it, unmoving.

We will be there.

Tears surged unexpectedly at that simple message.

We. We will be there. If things went as hoped tomorrow night, there would no longer be a *we* in Nikolai's body.

Curling up on the sofa, Sarah let herself have a moment to cry for Nikolai, Mies, and herself for her part in all of this and the fact that she could not save them both.

Warm arms came around her and Sarah turned into him. She knew who it was instantly, his scent filled her nose. His embrace tightened and she felt his head buried into hers.

"*Bezolian szvilo xan*, Sarah," he whispered.

They sat holding each other, and at one point, Sarah lifted her head and looked up into Mies's eyes.

"I feel him. Nikolai. I feel him here with us," she said.

Mies nodded. "He is as sad for this as we are. Even if he gets to stay, he says that he will miss my presence. I heightened his human lifeforce so that we could all be together for the last time."

Laying her head back against Mies's chest, Sarah embraced him and Nikolai until she had to push away and stand.

"We need to get to the airport so that we can be safe by daylight tomorrow."

"We are ready."

Sarah went to her closet, pulled her overnight bag out, set it on the table and paused to look back at Mies. His presence in her small apartment still surprised her.

"Mies, thank you for giving me that moment. What you said was very comforting, but I don't know what it means."

"You wouldn't. The language is long dead. It is what my people spoke thousands of years ago. It was the only thing I could think of when I came into this room and saw your tears. It means *your sorrow breaks my heart*."

"Oh. It's beautiful."

"I meant it. I cannot abide watching you in pain."

"I'll be okay. I learned a long time ago that we must do what we must do, no matter how desperately we don't want to."

"Nothing truer ever spoken."

Nodding, Sarah picked up her bag. "The taxi should be here now. We should go."

On Koen's jet bound for the U.S.

"What do ya mean there's no booze?"

Xavier leaned way out of his seat, his body tight, his voice agitated.

Eillia smiled as she might to her toddler.

"No Scotch. No beer. No wine. No alcohol. Any other *awed* inquiries?"

The huge vampire dropped back into his seat, a hand covering his brow and eyes. "Nay. This is gonna be a bitch of a flight, isn't it?"

"Xavier, why don't you just talk with us? This is the first time we've actually been alone like this, so why don't we use the time to get to know each other better? Your brother is one of my dearest friends and yet you and I have barely exchanged words over the centuries."

With nearly his entire face covered now by his hand, the three women on board had to lean in to hear him.

"This is why I remain drunk. So that I don't *have* to listen to female caterwaulin'."

Eillia started to stand, but Park put a hand on her knee.

She turned to Park and smiled.

"It's okay, Park. I'll remain civil," she promised, then faced the slouching male. "Xavier. What is it about women that bothers you?"

He dropped the hand and stared at Eillia. "Bothers me? Nothin' at all, I *love* women! Ya can get a bit chatty, is all."

Park shrugged. "You know he's right. We do seem to go on. It's a built-in gender imperative across all species."

"Aye, this is what I mean. I have a bitch..." Xavier stopped when he saw Eillia upset again. "Female dog," he clarified. "The thing howls more than any ten of me male dogs combined." He grinned. "But I love the little pup to death, 'tis true enough."

Still shaking her head, Park leaned back again. "Let's just talk about the mission. Tam, we hopped on board with little notice because we know that if you need us, we're there, no questions asked. We're going to Boston to find Sarah, so it seems the time to ask. Why?"

"Sarah called me from Boston, where she has returned to live out her human life."

"She isn't blood-bonded to you anymore?" Park asked Xavier.

"Sadly, no. I miss the little lady daily, but when she earnestly asked, I could never refuse her. It's been over three months now."

"All right, she's human now. I hope that it is all that she wanted it to be. Why are *we* here?"

"Because of a phone call from Sarah, and the question that she asked. Then, a strange comment that leads me to believe that she may be in trouble, first blood magics kind of trouble, and that means she needs *us*."

"And Xavier?"

Xavier shot Eillia a hard look. "Aye, she needs me!"

Tamesine glanced at him. "He wanted to come. Anyway." She paused. "Ladies, Sarah asked me how to access the power of the universe through a first blood amulet."

Park and Eillia didn't react to the startling statement, well aware that the question held serious implications. Xavier, however, went with a knee-jerk reaction.

"What the fuck would she want to know somethin' like that for? She's human now, she shouldn't be botherin' with any type of vampire matter, let alone a first blood's power source."

"You see my concern. Xavier, I know the answer to this before I ask it, but I must. Have you and Sarah ever had any discussion about the amulets?"

He shook his head, his hands curling over the armrests of his seat. "Never. Even as me blood-bond, she had no real exposure to them until we went to that forsaken island of ice in Siberia."

"I wouldn't have expected you to. Here's the comment that has me most worried. I mentioned to her that a first blood's spirit amulet stayed with them and doesn't die, even when the vampire does. She responded to me by saying, 'I know.'"

Now, all three of Tamesine's traveling companions were quiet. Park finally spoke. "How would she know?"

"And there's the reason I brought you from your homes to go to Boston with me to find her."

"She doesn't have the ability to safely do anything with an amulet," Eillia commented.

"And yet I believe that she is. Whatever it is, whoever she's involved with, we need to get to her as soon as possible."

"We need to *stop* her." Eillia glanced around the cabin suddenly. "I know you said there's no wine, but food, right?"

"You know Koen. He wouldn't let this bird out of the hangar without the equivalent of several feasts on board."

"Good. I'm famished. In the galley?"

"Absolutely. So, I guess we'll just enjoy the flight. Xavier, there are several wonderful beverages and a lot of refined sugar in the galley."

Xavier grimaced. "Och, lassie, ye're killin' me. Still, I'll take what I can get."

He rose and followed Eillia into the galley. This was going to be a *long* flight. How long had it been since he'd gone over 24 hours without a drink?

AT MOUNT MITCHELL IN THE APPALAICHIANS

"The pilot has taken the plane to a small airport. He'll be back for us tomorrow night."

Sarah watched Mies as he responded with a single nod. Yeah, she wasn't feeling very chatty either. It was going to be a terrible twenty-four hours.

Mies placed the small pack that Nikolai had prepared for this journey on the ground. The intention was that Mies may need some clothes or ablutions for the next day, but Mies didn't care. He was vampire, he could get anything he wanted anywhere he went. All he wanted now was for this to be over.

Clearing her throat to get his attention, Sarah pointed to her right. "There's a cavern here that should have no daylight exposure. We'll spend the day here and then tonight, we'll do the ritual."

Again, Mies nodded without answering, but when he finally lifted his eyes to hers, Sarah's heart plunged. Pain flashed, and regret, his eyes reflecting his emotions…raw, ragged, exposed. Before she could speak, he turned away and headed into the dark cave with one of the several flashlights she'd brought.

He wouldn't tell her how he felt, but he couldn't stop her from seeing it. There was nothing else to do but follow him with the two bedrolls she'd brought, her own flashlight filling the pitch black cave with a hard column of light. He had already gone too deep.

When she'd found the caves online, she'd called a man who claimed to know this region inside out, and he'd confirmed that the caves went deep, but a series of tunnels provided access so that people could hike down without too much trouble. Still, she'd chosen full-on hiking gear for this trip. Mies, as vampire, would have no trouble with any of the terrain, but a human might. So far, the narrow tunnel that led through the cave was easily passable.

Rounding a sharp turn, she stopped when she saw Mies scoping a chamber. He looked at her, his eyes hard now, all business.

"This will suffice. I see no crevices or cracks that should allow daylight to penetrate. This was a good call, little doctor, thank you."

"It's my gift. Just call me the Fixer, I fix things."

147

She pitched one of the bedrolls to him, which he caught effortlessly, and began to unroll the second one to make a pallet that would be at least marginally comfortable. Dry, at least.

Finished settling in, Sarah placed four LED lights around the edge of the chamber that would burn for up to thirty hours, then dropped onto her bedroll and pulled a bag from her luggage.

"Mies, I brought some meal bars so that you wouldn't get too hungry tonight. They may not provide what a first meal would, but they're quite good and very filling. Here, I brought four different flavors, and plenty of them, so take what you want."

Mies didn't move. He'd dropped his roll onto the ground, but hadn't spread it out. It would be several hours until daylight so it wasn't necessary that he do so right away. He glanced towards Sarah, lit now by the little devices, leaning against the wall of rock, an unwrapped tube in her hand that reminded him of a candy bar. Even in such harsh light, she looked stunning. He wanted her, right now, so desperately he had to force himself to stay away from her. It wouldn't be right, to take her again, to continue his ruin of this human life she was so intent on.

It was the bond they'd already formed that would make it hard for her after he was gone. So if he took her again, it would further complicate her sexual need. She would probably be alone the rest of her life…and he couldn't do that to her. He already loved her too much. This woman who would have been mate to a first blood meant everything to him. Which is why he couldn't stay in this small space with her. Not right now, at least, until he got hold of himself and his raging sexual need for her.

"Thank you. I want to check out the area, so I'll take a few with me if you don't mind."

Sarah surged up from the bedroll. "How about I come with you?"

"No!"

Even Mies realized how bad that sounded. He winced when he saw the surprise on her face. "I didn't mean to bark at you. I just need a few moments, you understand?"

Sarah nodded. Relieved, she really did understand his need to walk away from this right now. "I get it. Okay. Here, one of each flavor. Go out, and just clear your mind."

"Thank you. For understanding."

He used air displacement and was gone before Sarah could respond.

She glanced around the cave, the little lights casting dancing shadows on the rocky walls. One of the lights had a flickering feature that simulated candlelight; pretty, in a post-apocalyptic sort of way. Sarah smiled at that comparison. It seemed appropriate, given what they would try tomorrow night.

With an uncontrolled plop, she returned to the bedroll and tore off too large of a piece of a meal bar. She understood why he wanted to be alone, and yet, *didn't*. After tomorrow, he might be gone. Why wouldn't he want to be with her if it were the final chance? Had he already checked out of the life that he'd been forced into here on the corporeal plane? Was he doing it for *her*?

"Fuck this!" Pitching the meal bar onto the dirt floor, Sarah raced from the cave. As she left the mouth of the cave into a light breeze, the moon immediately captured her gaze as it rose above the mountaintop. Its perceived proximity and brightness stopped her in her tracks. *How magnificent this place was!*

Distant lights didn't begin to interfere with the blackness of the sky and the densely scattered field of stars whose light was compromised by the nearly full moon. It had been the phase of the moon and the location that had convinced Sarah that they might really be able to do this. She'd taken into account everything she'd learned recently about first blood history, what Tamesine had told her, what Mies had, and her own instinct that had its own sort of power. No doubt remained…this was the time and place.

The rising moon bathed the clearing on the top of this mountain ridge with enough light that the flashlight was unnecessary, so she switched if off and put it on a large rock before she searched the skyline for Mies. His silhouette cut out a huge pattern against the star-studded, navy-painted sky. She approached slowly, well aware that he knew she was there. When she was near enough, he didn't turn, but he spoke.

"It's breathtaking. You couldn't have chosen a more perfect place. I can feel Mother Earth's heartbeat."

Sarah moved around in front of Mies. Was it possible that he was even more spectacular in moonlight? Seated on the edge of an embankment on top of a boulder, he lowered his eyes from the moonrise and caught her gaze.

"Your eyes are glowing," she said unnecessarily.

"You know why. It was probably not wise for you to follow me."

"It may be our last moments together. Why don't you want to spend that time with me?"

"Because I want you more than anything I've ever wanted in all of my centuries. Because I don't want to *talk* with you. Well, I do, but only after I bury myself inside you so deep, I couldn't ever find my way out. Sarah, you are the mate that I waited for thousands of years ago. I waited for you on the other side of forever, little doctor, and here you are, on this side of it. We were never meant to meet, it seems. Now that we have, I don't want to give you up."

Were there words to answer what he'd said? Something slid up from the pit of her belly, from the center of her womanhood that spread through her body, her heart nearly aching. She was this vampire's mate, and she had to touch him. Sliding down onto the grass, her hands on his thighs moved to the top of his jeans and slipped beneath the waistband.

"Then we should make every second count. We have none to spare, Mies."

"I don't want to leave you drowning in my wake. Sarah, you chose your path. You want to be human, and I don't want to destroy that for this one last night."

"If you do it right, it will be enough. Since it turns out, I'm yours anyway."

Neither moved. Had he heard right? She was willing to give up her dream for one more night with him?

"Mies, you're awfully slow for an ancient vampire. Send Nikolai away and make love to me."

Pushing off the ground, Mies walked closer to the end of the land. His toes reached beyond the cliff's edge, the landscape beneath nearly a sheer drop-off bathed in silvered light. "This will torture both of us for a long time."

"Then we'd better make it worth it."

Slowly, he turned to face Sarah. She had removed her shirt and was reaching for her bra, her eyes glistening.

He was there instantly, a hand on hers, stilling her from removing the bra. She dropped her hands as he finished the job for her, and pitched the bra yards away.

"You won't be needing that again," he whispered.

Vampire speed came in handy sometimes and this was one of those times. Aroused beyond endurance, Mies had them both naked and lifted Sarah up, her arms around his neck and her legs wrapped around his waist. She leaned in and nipped at his chest, her tongue hot as it slid across one of his nipples. "Nikolai?"

"Gone. It's just you and me and *eternity in an hour.*"

Sarah moaned as he hiked her higher, her clitoris rubbing against his hard belly, the contact extremely stimulating. "The sexiest man who ever lived, naked beneath me, *and* William Blake. You've learned a lot since you've been here, haven't you? I'm a really happy girl, Mies."

"Not yet," he groaned, and had them on the ground, Sarah beneath him, his weight sensually heavy on top of her. Her legs spread to allow his filled cock to nestle between them.

"May I drink?" he asked.

"God, yes," she barely got out. Sex during a blood draw was a dream no woman could ever forget.

Mies licked all around her neck before he sunk his fangs in, but when he began to draw her blood into his body, his hardened cock moved and Sarah lifted up to him.

Responding instantly, he did the same but when he fitted himself to her, he paused before he surged into her.

Sarah thumped him on the back with a fist to let him know she wouldn't wait. "Waiting," she hissed into his ear. When he still did not enter her, she moved her thighs to capture his penis.

"Now, ancient one," she said into his ear.

His eyes glowing even brighter in the darkness, the silver swirls charged, Mies pulled from her throat.

"Ah, I'm getting inside you, all right, but I want to look at you when I thrust into you. I want to see your face when we connect as mates. You should have belonged to me in that other lifetime, Sarah, you were *always* my mate, even long before you were ever born."

He plunged, then, hard and fast, a surety tearing through Sarah that her body recognized. Yes, he belonged here inside her. Her arms tight around his back, he began to move, the friction already overwhelming, as if she'd been waiting for him to come to her, excited, ready, needy.

But when Mies dropped closer, his hands in her hair, his lips on hers, they tightened, her legs went around his and rested on his buttocks, each thrust pushing him deeper. She was entirely immersed in him, the sensations carrying her someplace else and she struggled to hear him, because she was aware that he spoke into her ear.

What? Oh, God…that was…beyond this world incredible…her body shuddered, but he kept moving…was he trying to tell her something? Mies, not now…oh…God!

"I miss you already," Mies told her as he kissed her again, let go, and pumped into his woman, an orgasm so wild, they held onto each other and just watched the moon as it smiled down. It approved of the lovers who held each other as they climaxed, tears in their eyes, hearts filled and breaking at the same time. Love, found against all odds, even while they accepted that it would likely be lost.

Sarah and Mies lay tangled together, his spent cock slowly sliding from her. She already felt empty without him inside her.

They did not speak at first, just held each other and watched the moon slowly move across the wide sky, pushing stars out of the way as it went. The night air became cooler but Mies's body heat warmed them both.

Some long minutes later, Sarah sighed. "We should move into the cave in case we fall asleep."

Instantly, she was standing in the middle of the cave, a huge naked vampire grinning at her. Smiling back at him, she glanced around.

"You might want to bring our clothes in, too."

"Why? We won't be needing them."

With a laugh, she reached for him. "We will, at some point."

He lifted her into his arms again and carried her slowly, human style, over to her pallet to lay her down.

"Not yet." In the flickering light of the small cavern room, Mies slid down Sarah's body, leaving a hot trail as he went, teeth nipping tender skin, lifting Sarah off the bedroll.

"Mies, that's…heaven."

"Good. I want to take you to the stars."

With his tongue, he did just that, pulling her knees apart and sliding up to burn another path from inside of each knee to her belly. He stopped momentarily to tease her where her legs ended, heaven for him, a place he wished he could bury himself over and over for the *next* 6000 years. He plunged his tongue deep as she grabbed his hair, then traveled up to hard erect nipples that needed the same attention.

"Mies…" she whispered, and he smiled, his eyes swirling silver again, as he nipped round the nipples and then moved back to her neck to drink again.

"I can't get enough of you."

His comment stopped them both, *stilled* him at her neck, stilled *her* underneath him. *Can't get enough of you,* he'd said, when they both knew that the day just beginning to dawn was likely all they would ever have.

Sarah pushed Mies away from her and shoved him onto his back. She would not let this turn maudlin if it were all the time they had left.

"My turn, vampire," she said out loud, and bit him on the shoulder, hard, with blunt teeth that he found oddly erotic. While she didn't break the skin, his shoulder tingled where she bit.

"You may feed again later, but for now, I want to practice something I read about online. Are you game?"

Mies watched the beautiful ex blood-bond as she dropped down between his legs and looked up at him from that location. Something she'd learned online? It was probably spectacular if Sarah had researched and chosen the action.

"I am game for anything," he bragged, but when she slid her fingers around his cock, which had been ready to enter her again, he closed his eyes, just to *feel* her touch him in that most intimate place. His eyes shot open moments later when her tongue began an excursion from top to bottom, lingering on the tip. When she nipped him gently there, too, he dropped onto the pallet and let her show him that she had, indeed, learned something extraordinary online.

Teeth, tongue, and active fingers pushed him to stone hard, and when she took him into her mouth to continue the oral assault, he sighed and groaned as his body quaked.

While his body quieted from the orgasm she'd created, Mies looked down to see Sarah grinning at the results of her work.

How satisfying it had been to bring such a pleasurable climax to Mies with the inventive things she'd learned on a site that taught women how to "*keep their men.*"

Mies lay still beside her, the orgasm so intense, he couldn't move.

Mies blew out an extracted breath. "I've never actually had anyone do anything like that before."

"It's ancient. Kama sutra, I think. Well, that won't mean much to you, but I, uh, became curious about different ways of making love. Recently."

Shaking his head, Mies wanted to bitch at the universe for doing this to her, to him. In the end, though, he couldn't fault the powers that sent him here for letting them have this time together, even if it was for just these few days.

"Sarah…"

She had been lying against his chest, her fingers playing along the hard contours, unable to stop touching him, when he began to speak. Sarah could tell by his tone that he was going to address their situation and she didn't want to.

"No," she said, to stop him. "No. We both know the score. We are aware now how we feel about each other. All I want to do is to be with you, so please let me have this."

After a long hesitation, he nodded. "All right. Then, I have an announcement to make."

"What?"

The world spun, and he had her beneath him again. "I can move again. Remember what I promised?"

"I do, but I have another request. I would like to ride *you*. I've never done that."

"Take control, my lady and do what you wish."

"A compliant vampire. Umm, that does sound right."

She slid out from under him and when he turned over, she pushed him down hard against the soft bedding. Slowly lifting a leg, she mounted him like she might a stallion.

Beneath her, Mies let his eyes move over every inch of her body as she moved, and when she lifted a leg, his view of the slit went straight to his cock.

Even though she didn't want him to say it, he was going to miss her more than anything he'd ever known. Although she was aware that he came from 6000 years in the past, she still had no concept of how long that would be. Watching her discover her sexuality with him was still worth it. *She was sublime!*

Lifting up, Sarah moved just high enough to slide him in and out of her so that his orgasm was already building before she had a chance to play. He worked to control himself so that he wouldn't go before she did. Sarah went wild playing cowgirl to his steed. She planted her hands on each side of his head, rode him hard, and just when he knew that he was finished, ready to explode into her, she orgasmed as well and dropped onto his chest as they finished together. *This*, her above him, riding him so gloriously, her hair flying, her face lit by pure joy, was what he would remember most.

Sarah rolled off Mies. "Whew. I never..." She took a moment to catch her breath. "I never knew sex could be like this. I never knew that *I* would love it like this."

Turning, she pushed up onto her side and slid a hand over his chest. "You're so beautiful," she whispered.

Although she'd told him that she didn't want to talk about what would happen tomorrow night, her mind went there anyway. "I'll miss you forever, just so you know," she continued in the same hushed voice.

"I know. In my place of rest, I will relive these moments forever and hope that the universe might see fit to bring you to me when the day comes."

Sarah dropped onto his chest, her ear against his strong heartbeat. Moisture welled in her eyes as she wondered if his wish could be granted. She didn't think that humans ended up in the same place, but she held the same hope.

They fell asleep, wrapped together, hearts beating, one on top of the other.

AT LOGAN INTERNATIONAL AIRPORT IN BOSTON

"Xavier, are you serious?" Park shook her head as she watched the shrugging man pace.

At a table in the airport cafeteria, Park, Eillia, and Tamesine stared at Xavier.

"I'm sorry, ladies, she isn't here. When I did the first trace in Paris, she was. Now, all I can tell you is I don't find her here. I'll have to have a quiet room to do another blood trace."

Tamesine stood. "No, you don't. Come over here."

Xavier winced at her. "What are ya gonna do?"

"For the love of all that is holy, Xavier, I'm just going to help you do the trace. Basically, I'm going to hold your hand and lend my power to you."

156

"Ah. Aye, then."

Xavier carefully took a seat beside Tamesine, a woman who he had been attracted to some time ago when she was still somewhat mental. He had known her centuries ago when she'd been full-on psychotic, but her attachment to her race and some serious soul-searching had helped her heal. He still considered her one of the most stunning women he'd ever met.

And a bit bossy.

"Put your hands in mine," she said.

Xavier knew it was a demand. Kindly said, but a demand nonetheless, so he did as commanded. Someone else in control…it didn't sit well with him, but this required diplomacy, and he really *did* need her help. They *must* find Sarah.

"Clear your mind. You will feel me push against your thoughts, try to relax and let me in."

"Lassie, I've never done anythin' like this before."

"I know. Most males haven't had a spirit trip and we won't do that, but I need to add my power to your search. It's simple, just relax and accept me."

That might have been one of the hardest things he'd faced in his long life. Xavier had always been an extremely private person, and the idea of having someone inside his mind was unacceptable.

Tamesine saw his reaction and felt him pull away. She tightened her grip on his hands and pulled him back to her.

"For Sarah," she said.

Nearly a minute passed before he relaxed and let her in. "For Sarah," he agreed. "I'm goin' to need to close me eyes."

"That's fine. Relax, clear everything from your mind. Visualize a white room and go there. Nothing, no sound, no images, nothing interferes. Can you feel me?"

Tamesine knew that she was in, she could feel him, but he had frozen, the intrusion overwhelming.

Inside his mind, she embraced him carefully. "It's all right, Xavier. I am only here to give you power. Calm down, enjoy it. A spiritual merge is wonderful if you allow yourself to experience it."

He didn't see it that way. Having another person that close was an invasion. Still, there was a task at hand and his job was to do exactly as she required him to do so they could find Sarah. For the first time in his life, Xavier let go and gave control to someone else.

Tamesine felt it the moment that he did and swept in, her own magic weaved around his and within moments, both vampires laser-focused on Sarah's location, separated easily less than a minute later.

Tamesine released Xavier. "The Appalachian mountains? Why in the world…"

She stopped, her eyes searching the air when she smiled. "Ah, of course. She's doing exactly what I told her to do. Well, my friends, we're air bound again. Next stop, North Carolina. Thank you, Xavier."

He stood, uneasy. "Aye, well, if we're gettin' back on that jet after that, I'm makin' a stop first."

The three women agreed with him. This trip had taken another turn and Xavier wasn't the only one who could use a mood enhancer. They headed for the airport bar.

SUNSET ON MOUNT MITCHELL

When Sarah opened her eyes, the first thing that she saw was Mies, his face above her, his fingers caressing her belly. After a soft smile and a moment of joy, memory and reality slammed into her.

"It's night," she said emotionlessly.

"It is."

For several seconds, she couldn't speak. It was time to go. She couldn't move. If she stayed right here, he would stay with her and everything would be all right. So she gave in and closed her eyes again.

Mies dropped down and pulled her to him, his lips on her forehead. There were no words now, all had been said, the future would take the course that is must take, and tomorrow, when the sun rose again, someone irreplaceable would be lost.

They stayed still, silent, until Sarah forced her eyelids open again.

"All right," was all she said, and pushed off the pallet to stand, naked, searching…for what? She couldn't function. The ever-reliable, always ready, brilliant Sarah couldn't function. There was something that she needed to do.

Mies handed her the clothes they'd left lying all over the mountaintop last night. Oh. Of course, she needed to dress.

Tonight, get it over with, get on to living life as I chose it to be, no more interference from the vampire world this time, Mies would be gone, Nikolai would return to Russia, time to have that date with Leo, back to work…

The stream of consciousness babble in her mind wouldn't stop. *Get hold of yourself, both of these men are depending on you. This must be done, and done right, and it is all up to you, human girl, to help sort out the crazy chaos of the universe, destiny, fate…whatever drove this mess.*

"All right," Sarah repeated and dressed quickly, efficiently, doing everything by automation now. She knew what she had to do and she *would* do it. For the moment, she couldn't look at Mies.

"I'm ready," she announced, minutes later.

He stood at the entrance to the chamber. "Where do you want to go?"

"To the summit. We want the highest point. It's why I chose here, at Mount Mitchell, it's the highest point in the U.S. east of the Mississippi."

After tying her boots, Sarah took a small backpack and led Mies from the cavern wordlessly. He followed the same way until they stood at the edge of the land, the moon rising again, a reminder of the night they'd had. Now, she couldn't help it, she looked at Mies, who hadn't taken his eyes off her the entire way to this destination.

After a soul-deep sigh, Sarah finally spoke again.

"Here. Tamesine said that we must channel your power through the living planet and the universe. Here, as near to the earth and as close to the sky as we can get. *Here* is where we make our stand and try to undo this deed."

Squatting, Sarah unzipped the backpack and pulled out four candles, placed them in a large square and lit them. She looked up at Mies.

"Sit, please, in the center of the grid."

He did so, and she joined him, facing him, the moon over his shoulder.

"The candles represent the four quarters of the earth, and should help bind your magic within so that we can channel it and get the results we seek." Sarah paused.

"Mies, I need you to clearly declare your intentions and desires."

"I will. But first, Sarah, Nikolai would like to speak with you. He speaks for both of us, my love."

My love? Sarah kept her teeth clinched. She couldn't respond. *My love?* Oh, God, nothing in this life would ever hurt more than this night. She nodded.

Mies did too, closed his eyes, and a moment later, Nikolai was there.

"Sarah, my friend," Nikolai said, and leaned in to give her a hug.

"Nik, I'm sorry that we kept you gone last night."

"I understand. I had already had my night with Naji, and you two needed to take yours. I assume that you did."

Nikolai thought that Sarah's smile was the saddest he'd ever seen.

"Yes, we did."

"*Da.* That is what I wished for you both. We do not know how this will go tonight."

"No idea. You know that Mies is intending to sacrifice himself so that you can have your life back. He's quite noble."

"I know this. I also know that the universe sent him here and it was willing to sacrifice me to bring him back. I have no doubt that it will try to protect its choice. I am human, powerless and disposable, there is just as high a

160

chance that, when this is finished, I will be gone. Sarah, this is what Mies and I wish you to know. Whatever the outcome, no matter who remains or who goes, none of this is your fault. You must carry no guilt or sense of responsibility for this. We asked for your help and we are both okay with this. You understand this, *da*?"

She didn't answer Nikolai because Sarah knew that she would carry this heavy burden until she left this world.

"Sarah?"

Unaware that she was shaking her head, Sarah finally answered. "Sure, sure I do."

"Sarah, I wish I could let you know how much we both honor and love you for helping us. We know it is a terrible thing to ask, but you must promise to remember these words, my angel. You are not to take on any guilt for this act. If you try, the one of us who remains has decided to kick your ass." He tilted his head. "Although, if it is Mies, he will more likely *kiss* your ass."

"I will try, that is all that I can promise."

"All right. The only thing I have left to say is, when you are with Naji, at some time, whatever moment seems right, will you just let her know that she touched me more than any other woman I have ever been with?"

That started the tears sliding down her cheeks, Sarah's voice still unwavering. She wasn't crying openly, but her eyes wouldn't stay dry, and she suspected that this was just the beginning of a month long crying jag.

"I will, Nik, I promise. She's okay, Mies took care of her, but I still think she's going to miss you."

"Good. As it should be. She will be my legacy then."

Nikolai suddenly looked at the bright moon, then back to Sarah. "It is time."

"Yes. The moon is here to channel the power of the amulet. It is a link between earth and sky."

"Okay, then. Mies is taking over now. If I never get to speak to you again, I just want to say that you have been a great pleasure to know, Sarah the brilliant."

"And you as well, Nikolai, earth protector."

He smiled. "Earth protector. I like that. Good-bye, Sarah." Nikolai closed his eyes.

161

Now, Mies opened the dark eyes and looked at Sarah. "How do we proceed?"

"Okay. We are here for you to tap into the power of the earth and sky. Tamesine says that you can touch the magic of the planet and the universe and channel it through your spirit amulet to achieve the power that you will need to do just about anything. I can feel it running through you right now, Mies. While I am fully human, with no skills beyond that, I have always been intuitive. For some reason, I can feel that you have the ability to connect to the source of first blood power, and here, with the earth, the sky, and the moon, you have all that you need. Take my hands, Mies. I am going to try to help keep you focused on what you must do."

Sarah watched his strong hands reach for hers, and when their fingertips touched, sparks crackled and lit the air around them.

"I can feel it too. The power moves through me."

His eyes lifted to Sarah's. "I love you, my mate. One day, I will find you again."

"Mies." After she croaked his name, Sarah couldn't speak. Knowing he knew how much she loved him, that words were not necessary, she held his hands tightly as she stood, pulling him up too.

Lifting all four of their arms high, Sarah on a stone to raise her to Mies's height, hands still intertwined, she spoke out loud as the air began to swirl. Electricity still crackled from their hands and began to move around their bodies as well.

"Feet and soul to earth, head and heart to sky, spirit amulet that guides this first blood soul, this man who seeks to undo an act of fate, Mother Earth, let your child in to seek your solace and return to his immortal rest above the sky and beyond the stars."

Mies felt the power enter his body, his spirit, all that he was, and all that he'd ever been, the magic as tangible as the ground he stood upon and as ethereal as the air that sailed above him. It weaved through him, exactly as Sarah had said it would, and it placed its magic in his hands. He could guide this, the power at his will, the chance to fix this, to give Nikolai his life, to return to where he should never have left.

He hesitated, though, as his gaze went to the woman who still held on to him, her hair wild, her eyes locked on his, her lips parted. She would not know that he stopped just long enough to burn that final image into his mind before he left. He knew now, the control was his, he *would* be able to make sure that Nikolai was the one left behind, he had the unimpeachable power to choose.

Mies felt Nikolai's sorrow as he slipped from the body he'd enjoyed inhabiting and began to leave the new world he would have loved to have explored with his newfound mate at his side.

"Make your life amazing," he whispered to his new brother. "Thank you for sharing it with me for a little while."

With one last look at Sarah, he felt his lifeforce lift, the amulet too, and began to leave the plane of the living.

"I unmake this unholy merge," he said to the powers that drove the universe, and separated, left, as white light surrounded him and Mies saw nothing but brightness. He felt, long before he saw, that he was no longer among the living. An ache set up in his chest, and he knew now why that particular organ was said to be where love came from. His heart was not needed here, and it was a good thing. It was irreparably broken.

When the brightness faded, he recognized the soupy existence he'd been immersed in for millennia that felt like moments lost in eternity. His lifeforce made up all that he was, the physical body a manifestation of life below, unnecessary in this realm. His mind active, though, he could access images, emotions, moments from the living realm. Touch, feelings, every detail about what he'd left behind. He'd adjusted to all the losses when he first died six thousand years ago, he would do so again.

But not yet. And although time meant nothing here, he still knew that this pain would last. He released the final tether to the earth, her own magic easing back from whence it came, his gratitude sent with it.

163

It was done. He wished a long and lovely life for Nikolai and Naji. For Sarah, he hoped, with all of his shattered heart, that she would find love again.

Nikolai lay on the hard ground, his eyes open, but he couldn't move. Someone knelt at his side, he could tell that, but he couldn't tell who it was or why they were there. Or why he was *here*. Eventually, a voice penetrated, feminine, soft, insistent.

"Nikolai, I need to help you to sit up. Nikolai! Can you hear me?"

Sarah. Why was Sarah here? God, he hurt. His head…as if someone slammed a crane into him. His vision was blurry, like he'd been on a 24 hour bender.

Sarah was persistent. "Nik?"

"Da…" he groaned. "I hear ya. Where am I and why would ya let me do that to myself?"

"Nik, I need you to sit up. I need to make sure that you are all right."

Why wouldn't he be? Using her assistance, Nikolai gained an upright position and glanced around him. An epic landscape spread beneath them, valley after valley, mountaintop after mountaintop. A moon that seemed far too close hung suspended over their heads. Memories returned like rushing water and he knew, he remembered…Mies. Mies, gone now… They'd passed as Mies left and Nikolai took ownership of the body they had shared.

"Are you okay? Do you remember what happened?"

Sarah wasn't letting up. Nikolai nodded.

"I do now. I was confused at first. I think I'd gotten out of the habit of thinking for myself. Mies and I had become one in spirit." He fell silent, his eyes lifted to Sarah's.

"I felt him go," she whispered, and accepted his arms around her as Nikolai gathered her near.

"I wanted to have my mind and my body back, but now, Sarah, I feel…empty."

"I think we always will. His presence was pretty huge."

They sat on the cool grass, buffeted by increasing winds, and held each other, lost in their own thoughts, their own efforts to find a way to deal with this, to be okay with never being with this extraordinary man who came into their lives and transformed them.

Nikolai glanced at the sky anxiously at one point, then smiled with a scoffing snicker as Sarah pulled back.

"What?" she asked.

"I looked at the sky to assess the nearness of daylight. I'm used to having to watch out for that, but that isn't an issue anymore. I assume that this body is fully human again. I don't know how to explain it, but I felt a change there too when Mies's lifeforce left."

"I think you're right. Your scent was never the same as Mies's, but it's different now, even from when Mies gave the body over to you. If you aren't fully human yet, I believe you will be soon."

"Oh. In that case, I guess it is prudent to go inside."

Sarah stood and began to gather the candles and supplies as Nikolai found his balance.

"It feels weird. Like I'm not sure how to walk anymore."

She turned to hold his forearms. "I've got you."

He nodded. "I know you do. Sarah, you're going to be all right."

"I know. It will take a lot of time to stop missing him."

"*Da.*"

"Nik, let's get out of here."

Ten

"I've found her. She's here, she's on this mountaintop," Xavier announced, pleased to have provided Sarah's exact location.

"As I suspected. She's accessing a spirit amulet. My God, what in the world could she be doing? Who would put her up to this?" Tamesine queried.

All three women looked at Xavier, who finished off a tall glass of Scotch and shrugged. "Ladies, ya forget that I said goodbye to my little blood-bond months ago. I've had no contact with her since then, at her request. Vampires apparently tend to mess up human doin's. So I can't be of aid to ya. I truly have no idea."

"I've checked with anyone that I've known had contact with Sarah. Neither Dez or Olivia have spoken with her since they parted in France. Your lab manager seemed the most likely, Park, but he has had no correspondence either. The only other person she spent time with was Olivia's friend in Russia and he's human. I guess we'll find out when we find her."

"The plane is on descent. There's a small landing strip nearby and our pilot said that another private plane landed here last night. I hope we're in time," Eillia announced as she looked at an update from the pilot.

"Good. I want to protect Sarah, but I'm also incredibly curious to know what she's up to. Things have been so calm lately, and this is a fine mystery."

"Tamesine, oh, my dear, you've invited temptation, and chaos likes to answer. All we've wanted for years was a calm ordinary life," Park *tsked* her friend.

Laughing, Tamesine reached for a Chinese dumpling off a tray Eillia set on the little table between them. "I know. I still haven't found my greatest enemy, Claude. When that happens, I guarantee, I won't be bored."

"I do admit that I'm very curious too. Sarah is too smart to get involved in something dangerous or beyond her ability to control."

Park looked out the window, the landscape lit by only the moon, no other lights visible, no homes, no businesses, no parking lots. "We're going in."

Sarah watched the earth fall away beneath them as the little Cessna rose into the sky. She glanced at Nikolai and then the pilot, aware that, to the pilot, nothing had changed, and to her and Nikolai, *everything* had. It was odd the way the world worked, so many people so clueless as to its real nature. Most people had no idea that supernatural beings really existed, often living and working right alongside them.

To this kind older man who had been flying these mountains for decades, Sarah was returning from a night on the mountain with her beau. In reality, she'd rescued an unexpected hero and sent away the man she would likely love for the rest of her life, all in that one night.

"Life's funny," she whispered to herself, and if either of the men in the lightweight aircraft heard her, they didn't say a word.

Hours later, Nikolai followed Sarah from the airport terminal. Neither had spoken for most of that time, both too consumed by dialogues in their own minds about what had happened on Mount Mitchell.

Waiting on the curb for a taxi to take them back into the city, Sarah caught one of Nikolai's frequent glances at her.

"Come home with me. I don't want to be alone tonight and I don't think you do either. We'll get a buffet of junk food and just take care of each other. Tomorrow, we'll deal with the rest of our lives."

Nikolai nodded. "I am grateful. The idea of returning to our hotel room…" He stopped suddenly, his eyes filling with moisture. "Our. I wonder how long it will take before I don't automatically use that word. Sarah, I wanted my life back, my mind, my body, and I am grateful to have it so, but this silence inside my head is unnerving. It feels wrong."

"I know. That's what I mean. We need to be with each other and help each other through this. No one else on earth has any idea what we've been through. We need each other, Niko."

Niko. That had been Mies's word. Sarah vowed she would never use it again. Just hearing the word hurt.

On the way through downtown, Sarah did exactly what she'd said she would do. After stopping at three different cafes, they carried pizza, subs, cakes, and cookies up to the third floor apartment.

Opening the door felt like shelter from the world, and when she and Nikolai stepped through, she closed it firmly and placed the safety chain on to keep out tomorrow. Tonight, they would support each other, eat, discuss, complain, cry, and get some rest. When she opened the door tomorrow, *then* they would get on with the process of living.

ON MOUNT MITCHELL

"I don't know why I'm surprised." Tamesine waited for the rest of her party to get back into the small private prop-engine plane they'd compelled.

"She's on the move, I cannot be responsible for that, ladies." Xavier took his seat and lifted a bottle of whisky from where he'd stashed it earlier. "Are we safe here?"

"We are. We'll be back in Boston just before daybreak and seek shelter. Then when we rise, we will find our little globetrotter, see what happened on this mountain tonight, and get home to France."

Tamesine leaned back to Park and Eillia. "Did you notice?"

Eillia nodded. "Yes. Powerful magic was drawn here tonight."

"We'll find her and know why. Any more cake?"

"Oh, yes. I heated up three of Koen's best. I half expected to have a nice reunion with Sarah, hoped there was nothing serious or nefarious occurring, and get home to our children and mates. This has just been kind of nuts. Here, a nice vanilla chocolate, perfect for this situation."

In Boston

"How are you feeling, Nikolai? I mean, how does your singly occupied *body* feel without the *first blood* infusion? Is all of it gone?"

Nikolai had to finish chewing a slice of buffalo chicken pizza. Wiping his mouth, he cleared his throat. "It's changing. There may be small amounts of residual first blood magics, but they are already waning. I don't think it will be very long before I am fully human again."

"I know a little about how that feels, but your change must be far more extreme. My body was never vampire, and yours was."

"I ache, which is the first thing that I noticed when I woke after realizing that you were calling me. Being vampire, it was incredible. I will miss that along with Mies's absence. I can't believe that this happened. And as much as that, I can't believe now that it is finally over. We will be able to move on, *da*?"

"We will, because we're both strong to have even survived the pain of this event. And we have each other. I know that you will return to your home, but what we've shared has changed us forever. I hope we can be there for each other whenever the need arises, even if it is just to reach out to say hello?"

"Always. Thank you for coming to our rescue, Sarah. I don't know that I can ever say that enough."

"You can, so stop. Here, try this. It's a lemon bar, and while I've never really cared for the taste of lemon, these are truly scrumptious."

Sarah held the sugar-covered pastry up to him and he took a bite.

After eating enough comfort food to satisfy even the voracious appetites of a vampire, both Sarah and Nikolai gave in to the exhaustion that had been plaguing them all night.

"Why don't we get some rest?" she suggested.

"God, yes. Everything on my body hurts, inside and out. And my heart hurts. Sleep sounds like heaven."

Nodding, Sarah slipped off the sofa and closed the bathroom door behind her. Twenty minutes later, teeth cleaned, face washed, she stared into the mirror for several long moments.

"Back to normal day-to-day," she told the pale face that stared back at her with haunted eyes. After she'd changed into a long tee shirt, Sarah came out of the bathroom to find Nikolai stretched out on the sofa. He looked every bit as whipped as she did.

Killing the last light, other than a bright blue night light in the corner of the room, she said, "Good night, Nik."

"Sleep well, Sarah," he answered with a yawn.

Sliding beneath her sheet, she tried to will herself into blessed unconsciousness, but sleep eluded her. She could hear Nikolai's soft breathing and knew that he was trying to do the same thing. She needed solace where there was none to be found.

Sarah pushed up onto her elbows. "Nikolai, would you just hold me tonight?"

"*Da*," he said, and with the simplest word in the world, that solace came. He slid in beside her and pulled her close. Now, with loving arms around them, Sarah and Nikolai finally fell into restful, dreamless sleep.

Persistent knocking slowly brought Sarah up from wonderful oblivion. She tried to ignore it and stay asleep but it was relentless. Still half-asleep, she tried to slide from her bed, but something was holding her there. What in the…?

Awareness struck at once that someone was in bed with her and that someone else was at the door.

It was Nikolai's arm stretched across her, so Sarah gently picked it up and laid it aside, hurried to the door, unlocked it, and peeked out.

"Tamesine?" she said, shocked, total wakefulness finally hitting her.

"Hi, little one. *You* are a tough human to find."

Tamesine swept in, Eillia and Park following her, as Sarah stepped back. Her eyes shot even wider when Xavier, who had been waiting against the wall out of sight, faced her.

"It's a party, my Sarah."

Sarah finally found her voice. "Xavier, what are you guys doing here?"

Eillia scanned the room to see if they were alone, but the man in the bed, now waking, clearly showed that they weren't. "It *is* the Russian scientist," she commented. "I think we've found our source."

Taking Sarah's hand, Tamesine led her to the sofa to sit beside her. "Sarah, our conversation worried me. I knew that you were in trouble. So here we are, powerful vampires, come to help. Are you two okay? What have you been involved with, Sarah? We need to know what happened up on that mountaintop."

Sarah stood and walked into the kitchen to switch on a light over the counter. They were going to need coffee.

"It's finished. I thank you all for your concern, but I actually was able to achieve what I needed to do, thanks to your advice."

"While I'm thrilled to hear that, it doesn't mean that you don't have to let us know what happened. Sarah, what you said, that you knew an amulet didn't die with the vampire, you couldn't have known that. We need to know why you do."

"It was because of me."

Nikolai interrupted Sarah before she could respond. "Sarah was helping me."

The four vampires turned their attention to the large man who lifted out of Sarah's bed easily. He wore loose-fitting jeans that sagged everywhere.

Eillia stared at him. "Nikolai, you look markedly bigger than the last time that I saw you just three months ago. And I can read...*something*..."

She walked over to him and touched his hand, then moved her fingers up his arm. "There's a residual."

Her eyes opened wider and they shot to her vampire companions. "He's had first blood magic."

"What?" Tamesine stood, her eyes moving between Sarah and Nikolai. "That isn't possible. My friends, we need to have a discussion."

Sarah nodded. "Okay. I actually agree with you, but let me get some coffee going and order up some food. You guys have to be hungry. I'm guessing it's just now night and you haven't had first meal."

"That is correct, lassie."

Xavier took a seat on a stool near the counter barely big enough for one buttock. "Sarah, ya look bad, and I'm not bein' insensitive. Are ya okay?"

"Thank you, Xavier, I am. Or I will be. You'll find out what I mean in a few minutes when Nikolai and I tell you what we've experienced. Let me just say that I don't think any of you have ever heard of anything like this before."

"Intriguing. Scary. Okay, I tell you what. Xavier and I will go get food and drink, you guys get dressed if you want to."

Park grabbed Xavier's arm and they were gone.

Half an hour later, the vampires and two humans sat on the sofa, a wicker rocking chair and on the rug beside the sofa.

"I think it best that I begin," Nikolai said. Sitting on the floor, his knees drawn up, he hesitated.

Impatient, Eillia got things started. "So you are the one Sarah had to help with a first blood amulet. That makes no sense, you aren't even vampire, let alone first blood."

"That will reveal itself with my tale. It's quite illuminating about your world and the afterlife."

Park's eyebrows lifted. "Afterlife?"

"*Da*. Okay, it happened right after I returned to Lake Baikal. You are all aware of the ancient vampire gravesite I uncovered beneath the frozen lake this past winter?"

Xavier snorted. "Aye. Most miserable place I've ever had the misfortune to visit."

"I see that in my absence, you haven't enrolled in any sensitivity training classes," Sarah commented.

"Ya see why I need ya back, now, lass. Nobody else dare say anythin' like that to me."

She smiled. As much as she'd wanted her human life, she had missed this vampire that she'd served for many decades. "Nik, continue."

"One weekend night, all the other workers were gone, I'd turned off the lights, and started to leave. Something bright caught my eye and I looked back to see a glow in the corner of the cave. One of the dead amulets was alive. I tried to get it free of the ice when the floor of the cave gave way and I fell into a chamber deep beneath. I was badly injured, sure that I would die right there. For some reason, all I could focus on was that amulet, which had fallen through with me. I crawled over and put the amulet around my neck. I knew they held power, and although it likely couldn't help, I was desperate. Once it was in place, it did something amazing. The thing transported me to your spiritual plane."

Everyone was silent until Eillia spoke. "It cannot do that."

"Perhaps not under ordinary circumstances. I came to know that it did not do so alone. It turned out, the universe had a plan for me."

"Oh, I cannot wait to hear this, the hair is standing up on my arms." Park leaned in. "Continue."

"While there, I met a man, an ancient first blood. The spirit amulet that I wore had been his, when he was alive, six thousand years ago."

"What the hell? Are you saying that you met a first blood from that group that lived before our clan? Nikolai, are you saying that you were taken to the spiritual plane to meet a long-dead vampire?" Eillia was visibly shaken.

"Not just to meet him, but to discover a plan by the universe to return this extraordinary vampire to the living world."

Everyone was so shocked and mesmerized by the story unfolding that they didn't speak or move. Nikolai noticed their disbelief and rapt attention. He continued.

"Simply, I was dying. My body was torn to pieces by the fall, my wounds not survivable. Mies, that's the vampire, would enter my body, his first blood magics would enter as well, and repair the body. We believe that the intention of the powers-that-be were that when the body was repaired, Mies would take ownership of the body and my lifeforce would be *forced* out. They didn't take into account that Mies was an honorable man and could not do that. So, my friends, you will have to tell me if you've ever encountered anything like this before, but Mies and I shared this newly changed first blood vampire body for three months. *Shared*, mind and body."

Dead silence met his question. Eventually, Xavier stood, pinching his bum. "That seat is so inadequate for a vampire it isn't possible to overemphasize it. Let me say, though, that I have never in a thousand years heard anythin' like that."

Tamesine sighed. "Never. I can't even imagine it. Nikolai, the vampire, Mies, what happened to him? Eillia said there is only a remnant of the magic now."

"He is gone. Returned to the spirit realm, I hope. He was a fine man, as great a man as I will ever know. Sharing this body and mind were difficult, but now that I am alone, I miss him. It has only been a day, but I feel empty, I guess, is the word that seems to fit most. Lonely, perhaps, because we had become accustomed to sharing our thoughts and ideas, our plans. We couldn't have stayed like that, we both knew it, but having him gone isn't very good either."

Park came to Nikolai, her palms against his cheeks.

"You will be fine. Look at me, Nikolai." She was reading him, he knew, Olivia had filled him in on each vampire's unique skill and hers was an empathic connection much like Eillia's. "You are stronger than you can imagine. I have a request. When you return home, could I have you stop by my lab and let me take some samples and do some simple tests? If this has never happened before, I would really like to document it."

"Uh, sure. I will do that, in the name of science."

"Splendid."

Tamesine cleared her throat to get everyone's attention back to the subject. "What happened on the mountain? Sarah, everything went all right?"

"It did," Sarah answered. "I used your idea to help Mies tap into the power of the earth and sky so that he could untangle the two lifeforces and lift himself from Nikolai's body. He was determined to be the one to go. If the powers of the universe had known what we were doing, it may have gone differently. It's why he insisted that we did not include any first blood in the ritual."

"The power that can be created with a spirit amulet and universal access is tremendous. It can be dangerous in the wrong hands. You should have called me, Sarah."

Tamesine wasn't letting this go.

"It turned out okay. Mies is gone and Nikolai has his body and his life back. It's all right."

"It might not have been, you realize that?"

"We *all* did, but we had to do it anyway. Mies and Nikolai deserved nothing less."

"You were all very lucky. I'm glad it went okay, and I hope there is no unforeseen fallout."

"What kind of fallout?"

"Anything you can imagine. Sometimes magic has a price and consequences must be faced. But with this unique situation, I really wouldn't hazard a guess. In the end, I pray that everything is okay and we can all go home."

Nikolai caught Park's attention. "I will need some time before I come to you, Ms. Park. There is someone in this city that I need to see."

Sarah smiled. Naji was going to get her man back. It pleased her to know that they could be together. For now, she refused to even think about her own life ahead.

Park clapped her hands together gently.

"Why don't we all go out for a nice dinner before we leave Boston? I've been to New York but never here before."

Sarah was ready to put all of this behind her. Later, when she was alone, truly alone, she knew the worst would come. For now, though, she was grateful for the company of old friends.

The evening was a much-needed distraction, a chance to catch up with her life from France. Xavier, Sarah freely admitted, was a hot-tempered alpha male who loved women and found them exasperating all at once. He also had the heart of a gentleman. She had loved him from the time she was a little girl with a big crush on him.

The vampire women were from widely diverse backgrounds, yet they came together as one of the most unbeatable forces on earth. That they'd flown around the world to help *her,* a simple human, meant so much to Sarah.

It was a wonderful visit. When the taxi pulled back up outside of Sarah's apartment, everyone got out to say a final farewell. As they parted, hugs and kisses went all around, even the normally standoff-ish Xavier gave Sarah a long hug and an even longer gaze.

"I'm gonna miss ya worse than ever now, lass," he told her.

"We'll keep in touch, I promise. I've missed you a great deal, and everyone at the mansion. I promise that once I get my life sorted, I'll be back to visit." She knew that if she ever needed him again, he'd be there in an instant.

Tamesine had been leaning against the taxi as Xavier said goodbye. She gave Sarah one last quick hug. "You call me if something like this ever, oh, shit, I hope not, but if you need me, for any reason, call, okay?"

Her eyes went to Nikolai.

He touched her hand lightly. "We're going to stay in touch." He looked toward Park. "Right, Park?"

"Very right, Nikolai. I need to monitor you as your body returns to normal and see if there are any lasting echoes of the magic or the first blood physical enhancements."

"I will comply. I will stop on my way to Russia in a few weeks. Have a safe journey."

After another brief hesitation, Xavier coughed. "We'd better go, ladies. We're burnin' through the dark."

Park nodded and took a seat beside Xavier as the other two women got into the private taxi with two backseats facing each other much like a limousine would have. The car pulled away from the curb, leaving the two humans alone finally.

Nikolai escorted Sarah back into the building. Slowly, because they were both still spent, they trudged up the stairs, one and then the next, then the next, then the next. At one point, Sarah realized that she was counting them.

"Oh, I don't know if I can make it, Nik," she sighed, grateful for his hand on her back to help push her forward.

"If I were Mies, I would swing you up into my massive arms and have you in bed in a fraction of a second."

"We must make the adjustments again. I'd made the switch to living like a normal human, but I'd never had vampire abilities. I can't even imagine how hard it is going to be for you after living like a first blood for three months."

"It is okay. I am ready to be Nikolai Zalesky again. There is a certain woman I would like to properly introduce myself to."

Sarah smiled and dropped back to take his arm, but then leaned into him. "Would you like me to set up a date?"

"No. I think this time, it is I who will set up everything. I like the idea of it being just Naji and me."

"Good luck, then, my friend. You don't need it, though, because I already know that she's crazy about you."

"We will see. For now, let me try this."

Nikolai lifted Sarah into his arms and carried her up the last four stairs to place her on the landing. Laughing, she kept her arms tight around his neck.

"Don't try this with Naji."

Nikolai nodded, grinning. "She is an armload of woman."

"She's much larger than I am."

"I know. Perfect for a six foot two Russian, I think."

After they entered the apartment, Sarah opened a bottle of white wine and led him to the sofa. "One last night of commiseration, and then we go our separate ways. We'll get back to our lives, but remain in touch, yeah?"

"As we have decided, we are forever part of each other."

"Forever. Who knows what will happen anyway? You may end up here in Boston."

Nikolai visualized Naji. "I do not know what I would do here."

"Bridges, Nik. We cross them when we come to them."

"You are wise, little doctor."

Sarah's eyes misted and she looked away.

"I'm sorry, Sarah. I remember now that was what Mies liked to call you."

"It's all right. *I'm* all right. Shall we get some rest?"

Too tired to undress, Sarah and Nikolai crawled back into her bed and curled up together. Tonight, Sarah had turned out all of the lights including the night light. Its eerie glow had freaked her out last night when she woke, sweating and confused. She just wanted to sleep, that's all, so she made the room as dark as she could.

Sleep, they did, and well. When the sun rose the next morning, they had a quiet breakfast, Sarah said good-bye and held Nikolai a little too long, then closed the door and turned to face her empty apartment.

"Well," she said aloud. It was done. Nikolai would return to his life and she would return to hers. Mies was gone and no matter how painful it was, there was nothing else to be done.

Sarah sat on the sofa, the blinds drawn, the lights still out, her eyes closed, and tried to convince herself that everything was okay. When she couldn't do it, she picked up the phone. "Lucy, hi, it's Doctor Smith. Can you put me back on the schedule? I need to work. Tonight? Yeah, I can make that. Thank you, Lucy."

Ending the phone call, she nodded to the darkness. Good. They had a call-off for tonight, and that was exactly what Sarah needed. "Get back to work, to the plan. Don't deviate. It's in the deviation that good plans go awry."

She glanced at the clock. Six hours. Perhaps a little more rest, then a quick shower, and back to doing what she was trained to do. Back to her *normal human life.*

Later, she cried the entire length of the shower, tears blending with the water as she admitted, nothing would be normal again for a very, *very* long time.

The hotel room was exactly as they'd left it. Nikolai wandered in, his fingers moving over the edge of a wine glass left on the bar, then across a plate still half full of the potato chips that Mies loved, over a zipper of the satchel he'd packed when they left Siberia, clothes still strewn where they'd dressed and paid little attention to tidiness over the days they'd been here.

Yes, the hotel room was exactly as they'd left it, and yet nothing was the same. Nikolai fell onto the bed, clothes and boots still on, and rolled over to bury his face in the pillow. He would sleep but then he wanted to see Naji tonight, to explain to her…

No, that wasn't necessary. Mies had left her prepared for the possibility that she might not ever see him again. So he would let her know his intentions and see where they might go from there. In his thirty-six years, he'd never been in love. Not really in love, not the "'til death do us part" kind, and he was ready.

"You've motivated me," he thought, and then listened for a reply in his head that would not come. Punching the pillow, he rolled onto his back and slammed his head against it. "I hope you are okay tonight, my friend," he whispered, and prayed that he was.

Perhaps one of the most difficult things of all with this situation was that he would never know what really happened to Mies and where he was.

Sarah noticed four calls from Naji on her cell phone. She dried her hair and used a silver clip over the length to secure it before she began the minimal make-up application she usually did before she went to the hospital. Twice, she picked up the phone and started to dial, but stopped. Not yet. It was too soon for that kind of normal. She'd call her friend tomorrow morning after she finished the shift.

One step at a time, that's how you climb up a hill.

Tonight, she'd do what she was best at; medicine. It was truly one of the most satisfying things in her life.

When Sarah walked into the E.R. later that evening, Tracy, waiting at the front desk, looked up at her.

"Stranger! Nice to have you back."

"Family emergency."

"Aw. I hope everything is all right."

"It is now, thank you. So, what have we got?"

"Two ambulances coming in, a bad skateboarding accident, severe head injury, and a heart attack."

"I'll take the skateboarder."

"I hoped you would. You know how I hate the sight of blood," Tracy responded with a laugh. "Still considering that career driving an ice cream truck. All you do is make kids happy all day, how can anything go wrong?"

Sarah nodded. "Yeah. Need an assistant?"

The doors flew open and Sarah's skateboarder was reeled in, the EMT giving her his stats. Time to go to work.

At the art gallery near the waterfront

Naji finished closing the ledger and tapped the controls for the main lighting in the show room to lower the overnight light level. She was anxious to get out of here tonight. As soon as she had everything secured, she planned to go by Sarah's apartment, and if she wasn't there, she would head to Massachusetts General.

Five phone calls and twelve texts had gone unanswered, and she wanted to know why.

Sarah was one of the most responsible people she'd ever known, and Naji knew that something was wrong. Friends were there for each other, and whether Sarah wanted her or not, she got her. The only thing left was to turn the alarm on for the front entrance. She would then exit through the back of the building to her car, safely parked undercover in the private lot.

As she reached for the panel to engage the security system, her eyes moved to the glass double-doors that welcomed artists and patrons when they were open. Right now, a face stared at her, white teeth glowing from behind a wide smile. *Nikolai!*

So that she did not seem too eager, which was never good, Naji continued to turn out lights and close off exhibits.

Finally, she turned to the man who waited patiently behind the etched glass. Oh, he was a sight for sore eyes! In spite of her desire to remain aloof, she unlocked the door and gave him a welcoming smile.

"I've missed you. May I come in?"

Naji lost the smile and tilted her head in an *I don't care* gesture, but she stepped back to allow him to enter.

"Nice of you to stop in," she said, keeping her voice level with little interest.

"We just arrived from out of town and I couldn't wait to see you tonight."

Oh. That made a difference. *Still, play it cool*, she told herself. She was the queen of cool, that's one of the reasons that men wanted her so badly. They always want the unattainable. Naji was attainable, but only on her terms and only with those she really wanted. God, she had to admit…she really wanted this sweet, sexy Russian friend of Sarah.

"You must be hungry, it is past dinnertime. May I escort you to dinner?" He asked.

181

Now her smile returned. "I seem to remember the first time we tried to go to dinner."

His eyes sparkled. "I seem to remember some pretty wild appetites that night."

"You know, when something is good, it's a good idea to try that same dish again to see if it really suited you."

"I wouldn't even dream of disagreeing with you."

"Are you in a car?"

"I have no vehicle here in America."

"Fine. I'll drive."

It would be inaccurate to say that butterflies tickled her belly, more like pterodactyls flew from one side to the other in circles. Why this man hit her this way, she didn't know, but everything about him made her tingle. It might mean that she was capable of love after all, and if it was with this gentle man who was a sexy beast in her bed, she would gladly accept him.

The shop closed and locked, Naji led Nikolai to her car, but before she could use the remote to unlock it, he was in front of her and pressed her back against the cool steel.

"I find that I cannot wait. I demand an appetizer."

His body felt right, his belly touching hers, her breasts touching his chest.

"Really?" Naji responded. "What did you have in mind, sir?"

She moved closer and fondled his crotch with gentle fingers. "This?"

Then she lifted his right hand to place it on her left breast. "Or *this*?"

Her voice dropped. "Perhaps this?" Both hands moved to his neck to pull him to her, her breath warm on his cheek. When her tongue slid between his lips, Nikolai was lost in her.

"This," he whispered minutes later when he could speak.

"Ummm," Naji moaned. "I could make a full-course meal of you." She kissed him again, her tongue moving through his mouth almost desperately. "I knew you might not come back. I hoped that you would."

Nikolai lifted her up onto the hood of the car and pulled her shirt over her head. A lace satin bra showed off her full breasts before he lifted one cup and nipped the tender skin above it. *Nipped?* He'd never done that with a woman before. Must be left over from Mies. She seemed to like it, she shuddered, and reached for him, so he continued to score a path beneath the bra to each nipple. Suddenly, he glanced around. No one else was in the parking lot, but there could be.

"I can't finish here. We must go." He lowered his voice as he leaned in to speak directly into her ear. "I did not want to leave you, I just didn't know if fate would let me come back."

Naji took his face in her hands and captured his eyes.

"Fate? My beautiful Russian lover, I don't let anything or anyone get in my way when I want something. You, I want."

She kissed him, then, like no other kiss she'd ever given anyone. This one was filled with promises, and hope, and the chance for a future. And that was all new to her. Moments later, she pushed him back.

"Get in the car. Do you have somewhere you have to be for the next few days?"

Nikolai shook his head.

"Good. You're mine, love. We're locking ourselves away for that time. Do you object?"

He smiled. "No."

She pulled her cell phone from her back pocket and punched a number, her eyes still frozen on his. The call connected and Naji began to speak.

"Isley, I have something urgent to tend to until Monday. The studio is yours. If you need something, text me, and I'll get back to you."

Ending the call, Naji nodded to Nikolai. "Get in the car."

Eleven

The E.R. was extremely busy for the next three weeks, giving Sarah exactly what she needed; no time for sadness or regret or to miss Mies. She'd volunteered for any open shift, and because they were short-handed, she worked every night and slept every day. It might not have been cathartic, but it was exhausting, which felt good, both mentally and physically.

The one bright spot had been a text from Naji and then a second one from Nikolai.

Nikolai and I connected. Boy, did we! Falling in love. Will see you soon and dish. Love U.

I hope you are well, Sarah. I am VERY well. Naji likes to dominate her men and it turns out I like to be dominated. Apparently. It is a match made in heaven. Ugh, you know what I mean. Please be well, my dear friend.

They were happy. Out of all of this, something really beautiful had happened; two people had found each other who really needed each other. After she'd received the texts, Sarah had spoken to the absent Mies for the first time since the week they'd said goodbye.

"Look what we did, Mies. You would be so proud."

Startled at herself, she found that she had waited, very, very briefly, for an answer.

The sadness had leveled out and she was doing okay again. Her work was more satisfying than ever, and, little by little, she felt better each day. Other than a persistent gastrointestinal bug, Sarah had gotten back to her routine.

There were moments alone at night when memory of him welled up and brought sorrow laced with tears, and then, the night was awful. But morning came, as it always did, work had to be done, a life had to be lived, and the pain managed.

Sarah had often been told that she was such a strong woman. It was true, she was, she had always believed that she could overcome or endure just about anything. This emptiness, the lost possibilities, Mie's second chance to have his life, to see this new world, just the knowledge that she would never see him again, had more a chance to be overwhelming than any other event in her life.

These days would likely be the saddest of her life, but she knew that time would soften the pain of his memory, if not the regret, and in some distant time, she would remember him without the chest crushing pain. The day would come when life would simply overtake the loss.

Today, rising with the sun, she'd picked up a bag of blueberry muffins and coffee, and headed out to watch the boats on the waterfront. Warm sunlight brought a pink flush to her pale skin.

When Sarah had first come to Boston, one of the things she'd loved the most was getting out into the sun. These past few weeks, she'd hibernated like a grizzly bear. Now, the brightness and warmth would do exactly what it had then…it would help her begin to heal.

She had a date with Naji and Nikolai the following Saturday for lunch since she hadn't seen either of them in quite some time. She'd missed them both.

And tonight, she was going to ask Leo for a date. It was time to get back on track with her original goal for coming to Boston. The past few weeks, working together

185

often, she and Leo had returned to the rapport they'd had from the beginning. When she went to work tonight, she planned to let him know that she was ready once again to try a romantic relationship with him.

Selecting a nice place to watch the boats on top of a hill, she bit into the fresh muffin. Sighing, she wished that she was more excited about the prospect of dating Leo.

"I told you that you'd spoil me for ordinary men," she whispered to Mies.

Two businessmen taking a walk on this pleasant morning gave Sarah long looks and warm smiles.

She glanced down as they passed, aware that if she smiled back, it might be an invitation to come over and begin a conversation. For some reason she didn't understand, for the past two weeks, men had been noticing her. *Really* noticing her. Naji would have been able to help her figure out why, but she was still in the "honeymoon" stage of her relationship with Nikolai and they were functionally absent. Naji went to work, briefly, then disappeared.

Sighing again, Sarah cleaned up her mess and headed back out of the park. She had a few tasks to accomplish today, wanted to send a text to Tamesine to assure her that everything here in Boston was okay, send another to Park to let her know why Nikolai hadn't stopped in her lab in southern France yet, and get her hair cut so that she could style it easier. She wanted to look more put together than she felt when she asked Leo to give her another chance.

Separating her recyclables from the rubbish, Sarah headed for the street when a wave of nausea overcame her. *Even the blueberry muffins upset her stomach? Ugh.*

As usual, it calmed down within twenty minutes and she headed home to prepare for her day. She'd taken some meds that should help her symptoms, but perhaps she should order some tests. Could she have picked up something from the mountains? They'd lain in grass that could have had any number of insects that could have made her ill. If this didn't settle down, she'd have Tracy run some diagnostics.

Even though he was outrageously expensive, Naji's hairdresser was the only one Sarah knew, and since he'd done such a wonderful job for her on the color, she decided to have *him* give her a new haircut. Seated in his big cushy chair, she tried to keep up with his ceaseless chatter, but her mind wandered half way into a story about a celebrity who had wanted a color similar to Sarah's.

"It was just too stark for her. Your skin is pale, but hers was absolutely ghastly ghostly. Blonde turned her into a gaudy zombie, oh, my God!"

He finally paused, suddenly looking Sarah over closely. "You know that you just glow, don't you?"

That comment got Sarah's attention. "No, I don't. Although lately I keep getting strange comments like that."

"Well, it's true, darling. Naji tells me that you are one of prettiest girls she's ever seen and I agree, but there's just something…I don't know. Glowy, is all I can come up with. I'm somewhat intuitive about things like this. It's what makes me so good at my job. For instance, I know that this cut will highlight your well-defined cheekbones, and although others won't know what it is that transforms your face, they'll respond to the result. You'll see."

Sarah smiled. Maybe. He'd transformed her pale one-dimensional hair color into something that did, indeed, glow, and perhaps that was what he saw, the product of his own work.

Once he was finished, the cut complete and the hair styled, Sarah approved immediately when he handed her a mirror so that she could see her hair from the front and back. He'd left it longer, but sliced varying lengths of layers that created a charming lift and brought attention straight to her eyes. Did she *want* people fascinated by her eyes? In this case, yes, one particular person, she did.

"Like Naji said, you are a miracle worker. Thanks, BenG." The unique single name he went by, created by merging his first and last name, replaced his given name, otherwise too common for his effervescent personality.

"You are an artist."

BenG beamed. He loved making women, or men, beautiful and particularly loved to be told when he had.

"Return soon, glowy lady," he said with an air kiss on each cheek.

On her way back to her apartment, she caught a glimpse of herself in a storefront that featured full length mirrors and a sign with a question to passersby:

Are you the best that you can be?

"Honestly, I look pretty hot," she answered out loud. Her hair was full, blowing in the breeze, and it did make her amber eyes pop. She planned to wear a low-cut top tonight under her lab coat so that at an appropriate moment, she would unbutton the coat, and ask Leo if he was still interested in getting together.

"I intend to knock your socks off, Dr. P."

Home now, to find the perfect top.

That night, the E.R. was a zoo. The roster included everything from pain to sliced fingers to car accidents. Two GSW's brought law enforcement. Sarah saw three cases of lower abdominal pain, one that turned out to be a badly enflamed appendix and two that seemed to be a recent virus that targeted the gastrointestinal tract.

It wasn't until well after 3 a.m. that Sarah had a break to intercept Leo.

"Hi, treat you to some bad coffee in the cafeteria?" she offered with a smile she hoped was charming.

"Deal. As long as it's obscenely caffeinated."

"Haven't you gotten coffee there before? It always is."

"I have a coffee maker in my office. It's easier and certainly better coffee."

"Ah."

"Would you, uh, like to join me in there to try it? I have a vanilla bean coffee from France that is really good."

"I would love to, Leo."

He nodded and smiled cautiously. They'd been careful to keep their relationship friendly but professional since the aborted attempt to meet for an official date. She knew that she had been vague about rescheduling and he must have

188

decided that she'd changed her mind. It was up to her to repair this if it were to be repaired.

His office was pristine, everything in what looked like its exact assigned space. The coffee-maker he'd mentioned was high-tech, a high-end stainless steel unit that looked more like a piece of contemporary art. Leo pointed to a nice loveseat-sized sofa along the back wall near the coffee maker.

"Please, have a seat. This thing fires up pretty quickly. I just hope that things stay calm out in the bays enough to let us get a cup when it's ready."

"So do I." Sarah paused as she slid off her lab coat before she sat.

Leo finished setting the automatic feature on the coffee maker and turned to her.

"Wow. You look so pretty sitting here in my office. I like seeing you here. That, uh, blouse is quite attractive on you."

Nodding, Sarah patted the place beside her. "Thanks. Listen, we need to talk. I need to clarify something."

"I like that idea. I have a few things I'd like to clarify as well."

"Perhaps they are the same thing."

Once he dropped down beside her, his gaze wandered to the full cleavage now displayed, then back to her eyes, as he ran his tongue around his lips. "Sarah..."

She'd decided to take the leap and see if they had any chance of getting this wreck of a relationship back on track. Sliding forward, she kissed him gently on the lips, then moved closer and went for a deeper kiss. Within seconds, his arms went around her and he pulled her tight enough to startle her a little.

The kiss was warm and encouraging, his scent pleasant. While it had yet to arouse her, Sarah allowed that it would take time to move past Mies's lovemaking, or more honestly, past Mies. He would be impossible to forget.

Leo was definitely aroused.

A gentle chime interrupted them, and they pulled apart. Leo blew a long breath and stood. His penis was hard and he was grateful that his lab jacket covered him. When he reached for the coffee pot, he paused.

"Yes, they were the same thing. I hope that was my answer?"

"It is if you want it to be. I'm sorry, Leo, things got kind of crazy after my friend arrived from Russia. I had some things to sort out, something that he needed my help with, and it was impossible to try to maintain a normal relationship with that going on, let alone start a new one, but I want you to know that I *am* interested. Could we reschedule that date?"

"How about this Sunday night? I'm off and after the past five days on, I can't imagine that you aren't too."

"I am. Saturday is another long one, but I'm home for two days after that."

"Then we're on. Sarah, I can't tell you how much I'm looking forward to this. I've been really attracted to you from the beginning, but these past few weeks, it's been almost impossible to keep my hands off you. I feel like a rutting bull."

What the hell? Leo too?

"I'm the same old dull Sarah I've always been, but this time, we'll make that date and see how it goes."

Sarah stood and joined him, sliding her lab coat back over cold arms. "I better get back out there. Tracy mentioned that she needed to get something to eat while it was slow, so I'll give her a break. Leo, Sunday night, I'll put on my prettiest dress."

"I'll take you somewhere fitting, then. I'm excited, Sarah."

Her eyes dropped to the bulge in his pants, revealed now that he'd put his hands into his pockets and the jacket had pulled back. When he saw where her eyes went, he let the coat drop back into place and gave her a boyish grin as he shrugged his shoulders.

"Um, hum," she said as she hurried out.

IN SOUTHERN FRANCE

Eillia had the kids washed and ready for bed. Lately, she and Tamesine had been trading off the task because her son and Tamesine's twins insisted on bathing together. Pre-bedtime cleaning was always tough enough before they were old enough to declare preferences, but she'd learned centuries ago that you had to choose your battles. The important ones, you never give in on, but when it came to bath time for three tykes, let the children have their say.

Tamesine poked her head in. "Spit-shined and polished?"

Caedmon giggled. Tamesine chased him around the large bathroom with tell-tale bubbles all over the floor and walls, and caught him easily. "Not yet? I guess you still need some spit!"

The little boy shrieked and giggled so hard he went into a coughing fit.

"Calm down, little guy. Let's take a walk to the balcony for some fresh air."

Tamesine led him out of the bathroom and onto the huge balcony suspended out over the sea from Eillia and Daniel's bedroom suite. "Can you breathe better now?"

With a small gulp of air, the curly-headed boy nodded. "Uh, huh."

"Good. You're all right, sweetheart."

They'd been watching Eillia's son closely. For some reason, he seemed to have developed a slight medical problem...and that was not normal for a first blood child.

The children of first bloods grew up like any fully human child until they reached adult maturity. At that point, the vampire genome would take over and the body would continue the change to become a first blood.

But although the children were mostly just like ordinary human children, one thing was certain...first bloods, children or not, did not get sick. The only exception that they had ever found was a recent virus that had the ability to kill vampires. With much focus and a lot of ancient universal luck and aid, Park's medical lab and staff had managed to purge that virus and create a vaccine and cure.

But Caedmon should not sneeze or wheeze, or lose his breath after running in a small circle.

Tamesine watched him with concern, but he seemed to be fine now. The symptoms were slight and had only started two nights ago. Eillia and Daniel were holding it together, but every vampire in both households here in the Orientales was on alert. The virus earlier this year had been deadly, and the idea that they might be facing something else that targeted their children was by far their worst-case-scenario.

They were using Park's lab to monitor Caedmon and the other four children in the two villas. Just the idea that one or more of their children could have an unprecedented illness was terrifying.

"He's calmed down?" Eillia inquired from behind Tamesine.

Turning, Tamesine clasped Eillia's upper arm. "He's fine. It's his wonderfully silly sense of humor. He cracks up at his own jokes!"

"I love that about him."

"He's all right, Eillia. We have to trust that. Don't forget how powerful we are."

"I know, it's just the ever-changing tide of fortunes lately in our communities. What if this is another test?"

"You think the events we've been experiencing are tests?"

"I don't know. What I do know is that if any of our children get sick, I'll rain hell up into the spirit realm."

"You'll have help. For now, though, Caedmon is okay. I'll take him to Park tomorrow night for his next check-up if you'd like."

"No, Daniel and I will take him. Thank you, though."

Eillia scooped up her naked giggling son and carried him back to the bathroom to slip him into his Star Wars pajamas. He would join in a brief playtime with the others before they went to their rooms to sleep.

192

Two hours later, just before dawn, back in her own suite, her babies finally in bed, Tamesine leaned on the railing of her own balcony and let her mind wander. There were times when channeling such strong magics wasn't easy.

Her connection to the spiritual realm had remained open since she'd used the combined power of five vampire first bloods to change the course of history.

They'd eradicated a virus meant to kill vampires using forces borrowed from the universe. Whether it was sanctioned or not, she did not know, nor did she care. What mattered was that she had protected her family and race, and possibly all human life on this world. So if the universe was pissed at her, *too fucking bad*.

Now, though, a new concern, a possible threat to the most precious things in their lives, the first blood children, their own blood, their babies…what was happening? She'd tried to put a positive spin on it for Eillia, who didn't need the constant worry, but the truth was, she had no idea what to expect.

Caedmon should not be sick. At all. His vampire blood and power, the heritage of first blood magic, protected its vampire progeny. Why, then, was he showing these symptoms?

Warm hands slid around her neck, massaging tight muscles.

"Ready to turn in?" Marc asked.

"Yes. I can't let my mind rest though."

"The children," he said simply.

"It won't be only Caedmon, not that that matters. We cannot lose him any more than any other, but I feel something black in the pit of my stomach. Another egregious thing. Something else to break us into pieces and force us to find a way to go on. I can't get it off my mind, Marc. We all know that these children have a destiny vital to the world someday, but what the hell do we have to endure to get there?"

"You told me once, fix the things you can, and have faith for those you can't. When something happens that needs fixing, you always rise to it. Every first blood that

193

walks this earth knows that if something comes for our children, nothing will stop us from stopping it."

"My hero, once again. You're right, of course. I wonder, though, if this has anything to do with the virus we destroyed this winter. Or if it has something to do with that odd event involving the ancient vampire in Siberia. I believe coincidences happen, but I suspect it too."

"As of now, there's nothing to fix. And even if there were, you need your rest. The sun will peek in soon."

"Okay. I'll get the barrier."

Back in Boston

Saturday morning, Sarah threw up, the nausea hitting its stride and knocking her way off balance. Even some weak coffee didn't stay down. Regretfully, she called in and let them know that she was too sick to work.

For Sarah, this was a new experience. Through her entire life, there had been no aches or pains or illness. Now, she felt sick inside of every cell in her body. Even though the temperature in her apartment was seventy-five degrees, she had chills. She still had trouble imagining herself lying in bed unable to do normal things.

This moment, being human, really *sucked*.

She had one more text to send, her fingers paused over her cell phone, but she forced herself to push the keys. Breaking this date with Leo had been incredibly hard, but if she was *this* sick, she was likely contagious. Considering what they'd done a few days ago in his office, Sarah just hoped she hadn't already given whatever this was to him.

Lying flat on her bed, two sheets and a blanket covering her but her feet hanging out, she groaned.

"Holy shit, is this what humans go through when they're sick? Often, over a lifetime? Ugh. Xavier, blood please!"

Leo sent back a text and let her know that he felt for her, that he understood, and *was there anything she*

194

needed? Kind man. She sent a brief text, *thanks, no, call soon*, and dropped back onto her bed.

When she woke some time later, she threw up again just before she collapsed immediately back into bed.

Hours later yet, Sarah rose to get some water, she knew that she was dehydrated, and stopped when a text arrived from Tamesine:

Sarah, it seems like you are picking back up and moving forward. I am proud of you. Please encourage Nikolai to stop in soon to let us check his stats and take some samples. Best to you, call if you need help.

Staring at the text for several long moments, Sarah processed the message. Help? Boy, did she need help, but humans didn't have that kind of help available.

Thanks, Tam. Sick right now, puking up my guts. Wish I had some of Xavier's blood. I'll talk to Nik.

Another text arrived seconds later.

Cherise and David are in NYC. Do you want them to come?

The text message lay there, Sarah staring at it unblinking. A first blood was just south of her, she could get well immediately.

God! Tempting, but no. Human now, guess I'll adapt.

No problem if you want help. They can be there in no time.

Thanks. Gonna try to do this right.

Only she felt sicker when evening came. Like her guts were being rearranged. After all that she'd been through, this felt like punishment. Was that possible? Could this be a little karmic payback for messing with fate? It felt much

195

deeper than an ordinary illness, more invasive and systemic. If it were, then she would likely not heal on her own very easily.

First blood's blood, immediate healing, damn it was tempting. No, beyond tempting. She'd had enough crap these past few weeks for a lifetime.

Tam, can you let them know I need their help? I can't do this anymore. Appreciated more than you know.

Right away. They'll be there tonight. Try to rest.

Oh, thank God and all that was holy in the vampire's world. After David gave her his blood, she could get back to her life. More and more as the evening progressed, Sarah felt sure that this sickness was supernatural in nature and without first blood magics, she might never be well again.

She'd never met David or Cherise, but she was familiar with David's history, a first blood who had been held and tortured for decades by the Supernatural Research Society. Cherise, his mate, was an empath who converted, making her the first vampire empath ever known. She'd heard that Cherise's talents had been intensely strengthened by her vampire blood.

After convincing her stomach to accept a little organic tea, she fell back onto her bed and finally drifted into a fitful sleep.

"Sarah, wake up. Sarah?"

The soft musical voice filtered through Sarah's sleep-infused, foggy mind. Who did she know with a French accent here in Boston? With great effort, she focused on the voice and tried to reach it. Eventually, when she opened her eyes, Sarah saw a sweet smile. Then she felt a hand on her forearm, immediately recognizing the sensation. *Impression.* The woman calmed Sarah's confused mind.

"Hi," Sarah said. "You're Cherise."

196

"I am. It is surprising that you could recall that so easily considering how sick you are."

"Can you tell, is it supernatural?"

"I do not believe so."

"Natural things can kick your ass too." A deep masculine voice penetrated their conversation.

Sarah looked up to the huge man who'd come up behind Cherise. David was big all over, like most first blood males, and he emitted that same sexually stimulating pheromone, she could smell it, but it did not turn her on like Mies's had. She recognized its purpose, but the biochemical makeup must have been all wrong for her. Or the pheromones were targeted to the one person meant to be mate to the vampire. Her mind went to Mies, and the sadness returned.

"*Chérie*, you are not doing well. I can feel the physical exhaustion and some type of virus invading you. Not to mention the emotional pain. You are grieving. David can make you feel much better. Do you want him to give you some blood now?"

"Yes, please, thank you," Sarah said weakly, the helplessness frustrating.

David slit his fingertip and dripped his blood into the mug that still held some of the organic tea, and handed it to her.

"Here you go," he announced.

Sarah held the mug reverently, aware that this was a step back from her progress in becoming fully human, but she sipped it anyway, and even slid her tongue around the rim to get the last of it. Strange. She'd always expected that it would be nice someday to *not* drink blood, but this was satisfying, and she wanted to ask for more. Too much vampire blood, though, especially that of a first blood, would trigger conversion and that was something that she *definitely* didn't want.

Setting the mug on the floor beside the bed, she swung her legs over the side and stood. The blood was working already, the queasiness gone, the pain easing.

She sighed and smiled at Cherise and David.

"I can never thank you enough. I haven't the coping skills for this kind of illness I guess. I was blood-bonded for most of my life and this is the first time I've ever been sick like this."

"It *is* dreadful." Cherise looked up at David, her eyes wide.

He nodded.

After an obvious hesitation, Cherise caught Sarah's attention again. "Sarah, do you know that you are pregnant?"

Sarah didn't move. Her eyes shifted from Cherise, landed on David, who looked amused, and then back to Cherise.

"I'm sorry, what?"

"You are with child, my dear. And the father is not your average guy, is he?"

What? Pregnant? Not possible. *Not* possible! *Was it?*

The reality hit her suddenly, slamming into her consciousness.

"I'm Shoazan?" Then again, even more incredulous, believing it less, "I'm Shoazan? I can't be!"

"Apparently you can. You carry a first blood child."

"I…" Sarah was ready to repeat that she couldn't be, but she knew different. There was a chance, and if she was, Mies had left something behind.

Her hands went to her belly where this shocking life grew inside her body without her knowledge until now.

"Why didn't I know?"

"You are not in touch with your body or mind right now. The child senses that. She has remained quiet and unobtrusive until she believes you are ready for her."

Oh God, oh God, oh God! There went *normal* forever.

"It was this ghost from the past, yes? Tamesine told me about his appearance. I find the whole thing fascinating." Cherise watched her mate wander into the kitchen and pick up a kettle.

Sarah moved to the sofa almost trancelike. "I'm going to have Mies's child." Her eyes shot back to Cherise. "Uh, yeah, the ghost. His name is Mies. He lived with that first group of vampires whose graves were uncovered under Lake Baikal recently." She winced. "You're sure?"

Cherise nodded and joined her on the sofa. "Here. Remain calm."

Placing her hands on Sarah's belly, Cherise closed her eyes.

"Yes, it is a little girl who has dark hair and eyes like her father. And a heart as wide as the world."

The empath touched Sarah's cheek as she opened her eyes. "You can feel her if you are ready. Listen and see with your heart, not that brilliant mind you are so famous for."

Quiet, trying to follow directions, Sarah forced herself to control her breathing, which was difficult considering she was freaking out. Thoughts and images pounded her and nearly overcame her when she felt another hand on her shoulder and looked up to see David behind her. All of the wild thoughts faded away and she was able to lower her respiration and focus on her own lifeforce.

There she was, the child, lying nestled inside her, warm, happy, waiting for nature to take her from the echo of life she had been to the sweet baby girl she would be someday soon.

A message sent to Sarah, over and over, not in any voice, but in a feeling that translated nonetheless, still recognizable: *hi mommy, hi mommy, hi mommy.*

Standing, Cherise lifted her hands from Sarah, but David stayed with her to guide her forward from the inward journey. He felt Sarah's hand on his as her eyes lifted.

"Thank you, both of you. She's here, she's real. I am Shoazan."

"Yes, your kind are coming out of the woodwork lately," Cherise commented. "I'm teasing. I know, though, that this child is here for a reason. You wondered why the universe sent this man." She tilted her head toward Sarah's belly. "She's why. None of us have any specifics, but that young lady will be right beside our other children when the time comes. The future looks very interesting."

David carried three cups of tea from the little kitchen, all infused with honey and whisky.

Sarah started to protest when he shook his head. "It won't hurt the child, but it will help you cope. Believe me, Sarah, you have a lot to cope with. Your life is changed forever."

"I realize that. Honestly, I've just barely moved past the trauma of this entire event. Losing Mies, adjusting to life without him, helping Nikolai deal with all of this, and now this little girl. She's going to need her father and he's gone forever."

Silent again, Sarah drew small circles around her belly.

"How do I do this? Raise a magic-infused child on my own as a normal human woman?"

"You don't," Cherise answered quickly. "You must return to France to Xavier's home. Or you can come to Iceland. You are always welcome to stay with us. But Sarah, you cannot raise a first blood child by yourself."

"I don't know. Thank you both for all you've done. And this situation, Cherise, I can't ever thank you enough for letting me know. My own child didn't trust me."

"She trusts you. She just knew that you weren't ready for her."

"I am. It doesn't take me long to adapt to anything, although I admit this is the biggest adaption ever, but I'll be okay. I'll be there for this beautiful child. I will be a great mother, I promise."

"I sense that, and my senses are highly accurate. Do you need anything else before we go?"

"No. I think that my daughter and I just need to be alone to get to know each other."

"That is very true. Sarah, you'll call Xavier or Tamesine and let them know that you'll be home before she arrives? You are aware that vampire babies come in six months, not nine, aren't you?"

"Yes. I know most of your race's history. Not too much would surprise me. Other than anything about this particular situation with Nikolai and Mies and now, a child from a long-deceased vampire. Yeah, the word crazy doesn't quite cut it, does it?"

"Not really, no. All right, we need to go. Take care of yourself."

David leaned over and kissed Sarah on the cheek.

"Sleep well, little Shoazan."

As with most vampires, they were gone the instant the door opened. Sarah stood looking at the wide open door to her apartment, unable to concentrate on the simple task of closing it.

"Mies," she whispered. "I have something of yours."

Outside Sarah's apartment building, David and Cherise stopped.

"She's not going to return to France or come to Iceland," David commented.

"She isn't. My guess is she'll try to do this here in Boston on her own."

"It's a mistake."

"It's hers to make. And we'll always be there for her."

"I should let Park know."

"Yes, you should."

Twelve

Now that her life's course had been changed once again, Sarah had a lot of decisions to make. This child must take precedence over everything and that included her own desires. Her own needs fell very low on her list of priorities.

Cherise and David had told her that she must raise her daughter with the first blood community. And while that made perfect sense, and she understood the reasoning, something held her back from buying a ticket and returning to France.

Yes, this child was going to be powerful, and yes, she would need the instruction and legacy of her race. *Someday*. Until that day, she could live a normal life with guidance from a mother who understood her vampire heritage almost as much as the first bloods themselves.

In the end, that is exactly what Sarah wanted for her little girl. She wanted her to grow up as any child should, with no expectations of destiny or fate facing her; just a carefree childhood built on learning the basics of life, to learn to love and have fun, to feel safe every minute.

That's why she decided to stay in Boston. Here is where her life was. She would raise her daughter to be part of the world, to see all of its beauty and know that there were things to be cautious of. She would shine here, have friends, go to school and learn her ABC's. When the day came to introduce her to the first blood community in Europe, then Sarah would take her to southern France. After all, that part of her heritage would control her choices in the future. Either way, this child would grow up in both worlds.

However, it couldn't include Leo. Sarah made the decision this morning over a strong cup of coffee. This is where the sacrifice must be made for now. A vampire was essentially a normal human child until full maturity, but there were some things that happened around them that were not normal. She would be too unpredictable and that meant that only those read in could be really close to her.

"I will manage to do this," promised Sarah, her hand on her belly as it had been most of the day since Cherise told her that she was pregnant.

A warm tickle had invaded Sarah all day, little surges of joy that coursed through her. It was the child. Now that she had accepted the baby, the child was interacting with her. Sarah had heard unbelievable stories about how these children respond, even in utero, to their parents.

Love and gratitude overwhelmed Sarah several times while she wandered around the apartment and then took a walk in the park to think about how to proceed with her life. The decision made, Sarah was already making plans. First, she needed to let Nikolai know, but not in a text or phone call.

So she sent a brief text: *Nik, meet me for lunch Monday at noon at Friday Next. Please. Don't bring Naji. Miss you.*

Friday Next was a family owned sandwich shop that had perhaps the best bread and soup she'd ever tasted. She'd been craving food from there all morning. And now that she knew that she was pregnant, whether it was psychosomatic or not, she felt ravenous.

"That *eating for two* thing…is it real?" she asked her daughter. "I'm going to go for *yes it is* and order a large pizza tonight for dinner. Oh, this could get ugly."

As night settled in, so did Sarah and the large pizza, curled up on the sofa, along with a big bottle of cherry cola and an old romantic movie starring Doris Day and Rock Hudson. It was silly shit, and she loved it. At the end of the movie, Doris's character was pregnant and alone until, just in time, Rock Hudson's hero comes back into her life and they marry. *Happy Ending* ensured.

Briefly, Sarah allowed a moment to feel sorry for Mies, for herself, for this little girl who would never know her father.

"He is a hero," she told her unborn child. "Someday, we'll have a long discussion about him. I intend to make sure you grow up knowing him. For now, I need to go to the bathroom, clean up, and get some sleep. It's been a good night, my darling."

Monday at *Friday Next*

"What is it, Sarah? You would never have told me to leave Naji out of this, so what is it? Are you okay? Have the vampires gotten pissed or something? Is the universe retaliating already? Sarah?"

"Nik, God, calm down. I can't tell you what I came to tell you if I can't get a word in. No, everything is fine. Why don't we order and *then* we can talk."

"Sarah, you have me freaked out. Right now, I *can't* eat. What is going on?"

"I'm starved, so if you'll give me a moment. Ah, hi, good timing," Sarah said as the waiter arrived at their outdoor table. "I will take the soup of the day combo with your chicken pecan sandwich, an order of onion rings, and a basket full of the focaccia bread. Oh, yeah, and that cinnamon encrusted apple dumpling. To start."

Nikolai watched Sarah lay the menu back on the table. When she looked up at him, she beamed. He could see her intense joy at the prospect of eating the food she'd ordered. Intense? That word didn't quite apply. She was over-the-top crazed about receiving her order.

"What's going on? Please, tell me now. I won't be able to eat a bite until you do."

Sighing, Sarah pushed the menu and napkin aside and leaned in. "In about five months, I'm going to have a baby. Mies's little girl."

At first, Nikolai just stared at Sarah. He began to speak, stopped, tears welled in his eyes and he scooted out of his chair to come to hers. Pulling her up and into his arms, he held her so tightly, she had difficulty breathing. She held him back just as tightly.

This was something that she could share with no one else, because he was the only other person alive on this earth that knew Mies. They both had come to love and admire him and that a piece of him was left behind, *his child*, meant more than either of them had words to describe.

When he backed away, Nikolai wiped his eyes.

"I'm sorry, my friend, I couldn't stop myself. You're pregnant. With Mies's baby. I can't imagine too many things that would make me happier right now. Ah, Sarah, how are you feeling? Do the others know? It's a girl? Is she all right?"

"Whoa, Nik, my goodness, rapid fire Q and A! Sit back down, order, and we'll talk. I've needed this for a while now. But first, how are you and Naji doing? You've been incommunicado for two weeks."

He smiled as he finished giving the returned waiter his order for nearly as much food as Sarah had ordered.

"There hasn't been much "communicado" between *us* either. It's been a whirlwind of wine and lovemaking. We just fit so well together, Sarah. I've never met anyone like Naji, and the more I get to know about her, the more I *want* to know. It's pretty magical. I have no idea where this might go, but I suspect, I hope, that we have started something lasting. I've never really been in love before, and while this is still too new to say that, I'm willing to admit that it's where I'm heading. I just hope it is for her too."

"Oh, she's hooked, Nik. I'm pleased for you. Naji doesn't spend weeks or even days with anyone. She's really taken with you. And why not, you're a beautiful man with a huge heart, the best smile, and a nice bod."

"And some residual vampire skills."

"Really? Like what?"

"Sex things, Sarah, and things I won't tell you. Just suffice it to say that I can do some things normal men cannot, and she's pretty thrilled. Don't worry, I told her I had vampire skills and she laughed. She doesn't suspect anything."

"I'm glad to hear that. She deserves an uncomplicated life. Although, Nikolai, if you two remain together, then we will need to tell her eventually."

"I know. We'll hop over that bridge when we come to fall off it."

English as a second language. He cracked her up and she adored him. It amazed her how easy it was to look at his body and not see Mies. She saw only Nikolai as she watched him lift a glass of iced tea.

"I can't wait to see you two together. Okay, my news is epic, but you know about all *I* know now. I only found out two nights ago. The empath Cherise came to my apartment and was able to feel the baby's lifeforce inside of me. I'm having a daughter, and she's not fully human so it's a little scary."

"I will help you with our baby. I am sorry to lay claim, too, but as you know, her father and I were very close. He would be so thrilled to know that he was going to have a daughter. I wish he could be here."

"Oh, so do I. I've been assured that I can't do this on my own."

"You are *not* on your own! I will be here. There must be a museum in Boston that can use an historical specialist. I have a very unique perspective of human life *and* vampire through the centuries."

"Which will get you killed. The rule applies doubly in big cities, so you can't let anyone know about them."

"No, Sarah, you know I joke. This secret does not leave me. I always realized how fortunate I was to be in on one of the greatest anthropological finds in the history of mankind, well aware that I must keep it to myself."

"It's also a great honor to be trusted."

Nikolai bowed his head. "I know this. Okay, so in about five months, I will be an uncle."

"Before we even know it, we will welcome her home."

"How are you doing with this? I know you were falling in love with Mies and now, you will have a reminder that he is gone."

"No, I will have a reminder that he was *here*. She'll be beautiful, Nik, more than anything I've ever seen. She'll be his but she'll also be *mine*. I already love her more than I ever thought possible."

"I do too. You must let me know anytime you need me, and Sarah, you must promise. I know you, you'll do everything on your own before you ask. Raising a child on your own is not easy. My father left just after I was born and my mother struggled every day to take care of herself and me."

"It won't be easy, but there are millions of single parents all over this world. I have a good job in a great city with every convenience I could need. And I have you. If I ever have to ask for help beyond that, I know that the vampires will come immediately. So I have no worries about whether I can raise this little girl safely and happily."

"And Naji?"

"If I read her in, then she can stay close to me. If I can't, then I will have one of the vampires use compulsion to erase me from her life. I have mixed feelings about that. We love each other, but she's had a hard life, and being introduced to the existence of vampires won't make it easier. I have to think of what is best for Naji. There is so much to consider before this child comes out to meet us."

"*Da*, knowledge of supernaturals has been difficult at times, but also fascinating. I would not wish to have my memories purged, even with what I have experienced with Mies. Sarah, if they ever tell you that they want to do so, please try not to let them. The past few months have been difficult, but now, having made it through it all, I wouldn't want to lose those experiences. In many ways, I am stronger for having known Mies and I am *grateful* to have known him and for what we endured together. I am more of a man, and less afraid than I would be having never known him."

"I feel the same. And now, I have this little girl. I already believe she'll outshine the sun."

The waiter arrived with the first of their plates.

"It's here! I am insatiable since I found out that I'm pregnant. I eat everything in sight now."

For the next forty minutes that is exactly what Sarah and Nikolai did. He felt he needed to support her, so he kept up. It wasn't easy. The following night, Sarah returned to work to face another difficult task.

"I don't understand."

"Leo, I'm not sure if I can make it any clearer. In the past few days, some things have changed in my life over which I have no control. Because of these changes, I can't begin a relationship with you after all. You are a wonderful man, you deserve someone who can give you all of her attention, and right now, that isn't me. You know that I've been attracted to you, I still am, but until things change, I'm not dating. Anyone. I'm really sorry, but nothing can change my mind because the situation that I face is unchangeable. I hope we can remain friends."

Leo threw his hands up. "I give up. Uh, yeah, sure, we work together, I admire you, of course we'll remain friends. But if you ever decide you're interested in me again, it's all up to you, okay?"

Sarah smiled. "Yes, that's fair enough. It means a lot that you want to remain friends. If I lost your friendship at this point, I really would be upset. You know this has nothing to do with you personally, right?"

"Of course it doesn't! Who can resist this?" He held his hands out to present himself.

Laughing now, Sarah touched his forearm. "I couldn't, if things were different, I promise. Okay, I guess I'll see you tomorrow night."

Dropping his grin, Leo nodded. "I guess so. You know, I accept that something is keeping you from going out with me, but I still have hope."

"You're a really good man with a good heart. I'm the one losing out here. See you tomorrow."

It was done. One more tie broken to the life she had hoped to build here. The next challenge that remained would be the deepest cut of all. She would have to discover if Naji would also become the casualty of a bitter choice.

Tonight, though, she needed to call Tamesine.

IN SOUTHERN FRANCE

The phone interrupted Marc just as he'd fallen asleep. Fishing it off the bedside table, he saw it was Sarah in Boston.

"Tam, baby, wake up," he moaned into his mate's ear.

"Why…do the children need me?"

"Your girl in Boston's calling."

"Oh." Tamesine rolled into a sitting position and took the phone from Marc, grimaced when he dropped and pulled his pillow under his head to fall off quickly.

Pressing the button, she answered softly. "Sarah?"

"Tamesine, hi, I know it's late for you, I'm sorry. I just needed to check in and I couldn't wait. I'll be brief."

"Okay, dear, what did you need?"

"You know, don't you?"

Sliding from her bed, Tamesine walked past the children's beds into the bathroom attached to their suite.

"Of course. Cherise called as soon as she left you. We care about you and know what a difficult time you'll have raising this child."

"Are you sure? I mean, I think I can do it quite well here in Boston. There's a lot of support for single parents."

"Single parents raising a vampire child?"

"Is that really going to be that much of an issue until she's older?"

"Perhaps. The thing is, we've discovered that the children of this generation are more powerful than we were and they get their skills earlier. I think the worst part is the unpredictability. You will never know what she might do. In that, yes, I think it will be an issue. And you don't have the ability to wipe memories to clean up any mess she might make. You see my point?"

Tamesine heard a long sigh and some movement. Sarah was pacing in her small apartment.

"I want to stay here, at least for a little while."

"I do understand, you've made that city home. You can try it while she's a baby, see how it goes, and come to us when you are either ready or hit a time when it is necessary. Cherise and I agree that you are a smart, headstrong woman and that you will choose the right course when the time comes. Sarah, we trust you and we know that, ultimately, you will do what is best for the child. So stay, enjoy, be a doctor, and let us know when I need to send the jet for you. Does that help?"

"It really does. You know how much I value your community, but I feel like I need to embrace my humanity and I feel like it's the first lesson I'd like to teach my daughter someday."

"Those are fair goals. She'll be with us in the end anyway, you *do* know that?"

Tamesine felt as well as heard Sarah's heart-stopping hesitation as she prepared to admit what she did not want to admit. Finally, she spoke.

"I know that. I assume that I'll be welcomed back into the community as well."

"Oh, darling, of course you will be." Now Tamesine paused. "Sarah, you need to think about the future. You know what I mean by that."

Another long pause from across the sea made Tamesine ache for the young human woman whose life was no longer her own to control.

"I know."

That was all there was to say and Tamesine found herself nodding. No decisions had to be made now, there was plenty of time, but if Sarah wanted to remain a part of her daughter's life for the coming years, she would have to convert and become vampire.

"I should let you go," Sarah commented suddenly.

"Yes, I need to rest. Thank you for letting me know about your choices and situation. Again, anything you need, you know we are here."

"I really do know that and it gives me great comfort. Goodnight, Tamesine."

"*Bonne nuit.*"

Sarah slid her phone onto the tabletop in front of her sofa and lay her head back on one of the arms.

Okay, that was done.

The relationship with Leo was settled in that she wouldn't have one now. Tamesine, and as such, the vampire community, was apprised and okay with her choice to try to raise the baby here in Boston. Nikolai had been told and was overjoyed. She was fairly sure that he would stay and help her. Thank God, too, because she *would* need help.

The only thing that remained was how to deal with Naji. This weekend, she would sit down with Nikolai and Naji, find out how their relationship was going and make a final choice.

This was not the life she'd built when she came here three months ago. It reminded her of when her parents left Xavier's household. "I remember, Mom, when you told me that life is what happens to you while you are making other plans."

While that was true for most people, it was particularly true when an omnipotent universal force made those choices for you.

Aware that everything she thought and felt could be felt by the baby growing inside of her, Sarah quickly smoothed her fingers across her abdomen that was just beginning to swell.

"I wouldn't wish you away, my sweetheart, for anything in this world, though, I promise."

An overwhelming warmth began in her womb and moved throughout her body. Her daughter approved.

The rest of the week flew by.

Saturdays were busy in the city. With bright sunlight moving through the streets, the air warm with a light

211

breeze, the crowds followed that sunshine to the parks, several local festivals, and great restaurants.

Finally, looking forward to seeing the couple together for the first time, Sarah waited for Naji and Nikolai at a popular café on Liberty Wharf. Luxury yachts moved gently on the calm sea, elegantly serene in a loud frantic world. It felt good to be out of the apartment for something other than work.

"Ahhh!"

The scream broke her concentration as Sarah looked up to see Naji advancing on her quickly, a smiling Nikolai just behind her. Naji filled the space with her presence as she grabbed Sarah and hauled her from her seat to hug her. Sarah hugged back, so grateful to see her friend again after all the life-changing moments this past month.

Stepping back, Naji held Sarah at arm's length, her coal dark eyes glittering. "It's been too long, love." Then her eyes shot to Nikolai and back to Sarah with a sly smile.

"Of course, I've been busy!"

"No details! But I'm happy for you. Here, sit beside me and tell me how you've been." Sarah kept her eyes on Nikolai as he sat on the other side of the table. He looked happier than she could have imagined when she first saw him here in Boston weeks ago on that examination table in the E.R.

"I assume things are going well?" she asked, the question general to Naji, more focused to Nikolai. She had to know how close they were.

The answer came seconds later when Naji looked directly at Nikolai and he bowed his head. *Love.* Pure and simple, Naji was in love with Nikolai.

"It's going well," was all Naji said though.

Nikolai slid a hand across the table and underneath Naji's. Their eyes locked.

Sarah looked back and forth between the two serious expressions. "You two are together, aren't you? *Really* together, am I right?"

Nikolai looked back into Sarah's eyes. "We are. These weeks have shown us that we are a perfect match. We have found what many seek all their lives and never find; the perfect partner to share life with."

Naji took Sarah's hand. "He has made me believe in love. That I am worthy of it when I never thought that I was. I could never get beyond the lonely little girl who desperately wanted a hug and never got one because I was sure that I didn't deserve it. He's knocked all the cobwebs off memories and showed them for what they are. Other people's failures, not mine. I love this man, Sarah. I am so grateful that you brought him into my life."

Sarah surged out of her seat to hug Naji again, her eyes on Nikolai. He saw the question in them and nodded. All right, Naji would remain a part of their lives.

Pulling back, she slipped into her chair. "I am so happy for you both. Let's have a great lunch, my treat, and then go back to my apartment. I have something I need to go over with you."

"More surprises?"

"You have no idea. So, what would you like?"

Three hours later, Nikolai waited for the two women to pass him into Sarah's apartment.

"I have some decadent ice cream if anyone would like to make a sundae."

"Sarah, that lunch has already pushed me up another size. How am I gonna keep my man happy if I my hot ass keeps growing?"

"He's not in love with you for your size 8 ass, Naj."

Nikolai came up behind her and slid a hand over her bum. "Not for its size, no," he commented.

"Ugh! I told you, no sex talk. Generally, and also specifically, because I am celibate now."

"No, you're not, I'm going to find you the perfect man since you found one for me," Naji promised.

"That isn't necessary. And now, I'm going to explain why. Nik, why don't you get Naji a hot tea and some of that cake on the counter?"

"Of course."

He went into the kitchen to put the kettle on and prepare the dessert. Fifteen minutes later, he brought three cups of sweet tea and a slice of cake into the living room and placed it all on the table in front of the sofa.

Seated now on the sofa, relaxed at first, Sarah beside her, Naji suddenly found herself watching her companion's faces. She was intuitive enough to notice that their behavior was different now, odd, maybe suspicious. "I know something is going on here. You are both acting strange. What is it? Sarah, you know I hate lies."

"I do. Which is why Nikolai and I have something to tell you. It's crazy, Naj, and you'll have trouble believing it, but you have to trust us that it's true. Because I'm really going to need you in the future."

"I'll be here for you no matter what, love, you know that. Just because Nik and I are hooking up doesn't mean that I abandon you. What's going on? You two look so serious and it's fucking scaring me."

"There isn't anything to be afraid of. It's actually good news. Incredible news. But there's a bit of a tale to tell before we get to that part."

"Then begin the tale, damn't!" Naji reached for the cake.

Sarah looked at Nikolai. "Do you want to start?"

"*Da*, I think that is the best place." He turned to Naji.

"Please, keep an open mind and remember that the universe is a big place and that things happen in this world that are far beyond anything we can imagine. It is an incredibly complex place."

He paused, looked to Sarah for support that this was indeed the right thing to do. She nodded. He turned back to Naji. "Okay, this is what happened to me one night in Siberia."

Naji hadn't moved in over half an hour, the cake she'd taken off the table still perched untouched on her lap. Her face expressionless, she sat stone still as her eyes moved from Sarah back to Nikolai now that Sarah was finished with her part of the story she'd just heard. All three sat wordless for several long minutes of deep breaths and long shocked stares.

Finally, Sarah broke the silence. "Naji. Tell me what you're thinking."

"You don't want me to. Not yet."

Nikolai slipped from his chair, knelt at Naji's knees, and rested his arms down the sides of her thighs. "We need to talk about what we just revealed. Do you understand that all of it is completely true? We are not crazy?"

Naji rolled her eyes up to the white ceiling and noticed the shapes made by past water leaks in the stucco. What did they want her to say? She dropped her gaze back to Nikolai. This man she had fallen for was at her feet, begging for her to believe something entirely impossible.

Vampires? Really? People from thousands of years ago reviving? Possessing Nikolai's body? And Sarah had lived with vampires since she was born? Now, she was pregnant with one of their children? It *was* impossible.

"Nik, I've fallen in love with you, and I'm in this with you until the end. For both of you. But this vampire story, the tales, the elaborate possession, it's too weird for me."

Her eyes moved to Sarah. "I loved you almost from that first morning we met in the bakery; you, desperate for that last cupcake, me, determined not to give it up, and how we recognized each other's souls right away. I've trusted you like no one else in my life because I could see you. So, when two people who I love and want to spend my life with tell me a fantasy about things that I know cannot be true, and I can see that you both really believe it, then there is only one response."

Shaking her head, Naji smiled. "I have to trust you, to have faith in you, because you are my family."

Nikolai pulled Naji off the sofa into a tight embrace. He kissed her forehead several times before he let her wiggle free.

"That doesn't mean that I don't want proof. One of you is going to introduce me to one of these vampires."

Sarah stood. "That is a deal. In a few weeks, I'll introduce you to the one that is sleeping inside of me right now."

"So you're really pregnant?"

215

Nodding, Sarah pulled Naji's hand to her belly and curved her long fingers over the expanding bubble.

"It's a girl."

"And the father is a vampire who died six thousand years ago?"

"Uh huh," Sarah mumbled through relief and joy. Naji had taken this better than she was afraid that she would. Did she fully believe everything that they told her? No. But she believed that *they* believed it and it would give them time to prove that they were not certifiably insane. Love could overcome a lot of barriers.

"Naj, thank you for taking the leap of faith. I promise you, this is the most bizarre thing you'll ever be told and it is one hundred percent true."

"Okay. You know, I'm going to walk into that fog with you knowing that you both have my back, but I'm gonna keep my eyes wide open!"

Laughing, Nikolai came back from the kitchen with a bottle of wine. "This is a celebration. We have much to look forward to in the years ahead. We are a team now, the three of us, and we take care of each other."

"The four of us," Sarah commented, hands on her belly.

"Ah, yes, four of us. Dinner, tonight, on me, the restaurant of your choice."

"Nik, you can't afford that. Let me take you guys out."

"I will find work soon. For now, I have a savings account that needs to be deflated some. Dress in your pretty clothes ladies. Sarah, we will be back to pick you up in two hours."

Giving Naji and Nikolai a hug, Sarah closed the door behind them and wandered into the living room to pick up the cups and saucers from her table.

"So, we're doing this. We have a support team, and everyone is read in. Yeah." She looked down at the saucer with Naji's uneaten dessert. "Yeah, it's going to be a piece of cake."

Shaking her head, she placed the saucer in the sink.

Piece of cake? *No.* Life never was.

Thirteen

FIVE MONTHS LATER

Cooler air pushed in off the water as Sarah watched the seagulls. Her belly was enormous now, and she mostly just used it for an armrest. She was starving again, though, as she had been for the past five months.

Nikolai carried a cooler to the water's edge and sat beside her on the rustic bench.

"Oh, thank God. I've been eyeing those seagulls and if you hadn't gotten here soon, it might have become a bloodbath."

"As if you could kill a seagull. You'd wrap it up and take it home to feed it, maybe."

"Gimme," she hissed, as he pulled a thick sandwich from the plastic box.

"Crezia is going to eat me out of house when she gets here, isn't she?" Nikolai complained with a grin as he watched Sarah devour the sandwich. It wasn't pretty.

Between bites, Sarah glanced up at him. "She's going to be a normal kid. I think. Tamesine said that the big thing we need to watch for when she gets a little older is manifestation of her talent. All of the other kids have shown some of their ability by age two. Of course, this child is the progeny of an ancient vampire and no one really knows what to expect."

"When are they all coming?"

"Next week. Cherise will be here in two days to assess the day of birth. She says she can tell us exactly when the baby will come."

"Remarkable."

"When's Naji getting here?"

"She's held up. An important buyer arrived just before she was getting ready to leave and she couldn't pass him off to a lower associate, so she's working him. We need the commission."

"I'm sorry, Nik. I can get back to work soon. A Shoazan heals very quickly following childbirth."

"No, we're fine. The apartment is just a little grander than I expected. Who knew people paid that kind of money just to rent space in a building?"

"Naji. The girl has impeccable taste and lavish expectations. I love our place, though. Huge master bedroom for you two, a separate suite for me and Zia. A balcony so we can watch the sunrise. Italian tile throughout. It's almost as elegant as Xavier's apartment in Paris."

"As long as my women are pleased." He sighed as he bit into a sandwich before Sarah ate them all. "It *is* a pretty evening. I'm kind of exhausted."

"That new display at the museum?"

"*Da.* Everything weighs a ton. Literally. And I have too small a budget for staff, so I get to figure out how to move four tons of Egyptian stone into the main exhibition room. It will be a magnificent display once it is done."

"Do you miss being out on the dig yourself?"

"Sometimes, but I'd miss being here with my girls more, so it's worth the trade-on."

"I couldn't have done this without you, Nik. And it's trade-*off.*"

"Ah. You never will have to do this without me, I cannot wait to hold Mies's daughter in my arms. Do you think she will recognize me?"

"I know that she will. Cherise can actually let you communicate with her."

"That is what I wait for. Sometimes, I am sad because I know how overjoyed he would be to know that you are having his daughter. I wish that I could speak to him again. Even on the spiritual plane."

"I do too. We've tried, though, and our triad of first blood women can't find him up there. The dead must go to a different place."

Sarah stopped speaking suddenly, her eyes misting, her belly moving. "Dead. I hate that word. When I think of it in relation to Mies, I can't let myself imagine that he is *just gone*. That he isn't out there somewhere above the clouds watching us."

"Sarah, he may be. We cannot know these things."

She was silent again.

Nikolai's eyes teared. "It's all right, okay?"

"I know. I just kind of believe that if he was still *somewhere*, he might be able to communicate with us. That's why I think he's just really gone this time. For always."

The only thing that he could do was hold her, so he set the cooler on the ground and pulled her close. The belly *did* keep them from getting too near, but she found comfort from him as they sat on the bench, the night air growing cooler while the pink left the sky.

"Did you see that sequined scarf I had in my hands ten minutes ago?"

Getting Naji out of the house to work was not easy. Everything had to be perfect, and she was kind of a scatter-brain about her belongings.

"Did you leave it in the bathroom?" Nikolai asked.

"Would I *ask* you if you had seen it if I knew where it was? Baby, go look, please. And see if you can find those blue strappy sandals with the sequined bows on top."

Sarah sat on a plush recliner with two bowls in front of her, one with tortilla chips and a second one with spicy melted cheese.

She watched Nikolai racing around searching for Naji's clothes and shoes, Naji grabbing a last minute cup of strong coffee and a cinnamon roll, and looked back at the seventy inch television screen that Naji had brought with her to the apartment. It was like watching real life, the TV was so large and clear. Sarah had fallen in love with it.

God, though, it would be a pleasure when the baby was born and she could get back out and see the real world. Right now, she felt like a baby-making blimp. Her legs hurt and her feet felt like concrete blocks attached to her ankles. Eillia had told her that a human Shoazan would have all of the usual issues of any *normal* pregnancy.

However, Park wanted to deliver the baby. Her strong medical background and the fact that she was first blood meant the birth would be safer for the baby and risk no exposure to uninitiated humans. Sarah was thrilled that Park would be here to take care of her and Zia.

Pulling on the sequin-bowed shoes, Naji raced over to the sofa, kissed Sarah on the forehead, yelled, "Have a wonderful day, love," kissed Nikolai in a very different way, and raced out the door, satchel flying behind her, keys jingling wildly in her hand.

Nikolai began to walk back to their bedroom to prepare for work himself when Sarah, just getting ready to pop a chip in her mouth, squeaked.

"Sarah?"

"Um, I'm okay. Just a sharp pain, but it went away immediately. Nothing to worry about."

"You're sure?"

"Yeah, I'm just a week from delivery, so…"

With no warning, another pain hit and Sarah doubled over. Nikolai flew to her side.

"Sarah! What can I do? Should I call the hospital?"

"No! Get my cell…oh! Uh, call Park."

Nikolai grabbed her phone and did exactly as asked.

A sleepy voice answered. "Hello?"

"Park?" Nikolai inquired.

"Umm, yeah. Who am I speaking to? It's the middle of the day here and you woke me."

"I'm sorry. This is Nikolai, Sarah's friend, calling from Boston. She's having some sharp pain. It just started."

"Ah. Okay, do you have a tablet or laptop where I can see her?"

"Yeah, uh, let me get it…" Nikolai hurried across the apartment, which he now decided was definitely too big, and brought back a large tablet computer with a camera, set it up for videoconferencing, and brought it to Sarah.

"Sarah, it's Park. Sweetie, tell me about the pain and show me where it is located."

Collapsed over, holding her body with shaking arms, Sarah forced herself to sit upright.

"Here, sharp pains shot through from one side to the other and I couldn't sit up. They've subsided, but now I'm cramping. The cramps seem to encompass the entire womb. I can feel her, Park, she's panicking. What's wrong? What can I do to help her?"

"I can't say. Your symptoms are atypical of a vampire pregnancy. Recently, you haven't eaten anything strange that might have made you sick, or taken any falls, hurt yourself, anything that might have harmed your human body? It won't kill you or the child, but you could still be in a lot of pain."

"I don't think so. I can't think of anything. Park, what am I to do?"

"Sarah, the only thing that I can think of right now is vampire blood. I'm trying to think who might be close to you."

"Does it have to be a first blood?"

"Ideally, yes. Any vampire blood should help, but I'm going to send David, since he's the nearest geographically to you. Sarah, he won't be able to come until tonight. You realize this is unprecedented. Vampire pregnancies are uncomplicated, so I really don't know what may be going on. I suspect it has something to do with the unusual nature of the parentage."

"I'm afraid of that too. Park, I can't lose this baby."

"We'll do all that we can. Tamesine and I will leave at sundown, so we'll be there as soon as possible. Sweetie, I'm sure she's okay, vampire children are almost indestructible."

"Which is why I'm terrified."

221

"It won't help her if you're stressed. Nikolai, can you stay with Sarah?"

"Of course."

"Keep her calm, keep her hydrated, and get her to eat if you can do so. We'll be with you shortly."

After Park rang off, Nikolai went into the kitchen and then returned to sit beside Sarah. "They'll be here, and they'll help you. Here, drink this."

He handed Sarah bottled water with the cap already removed. She killed it in little more than one gulp.

"It's easing. Some. Nik, I can't let anything happen to Mies's child. It's all I have of him."

"She's going to be okay, I believe that. Sarah, you've had faith all along, don't abandon it now. Let me make you something to eat and then why don't you lie down for a while. I'll watch over you both."

Sarah cupped Nikolai's face with her hands. "You always do. We've carved a beautiful life out here with Naji. I pray that it will not change."

"It won't. Now, I'll be back with more pasta than a small woman can eat."

Sarah slept the rest of the day. She woke only twice with slight cramps but they subsided quickly and she fell back to sleep almost like she'd been drugged. Nikolai slid in beside her in the huge bed she'd chosen so that there would be plenty of room for the baby to sleep with her.

Wrapping his arms around her, he put his head against Sarah's belly and listened to the calm gurgles. He wouldn't tell her, but he was equally as terrified that they might lose this child.

"Stay with us, *kotyonok*."

Moments later, his eyes closed, he heard her speak quietly. "You call her kitten."

"She is to me, this tiny precious life that must be protected at all costs. I love her already, Sarah."

"I know." Sarah sighed and kissed Nikolai on the top of his head. "I know," she repeated.

They fell asleep and were still there, curled close, four hours later when Naji came home. She watched them together with no jealousy at all because they were family and she trusted them completely. There was also the fact that she knew Sarah's heart almost as much as she knew her own, and that girl was still very much in love with her missing baby daddy.

Although she accepted Sarah and Nikolai's story about the vampires existence, the evidence they'd said they would present had never happened. No *vampires* ever came to Boston or proved to Naji that they were real. She'd long ago forgotten about her initial knee-jerk response. She loved these people when she had never expected to love anyone, and that was all that mattered.

He was sleeping so nicely, but Naji couldn't help herself. Whenever she was with him, Naji had to touch Nikolai and this moment was no different. Her fingertips slid along his neck and up his left cheek into his hair. Even though her touch was light, he felt it and stirred. When his eyes opened, he smiled.

"Lady," he said. "You're home. Thank God. We've had a problem."

Naji's brows came together. "Problem?"

Nikolai rolled off the bed careful not to disturb Sarah, who seemed to be sleeping easily.

"Come," he whispered, and led Naji from Sarah's bedroom and out onto the balcony, easing the sliding door shut. He noticed, gratefully, that the sun was nearly gone. Taking her hand, he pulled Naji to the railing so that he could see Sarah's bedroom door from where they stood.

"There may be a problem with the baby."

"What?" Alarmed, Naji glanced in toward Sarah's bedroom.

"After you left for work this morning, she had some abdominal pain."

"Did you get her to the hospital?"

"They can't help her."

"Oh, Nik, you guys need to get a grip. If there's a problem, Sarah needs to see an OB. She has to know that."

"Vampire babies don't have problems like this."

Naji didn't say a word for the count of ten. She'd learned to hold her ire until she calmed down. Once she had, she captured Nikolai's eyes.

"We have to call an ambulance. Nikolai, don't fight me on this. I know what you two believe, and I honor that, but this is the baby's life. Maybe Sarah's life too. You understand?"

The sun was dropping quickly now, only a slight glow left at the waterline. Nikolai prayed that the vampires would be here soon. He put a hand on Naji's wrist.

"If you honor what we've told you, you'll give us a few more hours before you feel compelled to do something that won't help, and might hurt. Please, Naj, you have to trust us."

Shaking her head as she shook off Nikolai's grip, exhausted from standing on high heels all day and coming home to a serious concern for her friend and her baby, Naji walked back into the bedroom and knelt next to Sarah. She brushed her hair from where it had fallen over her face.

"Sarah? Love, wake up, I want to see how you're feeling. Sarah?"

As her eyes opened slowly, Sarah came aware quickly. She smiled at Naji and remembered immediately that she'd experienced significant pain earlier in the day. Shooting into a sitting position didn't help any, the tenderness caught her breath and made her gasp.

"Sarah, I'm going to call an ambulance and Dr. Leo, okay?"

"No!" Sarah spoke harsher than she'd intended to. To soften the response, she repeated it. "No, Naji, I have help coming."

Naji pushed off the bed, her arms folded. "Vampires?"

Sarah didn't miss the condescension in Naji's voice.

"Yes, the only ones who might really be able to help me protect Zia."

"I don't know how to get through to you two." Naji walked quickly from the bedroom into the main living room, frustrated and worried.

Nikolai followed her and headed to the kitchen, where he poured two glasses of wine and carried them back, gave one to Naji, and sipped the other. "I told you, we just need a little time to prove all of this to you. Two vampires will be here shortly, and two more will be here by tomorrow night."

After another interval, Naji sat on the sofa, still, her eyes closed. When Sarah showed up, moving slowly toward them, they popped open.

"I'm sorry, I'm calling for real help," Naji announced.

The knock on the door startled all three residents of the apartment.

Sarah sighed with relief and carefully lowered onto the sofa. "Nik, bring them in."

Nikolai hurried to the door, and when he opened it, Naji sat transfixed as an extraordinarily beautiful woman entered followed by a huge piece of sex on a heavily muscled stick. Her eyes wide, she couldn't tear them away from the mesmerizing couple.

"Naj?"

Several seconds passed before she realized that Sarah was trying to get her attention. "Naji, this is Cherise and David, from Iceland. And they are vampires."

Naji's head swiveled back to Sarah. "You're kidding, right?"

"You never really did believe us all of these months, did you?"

"Darling, I love you and Nikolai, but vampires don't exist."

"They do. You'll see."

Cherise moved closer and stepped between Naji and Sarah.

"May I?" she inquired.

Naji nodded and moved back to allow Cherise to sit beside Sarah.

"How are you two doing now?"

"Better once you talk to Zia."

"Zia?"

"Oh, yes, you don't know yet. We've named our daughter after the ancient vampire from Mies's time that

225

gave her life to help find a cure to the vampire virus. Her name was Crezia, and Mies said that she was one of the most warmhearted and devoted of their clan. I thought it a fitting name for our little lady. We've started calling her Zia for short."

"It's lovely. And a fitting homage to Mies. Okay, let's see how she's doing."

Naji watched, fascinated, when Cherise placed her hands on Sarah's belly and closed her eyes.

"She's okay. I sense…something…I'm not sure what it is, but there is something going on with her. I think…"

Cherise looked confused, and Sarah leaned in.

"What? What's wrong?" Sarah asked, so quietly, Cherise barely heard her.

"I'm not sure. I think Park is right. David, I believe Sarah needs some blood."

Naji had watched as the stunning woman did the bizarre thing with Sarah, but when the woman mentioned blood, she stepped closer, her hands out, ready to stop them.

"Hold on. I don't know what you're doing here, but I…"

"Naji, stop. Cherise, would you introduce Naji to Zia?"

"Happily." Motioning to Naji to come closer, Cherise caught her eyes. "Come here, young woman."

Naji, unsure, didn't move and then suddenly, against her will, she was beside Cherise. *What the hell?*

"Kneel," Cherise commanded, and Naji did so immediately, once again without intending to do so.

"Put your hands on Sarah's belly."

This time, she wasn't as stunned, but her hands moved of their own volition. Cherise placed her hands over Naji's and closed her eyes again.

The world fell away from Naji, a dizziness assaulted her and then, a feeling, a presence, invaded her mind and smiled to her. *Hello*, it said, *you have been with my mother from the beginning. I cannot wait to meet you.* No words, just sensations and images, the message clear and incontrovertible. Naji knew, without doubt, that this was the precious baby they had been waiting for and that she had just met her before she was even born. The emotion shocked her. She pulled her hands away and backed up into the big man, who steadied her when she lost balance.

"What was that? I mean, how did you..." She looked up into the handsome face above her.

David smiled. "My mate has some very special magic," he explained.

"Magic? That isn't... Sarah, what did she do to me?"

"Cherise is an empath. Her vampire nature has heightened her ability of empathic connection to all living things. She just allowed you to meet Crezia."

"It isn't possible. I mean, I feel like I did, but I couldn't have...could I? I'm freaking out a little here."

Nikolai came forward and pulled Naji from David's hold. "Naj, what we have been telling you for the past several months is true. We told you that we would eventually show you proof that we weren't nuts, and this is it. David and Cherise are vampires."

David grinned and gave Naji a two-finger salute. "They are telling the truth, pretty lady."

Cherise stood. "They are. First order now, though, is to get some vampire blood into Sarah to see if its healing power will help her pain. David?"

With a brisk nod, David slid in next to Sarah as Cherise backed away. He slit his wrist with a small stiletto and brought it to her lips as blood began to flow.

Sarah cupped his wrist with her fingers and held it as she drew the blood in.

Naji watched, amazed that this was really happening, that Sarah sucked this man's blood with no hesitation.

Even now, though, after the strange visit with the child, the obvious presence of people who were *beyond* ordinarily beautiful, Sarah and Nikolai's insistence that it was all true, a thread of understanding and acceptance began to weave into her mind.

Could it be true, then? Vampires, supernatural beings, actually existed? And there were two of them right here in her apartment? That were helping Sarah protect a vampire child?

Overwhelming didn't come close.

Naji pulled away from Nikolai to keep all of them at bay.

"Wait. Just let me think…"

Nikolai stepped close again. "It's true," he said. "Plain and simple. You must accept this because you're a very smart woman and evidence is in front of you that is unexplainable any other way. Also, the two people you love and trust most in this world are telling you that it is."

He was right. At the core of everything that Naji knew in her life, he was right. If she loved them, and she did, then she had to trust that, however impossible this claim seemed, it was true. Vampires were real.

She lifted her eyes to his. "Okay," was all she said.

Sarah watched her friend's reaction to all of this as she drew on David's blood. It was already interacting with the baby, moving through her body, redefining it, reactivating an embedded memory of blood traces, leaving her wholly human, but plumping up her immune system and aiding in her body's ability to function. It was what she needed.

David pulled from her and used a moist towel that Cherise handed to him to gently wipe Sarah's mouth.

"There you go, young woman. Your color is already better."

"Everything is. The baby is doing all right, too. Thank you both for coming so quickly. I really didn't know what was wrong."

Cherise took David's place at Sarah's side. "We still don't. Sarah, you should not have had this pain, it isn't normal. Park will do some tests when she gets here, but in the meantime, I'm glad your symptoms have improved. May I feel the child again?"

"Sure," Sarah agreed and leaned back while Cherise entered the spiritual realm to contact the baby.

When she pulled free moments later, Cherise smiled, but the smile was tight. "She's better, too."

Rising, Cherise looked around the apartment. "Very lovely. And what a gorgeous view. Can we bring in some food for a first meal?"

"I will take care of everything," Nikolai volunteered. "Naj, why don't you come with me?"

"Uh, yeah, I think that's a good idea." Getting out of there was a *great* idea. She might be able to accept that vampires existed, but it was still mind-blowing and getting some fresh air was exactly what she needed.

"We'll be back soon." Nikolai pushed Naji out of the apartment ahead of him.

They chose the stairs instead of taking the elevator. Until they exited the building and walked up the boardwalk, neither spoke. Nikolai waited for Naji to do so, but when she didn't, he couldn't stand the silence anymore.

"What are you thinking?"

"I'm thinking that I'm a fool. You guys told me, but I didn't believe you. Yeah, I've been a fool."

Even though Naji was nearly as tall as Nikolai, he came to her, lifted her off her feet, and gave her a long kiss. Her arms went around him, holding tight, afraid that he'd decide she wasn't worth the trouble.

When he pulled away, he buried his face in her hair.

"I won't have you say that about the woman I love. You are the best thing that has ever happened to me. Naj, the vampires believe that many people have a destiny, that the universe has a hand in much of what happens in this world. I believe that I was brought here for a reason. And I believe that reason is *you*. So, the things that have happened, the *way* they've happened…lady, we were meant to be."

"I've never had anyone believe in me the way that you and Sarah do. I'd follow you to the ends of this earth, vampires or no. I've never held much for things like destiny, but you make me want to believe in it."

"You will. Stick with us."

"Like glue, love. Like glue."

"We'd better go get that food. You have an interesting education coming tonight. Vampires eat more food in one night than we eat in three days, and they look like supermodels on steroids. Wait until you see it. It's pretty awesome."

All Naji cared about right now was that Nikolai still wanted her, that Sarah and the baby would be all right, and that hopefully, no vampire was going to want to munch down on her tonight.

The evening unfolded exactly as Nikolai had explained it to her. The vampires were kind and amusing, and did in fact eat most of the massive quantities of food that he and Naji had brought back.

Naji had warned him that he'd ordered too much food, but she'd been wrong. By the time this *first meal*, as they called it, was over, the oversized platters they'd brought from three different restaurants were empty.

"Show us Boston, Nikolai," David requested. "Other than that brief visit a few months ago, well, I won't tell you how long it's been since I walked this city. Suffice it to say, there were still British soldiers here."

"Uh, sure, but can Sarah come or should we leave someone with her?"

"I can go," Sarah answered, circumventing anyone else's assessment of her condition. "David's blood has worked and I feel better right now than I ever have. I'm more alert, my vision is sharper, and I may be able to superspeed."

Nikolai frowned at her. "That's possible?"

Sarah laughed. "I'm just messing with you. No, I'm still fully human, Nik." Her eyes landed on Naji, her face unreadable. "Sweet Naji, I am and will always be exactly who you've known from that first moment we met."

Releasing her held breath, Naji smiled. "Yeah, I know. Still getting my grip on all of this. Nikolai and I talked, I'm okay."

"Good. Tour?" David inquired, a big hand landing on Naji's shoulder.

She held her breath again.

Fourteen

"For now, you and the baby seem fine." Park sat back, her stethoscope in her hand, her eyes moving to Tamesine.

"You still look worried," Sarah commented, her eyes riveted on Park's.

"Well, I'm concerned. Your incident shouldn't have happened. To my knowledge, vampire pregnancies go without trouble. Unless there's shit like what happened to Starla, but even then, the baby never showed any sign of distress. Let's just keep our minds and eyes open. I'm glad we're here for the last few days of the pregnancy."

"Cherise said the baby will arrive on Thursday."

Tamesine took her hands. "Ah. So we have two days to prepare. Good. Sarah, don't worry, I'm sure it will all be okay. You're Shoazan, pretty much nothing can touch you or your child."

"Keep telling me that. David's blood seems to have stopped the pain for now."

Still holding onto Tamesine, Sarah pulled herself off the sofa. "I have been restless. Let's get out of here. Why don't we go for a walk?"

Park nodded. "Sure. I would like to see your hospital. May we go?"

"Yeah. Let me get dressed," Sarah said, tugging at her oversized tee shirt.

Tamesine stepped back. "I'll remain here and make the preparations for the birth. I'd like to speak with Nikolai anyway. He never did show up in France."

Park responded to her.

"It's probably too late now, but I took some samples after I arrived tonight. Nikolai and Mies's merge, from a medical standpoint, is just so fascinating. I would love to have recorded the transition back to human from that strange possession. Is that what we're calling it?"

The E.R. was bustling, too busy for the staff of only two doctors on a Tuesday night. When the head nurse, Callie, saw Sarah enter the waiting room, she smiled.

"Hey, you, ready to come back to work?"

"Not quite yet," Sarah said, pointing to the huge belly that had preceded her through the door.

"Umm, yep, gonna pop soon, I see. Well, we miss you. Tonight, especially. We had a school bus returning from a sports event overturn, filled with teenagers. They're okay, just a bunch of scrapes mostly, three with broken limbs, one head injury. Then we had a run on chest pain earlier, four people presenting with possible heart attacks, all negative."

"I wish I could stay and help. I just wanted to show my friend our new lab facilities. She has her own research lab in France and was curious about that new equipment for genetic identification."

"I don't think you can get in. The specialty departments are locked at night."

"I didn't think about that. Perhaps I'll just give her a general tour."

"Have a good time, then. Uh, Dr. Peretti is in tonight. Right now, he's with one of the kids, but I thought you might want to know."

"Thanks, I appreciate that. This way, Park."

As they moved down the corridor away from the E.R., Park caught Sarah's attention. "Dr. Peretti?"

"He's a handsome doctor, human, that I was attracted to before I got pregnant with the child of a 6000-year-old

232

vampire. I broke off the potential relationship when I found out. I didn't want to get closer with him and then have to mess up his life by introducing him to supernaturals. We weren't in love, so I did the right thing and let him go."

"As a blood-bond, you know what it means to bring someone in, and while I agree with your choice, I'm sorry."

"It was the only choice I could make. I had Nik and Naji to help me raise my child, so I didn't need another confused human. This is a deep responsibility and I think if most people were to understand how things change if they were to know, they would say no. I made that choice for him before it was necessary for him to do so."

"You're a wise woman."

"Just a practical one."

A heavy door with a silver placard that said "Specialty Laboratory" came up on the right of a long hallway.

"This is it?"

"Yes, it is."

Park used her skills to gain immediate access. Once she'd swept into the locked room, Sarah hit several switches which brought up the lights and turned on power to the equipment.

"Come see the height of technology in genetic medicine in the U.S."

Park, smiling ear to ear, walked forward into the dim room. This was her version of a candy store, so for the next hour, she devoured Sarah's guided tour.

Arriving back at the apartment, Sarah noticed that the barriers Nikolai had built two months ago were already pulled into place to guard the visiting vampires from the imminent daylight. She lowered her girth carefully into a reclining chair.

"Are you hungry?" Naji asked, her eyes moving between Sarah and Park.

"Yes," they answered in tandem.

"I got this," Naji told Nikolai when he started to rise to get the women some late dinner.

"I already ordered six entrees just before they left the hospital. How good am I? I think I'm getting the hang of this vampire thing."

"You are doing well, my love," Nikolai said, and wondered if the vampires might be offended by the phrase *this vampire thing*.

Naji carried two trays into the living room and set up a little buffet for Sarah and Park.

"All of these entrees are double portions and from the best chefs in Boston. If I'm going to feed vampires, I'm going to do this right."

"Naji, you're a sweetheart, but simple fare would have been fine."

Licking her fingers, Park moaned. "Speak for yourself, little mama. This shrimp is perhaps the best I've ever eaten. Naji, I need the recipe for my chef in France."

"They don't give those out."

"Just introduce me, okay?"

"Oh. You're gonna do that compulsion thing on him, aren't you?"

"Um, huh. Shrimp like this must be shared and I know a large group of people who will really appreciate it."

"Tomorrow night, then, I'll take you to him."

"Thanks. Meanwhile…" Park slipped half the order onto her plate and continued her love affair.

Sarah ate very little before she pushed up off the deeply cushioned chair. "Since I know that I'm only going to have two days of baby-free sleep left, I think I'll get all that I can now. You can have my share, Park. Goodnight everyone."

"I think I'll do the same. Coming?" Nikolai asked Naji.

"Not yet, love. Go on, I'll see you in a little while."

Park picked up the plates. "I'll finish in my room. Thanks, dear, for your excellent choices."

Naji nodded as Park entered the room she would share with Tamesine and closed the door behind her.

All members of the household had switched to the vampire's schedule. Nikolai and Sarah had no difficulty, but Naji felt tired. She was adaptable, she knew she'd get the hang of it, but for now, she dropped back onto the sofa, the living room abandoned, and flipped on the television.

"Morning TV sucks," she commented and searched for something dull enough to put her to sleep so she could join Nikolai in their bedroom.

Thursday had been a perfect day, mid 80's, soft breeze, sunshine, the city unusually quiet. Even now, on an evening normally bustling with patrons, the shops and restaurants that surrounded their apartment building were mostly empty.

Nikolai, Naji, and Sarah sat at an outdoor table finishing decadent crepes filled with sweet cream cheese covered with strawberries and whipped topping.

Twilight painted the sky magenta, reminding Sarah of the song *Red Sails in the Sunset*.

"What a lovely evening for our baby girl to come into the world." Sarah spoke softly, the reverence of the evening clear as the three friends who planned to parent this special child enjoyed their final evening alone.

Naji nodded. "It's like the sky planned a birthday party."

"Or it's smiling on this child who, according to Cherise and Park, has a place in an event of great importance in the future. Naji, you do realize that she'll still be here centuries from now?"

Her eyebrows lifted, and that was the only acknowledgment Naji made to the comment. *Still adjusting*, she said to herself, the idea that this baby would be nearly immortal was beyond her ability to process right now.

Nikolai leaned across the table to touch Sarah's hand.

"She is nearly here," he whispered.

Suddenly they all noticed that the brilliant burgundy skyline over the sea brightened, reds and pinks reflected off unusually shaped white clouds. The sea looked a deeper blue than it ever had before.

Her eyes moving across the horizon from the far right to the far left, the sky cut only by an occasional sail jutting up from the pier, Sarah looked at Nikolai. She loved sharing this with Naji and the others, but it was Nikolai who understood how she felt the most.

"I know." Her response to him was so simple. Then, her hands on the baby in her belly for perhaps the last time, she spoke again. "Crezia, my love, I wish you could see your party decorations."

On the way back to the apartment, the sky almost pitch black already, Sarah felt an odd sensation, a twisting in her abdomen that she'd never felt before.

"Sarah..." Nikolai called out as he reached for her. She buckled, but did not fall because he had her. "Sarah, is it time?"

"I don't know. Maybe..." The pain hit her harder. "Oh! Yeah, yeah, I think...*oh! Yes!*"

Swinging her up gently, Nikolai had her in his arms and carried her to the elevator.

"You'll be upstairs in moments. The vampires will take care of you."

He was nervous and felt completely helpless.

"I'm okay. This is just..." Another long moan tore her words away. Moments later, she finished. "Normal."

Naji held the doors open and Nikolai carried her onto the elevator.

Sarah lifted her head from a groan. "Do you have the leftovers? Can you get one out for me?"

"What?" barked Nikolai.

"Yeah, sweetheart, here you go." Naji put a napkin-wrapped crepe into Sarah's hand.

"This is crazy," Nikolai commented as they reached their floor and he rushed into the apartment.

Tamesine, Park, and Cherise waited inside the door.

"Everything is ready. Nikolai, bring her in here." Park led them to the right.

They'd prepared a birthing room in the spare bedroom, a pallet of heavy blankets covered a plastic sheet on the mattress, topped with soft eucalyptus sheets for Sarah to lie on.

Nikolai placed her carefully on the sheets and dropped onto his knees beside the bed. "You need anything, anything at all?"

Sarah gave him a pained smile. "Just a baby, out here, not in there. Guess I'm going to get my wish in a few minutes. Do you want to stay and watch her come into the world?"

He hesitated only a moment. "I think I do. I mean, of course I do, I've just never seen a birth before."

"You must be here for *this* one. You must be here for Mies."

His hand curled around hers, and he kissed the top of it. "I will be here for Mies, for Zia, and for *you.*"

Naji stood on the other side of the bed, tears in her eyes, more deeply in love with Nikolai than ever.

Sarah took Naji's hand with her other one, grateful that her closest friends were with her.

"Here she comes," Cherise announced.

Tamesine joined Naji near Sarah while Park stayed in position to help the baby come into the world. David stayed near the back of the room in case he was needed for anything, but wanted to be out of the way while the women did what they needed to do.

"I think she'll be ready soon. You're nearly fully dilated, Sarah, and you're doing well. Just continue to use your breathing technique."

Through labored moments of time-worn pain and joy borne by women from the beginning of life, on this magical night, the little girl who had waited patiently to join the world slid from her mother and out into loving arms to welcome her first breath.

Already carrying a destiny, Crezia cried and waved tiny hands as Park carried her around the bed to place her into the arms that would protect her for all of her life.

Sarah had been trying to decide whether she would do a conversion to become vampire and knew this very second that she would, absolutely, so that she could see this child become a woman, to see who she became then, and to watch her find her destiny.

Now, her eyes locked on the tiny face, dark eyes already open, thick dark hair still wet, Sarah did what any new mother does; she looked over every inch of the baby in her arms and proclaimed her perfect, more in love than she ever thought possible. Her heart filled with the beauty of this new life, and it ached that Mies would never get to hold his daughter.

Her gaze sought Nikolai, who leaned near, tears streaming down his cheeks, Naji holding him from behind, her eyes moist too, then up to Park and Tamesine.

"She's okay?" Sarah asked Park.

"She seems to be. I'll take some stats later, but she's breathing easily, her color is good, her heartbeat is strong. She's first blood, birth isn't traumatic for a vampire baby. You have a healthy and beautiful baby girl."

"I know, oh, God, I know! Thank you all for being here, for helping to welcome her safely, and for all that you will do for her in the future."

She dropped her eyes back to the baby now gurgling and staring up at her too. "Welcome home, Crezia. This is your family."

Sarah held the squirming baby up so that she could see all of the faces around the bed. Human babies couldn't see at birth, and she wasn't sure how much this child could, but she could feel the spiritual connection already reaching for every person in this room. This little girl recognized blood and accepted her family, that they belonged to her and that she belonged to them.

Later, after a thorough examination, Park nodded.

"All of her vitals seem great. I don't know what that pain was the other day, Sarah, but I believe she is completely healthy. Her smile is epic, have you noticed?"

"Noticed? Park, I *live* for her smile already."

"We all do. These children are gifts we never expected and treasure every second. Yours, especially so, because *your* first blood came through time for you."

"I don't know about that. At least, not necessarily for *me*."

Tamesine, who held a happy Zia, came closer and placed a hand on Sarah's forearm. "Yes, necessarily for *you*."

Shrugging, Sarah's smile didn't convey the joy within. "It would be nice to think so."

"Do, then. Mies was meant to come here, to you, and this little imp..." Tamesine touched Zia's nose with a fingertip. "She was destined to be exactly here, exactly now. I'm so pleased that it all worked out well for you and that you could stay here to birth her. But Sarah, you need to consider bringing her home to France. We can protect all of you."

"Give me some time." Sarah watched the baby reach for one of Tamesine's long blonde curls, now giggling because the springy thing evaded her. "Um, I have decided to have you do a conversion."

"I had no doubt. You need to be here to see what mischief this one gets into, and you can't do that in the only 40 or 50 years you would have if you remained human. It must have been a hard decision to make."

"No. I'd already given up on any semblance of a normal life when I knew about her. Then, as you said, I wouldn't want to miss a second of her life. Once I held her in my arms, there was no choice but that one. Just, maybe not immediately."

"You must take your time. Nothing is urgent now."

David entered from the bedroom he and Cherise had shared while they were here. "We're ready."

"Okay. Koen's jet is too." Park turned to Sarah. "You know..."

"Yes, I do. If I need anything at all, I'll call right away."

"Even me or David," Cherise said as she entered the room. "We *are* closer."

"Thank you. The best godparents ever."

"Family," Tamesine elaborated. She kissed the baby on the tummy and handed her over to her mother.

Park walked up behind Zia and sniffed her hair. "I love the smell of a baby's hair. My son still has that *new child* smell and I think I freak him out a little when I hover.

Having nearly lost him, I do that too much. Bas reminds me every once in a while."

Tamesine brushed Park's bright red hair back. "You'll always hover, I think. We all do. That's why they rebel when they're teenagers. They need to grow up and we need them to stay small." She looked around the apartment. "Where are your co-parents?"

"They're shopping. We're kind of out of food."

"Yeah, that happens with a house full of vampires. Goodbye, Sarah, little Zia." David carried his and Cherise's luggage out of the apartment.

Cherise hugged Zia and Sarah next, but stepped back with a serious expression. "I feel something in this child, Sarah, and I don't know what it is. She is healthy, that's not it, but my sensation may have something to do with her unique nature. You've embarked on a special journey, *chérie*. Zia's fine, really, but if you sense anything unusual, anything out of the ordinary, or have any concerns, call me or Park immediately."

"That I promise. This is all new to me, too. I already feel like I'm out of my element."

"You will be an excellent, loving mother. Doesn't mean that you won't screw up, we all do. Luckily, this is a pretty durable kid. Goodbye, my friend." Park was the last to hug Sarah as she entered the stairwell.

Once they were gone, Sarah stood at the opening of her apartment, the baby curled into her arms, and couldn't move. She could do this, she knew it, and yet there was suddenly a feeling of dread. Afraid that she would transfer that feeling to Zia, she smiled down at her. "Come on, sweetie."

Closing the door, she lifted Zia up to look at her, now dressed in a white onesie with a giraffe on the front that Cherise had brought.

"Hungry?"

Fifteen

Sarah had just finished dressing a nasty wound that should never have happened. Sometimes, often, she wished that she had first blood skills and could teach some of these shitty parents the lessons that they deserved.

The boy was eight, and had a long gash on his shoulder because his father happened to have a shovel in his hands when his son accidently dumped a wheelbarrow filled with soil as he tried to move it. Daddy hit the boy with the pointed end of the shovel, tearing open the tender skin beneath an un-protective thin tee shirt. Now, while she assured the timid boy that he had done nothing wrong, Sarah really wanted a shot at *Daddy Dearest* with that shovel.

"There you go, Lance. Just keep that clean, okay? Is your mother coming here?"

His pale blonde hair bounced as he nodded. "Yeah, she should be here in a few minutes."

"Okay. Wait here."

She went back into the waiting room where Lance's father sat reared back in a chair watching a sports program on the wall-mounted television.

"Mr. Spencer."

He had the decency to stand. "Yeah. The kid okay?"

"He's fine. That gash is deep and is going to need quite some time to heal. We'll need to watch for infection."

"Yeah, well…"

241

"Listen to me. What you did constitutes abuse in my book and if I ever see something like that again from you, I am going to come to your house and do the same fucking thing to you. You understand?"

"Hey, look, lady…"

"I don't give a shit about anything you have to say other than *I'm an asshole and I'm sorry*."

"I'll get your job, bitch…"

"Ooh, look at me all scared and everything. And if you want it, you can *have* my job. That way, I don't get the pleasure of meeting people like *you*. Be good to that boy."

She walked back to the desk and apprised one of the nurses. "Jane, will you call me when Lance's mother arrives?"

After getting Jane's promise, Sarah walked towards the back of the corridor, her phone at her ear.

"Hi, how's everything going?"

"Very well. She likes your breast milk whether you're at the other end or not," Naji answered. "She's slept most of the night."

"Good. I guess I've turned into one of those mothers who has to check in five times an hour."

"I guess you have. We're fine, love. How's the job?"

"First time back in two months, but it's like I never left. It's been fun at times and frustrating at times. Welcome to life in the E.R."

"You'll get back into it. Nikolai is sleeping, poor guy."

"He hasn't been getting much rest. I need to look at our schedule."

"We have a new baby, Sarah. *Nobody*'s getting much rest. That's okay, she'll be in college before we know it."

"Bite your tongue, wench! All right, I won't bug you again. I'll see you in about three hours."

She was still smiling when she clicked off the call and a voice behind her startled her.

"That's a pretty amazing smile."

Leo. Sarah turned and her stomach jumped a little. Damn, he was still incredibly handsome. No other human male had ever turned her on like he had. *Still did. No, stop, it isn't going to happen*.

"Hi, Leo. Yeah, I'm the woman now that everyone runs from in case she pulls out a wallet full of baby photos."

"You look happy."

"I am." Pausing, she searched his face and thought that he looked tired. "How are *you*?"

"Good. Good. Missing the friendship we'd started."

"Ah, Leo, so do I. I was a woman who had her exact life planned out. You were a part of that plan, but we both know that life doesn't take orders, does it? I don't regret my daughter, I am grateful every moment for her, but I do regret that we got derailed."

"Perhaps we can put things back on track."

No, that she couldn't do, no matter how much she would like it. How could she delicately turn him down again?

"Leo…"

He put his hands up at her hesitation. "I get it, I'm not pushing. Could we at least go back to working together without the awkwardness?"

"That, I would love. Yes, please."

He smiled and melted her resolve a little bit. *Maybe someday?* Even Sarah didn't rule out the possibility that she might love again someday.

They parted with safe comments and she hurried back to see if Lance's mother had arrived. She had, and Sarah put the idea in her mind that she needed to keep an eye on her husband. She could see in the woman's eyes that she understood and an unspoken agreement was made.

The rest of the night went quietly, Sarah feeling overtired and ready to get home to see Zia, to hold her, to smell her, and then to crash until morning. These second shifts were tough, leaving no real day and no real night to appreciate.

About half an hour before she was due to head home, her cell phone chimed. There were no patients waiting at that point, so she slid it out of her pocket. *Naji.* She smiled.

"Hey, Naj…" Sarah began casually.

"Sarah, you need to get home. Something's going on with the baby."

"*What?* What's going on?" Sarah paused long enough to call out to Jane.

"I have an emergency at home, Jane, I have to go!"

Jane gave her an understanding nod.

Sarah grabbed her bag and headed for the door. "Naji, what's happening?"

"I don't know. She's kind of...listless, all the sudden. I finished bathing her and she had a bottle, but when I picked her up to put her in her crib, she went limp, kind of like she fainted, only she's conscious." Naji sounded panicked. "Sarah, I don't know what to do!"

"Where's Nikolai?"

"He went to the museum because they had a late shipment of artifacts coming in. Sarah..."

"Naj, calm down. I'm on my way home right now. Answer me, she's still breathing okay, right?"

"Yeah, she seems to be."

"Okay, just lay her on the sofa and stay with her. I'm going to call Park right away. Just be there for her, Naj."

"Of course, but hurry. I'm scared, Sarah."

"It's all right."

It had to be! Quickly redialing, aware that in France, Park would be asleep, Sarah knew there was no choice.

A deep male voice answered.

"Bas, it's Sarah. I need to speak to Park immediately."

Bas got it right away and handed the phone to his mate. Sarah heard a sigh and then Park answered.

"Sweetie, what's wrong?"

"It's Zia. I went back to work tonight because everything was going so well. Naji called a few moments ago and said that she just went catatonic suddenly. She isn't in respiratory distress, but Naji says she can't rouse her."

"And to date there have been no problems? No flags?"

"None."

"All right. Get home and call me as soon as you arrive. Sarah, try not to worry. She's first blood, remember the history."

Sarah hung up without responding.

Because she did remember the history. Recent history. Things were changing, even for the first bloods.

Nothing was black and white anymore. First bloods had always thought that they were immune to any disease, but this past winter had shown them that there was a time in the past, and then this year, when a virus had the ability to wipe the vampires off the earth forever. It nearly had.

So Park reminding her that her baby was vampire and would be okay because of that, didn't bring the reassurance she thought it would. All Sarah needed now was to get home and help her child.

Naji kept her hand on Zia's belly, taking a breath with each one that the child drew, terrified that it would stop, and knew that if it did, she had no idea what to do to help her. She'd had no medical training of any kind, ever, so she prayed, *prayed*, that Sarah would get home as soon as possible.

She moved her other hand to Zia's forehead. Was she warm? Did the baby have a fever? One thing that she had noticed earlier today was that the baby's coloring was off, a little too pale this afternoon, but she hadn't thought that it meant anything. Was that a critical mistake?

The door burst open and Sarah raced through, stopped by nothing until she dropped onto her knees and looked at her two week old daughter.

"Naj, how's she doing?"

"No change. Sarah, I need to tell you that I noticed she looked pale this afternoon. I didn't mention it because I didn't think it was important, but now I think it was a symptom and if I'd just told you…"

"Slow down, slow down. This isn't your fault. She's sick, but I think it's much bigger than that. I'm afraid that it has to do with her father, and if that's the case, only first blood vampires can help her. Let me get a baseline for Park. Will you go get the thermometer and my med kit?"

Once Naji left, Sarah leaned closer, running her finger around the baby's chin.

"Hey, little lady, what are you doing? Hmmm?"

She could tell by the warmth of Zia's skin and the slight moisture that her temperature was up, and Naji was right...her color was poor.

Sarah's heart ached at even the thought that her baby was ill. She dialed Park.

"Hey, I'm home, she's still unresponsive. Her eyes are open, but she isn't reacting to my voice or any stimulus. Respiration appears normal but her color is pale and I think that her temperature is high. Naji's getting my med kit now."

"I'm actually preparing to board Koen's plane."

"Park it's fully daytime there!"

"Yeah, I can tell by that big bright thing in the sky," Park teased. "But I'm hoping that with minimal exposure, I can get to the jet without too much trouble. I don't want to wait for sundown."

"Just be careful."

"Sarah, we need to get some vampire blood into her again, but this time I'm sending Olivia. As fourth generation, her blood may have more potent properties and give Zia a fighting chance against whatever the hell is happening. She's coming from Seattle so she'll be there in about 5 hours. Just make sure that we have samples before and after she feeds Zia. We're going to need that lab at your hospital tonight."

"That won't be a problem. I'll take all the samples and have everything ready. Park, what do I do if she stops..."

Sarah couldn't say it.

"I don't have an answer. Obviously, use your medical training just as if she were human. Other than that, for now, we don't know why she's ill. I'm sorry, Sarah, I wish I could help more."

Sarah had been trying to keep it together, work this problem like she would for any patient, but this wasn't any patient, it was her child.

"Just get here," she finally said on a sob.

"I will, honey." Park's voice was full of emotion too as she rang off.

Sarah wiped the pooling tears when Naji returned. "Thanks. Now, we get to work."

Sarah took all the samples and readings for Park to use in her diagnosis before she lay down with Zia on her bed. She didn't sleep, but she curled up next to her unmoving baby, a hand on her chest just as Naji had done earlier, the other holding her close.

What worried Sarah most was that she couldn't feel her anymore. Until now, Zia would touch her mind, send her thoughts to her mother, but now there was nothing at all. That precious connection was gone.

Closing her eyes, Sarah squeezed them tight to push out the tears that lingered. "Oh, Mies, we need you."

Only the sound of the curtains lifting on the breeze from open balcony doors answered.

Naji touched Sarah's shoulder. "Sarah, Olivia's here."

Sarah startled awake, shocked that she'd fallen asleep. She pushed upright and looked Zia over, relieved that she seemed no worse, sad to see that she was no better.

"Thank God," she whispered, grateful that the baby still breathed. She'd been terrified that she might not be. Bundling her gently into her arms, she slid off the bed.

"Sarah, darling," Olivia said, coming up to kiss her on the cheek. "This is your little sweetheart? Come, let's do this right away and help her feel better."

Seating herself on the sofa, Olivia pulled a silver dagger with an ornate handle out of a small bag. She slit her wrist and drained hot red blood into a glass. Naji transferred the blood to a baby bottle, screwed on a nipple with the hole enlarged, and handed the bottle to Sarah.

"Thank you, ladies." Sarah turned to Zia. "I don't know how I'm going to get this down you. I hate to consider having to do a transfusion."

"That won't be necessary. Just get some on her tongue, Sarah. You know what it can do."

After only a brief hesitation, Sarah held Zia's mouth open and tipped the bottle up to drip several drops of Olivia's blood onto her tongue.

All three women focused on Zia, eyes unmoving.

247

Within moments, the baby began to cough. Her eyes opened and she coughed louder.

"She's weak, but she's responding," Sarah said, relief almost overwhelming as she repeated the dose of Olivia's vampire blood. Each small dose improved the child.

Once she'd taken in the entire four ounces that Olivia had drained, her cheeks pink, her eyes clear, she was alert, and in the dead silence of the apartment, her gurgle of glee seemed to bounce off the walls.

"Oh, God," Sarah murmured.

Abruptly, she surged from her seat while Olivia held Zia. She pushed out onto the balcony and sucked in the night air. Now, with her baby okay, at least for the moment, suddenly *Sarah* couldn't breathe. She began to hyperventilate and, although she knew that she was, she couldn't stop it.

A hand on her wrist was familiar, a soft *impression* from Olivia almost instantly calmed her runaway respiration and pounding heartbeat.

"She's okay."

"For now," Sarah amended. "But thank you. I can't ever convey the depth of my gratitude for what you've done for us."

"I saved a precious child, and that is a gift to me. What good are the tricks and magics I can do if I cannot do something good with them?"

"I've always felt that same way."

"I'm still a new first blood, as you know. You helped me when I needed it and I am honored to have the chance to return the favor. She's beautiful, your daughter."

"Thank you. I can't imagine my life without her and she's really only been in it for two weeks. If I lose her, I don't know how I'll manage."

"You won't. We'll do our circle thing where Tamesine controls the universe using our combined talents. You saw how well that works."

"I did, in that instance. I don't imagine that I'm too high on the universe's list for miracles, but Zia must be. I hope that she is protected."

"I know she is. So, she was fathered by a vampire whose body we found in the ice cave in Siberia? Damn, the impossible things that *are* possible these days. I wish I could have met him. He had to be extraordinary."

"He was. No one will ever replace him. I'd thought that perhaps once I get past the pain of his loss, and raising our daughter without him, I might find someone again, but I don't believe that I ever will. I told that damn vampire that I didn't want to have sex with him because who in the world could satisfy me after that. And I was right."

"I'm certain that he was an amazing lover, but I think it is also because you were falling in love with him."

"Nothing has more power over our lives."

"Never a truer word, my friend. Let's go get that girl of yours, I'll bring in some food and booze, and we'll catch up. I have to tell you how things are going with my grandmother."

"How *are* Dez and Zach?"

"Horny as hell! As her newfound granddaughter, it's embarrassing, and for a vampire to say that, well, you know *Dez*."

After several crazy days in Siberia, and several *even crazier* ones in the Orientales, she did.

Walking back from the balcony and seeing Zia in Naji's arms, Zia wiggling, Sarah felt as if someone had lifted the weight of the world from her. It didn't mean that everything was all right, but it meant that, for now, her daughter was well and happy and for that moment in time, so was she.

Park arrived two hours later from France, tired, but ready to do anything necessary to find out what was wrong with this new vampire child and to help her become healthy and remain safe.

She hugged Naji, Olivia and Sarah and took the baby immediately afterward. Holding her up, she perused Zia, intending to do an examination, but then that toothless baby smile got to her.

"You, young lady, you just want all the attention, yeah? That's why you're doing this, little imp. We'll figure out how and we'll just put a stop to it, right, *mama*?"

"Right. Please, oh, please, I hope that you are right."

"You have the samples? Okay. Ladies, we leave you to do some research. If you need us, just give one of us a call. Sarah, I have a car waiting."

After a last hug and kiss for Zia, Sarah followed Park out of the building to get into a local taxicab.

"We have a few hours before sun up to do this. I should have stayed when she was born. Cherise knew something wasn't right, but she seemed so good. We will find out what is going on, Sarah, I promise."

"We have to."

Two hours of blood and DNA tests later, Park and Sarah sat at a work bench in the lab.

"You're sure?"

Park nodded. "Sarah, it's right here. It's fact. At least we know now why Crezia has been sick. What Cherise sensed. To my knowledge, she is something that has never been before."

"A vampire/human hybrid. Incomplete DNA. I...I don't know where to start. What does it mean for her? Is she always going to be sick? Will she be mortal? Or is this a death sentence? How am I going to save my daughter, Park?"

"Sarah, this is new. I don't have any answers yet, but I'll find out. One thing that we do know is that vampire blood helps her. I don't know exactly how it's doing it, but I will. So, if nothing else, we can manage her symptoms using blood meals. You know that most vampire children live completely human lives until they're mature, but it's apparent that all bets are off when it comes to Zia. It doesn't have to be a bad thing, and no, Sarah, I don't think that this means a death sentence."

"Fine. We'll keep blood on hand in the refrigerator for her, but if it turns out that she needs a steadier supply, I'll make the move to France. It all has to be about Zia now."

"I agree. Don't despair, Sarah. You're a woman of science, and we'll approach your little girl's health logically and work the problem until we solve it. I'm just grateful we know what we're working against now."

Sighing, Sarah nodded. "Let's go tell the others."

Nikolai walked into the apartment, stunned to see the two vampire women. "What's going on?"

Park, who he had said goodbye to two weeks ago, motioned him over.

"We have something to tell you, Nikolai. Why don't you have a seat?"

Park lounged casually on the sofa. Olivia squealed, jumped up and gave him a tight hug, with Naji watching closely. Sarah sat on the loveseat with the baby asleep in her arms.

Hugging Olivia back, not quite as tightly, Nikolai joined Naji. "What is it?"

Naji slid her fingers into his as Sarah answered.

"The baby had another episode last night, Nikolai. A bad one. I called Park, who came right away, but not before she sent for Olivia. Olivia gave Zia some of her blood and probably saved her life. She's okay now, though, so you needn't worry."

His eyes on the sleeping baby, he shook his head. "Why didn't you call me?"

"We kind of had our hands full just figuring out how to help her. Plus, we didn't know how it would end and decided, for that moment, to protect you until we knew what was wrong. I'm sorry, it wasn't the best call. Forgive me."

Sarah stood and handed the baby to him.

Nikolai held Zia tenderly, his fingers moving along her body. "But she's okay?"

"Mostly," Park answered. "But we found out why she's sick. It's because of the bizarre nature of her birth and that of the shared body. Nik, here is the unexpected result of blood tests we did tonight. This child should have the DNA

251

of her father and her mother, but, strangely, she has your human DNA as well."

"What? How can she have DNA from 3 people? My body had been converted to first blood. It wasn't my DNA anymore, it was Mies's, right?"

"It would seem so, but apparently not completely. I mean, obviously, your body retained *your* genetic code, too, and now we have this odd complication. I guess it isn't much of a stretch considering the physical circumstances under which Mies and Sarah made love. What the unusual DNA is doing, though, is keeping this child from being either fully human or fully vampire. Even though she would not complete her conversion to vampire until maturity, she still needs her complete vampire genetic code to be intact. And it isn't."

"So what does this mean for her?"

"Nothing like this has ever happened before, and frankly, I have no idea. We think we've determined, though, that she can live perfectly well with frequent vampire blood draws. Unfortunately, she needs the blood now, unlike most first blood children who won't begin blood meals until they reach maturity. Until I can find a way to help Crezia find her *first blood* balance, that's how it must be."

"But she's okay for now? She isn't in any danger?"

Park hesitated before she answered. "I can't really say that. I have nothing to base this on, but my instincts are that the blood will keep her stable at this time. There is just no precedent for knowing her future. I can only tell you that we will do anything we can to make sure that she stays well."

"Then that is what we must do." Nikolai looked down at the baby sleeping comfortably in his arms. "Anything."

Sixteen

Nikolai refused to go to work.

"I will wait for her to arrive. You haven't finished a full week of work since you went back. Sarah, they're going to fire you."

"They understand. They know that I have a sick child and they're pretty lenient."

"Go to work, I will wait until Olivia arrives, feed Zia, and take her to the museum with me. All I'm doing tonight is paperwork and she can stay in her bouncer until I'm finished."

"You're sure?"

"I'm sure. You need to let me help more. Naji won't be home until Thursday and you can't do everything yourself."

"You're right. I'll go in tonight, then, but I'm taking tomorrow off so that you can get in a full shift too."

"I'll take that deal."

Sarah kissed Crezia on both cheeks and received a little giggle followed by two wildly waving plump arms.

The blood meals were working better than Park had expected. With one blood meal per week, just eight ounces, Zia was thriving. Her appetite was healthy, her coloring and activity level back to normal, and the spiritual connection with all three of her parents had heightened.

Sarah was beyond grateful for the support of the first blood community. Olivia came once a week to leave blood for the meals, and usually stayed to spend time in Boston. She had become a close friend with the three grateful parents. Park kept in touch every other day, pleased that her idea had worked, but Sarah could tell…she was also still concerned for Zia's future.

"Have a good night, babycakes. Bye, Nik, I'll stop by and pick her up after I'm done."

Nikolai took Zia from Sarah as he shot her an urgent glance.

Sarah grabbed her bag. "Yes, I know, I'll be late. Being a mother has made me less reliable."

"Get," Nikolai barked, his smile big.

"Later gators," she called back as she headed down the stairs.

"Holy shit, mama's on time tonight!"

"Funny, Tracy, I would laugh, but I'm too busy preparing to save lives."

"Funny, I've been doing that all summer while you've been baking that cute little bun."

"I'm sorry, but I'm back now. By way of penance, what would you like me to do?"

"Umm, rub my feet?"

"How about I hire a big sexy man to do that for you?"

"God, yes, please. My feet kill me after an all-nighter. Not *this* night, of course, it's one of the quietest we've had in a long time."

"How about I go get you some chocolate?"

"Twist my arm."

Sarah left her bag in the dressing room and headed down the long corridor to the coffee counter. As she fished coins from her lab coat pocket, she sighed a happy sigh.

This felt nice, finally getting back to normal, to a job she loved, to a peaceful, serene home, and to sharing the love and care of her own child. It would be nice if it could all remain calm for a little while.

Xavier was coming soon to see her daughter. His fascination with first blood children derived from the fact that in all of his centuries alive, he'd only seen three until the crazy rash of births over the past few years.

The coins dropped into the machine and began to dispense the first of two hot chocolates.

Xavier. *Normal?* Not quite. But when his visit was over, she and her two friends would settle down to live their lives as humans did, day to day, year after year, to allow Zia to have some type of normal life. It was just such a simple desire. Once she converted, all *normal* would be gone forever, but she'd be there for Zia's future.

"I wouldn't miss it," she whispered to the walls that didn't care. It was a promise, though, to her daughter and the memory of her father.

Tracy and Sarah had finished their second cups of hot chocolate when the overhead speaker came on.

"Trauma level 1, e.t.a. 5 minutes."

Without delay, they headed to the trauma bay where a team of nurses were already donning face masks and gowns.

"What do we have?" Sarah asked the head trauma nurse as she and Tracy began the same prep.

"Skydiving accident. Chute didn't open. Thirty-six year old male. He's really messed up."

"God," Tracy murmured.

"Dr. Sato and a respiratory anesthesiologist are on the way."

Sarah nodded. "We've got him until they arrive."

Once the chopper landed, the emergency team wheeled the gurney in while apprising the waiting trauma staff of his stats.

"He's unresponsive, had 2 rounds of acls, no shocks, pupils 6 and fixed, sats in the 60's, he is in svt," the EMT barked.

Trauma care wasn't Sarah's specialty, although she was completely confident of her ability to help any patient, regardless of the injury. All she and Tracy needed to do was assess and stabilize him until the trauma surgeon arrived in the bay shortly.

He was tubed, with fluids wide open, levo and epi running, but his injuries were extensive. Within minutes, Sarah and Tracy had done all that they could for the man.

Waiting for Dr. Sato, Sarah laid a hand on the man's cheek, aware that he was well past any act of comfort, but her natural empathy made her try. There was nothing else they could do for him now; there was no doubt that he would go into surgery immediately, but even the top trauma surgeon on the east coast may not be able to help someone who fell from the sky.

Dark blonde hair covered with dirt and blood had pulled loose from a leather tie and covered part of his face. She gently pulled the dirty sticky strands away. His face hadn't been injured in the fall, which was a miracle considering the speed at which he would have hit the hard earth. She noticed that he was handsome, with lines around his mouth that indicated he smiled and laughed a lot.

This was the hard part about her job, watching someone fight and lose their life. She thought about who he had been, the life that he'd lived, things he might have accomplished, things left undone. And how painful it would be for the people who loved him if he didn't make it.

Footfalls and loud voices let her know that Dr. Sato and his team had arrived.

Sarah and Tracy filled them in on all they needed to know, wished them luck, and left the area now that the full trauma team was present.

Tracy shook her head. "I can't imagine jumping out of an airplane, then the moment that you discover that your chute won't open, you know that you aren't likely to survive. What goes through your mind in a case like that?"

"Death comes to everyone at some time. Sky diving just makes the possibility a little more likely."

"Ooh, doctor, a fatalist today?"

"No. Maybe a little. I feel bad for his family."

"Yeah. He's really gorgeous. Paula said that she thinks he's a celebrity, but I didn't recognize him. Did you?"

"No, but I wouldn't know anyone in this area, celebrity or not. I hope he makes it, though."

Tracy sighed. "Yeah."

Twenty minutes later, after assuring a little girl that her mommy was fine, Sarah's shift was finished, and she made her way back to the doctor's locker room. As she finished putting her personal items in her locker, Tracy came through the door sighing.

"I am ready to drop into bed for *sixty* hours!"

As she pulled her lab coat off, Tracy lifted her hair to retighten her pony tail. "Did you hear? That skydiver? He didn't make it. His lungs had collapsed, he had massive internal bleeding, and he went into arrest on the table."

"I'm really sorry to hear that."

"Yeah. Joe told me that he was some important environmental activist and he was jumping for a charity with six other people. The others got down safely, but *his* chute failed to open."

"Death doesn't discriminate. It's sad, though, that a man's life is over in the middle of it."

"I know. Whew, okay, I'm out of here. Even though I'm beat, I think I'll swing into *Shay's* for a cocktail. Care to join me?"

"I'd love to, Trace, but I need to stop at the museum and get the baby. Nik is keeping her with him until I arrive."

"Ah, okay. See you this weekend."

"We'll do it all over again."

The locker room empty now, Sarah looked at the padded bench near the wall and almost went over to lie down for a few minutes. It seemed like the more energy her adorable little brat got, the less she had.

"There's a correlation," she commented, well aware what that was.

Her bag slipped onto her shoulder, the taxi already ordered, she stepped into the corridor. Her mind was spinning on the events of the night, as they often were after a shift. The skydiver. How sad. She took a moment to wish him a safe journey as he passed from this life, to acknowledge him.

"Sleep well in the cradle of the stars. Your journey is over, it's time to rest," she whispered. It was important to her to never become the type of doctor that sees her patients as a *number* or the *next in line*. So taking the time

257

to say a sincere goodbye to the man who'd lost his life tonight felt like the honorable thing to do.

There, she'd kept her humanity intact.

Now, though, she had her own life to continue. She needed to get to the museum to relieve Nikolai who had been off-the-charts supportive since all of this craziness with Mies had begun. She wished that she could do something really special for him.

"The man deserves a medal," she said out loud as she passed the ground floor and continued to the basement level. "Or a car."

That was it, she'd buy him a car. Now that she was back to work, and all three of them shared the rent on the apartment, she could afford to do that for him.

Things were going so well. She would admit, for the first time in a long time, she felt relaxed and happy. There were a lot of reasons that she was, but mostly, it was because everything seemed uncomplicated right now.

They wouldn't stay that way, she knew it, but for this moment in time, she really was living, mostly, as she'd hoped to.

Her taxi arrived and Sarah gratefully dropped onto the back seat.

In the morgue at Mass-Gen

Jasper was the only forensic technician on duty right now, and he had to get the case file started on the accident vic from trauma before he could get his dinner. It shouldn't take long, he didn't have to establish the file for the police…this was obviously a tragic accident.

He'd gotten up late tonight and didn't have time to get anything to eat before he left for work. Now, though, he was starving.

He lifted the sheet and scanned the big man.

"Come on, buddy. Let's you and me get this done fast, deal? We both got somewhere to be. Now me, I have this roast beef sandwich with mashed potatoes waiting for me.

258

There's this pretty little Latino girl that likes to sneak me an extra-large portion when I get to the cafeteria before her shift ends. I'd like to make that tonight."

Jasper liked to talk to his patients while he worked. Not only did it take some of the loneliness out of the job, but he liked to think he might give them some solace…keep them company while they headed out to wherever the hell they might end up next.

"Jasper!"

He jumped when the booming voice called his name from just behind him.

"Damn, Bill Bailey, don't I tell you not to sneak up on me in here? Some freaking day some stiff is gonna start talking to me and I won't know the difference. What?"

"Got a homicide. Takes precedence over that one. Put it in storage."

With a deep sigh, Jasper looked at the guy he'd already uncovered. "Guess you ain't my next dance partner, buddy. We'll still get that waltz later."

Pulling the sheet back over him, Jasper wheeled the table into the storage room kept at a cool 37 degrees to preserve the bodies. The freezer unit, the next room, dropped to 19 degrees if they needed to put the stiffs on ice.

"See ya," he called out as he closed the door.

He was so cold. Why the hell was he suddenly so cold? Temperature was not a problem on the spiritual plane, and physical discomfort just didn't exist.

So why the fuck was he so cold?

He tried to move his hand, but it stayed still. It should have been no effort at all to push upright and stand, but that didn't happen either.

This felt wrong…*and oddly familiar.* Were they messing with him again? Only recently had he been able to purge her memory and find peace in this place where peace was supposed to be the great reward once life moved beyond the corporeal. Dead, like he had been for thousands of years when gauged by earthly standards. Those earthly standards, though, did not apply here.

Using both arms, he pushed against a hard surface that felt frigid and metallic. Metallic? *There was nothing metallic in this realm! There was only one conclusion…he was no longer in the realm of spirits!*

Cold, and pain, that was what struck him first. The darkness, the physical awareness, weight, sound, nothing familiar at all. He tried to reach someone…someone who had been there once, who would help him to know where he was and what he was meant to do.

Niko, are you there? Niko, I need your help once again. If you are there, answer me. Niko?

No answer came. Mies pushed against the darkness, pushed through his mind, searched, reached. He was alone. Wherever they placed him this time, he was alone in this body and unprepared. All he wanted now was to scream at them and tell them they had no right to use him like this.

Not only did they hurt him, they hurt everyone who came into contact with him. He would never forget her, her pain. Or Nikolai, who he prayed had gotten his body and life back.

No! He would not be their pawn anymore. Mies was vampire and the universe had to answer for their choices this time.

All his ranting and raving left him exactly where he was when he woke, almost too cold to move.

But move he must. It felt like Lake Baikal, beneath the ice, when he lifted himself, bound to a human body for the first time in millennia, and the dying Nikolai, from certain death.

So, calling upon his first blood talents, upon the magics that moved through his spirit amulet, Mies gathered the momentum of power and magic and thrust it forth. He would see and know where he was!

Darkness was all that he could see at first, but light began to bleed through, so dim it barely registered. Once

Mies convinced his eyelids to stay open, he tried to scan the space that he occupied.

Musty, thick smells assaulted him, stale air and odd odors that made no sense. He couldn't identify anything, where he was, what he saw, what he smelled, what he felt.

Force, then, he thought, *force through it all. You can do anything. Nothing is more powerful than a first blood vampire.*

Determination and magics brought through his amulet let him bring the body upright, something moved and fell, and when he could see a few moments later, just barely in the small light available in the room, he realized it was a sheet that covered this body. It was naked and hurt worse than anything he'd ever known.

Luckily, he could feel this body trying to heal itself, but he had already known by this point that he was inside another human body and that he was alive again. And he could also tell that this body was far more severely damaged than Nikolai's had been. Niko had been close to dying when they'd merged, but Mies knew that the one who had been born to *this* one, *had*.

It took all of his strength to throw the sheet off and push from the table, but he had no control over the legs, so he crashed to the floor.

The floor was colder yet, and he began to shiver, aware that he was bare in a big freezing room with no idea where he was. This would take all of his concentration, but he was an ancient vampire with godlike powers, he could do this, he could fucking stand. He *would* fucking stand!

After lying there helpless for a period of time he did not know, Mies got his feet under him, but with no balance, he tumbled back over.

A squeak caught his attention and he looked to his right as a large heavy door opened, letting warmth and light flood into the dark and cold room.

A heavy-set, pale-skinned man entered, casually whistling, keys jingling in his hands. The man's eyes flew wide when he saw the corpse sitting up.

"Holy shit!" Jasper yelled, backing up, scrambling to step back from a man he *knew* was dead and should not be sitting up.

"No!" Mies yelled, reaching out. *"A little help here?"*

He smiled when he realized that he sounded like Nikolai.

When Mies spoke, Jasper, even more shocked, looked into his eyes and Mies began the compulsion. He was going to need this man's aid.

"You sure you're all right now?" Jasper asked, perched on the edge of the metal table beside the man who he had been prepared to cut up just an hour ago.

"As much as I can be," Mies answered, as he ate a strange sandwich with some kind of dark meat that didn't taste familiar. It didn't matter, it was succulent. At this moment, in this new body, his hunger was insatiable.

"Jasper, can you order a car for me?"

"Uh, you mean a taxi?"

He processed the word and finally recognized what Jasper meant. "Taxi? Yes, a hired car, that will do."

Memory of how this went with Nikolai's body in Siberia sharpened once he'd realized he was in another living body. He needed to get somewhere safe, take a good blood meal, and let his lifeforce convert this body to accept him.

God, he didn't want to go through this again!

And yet joy invaded his heart…he wanted, *needed,* to see Sarah.

Two hours later, Jasper left behind, properly wiped, no memory of him or the body he'd left in, Mies had finished a desperately needed blood meal. In a quiet alley, the small man who had donated the blood meal sat confused as his memory was wiped too.

Mies had found a basement room with no windows so that he could shelter safely from daylight, because he knew that this body was going to crash.

He'd looked into a mirror before he left the morgue at the alien face in the glass, the features unknown, a thick length of honey-colored hair long and filthy.

Sprawled wide on a smelly mattress, legs and arms stretched out, naked, sweating, trying to manage intense pain that stretched from the strange hair color to the big toes, he knew that he would not leave this sodden mattress for some time.

Seventeen

Xavier's visit had gone well. The man's vivacious attitude towards life infused everyone in the apartment, and that included the tiny baby girl already showing cognizance well beyond that of normal babies her age.

His devotion to Zia startled Sarah. In her nearly one hundred years in his household, they had never had a child. Honestly, if someone had asked her before, she would have been of the opinion that Xavier wouldn't be interested in children, they'd be too annoying or of no use to him.

In that case, she couldn't have been more wrong. He was so enamored with Zia, he wouldn't let anyone take her from him. Later, when Naji tried to carry her into the kitchen to give her some of Olivia's stored blood, he'd *tsk'd* that she'd prefer his *fresh* blood and that she would drink from him.

"The lass has good taste, ya know she does. My blood will fix her right up."

"Thank you, Xavier," Sarah said. There was no other response, Xavier wouldn't believe anything other than his own opinion. But she truly enjoyed watching his connection to her daughter, particularly since they may be living with him someday.

The baby had been content in his arms all night, but with no warning, she suddenly bucked and pulled away from him. Naji and Nikolai were startled by the abrupt change.

"I swear I didn't pinch the little thing," Xavier explained as he tried to calm her down. When she began an ear-splitting wail, he handed her to her mother immediately.

"It's at this point that the child needs her mother."

"It's at this point that everyone would agree with you. I don't mind, but it's strange how she went from being happy to inconsolable."

"I swear to ya, I didn't pinch her," Xavier teased. "But the next time I might, just to have a cause for this, ya little troublemaker."

Bouncing her in her arms, and doing the silly whispering thing that Park had taught her, Sarah was frustrated that she didn't know why Zia continued to cry, but it was softer now, with just a few hiccups.

"She's calming down. I'll go feed her and try to put her to bed. We keep her on a daylight schedule rather than the one vampires keep."

Xavier nodded, a finger curled around Zia's. "Aye, it's a good idea, especially since the day that she'll lose the sun forever is within spittin' distance."

Sarah sighed and carried Zia to their bedroom, slid her shirt off, and held her to her breast. Yes, the day would come when her daughter could no longer be in daylight, if her nature advanced like it should. Xavier was right that it would be here in the blink of an eye. *The days fly faster than we notice*, Sarah thought, never more aware of that than recently.

Because there was still a chance that Zia may never convert naturally, Sarah had decided to delay conversion until she knew. She looked into the small face lying against her chest. Zia's eyes were still wet, her cheeks streaked, her mouth attached with a death grip on Sarah's nipple. She stared, though, intense for a baby, unflinchingly, in spite of the tears. It was unnerving.

For several long moments, her hand moving in large caressing circles on the baby's head, Sarah returned the stare. It seemed like...was she...?

"What are you trying to tell me, Zia? I sense that you are, but I don't know what it is. I'm sorry, baby girl, but your mama is a normal human woman and I can't read you like a vampire could."

Once Zia finished feeding, Sarah dressed and carried her to the changing station to get her into her jammies. When she tried to put the baby down, Zia clung to her, those little watery eyes still on Sarah's, unwavering.

"I'll check your diaper, sweetheart, but if that's clean, I really don't know what else to do."

Twenty minutes later, Sarah joined the others in the living room. "She's down. I have no idea what happened, but I feel like I missed something that a vampire mother wouldn't have."

"Ya did fine, Sarah. Babies cry. They're the least rational thing on the earth."

Sarah shook her head. "No, I really feel that something specific was on her mind, that she needed me to know, but can't express it. It's disturbing to know that such a new baby is that aware."

"Ye'll get used to it. Come, join us for this American dinner. I'll be leavin' tomorrow as soon as the sun drops. Thank ya for welcomin' me to spend time with yer bairn."

"I hope you still feel that way if I have to come home to France."

Xavier surprised her by standing, formally pulling his shirt down to tidy up his appearance, and bowing.

"Lass, ya have to have known that ya would always be welcome in me home. I have a love for ya, child, like I would my own, if I had one. And that tyke ya made, she'll just bring joy to the dwellin', so both of ya come home whenever ya need to." He turned to Nikolai and Naji.

"Ye're both welcome too. That wee girl will need those who loves her as these years gather behind her."

Tears welled in Sarah's eyes now, too, because she'd never seen Xavier this gracious before. She'd always known, though, that he had it in him.

Bowing, too, she moved closer to give him a hug.

It took a few seconds for him to give in and accept the hug, but once he did, his arms moved around Sarah's slight body and he found himself holding on. This type of intimacy was much harder for him than a quick fuck with a pretty woman. This intimacy required emotions that Xavier had always had trouble with. Even with his brother, even after all of these centuries, hugging did not come naturally.

Still, though, this young woman had been born and raised in his household and he held her in high regard, cherished her even, surprised that tonight he'd told her so. It was in his heart and on his mind as he held the special baby that he did indeed hope would come to his keep outside of Paris.

As abruptly as Zia's change in manner, Xavier pushed Sarah away gently and said the one thing that was on his mind. "All right, now, who wants to get stinkin' bombed?"

When it was time to say goodbye, Sarah didn't want to do it. Xavier's visit had been alternately an incredible blast of excitement, frustration, moments of sadness, and moments of illumination. She would miss him deeply, and she told him so.

"Xavier, I believe that I will take you up on your offer to return to Paris when the baby needs to."

He tweaked a curl and slid a hand along her cheek.

"Ah, lass, ye're adventure to live like a normal human didn't work out too well, did it?"

"No, but I wouldn't change anything. Mies was unforeseen and I'd never wish away the time we had. You already know that the greatest moment of my life was giving birth to that little girl. I'm okay. Really."

"I think ya are. Ya always have been. Call me if ya need me."

He kissed her gently on each cheek and headed for the stairwell.

Sighing with contentment, Sarah needed to see her baby right now.

In a dirty basement downtown

267

Mies slept most of the next two days and nights. After the blood meal, he'd crashed for 24 hours, rose to find a second meal, and then crashed again. This body was converting completely, unlike what had happened with Nikolai. The only occupant this time, the DNA level changes were more brutal, and once they were completed, the damage repairs were almost as bad. He took the time to wonder who had been in this body before him? Had he been salvageable, like Niko? And if so, why had he been allowed to die? Was he a thief?

I'll come back, he whispered to the powers that made these awful choices, *if you have robbed an innocent man of his life.*

In this case, though, it seemed that they had fixed the problem they'd created last time by leaving the body's current lifeforce in residence. Even if Mies insisted on vacating, there was no one to come home *to* the body.

He groaned and his mind returned to the one subject he couldn't get off his mind. *Sarah.*

For a brief moment, he'd considered sending a spiritual message out to see if he could reach her, but that was crazy and selfish. If he *could* reach her, he would just frighten her. A lovely, vital woman, Sarah would have moved on by now, might *be* with someone else. He had no right to even consider interrupting her life again. She'd made it clear that she'd never wanted to be with a vampire.

It was only decent, though, to check on her and be certain that she was happy, that she'd suffered no ill effects from her time with him. *Wasn't it?*

For hours after convincing himself that he must check on Sarah's welfare, he still felt total exhaustion, but he couldn't sleep. He ran his hands over the chest of his new body, half again larger than it had been when he awakened, continued downward, and, yes, as expected, everything was enhanced, his fingers moving over the head of an excited cock. Things worked as they should, and a growling stomach showed that it wasn't just the impressive organ that was hungry for attention. He needed food now, and a lot of it.

Since sleep didn't happen, Mies pushed up from the mattress and slid on the pale blue scrubs he'd liberated from the hospital. They barely fit over the big muscles now, so, first, he needed to find clothes, then food, then a generous amount of alcohol.

Maybe with enough booze, he could forget about Sarah for a while. That left him with the awesome task of wondering about whatever the fuck *they* wanted from him now.

Dressed in the same type of clothes he'd worn when he shared Nikolai's body, tight jeans and a short-sleeved tee shirt, he compelled a taxicab driver to take him to Sarah's apartment. He didn't have to worry that she might see him, of course, because she would never know it was him. She'd just notice a stranger looking at her. As lovely as she was, he knew that he certainly wouldn't be the first strange man to stare at her.

After he sent the taxi on its way, he stood across the street from her apartment for twenty minutes hoping that she might come or go from the building and he could get a long, desperately desired peek at her. When she didn't show up, he walked over to the building and sat on the steps, at war with his better nature whether he should go up and introduce himself to her or not.

When the heavy door opened minutes later, Mies glanced back hopefully. Disappointed, he slid aside to allow an elderly woman room to come down the steps. She struggled with the first one, so he shot up to help her, and when it became apparent that even with help, the steps were too difficult, he gently swung her up and carried her down to set her carefully on the sidewalk.

Her watery eyes glistened as she looked up into his.

"Ooh, thank you, young man. These old bones lock up and refuse to do what I tell them to do. Stairs are not an old person's friend."

"I am happy to assist."

She moved her eyes over his body and smiled. "There are many times when I wish I were thirty or forty years younger. Your girl is a lucky girl. Are you waiting for her?"

"I am waiting to see someone, but she is not my girl."

"Forgive me for the assumption. I just can't imagine that they aren't standing in line."

"I would want only this one woman, but I do not believe that I am what she wants."

The woman's eyebrows went up. "You'd be surprised what a woman wants. It's always best to ask. Who is your girl?"

"Her name is Sarah."

"Sarah? Oh, honey, she hasn't lived here in months."

"She is gone?"

Nodding, the woman removed a foldable cane from a bag on her arm. "I'm sorry, but yes. All I know is that she moved to an apartment somewhere on the waterfront."

Mies bowed. "Thank you. Do you need further aid?"

"No. I'm just going two doors down to spend the night with an old friend. Well, good luck with finding Sarah."

She turned to go and stopped.

"I just remembered. She moved in with some guy. I think he had just gotten a new job at a museum."

"Do you remember which one?"

"Um, it's near the waterfront too, I think. That's all I can tell you."

"You've been exceptional, madam. I'm forever grateful."

This made her blush. "I hope you find her and I hope she accepts you. You would be good for her. Sarah's a sweet girl, but she needs to get out and raise a little hell. Life flies. You can't waste a moment of it, trust me on this."

She touched Mies's hand with a naughty gleam in her eye. "I imagine *you* would be fun to raise some hell with."

Mies laughed for the first time since he'd returned.

"*You*, madam, must have raised some in your time."

With her cane now extended, offering the support she needed, the woman turned away from Mies and looked back as she shook her booty. She grinned. "If the walls could talk! Good luck, young man."

Continuing the same direction that she faced, she slowly made her way down the sidewalk, just as she'd told Mies, two apartment buildings away.

Mies pulled out the cell phone he'd taken from a wireless shop downtown and dialed for a taxi. When it arrived, he slid into the seat.

"Where to, buddy?" The cab driver asked.

"I don't know. I'm looking for a museum located on the waterfront, but I don't know what kind. Would you know of any that you might be able to take me to?"

"Uh, yeah, I've got a map on my phone. Let's see. Locally, there's a children's museum, and an art museum. Looks pretty fancy. I haven't been to those. Hey, you might like the nautical museum. You can actually tour a big old cargo ship. And, oh, yeah, there's a new museum, I don't think it's open yet. Looks like it deals with foreign antiquities. Yeah, that isn't my scene."

Foreign antiquities. Perhaps Nikolai? Yes, that might be it.

"That last museum you mentioned, the new one, take me there please."

"Sure do, buddy."

Nikolai. Mies fell back against the worn seat and closed his eyes. Their connection was like nothing else in this world. They knew each other better than any other person could ever know someone else because they'd lived inside each other. As much as Mies wanted to see Sarah, he needed to also be sure that Nikolai had made it through without damage. If so, even if he hadn't made the choice to do this, Mies would have a lot to atone for.

The taxi stopped and the driver twisted to face Mies.

"It's right over there. That red brick building with the glass front."

Mies nodded, used compulsion to thank the driver and send him away with the belief that he'd had no fare tonight.

Multicolored lights glittered all along the pier, a magical setting, as Mies walked up aged wooden planks to cross a bridge meant to mimic an old fashioned rope bridge. Once he reached the door, he hesitated. Should he just observe

Nikolai and Sarah to confirm whether they were okay? Or should he let them know that he had returned?

He'd already decided that Sarah would be better off if he didn't interfere with the life she built now. Would it be okay, though, to tell Nikolai? The answer came when he entered the building moments later and saw Nikolai, distant, above him on a cantilevered floor actively engaging with a tall bald-headed man.

No, Mies decided that it would be best for everyone if he just disappeared once he made sure that those who knew him last time were all right. He could use compulsion to find out if their lives had continued undamaged.

The tall man walked away, and Mies watched as Nikolai glanced down at him.

"That shipment is delayed by at least two weeks, and it's half of the exhibit for room 4 for the open house. Can you see what you can do to replace it? Thanks, Brad."

Nikolai shook his head. Managing a museum this large with all of its political and financial obligations was exhausting. With all of the drama recently at home, Nikolai thought that he could sleep for a week if he had the chance.

He wouldn't, of course, with Sarah back to work, Naji traveling a great deal for a client, and all child care had to be handled by the three of them. A babysitter would be wonderful, but that couldn't happen, not with this child's parentage. They would manage, of that he had no doubt, details just had to be worked out.

Only a few more things needed attention so that he could get home to relieve Sarah, who had accepted an emergency overnight shift at the hospital. Thank God MGH had been so understanding about the strange schedule she needed.

He turned to follow Brad back to the offices when movement in the lobby caught his eyes. A big man he did not recognize stood just inside the doors.

Moving to the stairs, he called out. "Sir, excuse me, the museum is not open yet. How did you get in here?"

The man stood ramrod straight, still, his stare unsettling. As Nikolai approached him, he had an odd sensation, almost dizziness, but it cleared quickly. He stared back into the unusual pale green shade of the man's eyes.

Nikolai scanned and assessed the intruder; tall, model handsome face, ripped body, probably had a different gorgeous girl each night. He didn't know the man, nothing about his face was familiar. And yet, *something* was.

"The door was open," the guy said suddenly, his voice graveled, deep, commanding. "It looked interesting so I just wandered in."

"Huh. I apologize, that door should have been locked. I'll see to it, but you'll have to leave."

"I will. You run this place?"

"I am the administrative manager, so yes, I do."

"It's nice. You enjoy the job?"

Nikolai was getting strange vibes from the stranger. The man didn't seem inclined to leave, and now he was asking personal questions.

Nikolai answered abruptly this time, his voice coldly polite. "I do, very much. Sir, let me escort you out."

When he placed his hand on the man's shoulder, the dizziness he felt earlier returned, stronger, enough to nearly lose consciousness. His head cleared again and he pushed away from the man, who had steadied him with both of his hands on Nikolai's shoulders.

Nikolai pulled away. "Please, you need you go. I have a security team if you don't."

"I'll go. Can you look at me?"

Nikolai had walked over to the door and opened it as an urgent invitation for the guy to go through it when the question surprised him and he looked right up into the guy's eyes. "What do you want?"

Heat infused Nikolai's head. *What was happening?*

The stranger walked right up to Nikolai and stood in the opening of the museum. "Tell me if you're happy, if everything in your life is normal and you are satisfied with where you are in your life."

What the hell was this? He would call security, although, in truth, his security right now consisted of two gentlemen in their sixties long retired from the air force. He could easily imagine this giant of a man putting them down with no effort, so he would try once more to get the crazy asshole out of the museum without a confrontation.

"I don't know who you are, but if you want me to have you arrested for trespassing, just stay the fuck right where you are." Nikolai lifted his cell phone from his pocket and held it up to show he was ready to dial 911.

Holding his breath, Nikolai waited for the man to go or to punch him. When the stranger smiled and just walked out, Nikolai was surprised and relieved. He closed and locked the door quickly, talking to himself like he used to do when he was alone in his cabin in Siberia.

"What an odd duck. I guess you get all kinds, but that one needs some major mental healthcare. Wait until Sarah hears about this one."

Mies walked away from the newly erected building designed with an attractive blend of old architecture and new.

He'd learned something tonight that affected his plan to make sure that Nikolai and Sarah were well and happy.

Nikolai could not be compelled. Not by *him* anyway. Mies had tried to use compulsion to make Nikolai answer a direct question about his life, then he would have used compulsion to erase that question and any memory of the man who wandered into the museum after dark. In all of his centuries before, and even in this one, Mies had never met a human who could not be compelled.

"It had to be the merge. Somehow, it made him immune to my forced control. God, I depended on that skill to check on him and Sarah."

That wouldn't happen now. If he couldn't control their memories, it was too risky.

Using air displacement, Mies was on a sandy beach a good mile from the museum in minutes. Nikolai had looked well, and up until he'd frightened Niko, Mies had thought that Niko seemed quite content. What concerned him was that Mies knew that Nikolai had never had any intention of staying in Boston, and yet he had. Why? In spite of the situation, he still needed to check on Sarah. Surely, she would not be immune.

He'd do it quickly, carefully attempt compulsion on her, testing her before he asked his questions, and disappear afterward regardless of the outcome, no harm, no foul.

His best lead now to finding Sarah was Nikolai. He would follow him home tonight, stay near, and eventually, Nikolai would lead him to Sarah.

Leaving plenty of documents in a stack of bottomless paperwork, Nikolai squeezed the bridge of his nose with two fingers trying to get his tired eyes to focus. Glancing at the clock, he groaned. Midnight. He needed to get home.

When he got to the main entrance of the building, which was vacant now, he locked it, set the alarm, and stepped out to a waiting taxi.

"Home," he whispered, and the driver pulled out. Ivan was on most nights in this part of town and often drove Nikolai to his apartment building.

Ivan looked at Nikolai in the rearview mirror. "Another long one," he commented.

"Yep. I just want a quiet room and a warm bed for three weeks and I'll be good as new. Gonna have to talk to our little baby mama."

Strangely, because it wasn't common, Ivan knew a lot about Nikolai's life. They'd ridden together so often over the past three months, Ivan almost considered them friends. He'd met Nikolai's roommates, certainly two of the most beautiful women in Boston, and he'd told Nikolai so, and been invited for tea.

They pulled up outside the apartment building, Nikolai lifted his satchel, paid Ivan, and left. Ivan backed up to turn around. Out of the corner of his eye, he noticed a figure, a big man, standing across the street. Partially hidden by the cascading branch of an ornamental tree, the man stood, solid, unmoving, as he watched Nikolai enter the building.

Ivan pulled around the corner and did a little watching of his own. The man didn't move the entire time he was there. Fifteen minutes later, Ivan got a fare and had to leave, but as he pulled out, he decided that something wasn't right there.

Tomorrow night, he would let Nikolai know that someone might be watching him.

Mies watched Nikolai walk into the nice apartment building right on the waterfront. He could see that those properties were expensive, which meant that, financially, Nikolai must be doing well. That was good news. Financial stability was essential to human happiness.

Feeling much better after a long buffet meal at a downtown restaurant and a blood meal from a healthy-sized young man, Mies still tired easily. Eventually, he moved a park bench from deeper in the park and relaxed into it. Like many things in this century, he marveled at how it was made, smooth metal curved into the perfect shape for the human body. Flower designs molded into it gave it an artistic as well as functional feature. He approved, and particularly, his sore ass did.

Tonight, he'd sped all over town using his own vampire power. Tomorrow, he would get a car. Nikolai's knowledge of how to drive had been easy to assimilate, and although he'd never actually gotten behind the steering wheel of a car, he didn't think it would be a difficult task for him. If he was going to be here for very long, indefinitely, or perhaps forever, then this he must be able to do.

Sliding his hand into a small bag he carried, he pulled out a pack of chocolate bars, something he'd become addicted to when he was here before. He was halfway through the pack when he heard a laugh and recognized the voice. *Sarah's voice.*

Mies's head shot up. She laughed as Nikolai and she walked from the building. Nikolai handed her a satchel, kissed her on the cheek, and walked back inside as she got into a taxi that had just pulled up.

Nikolai and Sarah were living together? What did that mean? Were they *together...lovers?*

He had trouble wrapping his mind around the idea. It made an odd sort of sense. If it were true, if they were together and in love, he should be happy for them.

He should be happy for them. So why did his chest feel as if the universe had crushed it? Where did that lump come from that blocked his throat? And, what the fuck, vampires didn't get headaches, but between his eyes the pressure and pain was so great, he tried to force it away by holding his hands against his temples.

If Sarah and Nikolai had sought solace in each other's arms, it was natural and perfect. No one else would have understood what they'd been through, so it was good. *It was good.*

His heart was breaking. Mies realized now that it wasn't just Nikolai, but *any* man she would be with would have hurt. He was in love with Sarah, and to see the woman he wanted more than this second chance at life with someone else made him die inside.

It didn't matter, it didn't change anything. Now, he knew with absolute certainty, she was happy, she was with Nikolai, who was the finest man Mies had ever known, and she was living her desired human life.

He would go from here. After sheltering the coming day in his basement, Mies would go to the other side of the world and begin anew. Why they'd sent him here again, he might never know. But *this* part of his mission, he got it. Move on. *This* part of his new life was finished.

Several hours remained until he had to worry about sunrise, which was good since Mies could not use his air displacement to get back downtown to safety. He walked the entire distance at almost normal human speed because he was trying so hard to convince himself that he was okay with how things were. He didn't have the heart, the interest, or the energy to fight for speed.

Eighteen

"I missed you all so much!" Naji yelled as she came through the door, her bags abandoned in the hallway, her arms out. Nikolai reached her first, with Sarah right behind him carrying Zia.

Naji hugged and kissed Nikolai, then pushed him away to reach for the baby.

"Ooh, gimme, gimme. Damn, she's grown up so much in the past week!" Zia giggled as Naji hugged her close. "I don't think I can go away again! How could I walk away from this little princess, eh, love?"

Nikolai brought Naji's bags inside and closed the door.

"We're heading to *Shay's* to celebrate your return. Olivia is here to give us some blood and she's going to babysit. Go get gussied up, I know you want to clean up after the flight, and we'll go."

"Yes, yes, I've missed all of you, but I *can go* for a fine dinner and *Shay's* yummy cocktails. I'll be twenty minutes!"

Naji was ready exactly twenty minutes later, sparkling in sequins and shiny eye shadow. She stopped to give Nikolai a deep kiss before they headed out.

Throwing an arm over Sarah's shoulder, Naji hugged her. "I don't feel like I gave my man a proper hello. Later, he'll *really* get an idea how much I missed him!"

Nikolai nodded, a sly smile warning her that he was going to hold her to that.

They piled into a taxi and Naji pulled out a flask studded with shiny stones.

"Pretty," Sarah commented.

"Pretty? My darling, you don't realize that these stones aren't rhinestones or crystals, they're diamonds! Right? My client has way too much money to burn. Luckily, I lit a match for him. Not like that, Nik, he just liked my skills. Artistic skills, baby, artistic skills!"

Sarah pushed herself against the left side of the taxi while Naji apologized to Nikolai in case he misunderstood her comment about lighting her client's fire.

Shay's stood on the very edge of the waterfront and featured a deck that went right up to the waterline. The outdoor tables were romantic, spaced apart for privacy, with its own bar.

"We have reservations for the deck tonight."

"You spoil me, my friends, thank you. I promise I'm home for at least the next six weeks and I'll pitch in and make up for my absence. I meant it, leaving that baby is awful. She's growing so quickly."

"I know. Sometimes I stop and stare at her just to see if I can tell what's going to change next."

Naji reached for the menu as she looked into Sarah's eyes. "She's prettier every day."

"I agree. We'll be fighting the boys off too soon. Ah, Nikolai, get that waiter over here right away, I'm dying for a Hurricane Splash!"

They perused the menus, ordered four entrees to share, and several cocktails unique only to *Shay's.*

Halfway through the meal, relaxed, her arm over the back of her chair, Sarah laughed at one of Naji's many tales of extreme wealth and overindulgence. Her head back, she pushed a long curl over her ear as she glanced toward the water. Her eyes caught a man seated at the bar, his back to her, but she could see part of his profile.

The profile, the hair, the width of his back, all looked familiar. She kept staring.

Naji started another story, Nikolai leaned in to hear every word, but Sarah was still distracted by the man. She'd been watching him as she listened to Naji and once, when he turned his face a little more to the left, she caught a better glimpse of it.

Why was the face familiar, and why did it disturb her?

In a lightning flash, it came to her, and, shocked, she set her glass back down on the table.

She knew now why he looked so familiar. The man looked like the injured environmental activist she'd cared for in the hospital before he died. *Just* like him!

"Sarah?" Nikolai interrupted her thoughts. "What has your attention?"

She couldn't stop herself, she had to see him closer.

"Um, I'm not sure. A patient, maybe. I'll be right back."

Pushing back her chair, Sarah started to get up when Naji handed her a bright pink cocktail.

"Don't go empty handed."

"Thanks. I'll see you in a second."

Naji grabbed Nikolai's face and Sarah grinned because she knew that they wouldn't miss her.

The man she approached still had his back to her, a strong muscular back clad in a champagne-colored dress shirt that clearly showed his exceptional shape. Close enough now to him, she caught his attention, and he turned toward her, pastel green eyes so light they nearly glowed landed on her and locked like a guided missile. He looked shocked to see her.

"Hi," Sarah said, her voice barely above a whisper because it was true, this man looked exactly like the skydiver who died several nights ago.

"Hello," he responded, his voice deep, sensual. It went right to her core, surprising her further.

"Uh, forgive me, but you look exactly like someone else that I know."

"I get that all the time," he said.

Sarah took a quick sip of her drink, something to break the tension, because she could feel her libido spike.

"I doubt that. You're not…common."

"That might be one of the nicest things anyone has ever said to me. And I've been around for a long time."

With no warning, Sarah's head felt light, she knew that her balance wavered. What he said, it was something that Mies had said to her, and for some reason, the comment hit her emotions hard.

Mies couldn't believe she was here, in front of him, her respiration rapid, so he knew that, even in this body, she responded to his sensuality. The feeling's that they'd felt from the first time they met in the hospital were coming again. He really shouldn't have come here.

He'd followed them, then raced to the bar before they were seated, and tried to remain obscure. He shouldn't have. But gods in the heavens, now that she was this near, how had he ever thought that he could see her again and then leave her?

When she started to weave and her eyes slammed shut, without thinking about it, he reached for her.

And destroyed his hard-won resolve. Now, with his hands on her, he was lost. She opened her eyes then, looked into his, and grabbed his forearms. Everything he felt for her was in his eyes, he knew it was, nothing could have stopped the swell of pure love and need for her now that they touched. And he knew that she saw it all.

The dizziness subsided the moment he touched her, and her eyes dropped to where his fingers curled around her upper arms, supporting her, heating her. They gripped her like they would never let her go. What the hell was this?

Sarah looked up into the face of a stranger that she knew should be dead, only this time, there was something there, something that she *did* recognize, something that couldn't be…

"Mies?"

The man dropped his hands. "I'm sorry, miss, what was that?"

The dizziness returned and he moved closer.

"Are you all right? I think you've had too much to drink. Perhaps you should sit down?"

"No, I haven't had too much to drink. Who are you?"

"My name's, uh, Steve."

Sarah stared at him. Eyes the color of moss, long hair tied back like Mies had worn his, but a buttery soft mass that framed a hard square jaw. A handsome face, but it wasn't Mies. She remembered then, that the face she thought of as Mies's hadn't been his either.

There was something here, something not right, and so perfectly right at the same time. She pulled him closer; knew, somehow, that the name was wrong, that it didn't fit, that it wasn't who he was.

"No, it isn't. I see someone who cannot be here. Not just the man you were in this body, but another man who couldn't be here either. Neither of you, and yet..."

Desperation took over and she looked into the eyes again and saw beyond. *Mies...she knew it now.*

"Mies, oh, my God..."

The big hands moved from her arms to her face, curving along both cheeks, covering the side of her head. Heat licked into her skin and she felt tingling in her eyes, chest, and below.

"This was a mistake," he said.

Moments later, he made another. He leaned down and kissed her on the lips, the tiniest of pressure, before his tongue slid into her mouth to touch hers and he pulled back. "Forgive me."

He was gone.

Sarah, shocked, couldn't move.

Naji nipped Nikolai's ear, and started to whisper something when she felt him pull away.

"Son of a bitch!" he yelled. "That's the crazy-ass guy who tried to break into the museum the other night!"

Nikolai shot out of his seat, raced towards the bar as he saw the stranger kiss Sarah and then disappear off the edge of the deck. Fast. *Vampire fast.*

"Sarah!"

282

He watched her head swivel to face him, her eyes bathed in glistening moisture, unmoving.

"It was Mies."

"What?"

"That man, I saw him, last Sunday night, in the E.R. and he died. Just now, I looked into his eyes, and I saw Mies. I'm not crazy, Nik!"

Nikolai's gaze went to the beach below the deck, poorly lit, but he knew that he wouldn't find him anyway.

Nodding, he brushed away tears that had slid onto her cheeks. "I know you're not. That's the guy who I saw in the lobby of the museum. Remember the guy I told you was staring at me? He said that the door was unlocked. I'm an idiot! The door wasn't unlocked. Not to a vampire."

Both dropped onto barstools, their eyes downcast, searching the air in thought. Slowly, Sarah lifted her head.

"He's back."

Nikolai couldn't believe what they were thinking, what she was saying, and yet through all that, he knew the truth.

"My God, he is. Mies has been sent again."

Shaking her head, Sarah held out her hands. "But why would he take off? Why wouldn't he let us know that he was back? He has to know we missed him and need him. Nik, what the hell is going on?"

"I'm in the dark house, too, Sarah. I…I don't know. Now that I think about it, at the museum, I felt something when I got near him, a kind of dizziness. Then when I touched him, something odd. I think my body recognized him, Sarah. I think he knew that. Wait!"

Hanging on that word, she did, as she watched Nikolai sort something in his mind…a memory, she thought.

"He asked me if I was happy, if my life was normal. I didn't know at the time, but now I understand. He tried to compel me to forget him, but it didn't work. Of course not, this body knew him. I know what he's doing. He's trying to be magnanimous. He's giving us the normal, happy, supernatural-free life that he thinks you want."

"Running away from me? Leaving us? He thinks he's doing this for *us*?"

"I'm sure of it."

283

"I don't understand. He has to know that we need him. I need him." The moisture welled again. "His daughter needs him."

"Sweetheart, he can't know about Zia. If he did, I don't think all the powers in the universe could stop him from coming to her."

"Why wouldn't he do that for me? How can he not know that I fell hard for his sorry vampire ass?"

The bartender, who'd been wiping some glasses nearby, looked up when she said the word vampire.

Nikolai grinned. "She just means all men are blood-suckers. You know women."

Sarah wiped her nose with a napkin and squinted at Nikolai. "Really? Misogynist crap?"

"Sorry." He took Sarah's hand and led her away from the curious bartender. "You said the V word, not me."

"I did? I'm sorry, I'm a bit distraught. We have to find him."

"We'll find him."

Naji stood as they approached the table when she saw Sarah's face. "Have you been crying? Nik, what did that man do to her?"

"Family, let's finish our dinner, then we'll go back to the apartment to discuss the fact that Mies is back."

His eyes on Naji when he said that, he watched as understanding hit.

"Oh," she said and sat down wordlessly.

"Yes, this is not the place."

"I can't eat," Sarah said, looking at the empty plate in front of her that was waiting for some of the special food in four large dishes in the center of the table.

Naji picked up Sarah's plate and began to fill it. "You'll eat, and you'll enjoy it. We don't let men spoil our good times, and Mies is, essentially, just a man. So, we are going to celebrate my return and then we'll talk about the suddenly *not* AWOL you-know-what."

Coughing on a laugh, Sarah hesitated, shook her head, picked up her fork and stabbed a thin piece of beef.

"You never fail to amaze me. You guys are right, we'll find him. I am so hungry, and I don't want to ruin this."

"Right. So we enjoy our dinner, and then we deal with all the crazy vampire shit when we get home." Naji filled her plate even higher than Sarah's.

Miles from *Shay's*, Mies slowed to a walk, the sand cool under his bare feet. He'd slung his shoes over his shoulder, laces tied, and rolled up the bottom of his jeans to walk in the low surf.

He wanted her. Worse than ever. Why would they put him back here when all he would do was hurt her? Two nights ago he'd decided to leave this country and he wished he had done so. Once he established a friendship with a vampire in this century, he would send that vampire to remove Mies from her and Nikolai's memories, and fix this forever.

"Live happily and love deeply, Sarah," he whispered.

For the next hour he wandered along the gentle waters as the cold waves kissed his feet. This new body had adapted well, had adjusted to the power moving through it, and was ready to resume life as a vampire. Mies was ready, after all of the pain that last visit created, and the new hurt he'd unwittingly caused tonight to both himself and the woman he loved, to just live again in the new world.

He came upon an area where someone had carved stone seats into the solid rock wall that lined the edge of the water. A big man sat in one, the darkness barely illuminating him, but as Mies moved closer, he didn't need to see him to know that the man was vampire, and first blood as well. The unexpectedness of finding a first blood vampire here left Mies cautious.

The man looked up, eyes glittering in the limited light, and Mies knew that he had been tagged too.

"Good evenin'," the vampire said as Mies approached.

An obvious Scottish accent helped Mies place his origin. He didn't know him, but he doubted he would. It was unlikely anyone from his time had survived the six millennia that had passed since then.

"Good evening." Mies carefully dropped into one of the stone cutouts several feet from the vampire.

"How do ya find yerself on this stretch of lonely beach this night? It's highly unusual to find a first blood in America, let alone two in one place lookin' at the sea."

"Troubles of a long life, but I think you would understand."

The man sighed. "Aye." After a pause, he held out his hand. "I'm Xavier, from Paris."

"Paris?"

"Aye. Not me birthplace, no, but it's where me clan mostly resides. Easier there to maintain anonymity. And where might ya be from sir?"

Mies wasn't ready to declare himself. Truly, he wasn't sure he knew what to declare. He was new and that meant he had to build his world from scratch. So he chose convenience and caution.

"Nick. I travel a great deal, and don't declare one place home."

"That sounds genuinely brilliant. Responsibilities are exhaustin'. I'm here on family duty and now I'm done, so I'm headin' to a pub for some libation before I get back into that tin can. Would ya like to join me?"

It would be good for him to reconnect with a first blood, anything to take his mind from his Sarah. He needed to purge his desire for her.

"Sir, that is exactly what I need."

"I don't know Boston well, but I can't imagine two first bloods can't find a bar or two here. I've a car on the street out there."

Xavier stood. "Shall we go?"

Mies tore his eyes off the beach that led back to *Shay's*, and followed Xavier to his car.

"Och, this city welcomes the visitor. I've had four lovely ladies since I've been here and they've all been *very* hospitable. Ya should choose a pretty blonde and find a place to get together."

"You're right," Mies commented. His head felt too heavy. Both men had partaken liberally of various alcohols since they arrived an hour ago. "Have you ever been in love, Xavier?"

Shaking his head, Xavier finished off a glass of locally brewed beer. "Nay. It's my opinion that no one woman can keep me happy indefinitely."

"That's probably wise. I need to get there."

"I noticed, my friend. Ye're in love and it isn't reciprocated?"

"I don't know. Maybe. She's human and doesn't want anything to do with vampires. I'm trying to stay away from her."

"Ye've a big problem then. This is the real reason I don't stick around long enough to fall in love. I've seen love tear a strong man to pieces, and it's not pretty. By lovin' the way that I do, I've never suffered the pain of loss. One woman moves on and another takes her place."

"You have little respect for women?"

"Ah, *no*, lad! I've a great deal of respect! They're beautiful, all of them, inside and out. Ya know that they are every bit as satisfied afterward as I am. I don't use compulsion for sexual conquests, just to wipe memories when we're finished."

"I'm glad to hear it." Mies raised a glass of Scotch. "You're a good man, Xavier. I would be proud to call you friend."

"Ya can never have too many. To new friends, Nick. If ya ever need a place in France to rest yer head, ye're always welcome at my keep."

"Much appreciated."

After toasting their new friendship, Xavier grinned and raised up his eyebrows. "Now that's what I'm talkin' about. See that little blonde in the corner over there? She's been lookin' at ya for a while. Go get ya some, lad. Nothin' makes a man feel better than buryin' his cock in a fine warm place."

Mies agreed. The blonde Xavier pointed out was indeed fine, but she wasn't what he wanted. He shook his head.

Xavier set his drink down and touched Mies's hand.

"Ya have it bad."

"It may take some time before I can be with a woman again. I'm in love, and I have to get out of this country and leave her behind where she'll make love with another man. What can hurt more?"

Xavier tried to use impression to help his new buddy feel better, but from first blood to first blood, it usually didn't work. Some of the women in his clan had the talent, but he didn't.

"Let's get stinkin' drunk, forget all this shite, and collapse until sundown. Aye?"

"Aye."

When the sun began to rise, it couldn't penetrate the basement room where two first blood males lay passed out. Mies slept, free of dreams and memories, for the first time since he'd returned.

While Mies was using alcohol to numb his pain, Sarah held her baby in her arms as she stood on the balcony of her home watching a rising moon, and sent a prayer to the powers of the earth and sky.

"Bring him to us, please. You brought him to me to give this little girl life, so let us have her father to help guide her. I am not what she needs, not alone, so please, bring him home."

She kissed Crezia's brow. After she carried the child into their bedroom, she eased onto her bed, her usual nightgown abandoned at the foot. In the darkness, she visualized the face that Mies now wore.

Handsome, more so because she saw *him* inside, his touch had started the fire at her core again. For months, she'd had no sexual need, not even battery-powered. Now, strong spasms pushed through her. The need was back, intense, but she didn't want anyone but Mies, in whatever body he'd been placed.

Her mother slept, finally, Zia could feel her rest, her breathing even. Abstract thoughts and ideas assaulted her mind from all the input that came at her daily, but something new, something important, came to her through the air. It traveled along the spiritual plane and reached for her. *Father.* What she knew was that he did not know she waited for him, so she let her mind and spirit wander and reached out to him.

When daylight struck, the household exploded with activity. Naji prepared for work, Sarah had plans to shop for food and needed supplies, Nikolai had folders full of paperwork to do for the museum while he watched Zia, and Olivia watched them all. Leaning against a counter in the kitchen blocked from direct daylight, she sipped a cup of sweet coffee before she went to bed for the day, and sighed. Human life was just too busy. *Ugh!*

"Don't forget the meatballs. They're essential to the dish I'm planning for tomorrow night," Naji reminded Sarah.

"On the list. Have a good day, Naj."

"On the list. I've two big spenders coming in for lunch and to buy art to furnish their 20,000 square foot home they've built on an island somewhere. Yes, I'll have a good day."

Naji was off, Sarah kissed Zia and left. Nikolai fed the baby, gave her Olivia's blood meal, and put her down to sleep. Olivia did the same in the bedroom with no outside exposure.

Nikolai sighed to have everyone out and doing what they needed to do, the baby sleeping, and a chance to do some of his own work. Sometimes, things got just a little too chaotic.

After he pulled out the folders of display items he needed to research and vet, he stopped. Damn it, keeping his mind on his work was impossible. All he could think about was that Mies was out there in an unfamiliar world, trying to leave him and Sarah forever. *Damn it, vicious destiny!*

Zia slept deeply, her mind clear, her goal defined...*find him.* She weaved herself into the spiritual plane, and even at her age, she sent blood in search of blood. Somewhere inside of her she knew that she needed him, so if he was out there in the world, she would find him.

And out in the world, in a dingy basement...

There was something he must do, something waiting for him. Mies was in a hard sleep, this body had been infused with copious amounts of alcohol it still could not manage, but his mind was active and felt something reaching for him, searching and demanding that he...*what?*

What did the thing want? He couldn't identify it, but it came from the spiritual realm across skies laced with treetops. *Treetops?* No, the treetops were a clue...the thing that sought him was earthbound. But he couldn't make sense of it and he couldn't determine who or what reached out to find this displaced vampire. He felt its urgency but it was lost in space. Finally, it tore him from his sleep.

The basement room's dim lighting offered hard shadows in corners along with a musty smell that he'd hated from that first night. Snoring pulled his head around to Xavier, sleeping on a stack of old tarps, stretched out wide, a smile on his face, in as deep a sleep as he himself had been a few moments earlier.

Mies sat on a wood box and watched Xavier. Perhaps that was his best choice. Paris, around the world from Boston, was a safe distance from Sarah and Niko. Tonight he would get the address and leave the city.

It was time to get out and see what this world was really like. With vessels that flew in the sky, no corner of this globe was out of reach. In spite of the emotional trauma, he found he could be excited about seeing the new world.

His head throbbed, which was highly unusual for a vampire, but he knew the problem. Whatever had been prodding at him in sleep was still searching. It would have to try much harder if it wanted to do so. From here on out, Mies was nothing more than a man living his life.

They'd placed him here again, adrift, no idea why or if there was something he was meant to do, so he had only one response to something like it.

"Fuck it," he said out loud.

In the apartment on the waterfront

The baby finished her bottle of Sarah's breast milk, and Nikolai burped her. She'd had Olivia's blood yesterday so she was set to go for almost another week.

"What up, Zia lady?" he said as he lifted her and jiggled her in the air over his head. "Is that my girl?"

She smiled and popped another burp, her hands flailing.

"How are you this beautiful?" he commented as he brought her down and hugged her to him. That moist tiny body against his neck warmed him to his soul. He was deeply in love with this little girl.

No matter what else happened for the rest of his life, he regretted nothing that had led him here, with Sarah, with Naji, and this child that lit up the world. Or his crazy bond with Mies.

Now that it appeared that Mies was back, once they fixed things, the order of the world would be all right again and they would bring him home.

He looked around the room, the big open balcony that brought the daylight in. When Mies moved in with them, they would need a different place.

A strangled gurgle from Zia captured his attention immediately.

"Zia?" he said as he pulled her away to check on her.

She began gagging and struggling for air. He checked to make sure nothing was caught in her throat, and when there wasn't, he headed towards the phone.

Nineteen

"Olivia's blood isn't working anymore. Her system is breaking it down, but it isn't feeding her need for her vampire genome. Sarah, I don't have a cure for this. I don't know what to do to fix it."

Park smoothed Zia's hair off her forehead as she handed the baby back to Nikolai.

Sarah stood, shocked, her eyes searching, her hands clenched. "Um, are you telling me that Zia is dying?"

"I'm telling you that she's really sick and I don't know how to help her. You know how healing vampire blood is, and if it doesn't do it, I don't have another option. Olivia is fourth generation and we know that her blood is the most powerful we've ever seen, so I really don't have any idea at this time what else to try. It doesn't mean that I'll give up, of course I won't, but I have no answers right now."

Park didn't, but Sarah did. She turned and walked out onto the balcony to watch the waves. She had to find Mies.

Light footsteps let Sarah know that Park was behind her. "I'm going to do a power circle with Tamesine, Eillia, and Olivia," she announced. "Sarah, the universe created the situation that brought this child to you, so I must believe that it wants her here and if that's the case, we will be able to help her. She's meant to be, my friend, and the universe has a way of looking after those that destiny smiles upon."

"Have them find her father."

"I am not sure how that would help."

"He's here. In Boston. Park, they sent him back here in a different body, but he's here and I think he can help us."

"You've seen him?"

"We all have."

"Then why isn't he with you and Zia?"

Sarah shook her head as she leaned against the railing, her arms folded. "I think *he* thinks he's being noble. Letting me go to live my human life that I once told him I wanted. Holy shit that seems so long ago now. He doesn't know about Crezia."

"Then that is exactly what we must do. I've believed all along that *his* blood can fix this. *Her* blood will recognize *his*. The unique blending should repair the missing DNA. If I'm right, she's going to be perfectly okay, Sarah."

"Then that's our priority, we have to find him."

"I'll get the women here as soon as possible."

"Thank you, Park. In the meantime, I'm going out on the street and look for Mies. Naji will stay with Zia while the rest of us search for him."

"Count me in."

"Gladly."

Park suddenly stopped in her tracks. "Wait! Sometimes I can be so dense! I may be able to trace him. My skills are poor compared with Eillia's but it's worth a try. Blood recognizes blood. We can use Zia's blood to search for blood."

"Now?"

"Yes, Sarah, now! I just need the baby with me in a quiet room."

"Bless you, Park!"

In the basement

"I'm leavin' in two days and if ya want, ye're welcome to travel with me."

Mies held out a hand to Xavier. "I would like to, sir, until I can get on my feet again."

"It's nothin'. Do ya know where Logan International is?"

"I'll find it. I've been through it to get here, but that was some time ago."

"Okay, then. Just after dark in two days."

"I won't be late. Good luck with the women until then."

"Och, who needs luck with this kind of equipment, eh?"

Xavier cupped his crotch and grinned before he disappeared.

"What a wild man. I guess I'll be going to Paris."

Time for food, but thankfully this city had a lot of excellent restaurants. Afterward, he needed to find some clothes for the journey overseas.

In the apartment on the waterfront

"Nik, how's Zia?"

"She's not doing well, Sarah. Look how rough she's breathing. Is she in pain?"

Park did a quick examination. Dropping her stethoscope to fall back against her chest, she shook her head. "I don't think so, but she isn't comfortable, either. We have an idea that may help her. Nikolai, go get Naji. If this works out, she can watch the baby while we go and get her father."

He did as asked while Sarah picked her daughter up and held her to her chest. "No!"

Sarah didn't mean that word to bounce so loudly off the walls, so she repeated it seconds later. "No. We take her with us. You think she's well enough to travel?"

"I think it's all right," Park answered.

Desperation had crept into Sarah's eyes, Park recognized the emotion. When she had nearly lost her son, she had almost literally moved heaven and earth to save him. Even now, she had moments when the memory of how close she had come to dying, taking her unborn child with her, brought a split-second of fear that she had to tamp down. Usually, she had to go and hold him when that happened.

294

"Let's begin."

Lying in Sarah's arms, Zia sneezed, then sneezed again, her eyes watering as Sarah tried to wipe the moisture away.

Pain and worry marred Sarah's face.

"We'll find him," Park promised.

Lifting the baby from Sarah, Park laid her on the thick Aubusson rug and knelt beside her. Placing her right hand on Crezia's forehead, she buried her left one beneath the baby's clothes against her chest.

"Heart and mind," Park whispered to Sarah, who watched, rapt and silent.

Immediately, things changed. Park was surprised to feel Crezia's lifeforce move beside her own. The child was actively seeking her father, too, but she did not have the talent to achieve the link. She knew, though, that Park did.

Park reached inside the child to touch her blood, shared by either parent, but Sarah's would be overtaken by the legacy of her father. Everything first blood was dominant.

While Park was concerned that the baby would be frightened, she need not have been. This child knew what they were doing, wanted and needed the help, was grateful for it. Fully merged now with the blood, Park let it take her, track her across the city, through high-rises and past soul after soul until it charged downward, weaved through air trapped by more tall buildings, below ground to a sheltering basement. *There.*

Park heard the baby's emotional sigh, relief…here was blood, here was family, father, hope.

Wrapped up with the baby Crezia's lifeforce, traveling through the spiritual plane, Park could see that if they did not find him, this child would not survive. Her genetic makeup was too fractured, only her father's vampire blood could save her. She sent the message in feelings that the child could understand that they would find him and he would know her, he would love her, and he would fix her. Fear faded and the child clung to the promise.

Park would *not* fail this child.

She gently eased them back from the spiritual plane and Park noticed that the baby stayed right alongside her.

As a child, Crezia should not be this advanced at spirit walking. It would be very interesting to see where her talent lie as she became a young woman.

Once back from the inward journey, Park, awake and able to speak, smiled. "We've got him."

"He's not here. It looks like he might have been, but he's gone now. I don't see any sign that he might return."

"Park, we have to do another trace."

"Sarah," Nikolai, voice of reason, interjected. "He has to be near. I'm going to go up and check out the area. There are a lot of nice restaurants around here."

"No, we have to…"

Sarah had carried Zia into this dank basement where Mies had been traced less than an hour ago, and he wasn't here. God. *He wasn't here!*

The situation was desperate, and she was losing hope that they would find him in time.

Dizziness made her sway and she reach out to hold onto Nikolai as she closed her eyes. What the hell was this? An image came tearing through her mind.

"Sarah, are you okay?"

"I don't know. I'm receiving an image…*it's*…"

Suddenly the image was clear.

It was him…the man from the trauma bay who Mies now occupied.

"I see him," she shouted.

"Who? Mies?" Park asked.

"Yes. I don't know how." Sarah's head spun again, and something reached toward her. "The baby…she's tuned into him. I guess since he's so close, but she's got him. He's in Sailor's Square, there's a festival of some kind. Music, partiers, food…it's loud, and he's surrounded by people. He looks uncomfortable. We have to get there. Sailor's Square is just half a block up that way."

"Move," Nikolai said.

Naji took Zia from Sarah's arms. "Just in case you get dizzy going up the stairs."

"Thanks, Naj."

While Naji made sure the baby was safe, Nikolai followed Sarah up the stairs, anticipating the same possibility that Naji had, ready to catch her if she were dizzy again.

Out the door, Nikolai led Sarah down the street, Park and Naji just behind them.

Half a block away

"*Jason! Jason!*"

"Oh, my God, you're alive!"

"Jason! Over here!"

People were all over him, yelling that name. They were so certain that he was this Jason Stone that Mies assumed must have been the man who'd walked in this body before him.

Easily thirty people collected around him as he tried to get something to eat at this little street fair. Several tugged at him and he used compulsion to send them away, but he couldn't control this many at once. It was unfortunate for Mies, but it appeared that this Jason must have been a celebrity. A great many people seemed to know him and like him.

Mies came to the quick conclusion that he must have been a good man. He took a moment to feel sorrow for the lost life, but then he had to figure out how to get out of here without causing a bigger riot than he already was. Denying that he was not this Jason Stone hadn't worked, they continued to call out to him.

He felt overwhelmed, ready to push past them all and kick up his speed beyond human level enough that they could not follow him when. Moments before he was ready, scanning the crowds, he saw Sarah at the edge of the group, her eyes boring into his. Her face was drawn, worried, ecstatic, all at once, and it stopped him in his

297

tracks. Beside her stood Nikolai, a hand on her arm, a primal claim on *that* which was his. Mies must honor that claim.

He wanted to run, just turn and disappear, but he knew that he had to face them. Slowly, he began to make his way through the crowd, but every step he pushed towards them, he thought how much it hurt to see them together, and how much he loved them both.

"Jason, you remember me?" a pretty blonde girl screamed at him as she grabbed his arm. He shook her off and continued.

Two large men tried to block his way, cameras raised, snapping photo after photo, but he'd had enough and waved a hand to freeze them in place. Let them figure the fuck out what had happened to them later.

The crowd started to push in on him again as he cleared a small group of people and stopped just a few feet from Sarah and Nikolai.

"Jason Stone?" Sarah said to Mies, trying to sound serious.

Mies couldn't look away from her. "You know I'm not."

"Seems like an awful lot of admirers if you're not."

She really didn't know what else to say now that she was face to face with him, grateful that something had gone right and he was here now when he was so desperately needed.

Finally, he shifted his gaze to Nikolai. "Hello, my old friend. I am glad to see you as well."

"I'm shocked to see *you*." Nikolai moved forward and embraced Mies. "And happy to. We must talk about how that happened sometime."

Mies felt pressure behind his eyes and held onto Nikolai tighter than he should. "Perhaps."

Nikolai stepped back and Mies's eyes went back to Sarah. "You look lovely, of course."

"Thank you. That would mean more if you hadn't run away from me."

In the background, people were still calling for "Jason" and trying to push closer.

Park stepped forward and Mies noticed her for the first time. "We need to seek privacy," she stated.

Sarah nodded. "We do. Mies, will you come with us? I am in need of your help and it is a life and death situation."

He nodded as he assessed Park, aware that she was first blood. His eyes landed on Naji next, now revealed behind Nikolai with a bundle held to her chest. He bowed and smiled to both women.

"Come with me," he said, and led them from the crowds into an ice cream shop fifty feet away.

Only six people were inside, including two employees, so he sent them away. Closing the door, he waved a hand to spell it. The magic would keep anyone from attempting to enter, and, reluctantly, turned to Sarah and Nikolai.

He needed to acknowledge their relationship to show his support and avoid the awkwardness they all felt. "I am pleased that you and Nikolai are together."

Sarah had been reaching for the bundle in Naji's arms when her head swiveled to face him. "What?"

That had been impossibly hard to say the first time, he wasn't sure he could repeat it and remain convincing. "I merely…"

"I heard what you said, Mies. What makes you think that we are together?"

"I saw you two enter the same apartment. Do you not live together?"

"Yes, we do. So does Naji. The three of us share an apartment. Four."

Mies felt like his chest might explode. "You're not together?"

"That is *my* man you're talking about, vampire." Naji stepped closer to Nikolai and he put an arm around her.

"I'm in love with Naji, Mies. Sarah and I are good friends. I love her, but like a sister. You know that."

"I've been gone a long time and I thought that things had changed. I am sorry for the misunderstanding."

"Mies, I need to speak with you." Sarah turned to the others. "Could we have the room?"

"Yes, I think that's wise." Park moved towards the door, Nikolai behind her, then Naji, but not before Sarah stopped her and took the bundle.

Alone now, Mies focused on the bundle that was now moving. "It's a child."

Sarah hesitated, pulled the blanket away, and presented Zia to him. "Yours."

She wanted to shock him. She wanted him to know how wrong he was to run from her, to think that she was finished with him, to take away their chance to be together.

His eyes on the baby, Mies didn't move. "What?"

"Your daughter. Mine. What we made during the few days before you had to go."

"You're Shoazan."

"Aren't you quick? Mies, we need to sit and you need to hear me."

"Yes, yes, I am yours," he promised as he led Sarah and the baby to a wide blue and white vinyl-covered bench. He couldn't stop staring at the child who stared back at him. He recognized his eyes in her. Not these, the ones in the new body, but *his* eyes.

"May I hold her?"

"I would love to see you do so."

Carefully, Sarah handed Zia over to her father for the first time.

"She looks like you," he said without looking up.

"And you. She's a perfect blend of the two of us."

He held his daughter away from him at first to look at her, then folded her near his chest close enough to smell her hair.

"I couldn't know."

Sarah's eyes softened. "I know you couldn't. First things first, Mies. I need to tell you, Zia is sick."

His face buried in the baby's hair, a hand curved around her head, he lifted his head. "Vampire children do not get sick."

"This one is."

His expression changed to panic. "Is it the virus?"

"No! Mies, we've controlled that, so no. It's her odd parentage. She has DNA from you, from me, and from

Nikolai. Her vampire genome is unable to bond completely with her. We've kept her well for a while using blood meals, but they've stopped working. Park thinks that only your blood can heal her, blood to blood. Her incomplete vampire DNA needs your blood to finish the bond. Will you help us?"

"Sarah…" His eyes moved to Sarah's, his pain apparent, devotion apparent. "Of course. I would give her or you every last drop of my blood if you needed it. That you would even feel you need to ask cuts me."

"I knew the man that you were, and I'm hoping that nothing has changed, but we're kind of starting over. You misjudged the relationship I had with Nikolai, but the one we have is just as fragile. Let me get to know you again. That you are willing to stay with me and help Zia means everything to me."

"There is no other choice. This is my child too."

"She is. Why don't we take her home now and help her?"

"Immediately. I am completely yours."

Following a single nod of acceptance, they stood to join the others outside the shop. When Sarah started to take Zia, Mies kept the baby in his arms.

He would give anything for them. If she couldn't see how completely he meant that, then she indeed did not see him. He would save his daughter and save what he had with Sarah too.

It was a new world, he was a new man, and they *would* start over.

Mies stood in the elegant apartment shared by the three people he knew best when he was here in the new world seven months ago. He waited for the first blood woman who he now knew was called Park to do some blood tests on his baby before they began a healing process with his blood.

His eyes stayed on Sarah, across the large room as she consulted with Park about this blood infusion and how to most effectively treat his daughter.

Still having trouble wrapping his head around events, still stunned that he and Sarah made a first blood child, Mies knew one thing, he would never leave them. Even if Sarah decided that she didn't want him, he would still be here for her and Zia no matter what.

Sliding the cell phone from his pocket, he dialed the only number he had in it.

"Xavier, having fun?"

"I've three women in bed with me. What do ya think?"

"I think you're too busy for me to keep you. Listen, I appreciate your offer to stay with you but it seems I must stay in Boston after all."

"Aw, ye're sure?"

"I'm sure. Perhaps someday."

"Aye. All right then, back to me work. Now, where did I leave off, was it one, two, or three?"

The connection went dead and Mies closed the phone. It might have been quite an interesting time in Paris.

Sarah came over to him. "We're going for a blood transfusion, quick and direct, get it precisely where we want it as efficiently as possible. Our concern is triggering a conversion, which is *not* what we want with a child."

"I don't think you need to worry about that. Conversion for a first blood child won't trigger until maturity, and the spirit amulet guides that. I assume she doesn't have one yet."

"No. Tamesine was going to help me with it soon. That's good news, if it's so. All we need to do now is get your blood. Come with me."

She led him to a room near the back of the apartment, windowless, but dressed in pale colors with soft backlighting. "Why don't you have a seat here and we'll set up."

Daylight was nearing and fatigue beginning to set in, so Mies dropped happily into a big, light green, overstuffed chair. Sarah busied herself near him, setting up a small table with a tray on it.

"Zia," he said suddenly. "Where did you come up with the name?"

Sarah smiled. "It's short for Crezia. I remembered the story about the Shoazan who first gave her life to try to protect her race. It seemed the perfect name."

"Aye, it is."

"Aye?"

"Picked it up from a new friend. I met a first blood on the beach the night that we met in the bar."

"First blood, eh? Would his name have been Xavier?"

Jealousy fired off. Had she been with another first blood? "How do you know Xavier?"

"Settle down. I recognize the tone. I was blood-bonded to Xavier for almost a hundred years. He is like a father to me."

It took a few moments for Mies's respiration to drop back down. "He's a good man."

"He *is* a good man. I thought he'd left the city."

"Tomorrow. Right now he's ass deep in women."

"That is definitely my Xavier. A thousand years of sex and creative debauchery. From what I understand, he always leaves his lovers wanting more."

At that second, Sarah leaned across Mies to pull one of his arms forward. Her loose top gaped and his view, paired with the discussion earlier about sex, fired up his cock, which had been playing nice and keeping down since he saw Sarah tonight. It wanted in on the action now.

Down, boy, down, not now. Zia mattered more than anything right now. But his desire for Sarah had grown, not lessened, since he'd been here before. Was it possible that he could make a family with the woman who should have been his mate and the child that he'd never dreamed to hope for?

"I'm going to draw some blood now."

"Go ahead. You needn't worry that it'll hurt me."

"I know. Just doctor's habit, I guess."

Mies flexed his arm. Sarah tried to remain professional, although all she wanted to do was to lick this man until he cried for mercy. He presented a heavily muscled arm for his blood draw, and he reeked of the pheromones that got her into trouble in the first place, and did nothing for her self-control now.

Sarah drew ten tubes to make sure that they had enough. She started to put a bandage on the site when Mies smiled at her.

"I've got this."

Yeah, vampires had no problem closing wounds.

"Okay, uh, then, I'll, uh…get this to Park."

Sarah hurried from the room as Mies lifted himself off the chair. Had she been nervous? *Aye, she had.* That bode well for him. He'd gone tonight from thinking that he had a life ahead of him that he had no idea what to do with, to the possibility of building a new one with the most extraordinary woman at his side and a beautiful little girl.

Walking back into the living room, he noticed Nikolai in the big glass and chrome kitchen.

"Do you have any whisky?" he asked.

"God, I missed you. Yes, have a seat at the bar and I'll bring a bottle."

Drinks again with Nikolai. Mies didn't know what the universe had planned for him, but this, being with Nikolai and Sarah, felt like home.

"Here, Park, I pulled ten vials."

"Thanks, that should be enough."

As Park finished preparations to transfuse the blood to Zia, Sarah leaned back against the wall.

Shit! Just being close to him, even in that new body, *especially in that new body*, her libido hit her hard. The body was bigger and sexier, largely because she knew that it was entirely Mies. She wanted him, more than ever, and now, with the fact that he was the father of her child, and that her child was vampire, the normal human life impossible, there was no reason not to be with him.

"Sarah? Where were you?"

Pushing away from the wall, she joined Park at the center of the room. "I'm right here."

"No, where were you? I'd called you twice and you didn't respond."

"Oh. Sorry, yes, my head is somewhere else."

"I know where it is and I can't blame you. Your Mies is an uber first blood. Now that he is full-blooded, you have quite a ride ahead."

"I'm not sure that I should start that up again."

Park stopped, a vile of blood suspended in mid-air.

"Not sure? Oh, you're sure all right. I know the look. You're in love. You've been in love with him all along."

"I didn't want to be."

"You didn't have a choice. Real love slips in even when we try to keep it out. Don't deny him or yourself, or this child, the days ahead."

Placing a hand on her belly, which was doing flip-flops now, Sarah nodded. "So, we're ready?"

"Yes, just need to place this last vial. Okay, go get our girl."

The infusion went well. The needle didn't bother Zia at all. In fact, she giggled through the entire procedure. Sarah played mother and Park played doctor, so Sarah was free to sit near the head of the table they'd placed her on and kiss Zia all over the face to distract her.

Gathered around her bassinet, the baby's extended family waited for results. Naji sat on Nikolai's lap and Mies stood beside Sarah.

"Look at her color," Park pointed out. "She's already better than she was this morning. Mies, your blood is a genetic match to hers. The combination of that and vampire blood's healing properties should repair that odd genetic defect. It won't take long either. By tomorrow night, I'll be able to use the lab to determine if she's okay. I honestly think she will be."

With no forethought, Sarah turned into Mies's arms and he lifted her, held her, and kissed her gently on the forehead.

"Thank you," she whispered into his right ear.

He continued to hold her because the one thing on his mind after curing his daughter was to get Sarah back into his arms again. She was there, and he determined at that moment that she would stay there.

Daylight arrived and the vampires retired to the two light-tight bedrooms in the apartment. Park had hugged Sarah, Naji, and Nikolai, then brushed a hand lightly over Mies's shoulder before she went into her room, her step light, because she was sure that Zia was finally going to be healthy.

Mies nodded and headed into the room assigned to him without words. Before he closed the door, he glanced at Sarah, a long gaze, and then went inside.

Naji fixed breakfast for her roommates and they gathered for a quick bite before they, too, would get some sleep.

Nikolai nursed a big cup of decaffeinated coffee.

"It is so wonderful being with Mies again. To be able to interact with him normally, to touch him, to smile at him, to speak directly to him, I never could have hoped for this. My God, I hope they are not just fucking with us all and take him back away."

"You think?" Naji said.

"I think they are childish assholes to mess with lives like this. I mean, they took another life to put him in this body."

Sarah set her cup down. "I don't think so. Mies said that the body was empty and I believe it was. This Jason Stone, he was a daredevil and that last skydiving jump went horribly wrong. I saw him at the hospital, just before he died. Mies wasn't there."

"So you think they sent him back for good, that he might get to stay with us?"

Stretching, Sarah shook her head. "I don't know."

She yawned and slid out of her seat. "Naji, would you guys look after Zia? I need to take a shower."

"Sure, love. We'll just take her into our room with us. If you want to come get her, just come on in anytime and take her."

306

"Thanks, guys. This is one of those days when all I want to do is drop into bed and slip into oblivion for a while. I think I can finally do it, because it's the first time in a long time, I don't have to be afraid for Zia."

Nikolai pulled Sarah close and hugged her. "I think not. Mies is home, for now, and all is right with the world. Go get some good sleep, my darling."

She walked away from Nikolai and Naji, smiling. No, she didn't *think* that Zia was okay now, she *knew* it. Zia sent a spiritual message to her minutes after the transfusion that simply let her mother know that she was whole again. No more worries. Well, just one, and Sarah was going to take care of that tonight.

The water pressure in the apartment was strong, so when Sarah stood under the showerhead to let it pummel her back, the pulsating massage was beyond relaxing. Muscles loosened, and the headache she'd had for three days was gone. The past few days had been hell. When Nikolai had started talking about the cruel capriciousness of the universe, she'd almost screamed.

For now, her world might be back in order so, for the same reason, she wanted to thank the godless lot, or whatever the universal powers were, for Zia and for bringing Mies back to her. Nothing else mattered right now.

Ten minutes into the shower, she finally reached for the soap, scrubbed her skin clean, washed her hair, and then dried off. As she towel-dried her hair, she caught her image in the mirror, her eyes glittering. Mies was here, and she didn't know how long he might be, so she made a decision.

She ran her hand over her body, the fingertips lingering between her legs. They moved along the edge and dipped into the soft folds to remind herself what she'd missed, to prepare herself for what she was going to do as soon as she was finished with this shower.

Sarah was going to show that vampire real power.

After a quick shower, he dropped, still damp, spread out, legs wide, the damn cock refusing to stay down, and closed his eyes.

When this was done, when they knew that Zia was safe, he planned to remind Sarah how he felt buried inside her. He needed to let her know that she was his and that from this day forward, they were together, they would make a family, and happy lives in this modern world.

The powers-that-be would be wise to understand that this vampire was finished being their pawn, that he would move the stars in the heavens before he'd let them take him away from his mate and child again.

Sarah. Her nearness made it almost impossible for him to remain in this room and stay away from her. His fading consciousness kept him on the bed. When he woke tonight, he would take her out of the apartment to declare his intentions.

Sleep quickly invaded his exhausted mind as his hand wandered down to calm the stiff organ, to remind it that it would get no satisfaction today.

The room was pitch dark, no interior light burned and no outside light penetrated. Sarah brought a candle with her, and after she lit it and set it on a table several feet from the bed, she walked over to stare at the dark form spread out on the pale sheets.

Everything about this new body suited Mies's personality; it was big, strong, and hard. Hair the shade of summer wheat seemed to fit him more than Nikolai's rich dark color had, and those pastel green eyes had enchanted her the first time she looked into them.

Yes, the body was magnificent, and she couldn't wait to touch every square inch, but at the core of all of it, Mies was what she wanted...to touch him and make love to him, to feel him move inside her, connected, as they had been before.

A low moan let her know that he wasn't fully asleep now, that he might be aware of her presence. *Oh, she was going to make sure he was aware of her presence.*

Her thin dress abandoned on the floor, Sarah crawled over the naked body, her eyes resting on the big cock nestled between powerful thighs. She groaned. Her intention today had not been sex, but now…

She intended to let him know that he could not walk away from her and Zia. If he thought that he had done so because she didn't want him, she would show him how wrong he was.

Scaling his thighs, she finally landed on the other side of the bed, the only spot large enough for her with his arms and legs so wide. Lying beside him now, since he hadn't moved again, Sarah let her fingers slide over the cheeks and forehead of Mies's new face. If she had designed it herself, it couldn't have been more beautiful.

On their own, as she just watched them, her fingers continued their journey, over the chin, across curved shoulders, down the heavily muscled chest, over contour after contour of muscles. Those curious fingers did not stop. After scoring past tight abdominal muscles, and making circles around the belly button, they hesitated briefly before they began to move again and slid around the resting cock buried in soft hair.

The cock responded immediately and hardened in her hand, the tip pressing against her palm. Her eyes shot to his face to see if he had awakened. His eyes remained closed, but he released a sigh and his breathing quickened. Disappointed, she ran her fingertip around and around the head, then leaned down to lick across the top, and this time, when she glanced back to his face, he was lifting up on his arms, his eyes moving quickly over her.

Delicious. Erotic sensations eased Mies from his sleep, his cock rock hard again, his body tightening to stimulation that woke him from rest. His eyes opened slowly and he almost put a hand down to massage his cock when he felt something move across the head and nearly came off the bed.

He lifted up on his elbows, his eyes moving first to his penis, shocked to see Sarah there, her tongue moving across him, her eyes on him, her naked body stretched along his side. Could there ever have been a better dream?

"You're not dreaming," the vision said.

Sarah lifted herself and slid a leg over Mies, and as she positioned her buttocks in front of his cock, fully engaged now, she lowered her body to place a hand on the pillow on either side of his head. Mies didn't move.

"Do I have your attention now?" she asked.

Speechless, Mies nodded.

"Good. Now, listen to me, and hear me, old one. That dream of living out my average human lifetime died when I fell in love with a vampire who traveled centuries to be with me. If you think that you are leaving me and that perfect little girl we made, you are very much mistaken. Do you understand?"

Again, he nodded.

"Do you comply?"

One more nod, but a smile that had begun after the first nod continued to grow.

"Fine. Because we have guests, I can't do to you what I want to do, so this will have to work to seal the deal. Do you agree to my terms?"

Mies swallowed, so aroused he wasn't sure if he *could* speak. His hands went to her thighs, and he finally answered her. "To anything."

He watched as Sarah lifted up and slowly lowered her body over him, his firm penis sliding easily into her warm opening. She lifted again, and again and again, until he nearly shot into her too soon. As she began to move faster and faster, he pulled her down to his chest, her nipples grazing his skin.

"I love you, as well, Sarah the doctor. If you want this man torn out of place, he is the luckiest man in the universe to have found you across time. I would never leave you or our baby."

"Mies, I want all the years ahead of us when I join you and become vampire."

"Ah, Sarah…"

"Shut up and let me bring this home."

Mies held her thighs again as she sat up and began to ride harder while he thrust upward into her, erotic friction of skin against skin, and when the orgasms hit, he grabbed Sarah and pulled her down to turn them both over onto his side. He'd shot his seed into her again, a sense of satisfaction even greater because this was the first time they'd made love when they both knew that it really was love and that they could be together.

Were those shooting stars she saw around their heads? Bright lights weaved around them, grazing the two bodies entwined on the bed. When her body stopped shuddering from the orgasm, she looked into Mies's eyes, her hand on his back, pulling him close.

"The lights again."

"Magics. We were meant, my love. The universe approves."

Sarah rolled onto her back. Mies remained on his side because it was the perfect view and he could touch her anywhere, which, he planned to.

"Mies, the question is settled. You're staying?"

"I could never leave either of my women."

"Okay. I just wanted to make certain there was no misunderstanding. You belong with us."

His fingers moved along her belly, he couldn't pull his eyes away. "I belong to you," he whispered.

"Umm, all right. I guess I should let you get some rest."

"No, don't leave me Sarah."

"I have to go get Zia from Nik and Naji."

"Let me."

Pausing as she tried to get out of the bed, Sarah considered the request. "Okay. Stay in the hall and don't go into their room unless you know it's safe." It wasn't like Nikolai would be surprised.

Mies kissed Sarah's belly, then her knees, then her feet, before he lifted off the bed. Sliding his jeans on, he went to the bedroom two doors away where he knew Nikolai and Naji slept.

A muffled voice answered, and only his excellent vampire hearing let him know that someone invited him in. The door opened easily, it hadn't been locked, and he spoke from behind it.

"It's Mies. Is it safe for me to enter?"

Nikolai's voice traveled from beyond the door.

"It's safe. We have blocking in here too, and it's pulled closed. Mies, please, come in."

Stepping into view, Mies scanned Naji, still in bed, sitting up, the sheet pulled to her chest, but Nikolai was in front of him with a ready hug.

"Did you need something, my brother?" he asked, his usual smile bright.

Mies had missed that and hadn't realized how much until right now, so when he hugged his best male friend, Mies held on.

When Nikolai pulled away, he raised his eyebrows.

"You are here for your daughter?"

"I am. Sarah would like her with us."

The sentence said it all. Naji squealed, then quickly held the sheet over her mouth, but Nikolai just turned to pick the baby up out of her basket.

"I am pleased. You two belong together, I believe this almost from the first time you place eyes on each other."

"She is my heart. And now, this little lady is the other half. Thank you, Nikolai, Naji, for taking care of her and my child. If…"

Mies stopped, his throat blocked, the words hard to say because the idea tore him apart.

"If they take me away again, just love them, please, make sure that they have a happy life."

Shaking his head, tears filling his eyes, Nikolai handed the sleeping baby to her father. Zia nuzzled into Mies's bare chest.

"Take your daughter and go back to Sarah. We will not speak of things that shall not happen. When the sun drops, so will the celebration."

Mies's eyes stayed on Zia, resting comfortably in his arms, then to Nikolai.

"There is truth in what you say. Sleep well. We will celebrate all night."

With a final hug and a nod to Naji, who just lowered her chin with a smile, Mies carried Zia toward the room where her mother awaited them.

Coming through the door, he strode up to a naked Sarah lying on her belly, one leg in the air, her breasts displayed as she supported herself on her elbows.

"Hi, sweetheart," she said to the baby he placed on the soft sheets in front of her. "She didn't wake?"

"No. I felt her send a message to me. How can she do that so young?"

Sarah tucked her finger into the diaper to make sure it was dry. Luckily, it was. "Your first blood offspring, vampire, was cognitive before birth. She's been doing that from the very beginning. What was the message?"

Dropping onto his haunches, Mies placed his hand alongside Zia's sleeping face.

"She is overjoyed that her parents are together."

Her eyes nearly glowing, Sarah lifted the baby and crawled back to lay her in the center of the bed.

"Come, daddy, sleep with us. She is not the only one who is overjoyed."

Curled together, the new family slept undisturbed, restful, soul-repairing sleep that they all needed after all the pain they suffered to get here, safe, and finally together.

The happiest baby in the world woke once to send a tether from her small lifeforce to touch her mother on one side and her father on the other. Zia had the same talent as her namesake, an attachment beyond any other to all life on the mother planet. The weak tethers that she wielded now to bond with her parents would grow stronger as she matured, would bind her to the living planet and every other living thing on this world. She knew already that she had a part to play some day to protect the Mother planet. She accepted her destiny, but first, she wanted to love her parents and be a child.

313

Destiny smiled. She had accomplished her goal to bring this special baby to the world, although her task had never been easy. She had to put into place the two people who were meant to make her...from multitudes of centuries apart and two different worlds. It had been an impossible task...how would they ever get together to create the final warrior who would be needed in another one hundred years? Destiny had accomplished it by moving heaven and earth. The task done, even Destiny needed rest.

First meal was a generous spread provided by the un-daylight challenged Nikolai and Naji, who'd gone out that evening and made arrangements for the celebration that Nikolai had promised Mies earlier that day.

Sarah had risen with Zia hours before Mies did. The baby's diaper was changed, she was fed, and happily giggling in Naji's arms.

"So, you two do the nasty last night?" Naji asked.

"Naj! What we did was *not* nasty!" Sarah smiled and peeked past the kitchen area to see if Nikolai was coming back. "And yes, we did." Pausing, Sarah continued.

"Being with him, after all of this, when I never expected to see him again, Naj, we admitted our love for each other. When we were together, it was with our hearts and souls. Now, knowing that he might get to stay, it was like he said we would be...bound together by ancestry of blood, by our child."

"I'm starting to believe in destiny. Look at us, all finding the loves of our lives and getting our *happily ever afters*."

Mies walked into a busy kitchen where he saw Nikolai and Naji cooking, Sarah chopping vegetables, and in the corner of the room, a first blood vampire he did not know held his child.

The first blood looked up at him. "I'm Olivia, the babysitter. I'm here so often, I took an apartment nearby, but now, I guess I'm out of a job. Nice to meet you."

Mies nodded. "Hello, Olivia." Rubbing his eyes, he caught Sarah's.

"Good evening, sleepy-head," she said.

"Good evening. We're preparing first meal?"

"We are. Nik and Naji headed to the store before we rose for supplies."

"I am grateful. But," he looked at the other people in the room, all staring at him expectantly. "I wonder if I could convince you to walk with me at the beach."

"I don't know, we have a lot of things..."

"Please, Sarah. I need to speak with you."

She couldn't refuse him. "Okay, let me grab my shoes and a sweater."

As Sarah followed Mies along the shoreline, she wondered what he found so imperative. When he didn't speak at first, she stopped him suddenly with a hand on his arm.

"I know I thanked you last night for coming with us to help Zia. But I want to say it again, Mies, it means the world to us. If you hadn't come back, I don't think she would have survived."

"It would have been my fault."

That statement startled her. "How would it have been your fault? You had no say in how any of this happened."

"You told me right away that you did not want to be with a vampire."

"I did. I also remember that none of it was your decision. I walked into this with my eyes wide open, Mies. And by the way, I wouldn't change anything. That baby girl is my life. I hope that you come to think so too."

"I already love her and you more than my own life."

Sarah could barely speak. "Then, we're a family."

"If you want me, yes, without question, but Sarah, you must understand, I do not know if I can. It is impossible to know what they might do with me."

"Then I'll be clear. I want you. Forever, if I'm lucky. For less time, if it's all I get. We don't know what the fates and destiny have planned for any of us, and I won't live my life terrified that they will suddenly decide to take you back. Besides, I think they've gotten what they wanted from you."

Mies came to a dead stop. "What do you mean?"

"Zia. Cherise says that's why we were brought together, and I know it's true. You and I were meant to come together to create that little girl. It's happening all over the first blood community…children in numbers never before known. True, the other children came with less complications, but trust the universe to find a way to bring us together from thousands of years apart. Mies, our baby was your mission. Does that make sense to you?"

He didn't speak because he knew, instantly, that Sarah was right. "She was always meant to be, right here, right now, exactly as it happened."

"I believe so," Sarah answered. Seconds later, a scream interrupted her.

"*Jason!* Oh, my God, Jason, you're alive! I knew they got it wrong!"

The boisterous voice came from above Mies on the boardwalk where a frantically waving man insisted on his attention.

Sarah laughed and pulled Mies toward the beach, away from the speaker.

Moving fast, she hauled him behind her to put as much distance as possible between them and Jason's fan.

"We may have to leave Boston. It seems that your body belonged to a local celebrity. Interestingly, he was an environmentalist. If people keep seeing him walking around alive, you may never get any peace."

Mies lifted Sarah into his arms.

"I will go anywhere on this world with you and Zia. *You* tell me where and I'll make a home for us there. Xavier invited me to return to his home with him in France. Perhaps we could consider that."

"We have a standing invitation, so yes, it's possible someday."

"I liked the man. He wore a mantle of power and honesty."

"He does. My parents and grandparents were blood-bonded before me. His keep is the only home I've ever known until now."

"If you would like to go there, I will go with you, Sarah."

"I'm happy here. I think we can make it work. The Jason fans, eventually they'll stop asking. Until then, we just need to make sure we have a good explanation. We'll need to find better housing since we must have more permanent daylight protection."

"I didn't imagine you would take me back into your life. When I returned in this body, I felt lost."

"You will never be lost. You belong to us and we belong to you."

"I am yours, Sarah. Do with me what you will."

"Take us further down the beach."

Using his abilities, he moved them in seconds half a mile from where they were.

He watched her eyes sparkle as she glanced around the dark sands to see if they were alone. They were.

"Okay. Take your clothes off."

The End

EARLIER THAT NIGHT IN DOWNTOWN BOSTON

"Those are some fine women. I will have to return soon to continue that outstandin' pleasure."

Xavier swallowed the final swig of a bottle of Scotch he'd shared with the ladies and pitched the bottle into a bin. The tink as it hit the bottom seemed like a fitting homage to the end of this journey. It was time to go home.

He wished that his newfound friend had been able to join him. Those overseas flights were long and tedious, and this Nick seemed like he would have been an amusing companion.

Aye, though, he needed to rest anyway after several nights underneath various diversely gorgeous and talented American women.

"Thank ya for yer hospitality, Boston," he said as he enjoyed his last walk down a mostly abandoned street. When next a taxi came by, he'd use compulsion to get his ride to Logan International.

Watching the bright lights and remembering his experiences, Xavier decided that it was time that he got out more. Several long centuries tied to his keep outside of Paris left him restless, and it wasn't until this trip to visit Sarah and her child that he realized it. Travel, then, was his goal now. It was well past time for him to truly live again and see what the planet had to offer.

Distracted, he didn't see the shadow move out of an alley he'd passed two blocks past the bin where his final whisky bottle lay.

Claude stayed out of the light, unnoticed, and *hopefully*, off the big vampire's radar. He'd successfully blocked his lifeforce from his sire for the past year, but with this proximity to a first blood vampire, he wasn't sure he had the power to keep it blocked from *him*. Prudence and caution were his middle names.

Besides, if Xavier found out he was so near to him, Claude would be dead before he could protest. *That*, he knew.

318

Still, the tickle of joy he felt when he saw Xavier, alone in Boston, gave him a bit of a hard-on. The big-ass vampire was on Claude's list. It was a *long* list, and Xavier was near the top.

This was his first opportunity to kill one of his targets, and what a perfect one to start with. The arrogant prick, the Scottish bastard who killed Lamont and thought he was superior to Claude.

Lamont deserved it, he didn't mourn the slain creep, but this Xavier had been rude and irreverent, laughed at Claude and Lamont, and would have swatted them both like flies if he'd had the chance. Now, Claude had every element on his side. Surprise, a healthy need for vengeance, and the ability to do so.

Excitement swelled his organ even more. *He was going to kill Xavier tonight! A forever death!*

Scanning the street, no one was in sight at this late hour, so Claude pulled out his Glock 21 45-caliber semiauto handgun. It felt good against his palm, his finger finding the trigger like an old friend. When Xavier passed the alley, he used air displacement to move from the back of the alley to the street.

Claude smiled as the big vampire whirled, the expression of shock on his face a pleasure for Claude before he emptied the magazine into Xavier's brain. The first blood vampire went down fast, his heavy body crumbling on the sidewalk outside of a dive bar that had closed for the night.

Slowly, because there was no hurry now, Claude walked up to the body, stood over it for a moment, gloating, and then kicked him in the side as hard as he could. Once didn't satisfy him, so he continued to kick until reason resurfaced, and he backed away.

God that felt cathartic! It had been a long time coming! But if he was going to take the head, he needed to get to it before Xavier revived. Hoisting the body, the weight nothing for Claude now that he was vampire, he carried Xavier several streets from where he died, down concrete steps to the basement of an old factory that had made bagels at one time.

Claude dropped the body with force onto the hard floor before he walked away to get an ax that he'd carried with him almost from the first day he'd arrived on American soil again.

The ax on his shoulder the way Paul Bunyan would carry it, Claude began to whistle as he headed back to where Xavier's body lay, but as soon as he rounded a block wall that divided the basement, when his eyes went to where Xavier had been, the floor was empty. *Fuck!*

Panicked, because now this was going to be a battle for survival, and Xavier was better equipped, Claude raced over and grabbed the handgun he'd left lying carelessly on a table near the stairwell. He listened soundlessly, hoping to hear something that would alert him to Xavier's whereabouts, but the place was as silent as a tomb.

Had the asshole left?

Claude had thought about that, too, since this went wrong, just get the fuck out of here. Except it was too late for that. The vampire had him now, he knew he was in Boston, and there wasn't a chance on this *motherfuckingplanet* that Xavier would let him live.

All these months in hiding and he couldn't even pull off a simple assassination. He was a *professional assassin* for fuck's sake! He'd kept hidden from Tamesine all this time to finally get offed by that crude Scot? *Hell no!*

A footfall behind him shocked him and he whirled, the gun in hand, ready to answer.

Waiting for Xavier to charge him, Claude started to blast him again, but hesitated for just a moment when he noticed that Xavier just stood there, across the room and didn't move. Claude was stunned that Xavier wasn't already on him.

Suddenly Xavier shook his head. "Where am I? Who are *you?*"

Well, this was interesting…

Claude pumped Xavier's head full of bullets again.

Second meal was often chaotic now that there were five children in attendance. Things generally never went smoothly, and someone usually got in trouble.

Tonight, the two households were sharing this final meal before sunrise, the food nearly gone, the camaraderie deep, as the evening wound down. Finished, they abandoned the big dining room to reconvene on the first floor balcony.

Koen tagged his granddaughter, racing by with a huge piece of chocolate cake.

"Hey! Isn't that the last piece?" he called out. Cairine turned, grinned, and continued to make a beeline for the stairs before her grandfather caught her.

"Arrgghh!" he yelled, and chased her because he knew that she was expecting him to. Trying to *not* beat a four year old wasn't easy.

Squealing, Cairine shot up the stairs, then paused around the first curve to make sure her grandfather followed, squealed when she saw that he had, and continued up as quickly as her little feet could carry her. All Koen hoped was that his wicked little granddaughter wouldn't pull out some of her considerable magics and send something his way…*like a fireball!*

Tamesine carried Fia, her baby daughter, to the balcony to enjoy some fresh air with family and friends before they went to rest for the coming day.

Koen's wife Alisa carried Bryson, Fia's twin, giving him endless kisses on his face as he giggled. She'd become the twins' second mother, and Tamesine was grateful for her love and help with them.

Eillia wandered out, leaning over the balcony to wave to her mate and Caedmon as they prepared to fly a glow-in-the-dark kite. Her eyes were locked on her son.

Tamesine joined her. "That looks like fun."

"Uh, huh."

"He's doing fine, Lia."

"Yeah."

Tamesine couldn't reassure her any more than that. He was…for now. The strange moments when the little boy wasn't well continued to recur and so far, Park had not been able to find a reason for it. Everyone was deeply concerned.

Tamesine knew that there would likely be another power circle to ask the powers-that-be what was happening and if the child in danger. Did it mean the other children might be in danger too? Changes continued to come to the first blood clan. Centuries of expectations and history were being unmade.

The others slowly wandered out, talking about various topics as Tamesine's mate arrived and crashed onto the big cushioned bench. "We're going to begin the villa next week."

"Are we sure we want to do that?"

"Tam, yeah, we can't stay in Koen's home indefinitely. Besides, I've seen all of your pics from Instagram, and I know exactly what you want. You're going to love it."

"I'm sure that I will, it's just…"

"We're two minutes away, we'll be here for every meal, it's going to be fabulous."

"I know. I still haven't adapted to the concept of change as being a *good* thing."

Marc started to respond when he noticed Tamesine's expression change, her eyes closed. "Tam? Are you all right?"

Tamesine's head spun, and she knew.

"Claude," she whispered. "He's surfaced. I've got him."

Please join us for Book 12, Xavier's story, and then Days of Innocence, the final story before the Days of Awe...

We jump ahead one hundred years to find out how the special destiny of the unprecedented vampire children unfolds. Can they save the living planet?

You mustn't miss the Days of Awe.

Thanks for staying on the path with us once again!

Charlie Quinn

Made in the USA
Monee, IL
07 July 2024

61400659R00177